D0922890

Robert Jordan's
the WHEEL of TIME®
the EYE of the WORLD

The Wheel of Time®
Graphic Novels

Based on the Novels by Robert Jordan

New Spring:
The Graphic Novel
Robert Jordan, Chuck Dixon, Mike Miller, Harvey Tolibao

The Eye of the World:
The Graphic Novel, Volume One
Robert Jordan, Chuck Dixon, Chase Conley

The Eye of the World:
The Graphic Novel, Volume Two
Robert Jordan, Chuck Dixon, Andie Tong

The Eye of the World:
The Graphic Novel, Volume Three
Robert Jordan, Chuck Dixon, Marcio Fiorito, Francis Nuguit

Robert Jordan's

the WHEEL of TIME®

the EYE of the WORLD

Volume Three

TOR®

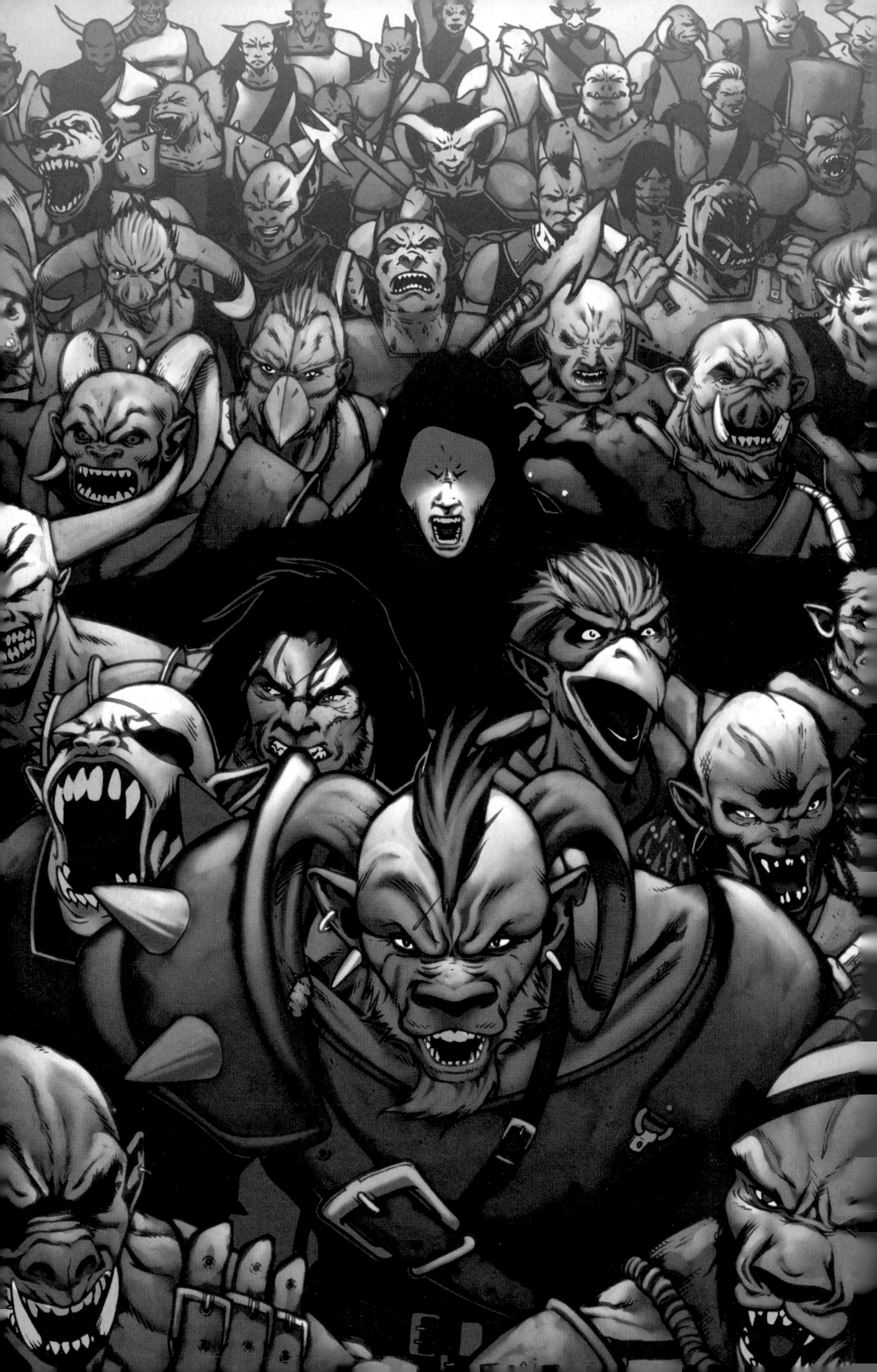

written by
ROBERT JORDAN

adapted by
CHUCK DIXON

artwork by
MARCIO FIORITO
FRANCIS NUGUIT

colors by
NICOLAS CHAPUIS

lettered by
BILL TORTOLINI

original series edited by
ERNST DABEL
RICH YOUNG

consultation
ERNST DABEL
LES DABEL

thematic consultants
MARIA SIMONS
BOB KLUTTZ
ALAN ROMANCZUK

Covers by Andie Tong
Collection edits by Rich Young
Collection design by Bill Tortolini

Dynamite Entertainment:

NICK BARRUCCI · PRESIDENT
JUAN COLLADO · CHIEF OPERATING OFFICER
JOSEPH RYBANDT · EDITOR
JOSH JOHNSON · CREATIVE DIRECTOR
RICH YOUNG · BUSINESS DEVELOPMENT
JASON ULLMEYER · GRAPHIC DESIGNER

www.dynamiteentertainment.com

Published in comic book form by Dynamite Entertainment, 155 Ninth Avenue, Suite B, Runnemede, NJ 08078. Dynamite, Dynamite Entertainment and the Dynamite Entertainment colophon are ® and © 2013 DFI. All rights reserved.

A Tor Book
Published by Tom Doherty Associates, LLC
175 Fifth Avenue
New York, NY 10010

www.tor-forge.com

Tor® is a registered trademark of Tom Doherty Associates, LLC.
ISBN 978-0-7653-3163-2
First Edition: January 2013
Printed in the United States of America

Table of Contents

WHAT CAME BEFORE...

The Emond's Fielders have learned much while
on the road to Baerlon.

Lan instructed Rand, Mat, and Perrin in the use of
their weapons, while Egwene discovered, with
Moiraine's help, that she has the ability to tap into the
One Power, and could one day become an Aes Sedai.

When they reached the city of Baerlon, Moiraine
allowed time for some rest and sightseeing before
they continued on their way to Tar Valon...

...But rest did not come easily for Rand. The Dark
One, Ba'alzamon, visited him in his dreams - not to
mention the dreams of Mat and Perrin – and tried to
tempt them all towards servitude.

Such dreams did not make one want to go back to
sleep... and so, after he woke, Rand decided to explore
the city... but before he could really get started, he
met Min – a young woman with an uncanny gift of
foresight – and she gave him an uncomfortable glimpse
into his own future, and how he was connected
with his traveling companions.

He later met up with Mat, and they stirred up a little bit of trouble by taunting the Children of the Light, an order that opposed both the Dark One and the Aes Sedai with a fervor bordering on the religious.

Rand and Mat then returned to the Stag and Lion Inn, surprised to find that Nynaeve, the Wisdom from Emond's Field, had tracked them there to bring them, Perrin, and Egwene all home.

She is convinced, instead, to join the party on their journey north, which she does... if only to see to the protection of the Emond's Fielders she had come to collect.

The group is forced to flee Baerlon earlier than they intended due to the Children of the Light, and once back on the open road, Trollocs swiftly caught their trail.

Moiraine is forced to lead them all down a path that the Trollocs will not follow...

chapter one

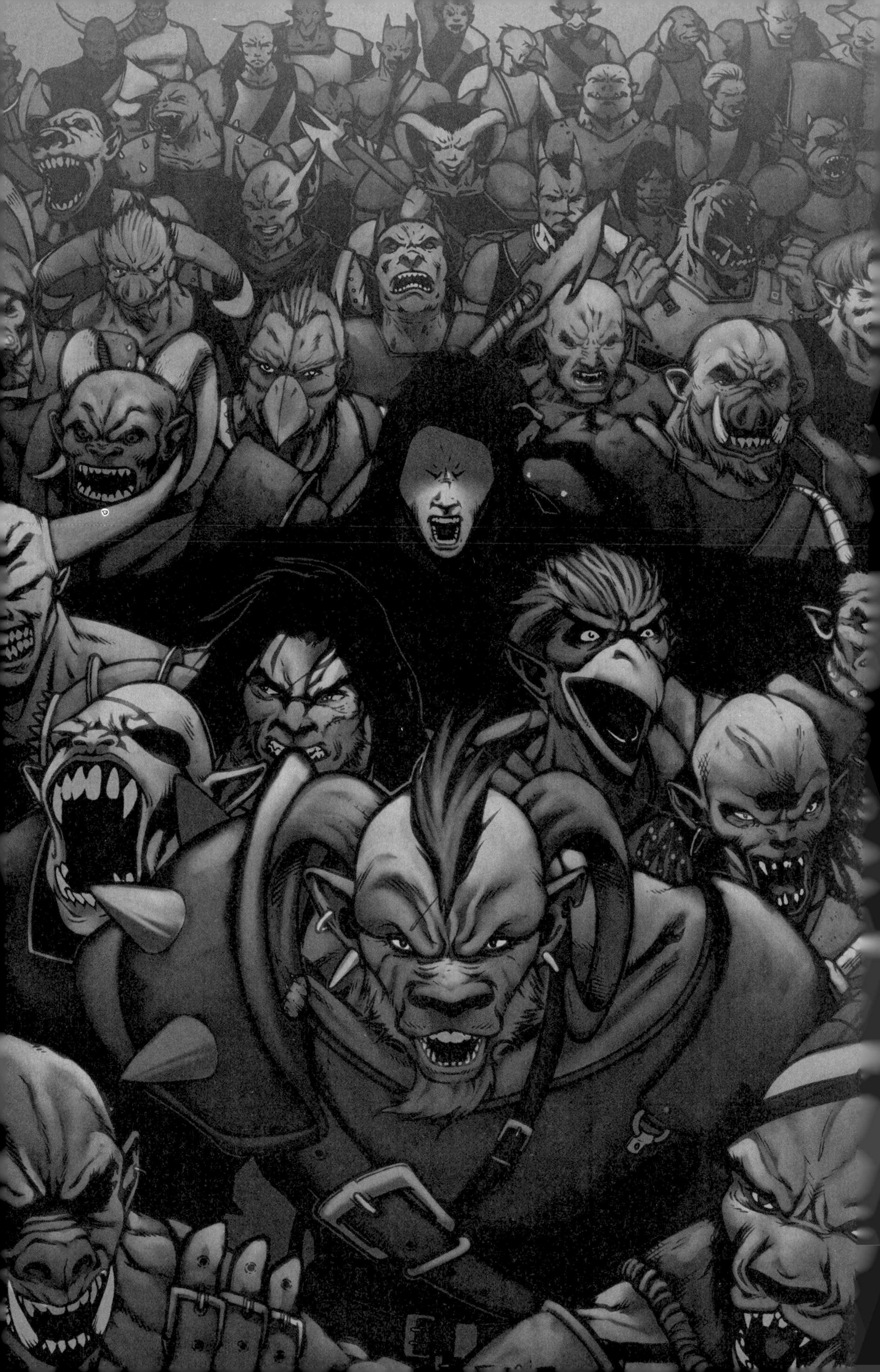

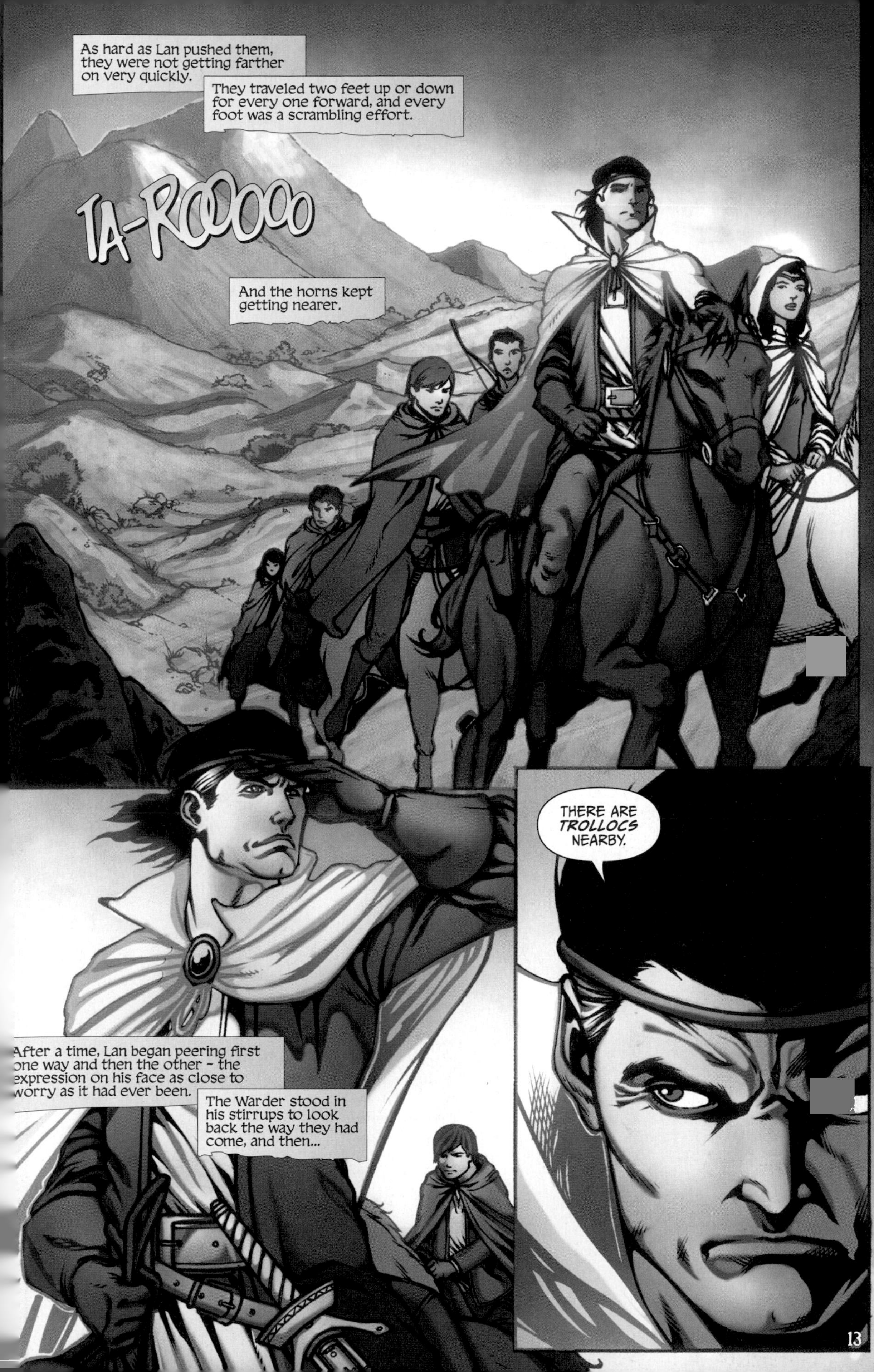
As hard as Lan pushed them, they were not getting farther on very quickly.
They traveled two feet up or down for every one forward, and every foot was a scrambling effort.
TA-ROOOOO
And the horns kept getting nearer.
After a time, Lan began peering first one way and then the other - the expression on his face as close to worry as it had ever been.
The Warder stood in his stirrups to look back the way they had come, and then...
THERE ARE *TROLLOCS* NEARBY.

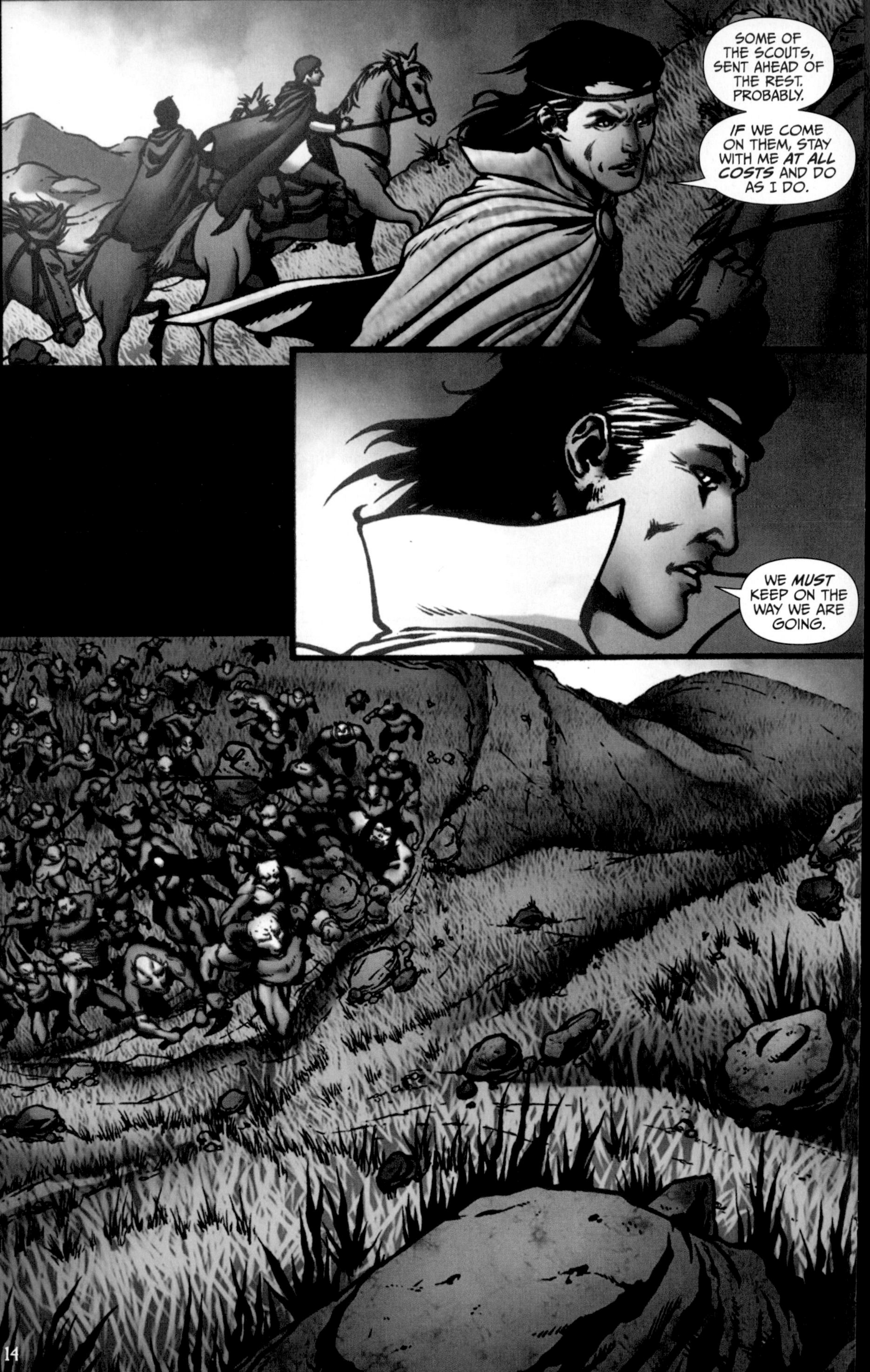
SOME OF THE SCOUTS, SENT AHEAD OF THE REST. PROBABLY.
IF WE COME ON THEM, STAY WITH ME ***AT ALL COSTS*** AND DO AS I DO.
WE ***MUST*** KEEP ON THE WAY WE ARE GOING.

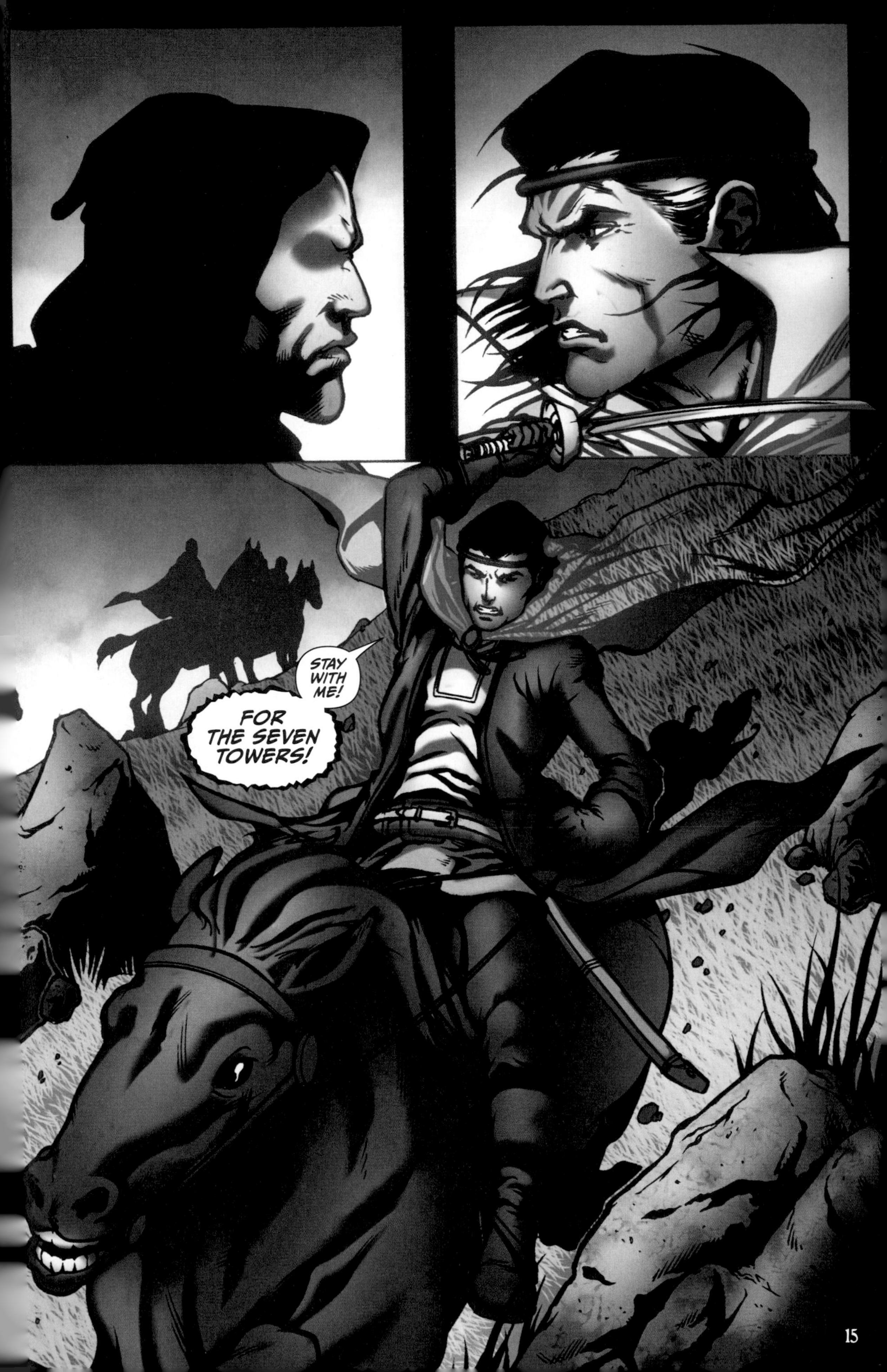
STAY WITH ME!
FOR THE SEVEN TOWERS!

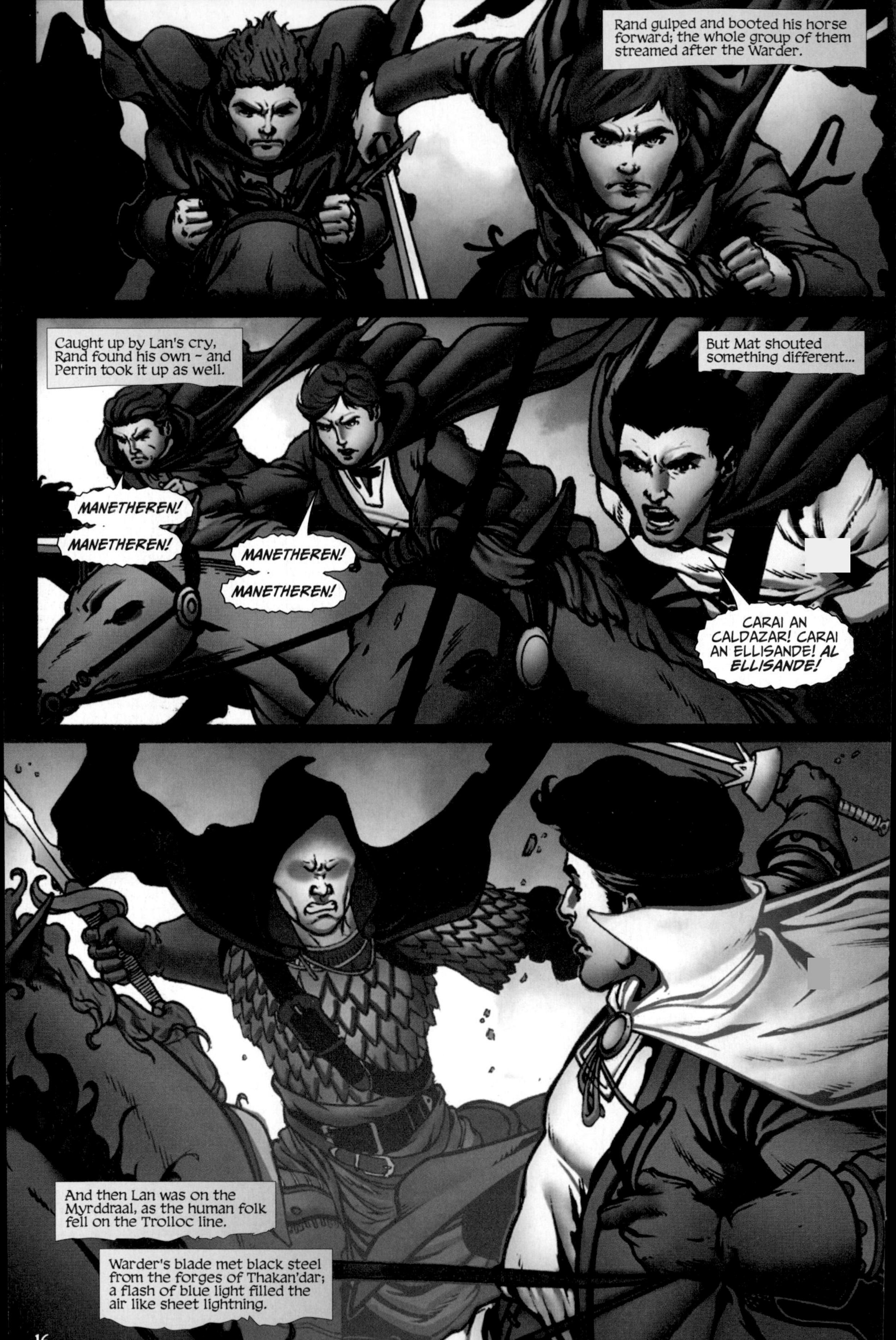

Rand gulped and booted his horse forward; the whole group of them streamed after the Warder.
Caught up by Lan's cry, Rand found his own ~ and Perrin took it up as well.
But Mat shouted something different...
MANETHEREN!
MANETHEREN!
MANETHEREN!
MANETHEREN!
CARAI AN CALDAZAR! CARAI AN ELLISANDE! AL ELLISANDE!
And then Lan was on the Myrddraal, as the human folk fell on the Trolloc line.
Warder's blade met black steel from the forges of Thakan'dar; a flash of blue light filled the air like sheet lightning.

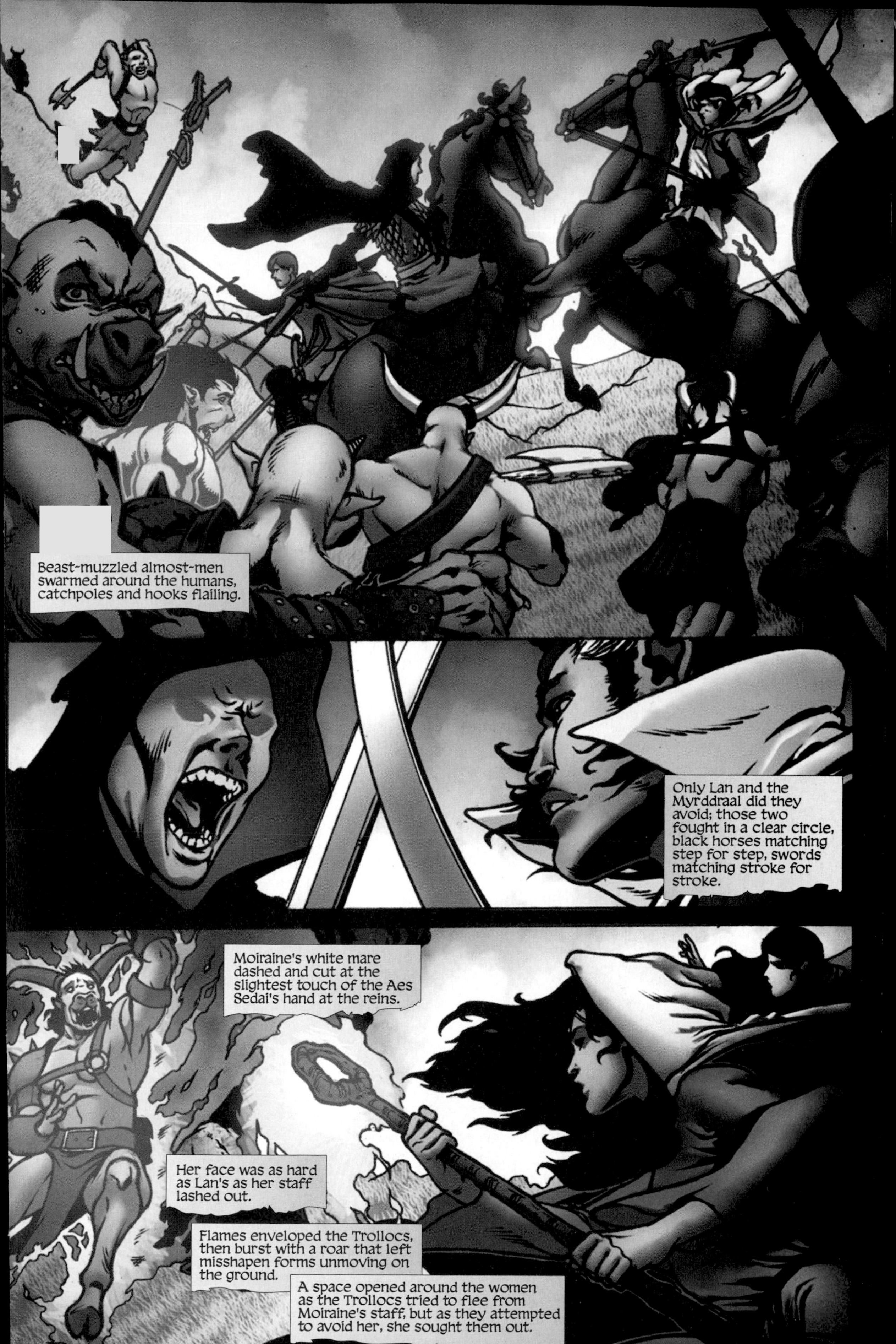
Beast-muzzled almost-men swarmed around the humans, catchpoles and hooks flailing.
Only Lan and the Myrddraal did they avoid; those two fought in a clear circle, black horses matching step for step, swords matching stroke for stroke.
Moiraine's white mare dashed and cut at the slightest touch of the Aes Sedai's hand at the reins.
Her face was as hard as Lan's as her staff lashed out.
Flames enveloped the Trollocs, then burst with a roar that left misshapen forms unmoving on the ground.
A space opened around the women as the Trollocs tried to flee from Moiraine's staff, but as they attempted to avoid her, she sought them out.

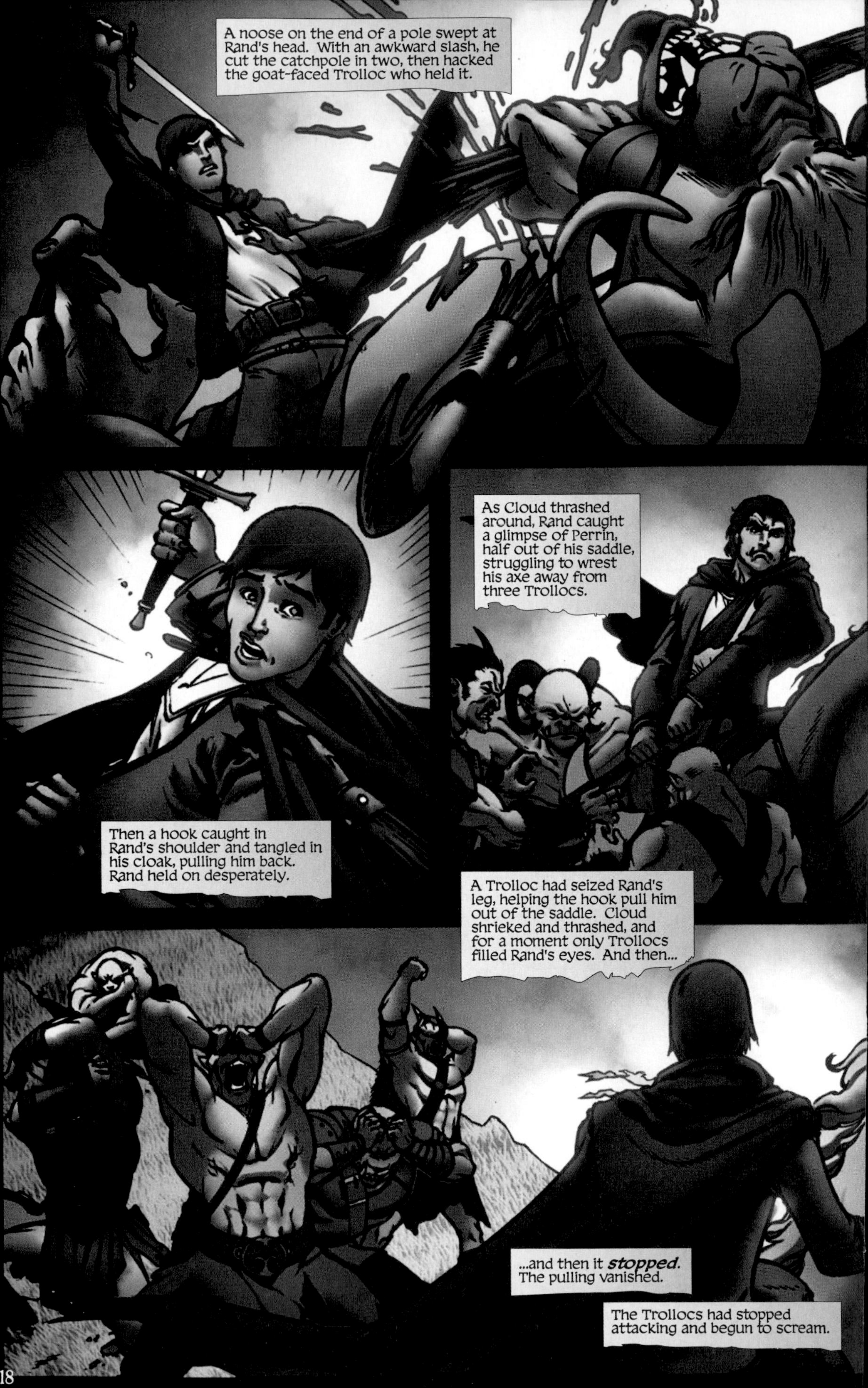
A noose on the end of a pole swept at Rand's head. With an awkward slash, he cut the catchpole in two, then hacked the goat-faced Trolloc who held it.
Then a hook caught in Rand's shoulder and tangled in his cloak, pulling him back. Rand held on desperately.
As Cloud thrashed around, Rand caught a glimpse of Perrin, half out of his saddle, struggling to wrest his axe away from three Trollocs.
A Trolloc had seized Rand's leg, helping the hook pull him out of the saddle. Cloud shrieked and thrashed, and for a moment only Trollocs filled Rand's eyes. And then...
...and then it ***stopped.*** The pulling vanished.
The Trollocs had stopped attacking and begun to scream.

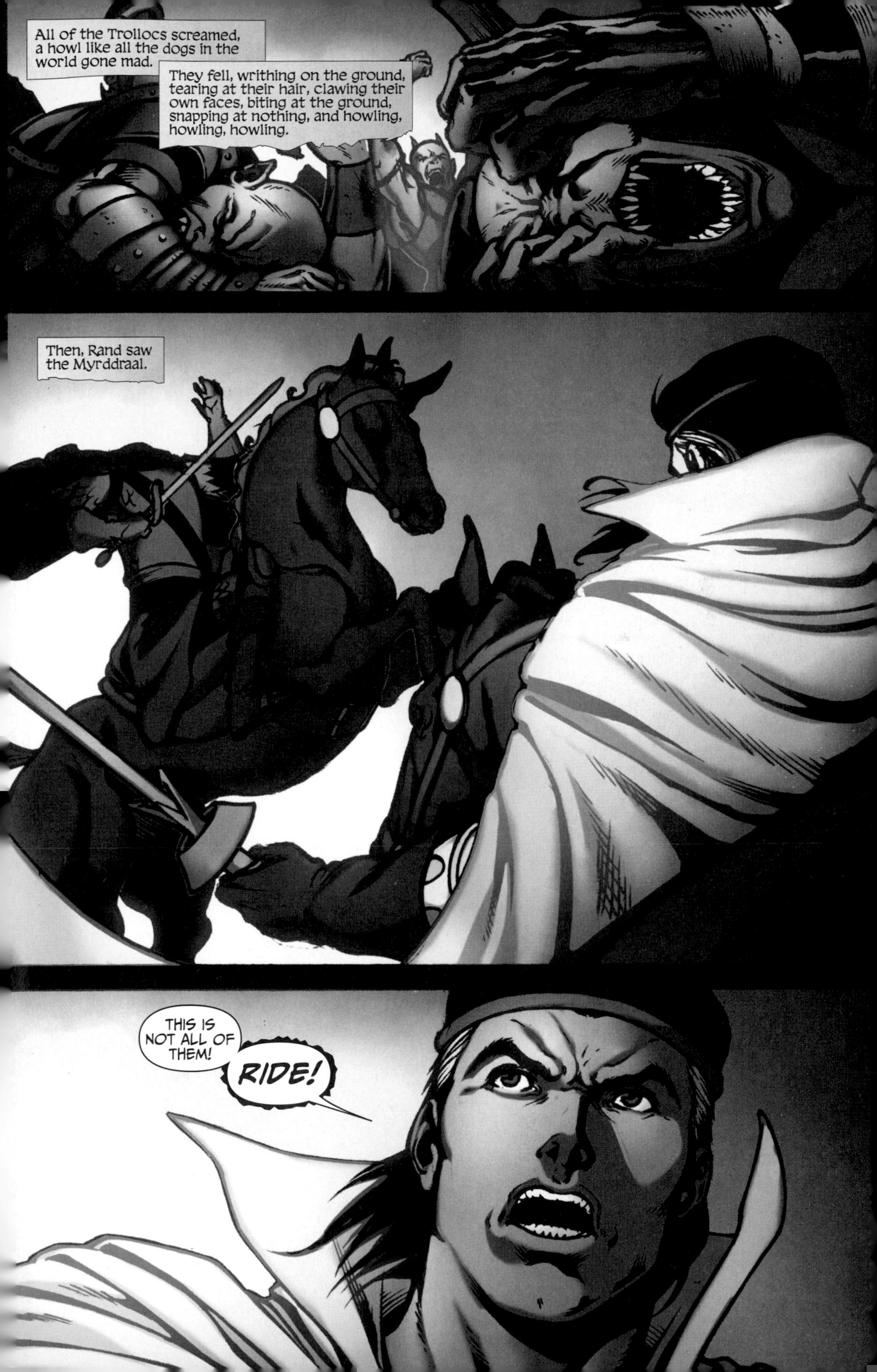
All of the Trollocs screamed, a howl like all the dogs in the world gone mad.
They fell, writhing on the ground, tearing at their hair, clawing their own faces, biting at the ground, snapping at nothing, and howling, howling, howling.
Then, Rand saw the Myrddraal.
THIS IS NOT ALL OF THEM!
RIDE!

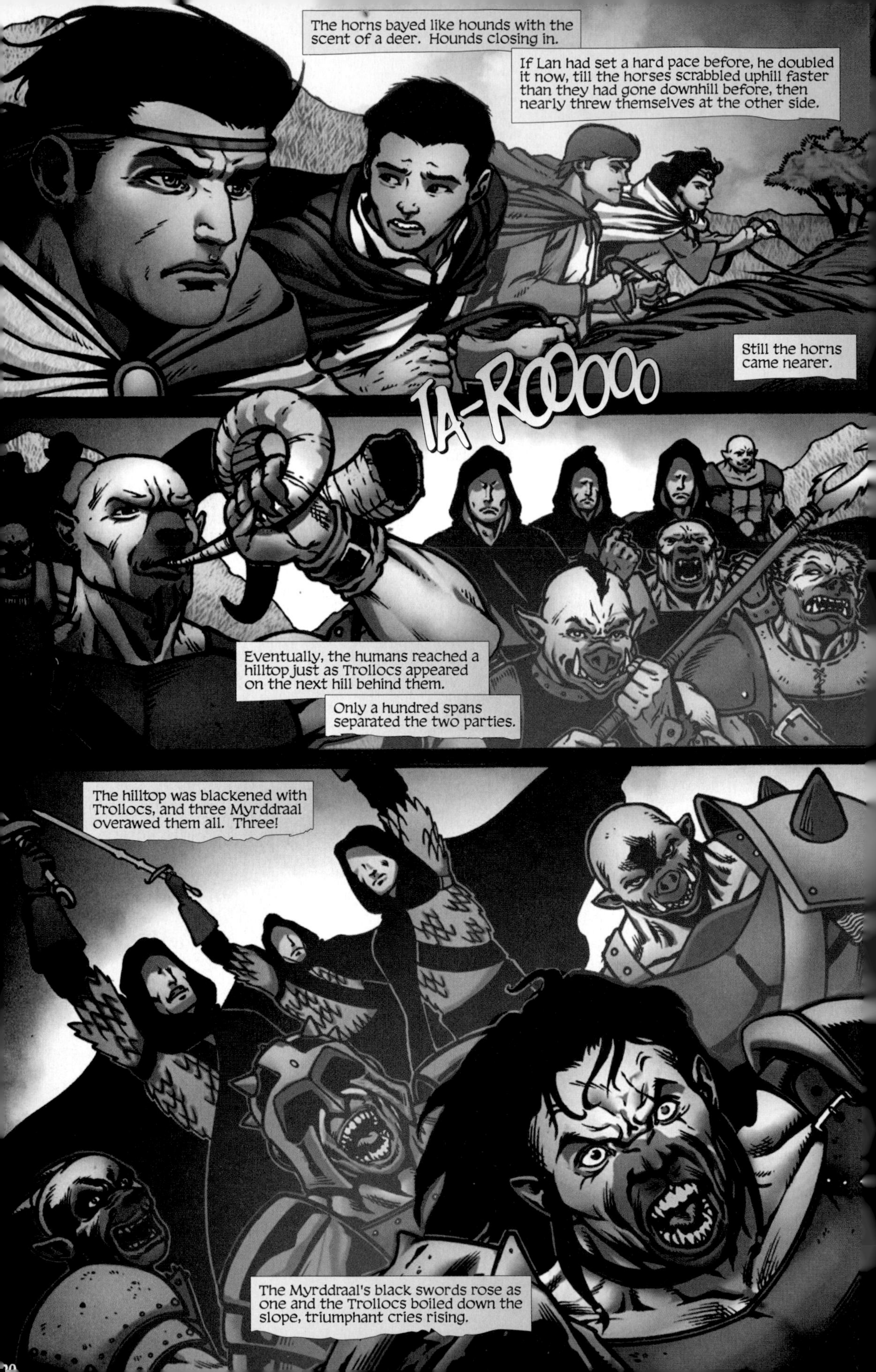

The horns bayed like hounds with the scent of a deer. Hounds closing in.
If Lan had set a hard pace before, he doubled it now, till the horses scrabbled uphill faster than they had gone downhill before, then nearly threw themselves at the other side.
Still the horns came nearer.
TA-ROOOOO
Eventually, the humans reached a hilltop just as Trollocs appeared on the next hill behind them.
Only a hundred spans separated the two parties.
The hilltop was blackened with Trollocs, and three Myrddraal overawed them all. Three!
The Myrddraal's black swords rose as one and the Trollocs boiled down the slope, triumphant cries rising.

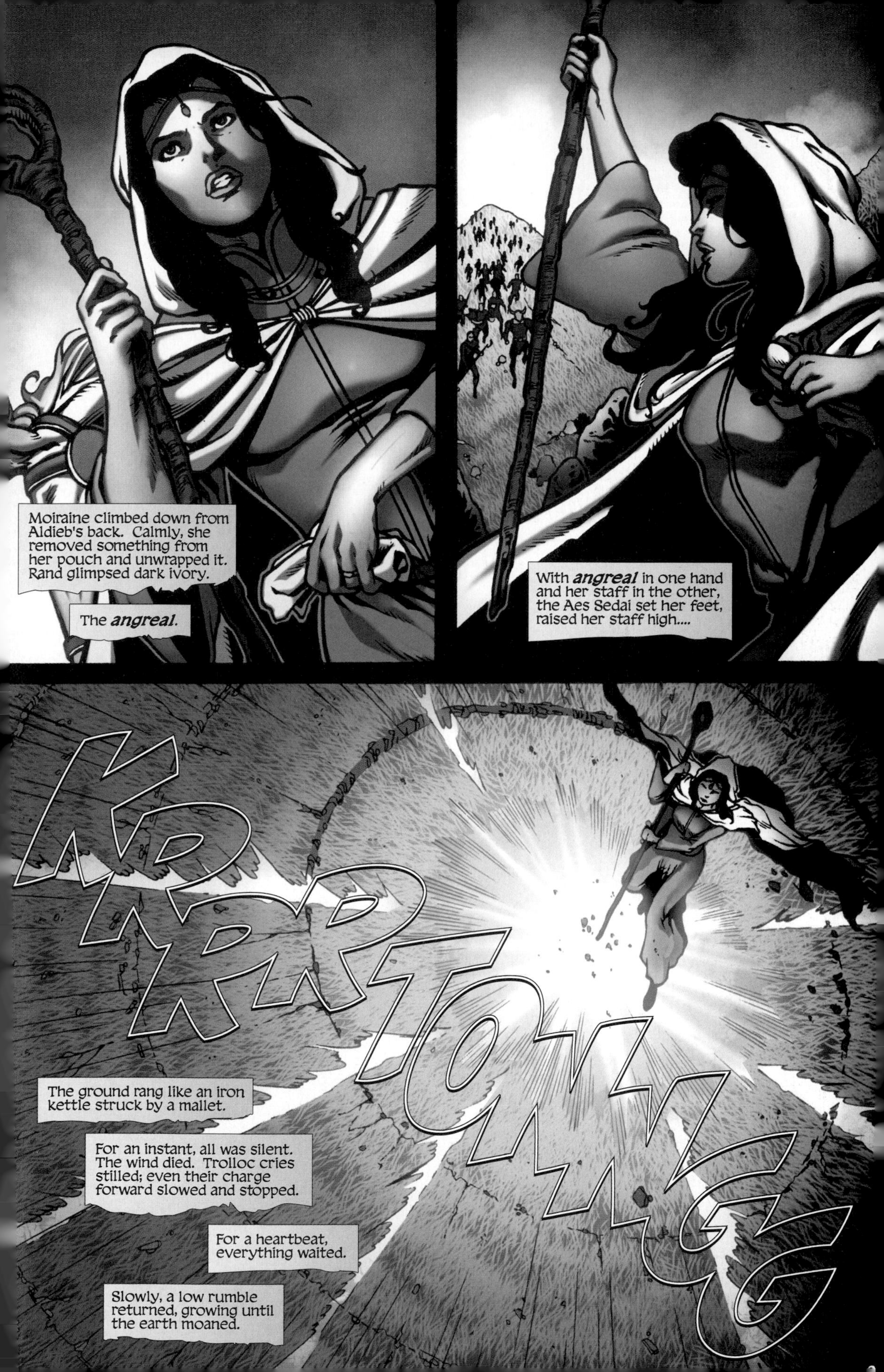

Moiraine climbed down from Aldieb's back. Calmly, she removed something from her pouch and unwrapped it. Rand glimpsed dark ivory.
The *angreal*.
With *angreal* in one hand and her staff in the other, the Aes Sedai set her feet, raised her staff high....
KRRTONNNG
The ground rang like an iron kettle struck by a mallet.
For an instant, all was silent. The wind died. Trolloc cries stilled; even their charge forward slowed and stopped.
For a heartbeat, everything waited.
Slowly, a low rumble returned, growing until the earth moaned.

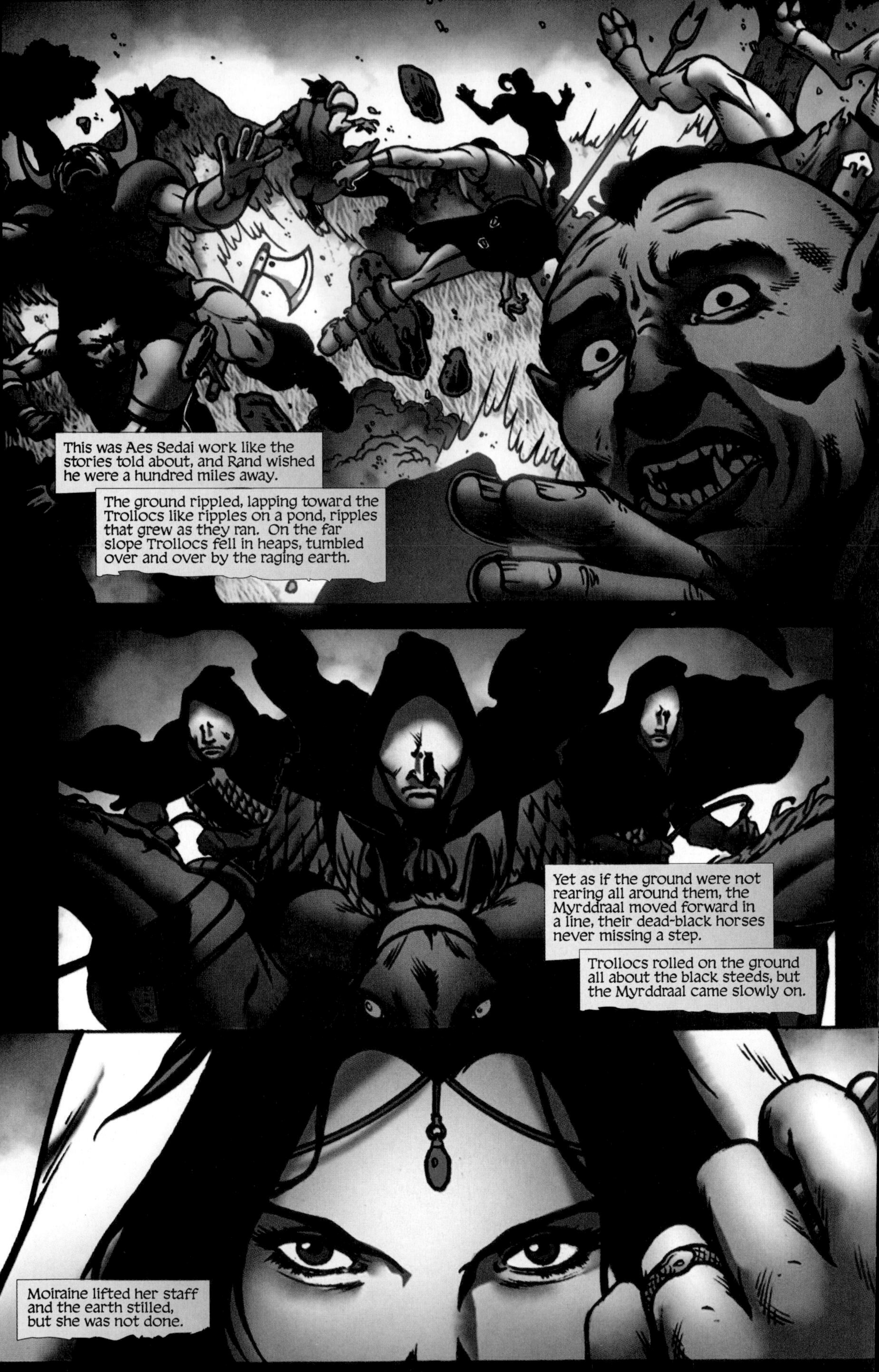
This was Aes Sedai work like the stories told about, and Rand wished he were a hundred miles away.
The ground rippled, lapping toward the Trollocs like ripples on a pond, ripples that grew as they ran. On the far slope Trollocs fell in heaps, tumbled over and over by the raging earth.
Yet as if the ground were not rearing all around them, the Myrddraal moved forward in a line, their dead-black horses never missing a step.
Trollocs rolled on the ground all about the black steeds, but the Myrddraal came slowly on.
Moiraine lifted her staff and the earth stilled, but she was not done.

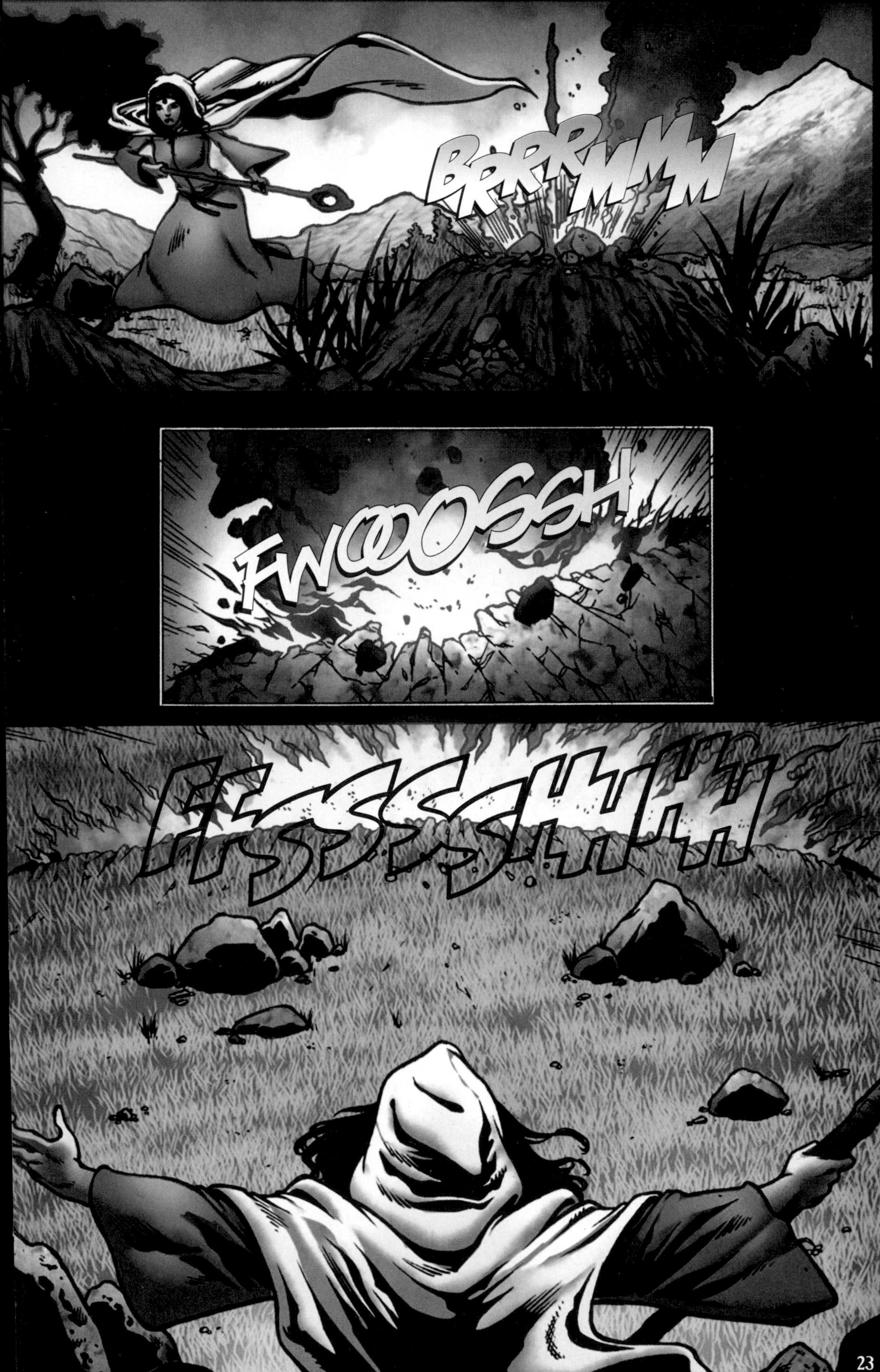
BRRRMMM
FWOOOSSH
FFSSSHHH

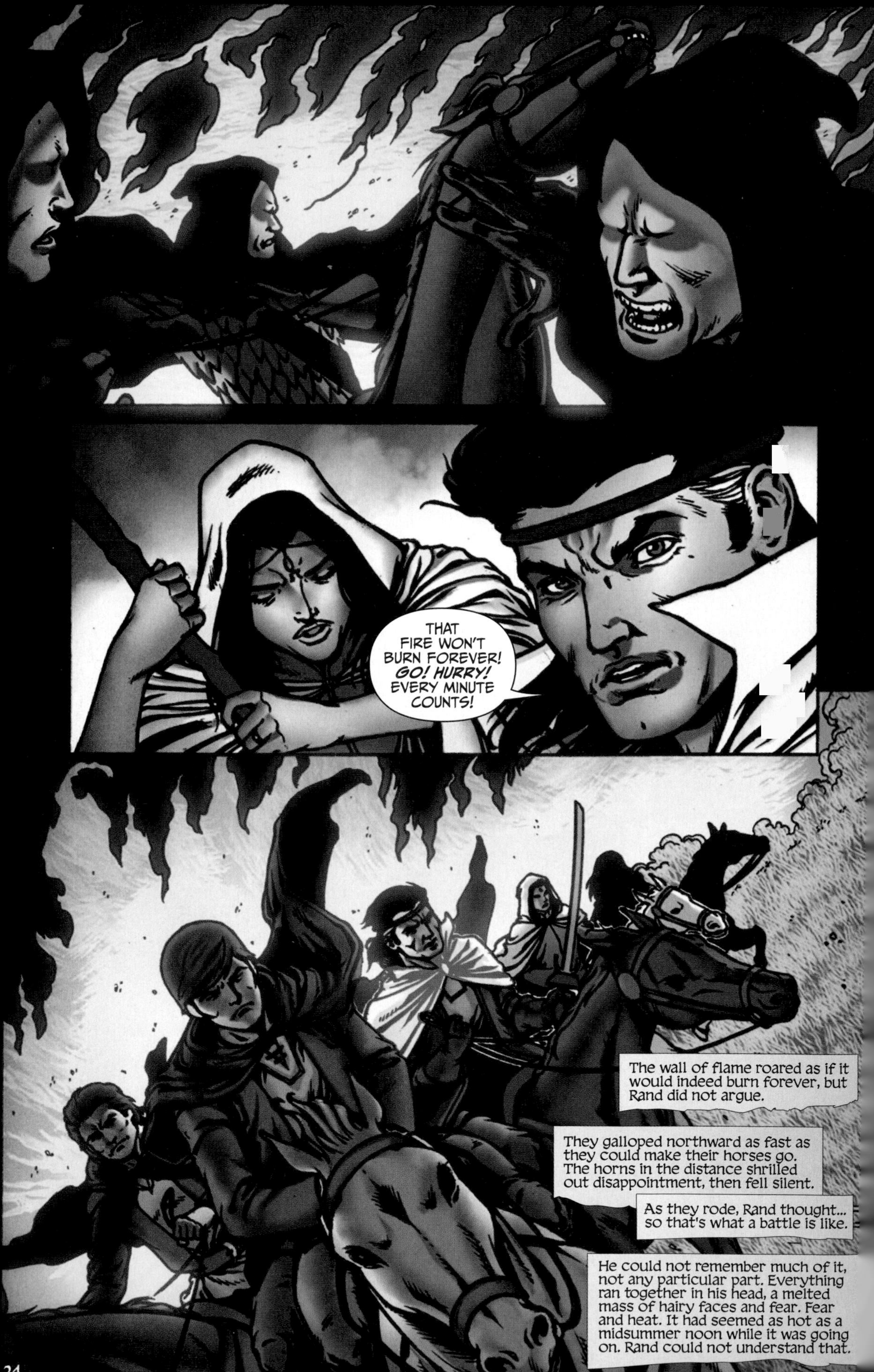
THAT FIRE WON'T BURN FOREVER! GO! HURRY! EVERY MINUTE COUNTS!
The wall of flame roared as if it would indeed burn forever, but Rand did not argue.
They galloped northward as fast as they could make their horses go. The horns in the distance shrilled out disappointment, then fell silent.
As they rode, Rand thought... so that's what a battle is like.
He could not remember much of it, not any particular part. Everything ran together in his head, a melted mass of hairy faces and fear. Fear and heat. It had seemed as hot as a midsummer noon while it was going on. Rand could not understand that.

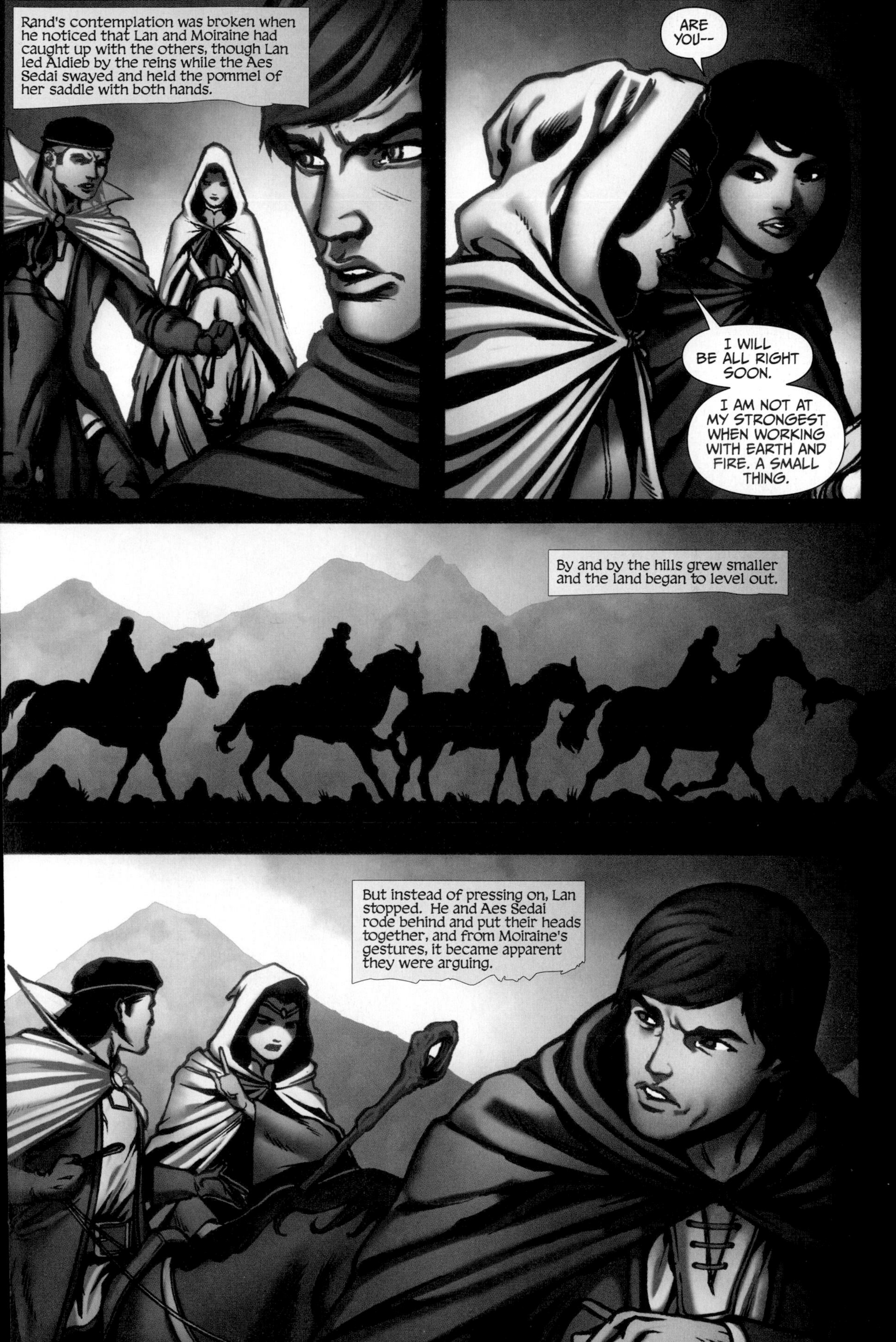
Rand's contemplation was broken when he noticed that Lan and Moiraine had caught up with the others, though Lan led Aldieb by the reins while the Aes Sedai swayed and held the pommel of her saddle with both hands.
ARE YOU--
I WILL BE ALL RIGHT SOON.
I AM NOT AT MY STRONGEST WHEN WORKING WITH EARTH AND FIRE. A SMALL THING.
By and by the hills grew smaller and the land began to level out.
But instead of pressing on, Lan stopped. He and Aes Sedai rode behind and put their heads together, and from Moiraine's gestures, it became apparent they were arguing.

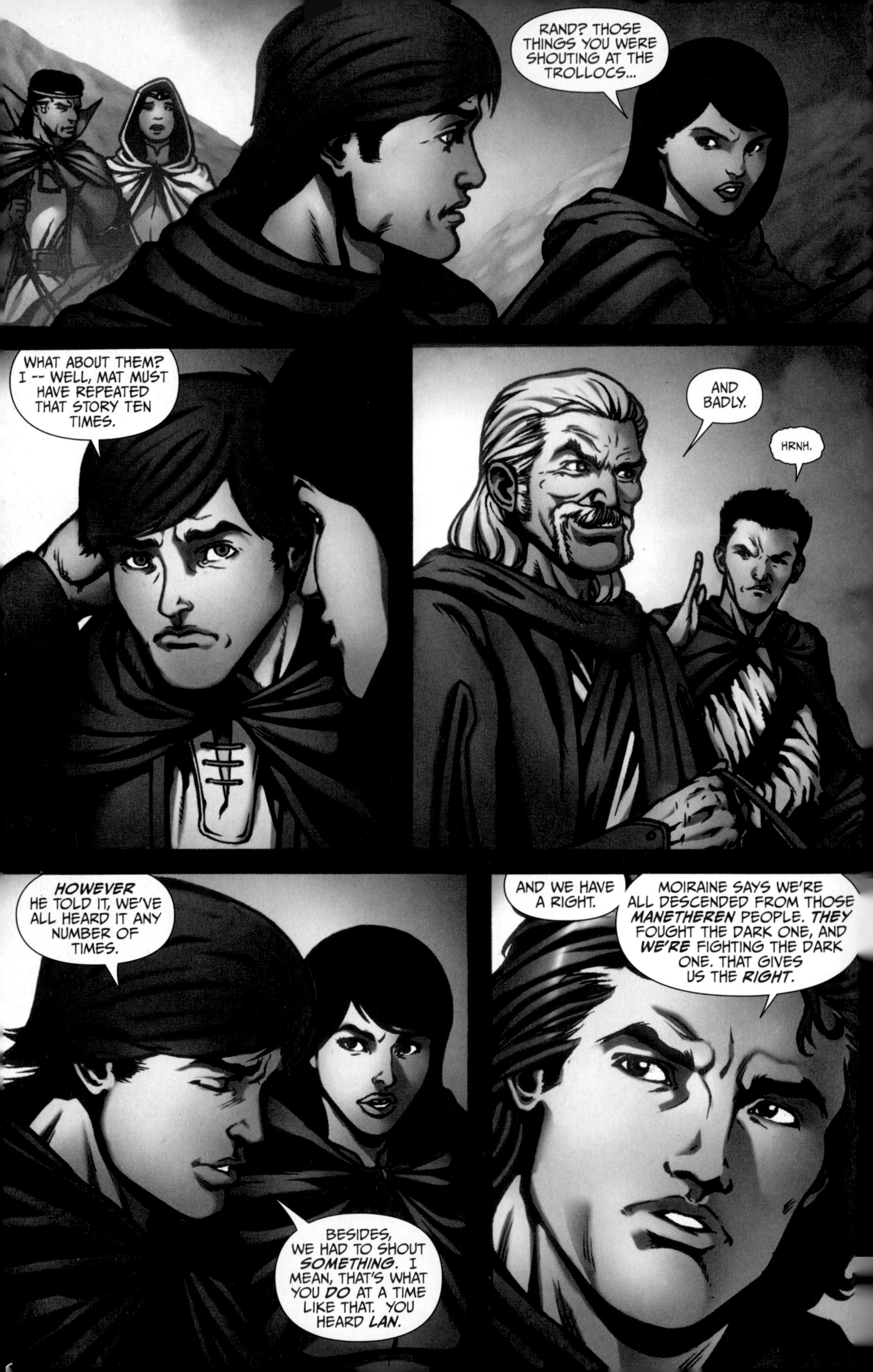
RAND? THOSE THINGS YOU WERE SHOUTING AT THE TROLLOCS...
WHAT ABOUT THEM? I -- WELL, MAT MUST HAVE REPEATED THAT STORY TEN TIMES.
AND BADLY.
HRNH.
HOWEVER HE TOLD IT, WE'VE ALL HEARD IT ANY NUMBER OF TIMES.
BESIDES, WE HAD TO SHOUT *SOMETHING*. I MEAN, THAT'S WHAT YOU *DO* AT A TIME LIKE THAT. YOU HEARD *LAN*.
AND WE HAVE A RIGHT.
MOIRAINE SAYS WE'RE ALL DESCENDED FROM THOSE *MANETHEREN* PEOPLE. *THEY* FOUGHT THE DARK ONE, AND *WE'RE* FIGHTING THE DARK ONE. THAT GIVES US THE *RIGHT*.

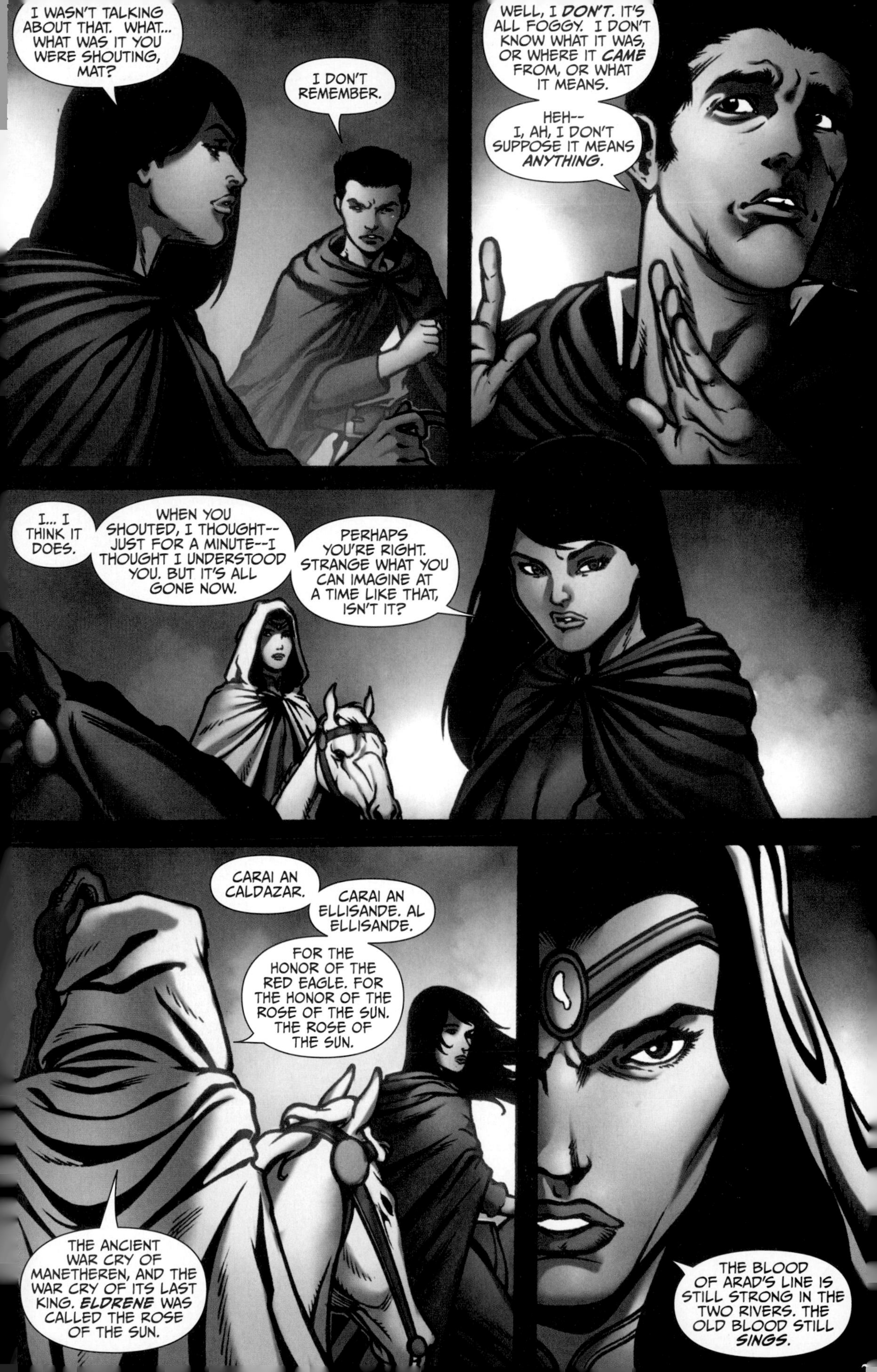
I WASN'T TALKING ABOUT THAT. WHAT... WHAT WAS IT YOU WERE SHOUTING, MAT?
I DON'T REMEMBER.
WELL, I *DON'T*. IT'S ALL FOGGY. I DON'T KNOW WHAT IT WAS, OR WHERE IT *CAME* FROM, OR WHAT IT MEANS.
HEH-- I, AH, I DON'T SUPPOSE IT MEANS *ANYTHING*.
I... I THINK IT DOES.
WHEN YOU SHOUTED, I THOUGHT-- JUST FOR A MINUTE--I THOUGHT I UNDERSTOOD YOU. BUT IT'S ALL GONE NOW.
PERHAPS YOU'RE RIGHT. STRANGE WHAT YOU CAN IMAGINE AT A TIME LIKE THAT, ISN'T IT?
CARAI AN CALDAZAR.
CARAI AN ELLISANDE. AL ELLISANDE.
FOR THE HONOR OF THE RED EAGLE. FOR THE HONOR OF THE ROSE OF THE SUN. THE ROSE OF THE SUN.
THE ANCIENT WAR CRY OF MANETHEREN, AND THE WAR CRY OF ITS LAST KING. *ELDRENE* WAS CALLED THE ROSE OF THE SUN.
THE BLOOD OF ARAD'S LINE IS STILL STRONG IN THE TWO RIVERS. THE OLD BLOOD STILL *SINGS*.

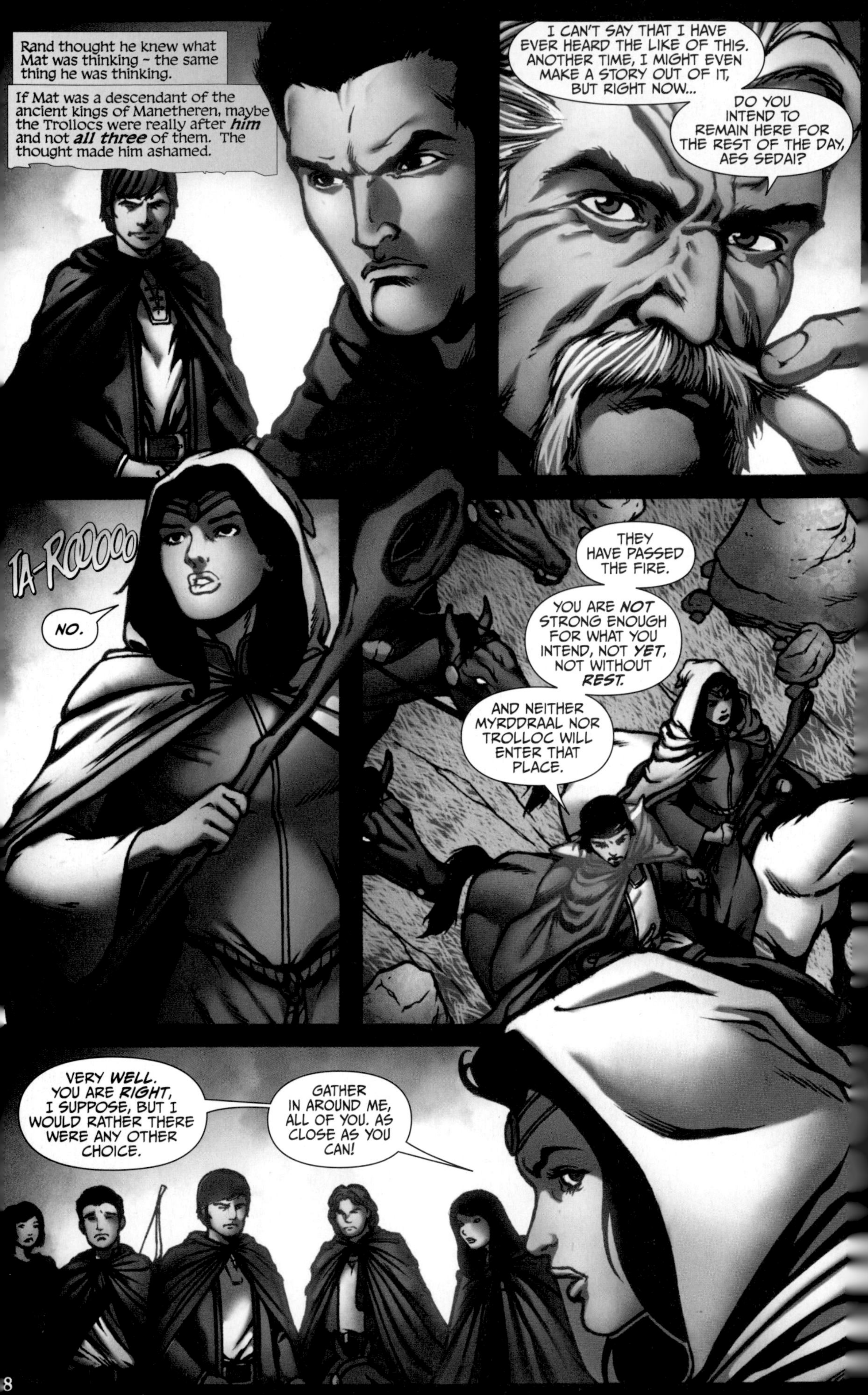

Rand thought he knew what Mat was thinking ~ the same thing he was thinking.
If Mat was a descendant of the ancient kings of Manetheren, maybe the Trollocs were really after *him* and not ***all three*** of them. The thought made him ashamed.
I CAN'T SAY THAT I HAVE EVER HEARD THE LIKE OF THIS. ANOTHER TIME, I MIGHT EVEN MAKE A STORY OUT OF IT, BUT RIGHT NOW...
DO YOU INTEND TO REMAIN HERE FOR THE REST OF THE DAY, AES SEDAI?
TA-ROOOOO
NO.
THEY HAVE PASSED THE FIRE.
YOU ARE *NOT* STRONG ENOUGH FOR WHAT YOU INTEND, NOT *YET*, NOT WITHOUT *REST.*
AND NEITHER MYRDDRAAL NOR TROLLOC WILL ENTER THAT PLACE.
VERY *WELL*. YOU ARE *RIGHT*, I SUPPOSE, BUT I WOULD RATHER THERE WERE ANY OTHER CHOICE.
GATHER IN AROUND ME, ALL OF YOU. AS CLOSE AS YOU CAN!

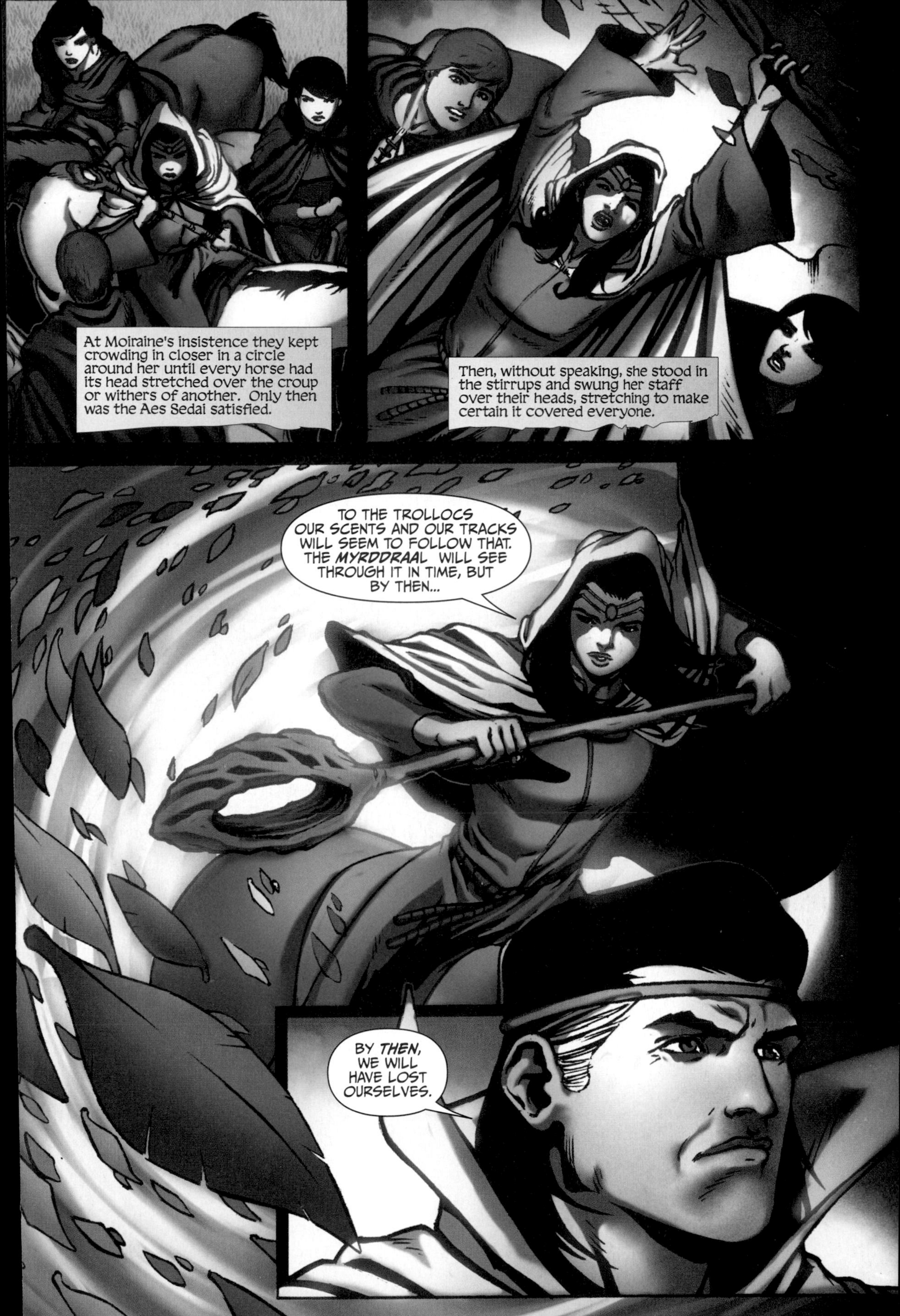
At Moiraine's insistence they kept crowding in closer in a circle around her until every horse had its head stretched over the croup or withers of another. Only then was the Aes Sedai satisfied.
Then, without speaking, she stood in the stirrups and swung her staff over their heads, stretching to make certain it covered everyone.
TO THE TROLLOCS OUR SCENTS AND OUR TRACKS WILL SEEM TO FOLLOW THAT. THE MYRDDRAAL WILL SEE THROUGH IT IN TIME, BUT BY THEN...
BY THEN, WE WILL HAVE LOST OURSELVES.

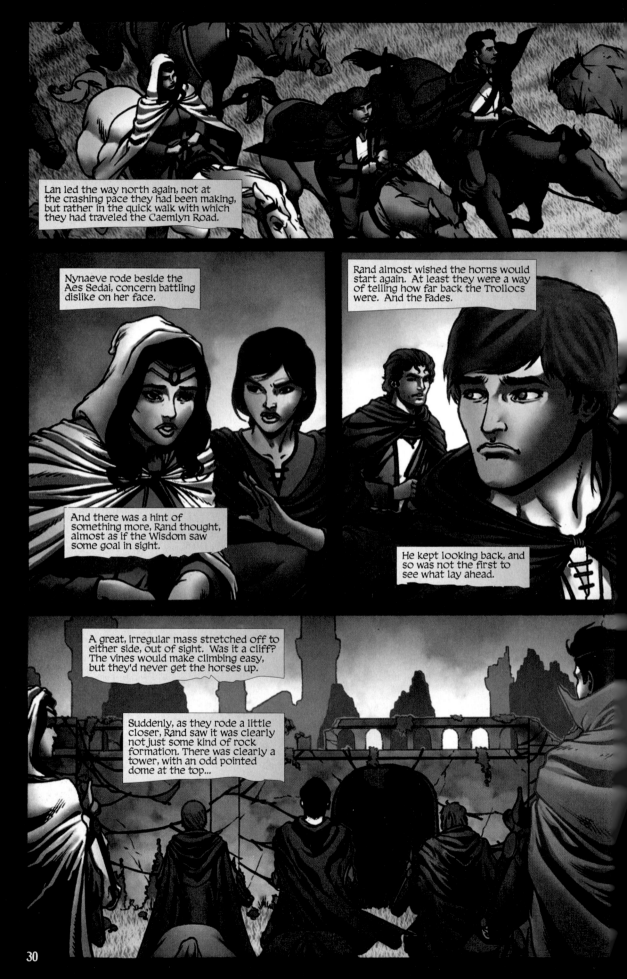

Lan led the way north again, not at the crashing pace they had been making, but rather in the quick walk with which they had traveled the Caemlyn Road.

Nynaeve rode beside the Aes Sedai, concern battling dislike on her face.

And there was a hint of something more, Rand thought, almost as if the Wisdom saw some goal in sight.

Rand almost wished the horns would start again. At least they were a way of telling how far back the Trollocs were. And the Fades.

He kept looking back, and so was not the first to see what lay ahead.

A great, irregular mass stretched off to either side, out of sight. Was it a cliff? The vines would make climbing easy, but they'd never get the horses up.

Suddenly, as they rode a little closer, Rand saw it was clearly not just some kind of rock formation. There was clearly a tower, with an odd pointed dome at the top...

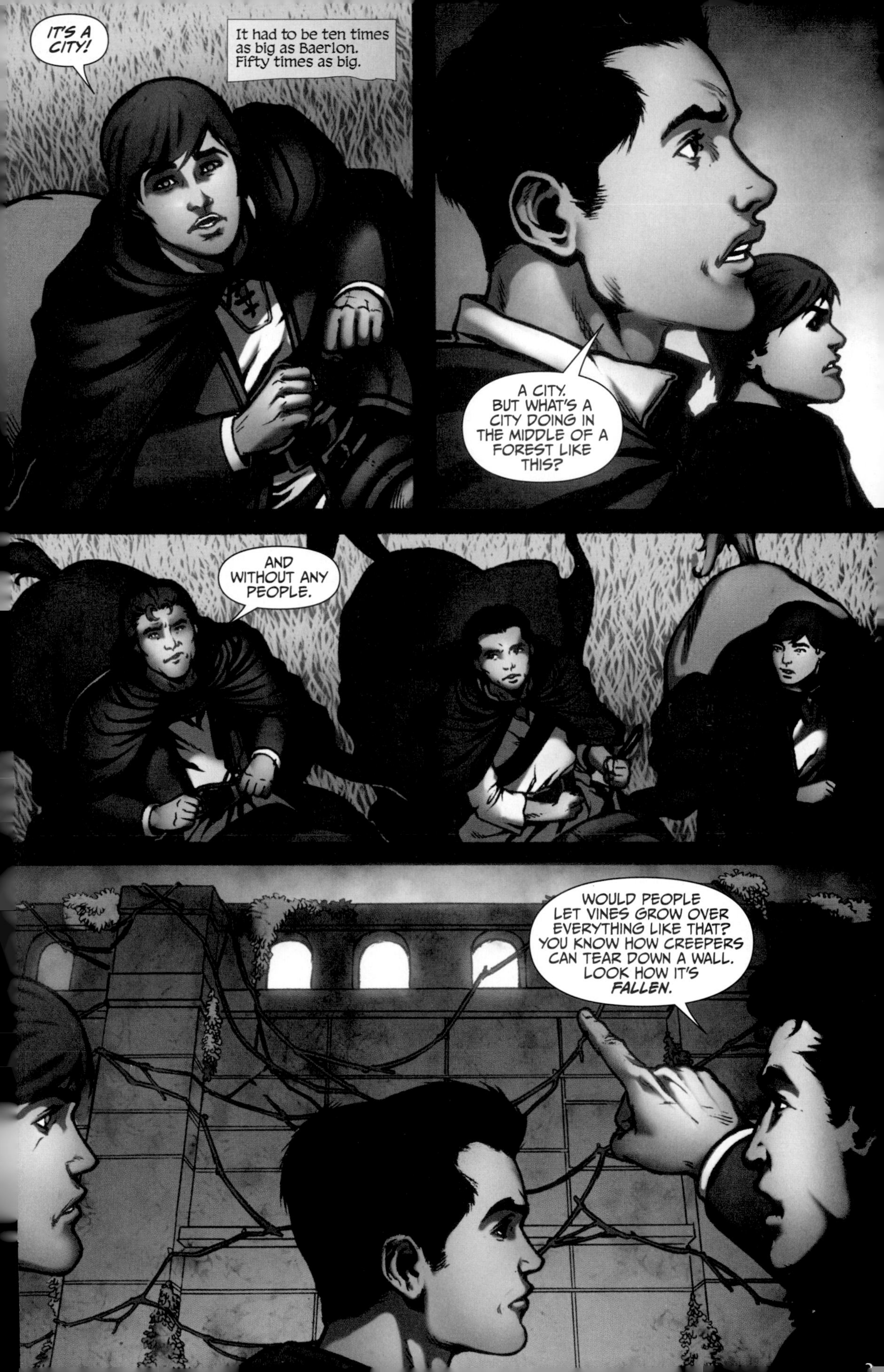
IT'S A CITY!
It had to be ten times as big as Baerlon. Fifty times as big.
A CITY. BUT WHAT'S A CITY DOING IN THE MIDDLE OF A FOREST LIKE THIS?
AND WITHOUT ANY PEOPLE.
WOULD PEOPLE LET VINES GROW OVER EVERYTHING LIKE THAT? YOU KNOW HOW CREEPERS CAN TEAR DOWN A WALL. LOOK HOW IT'S FALLEN.

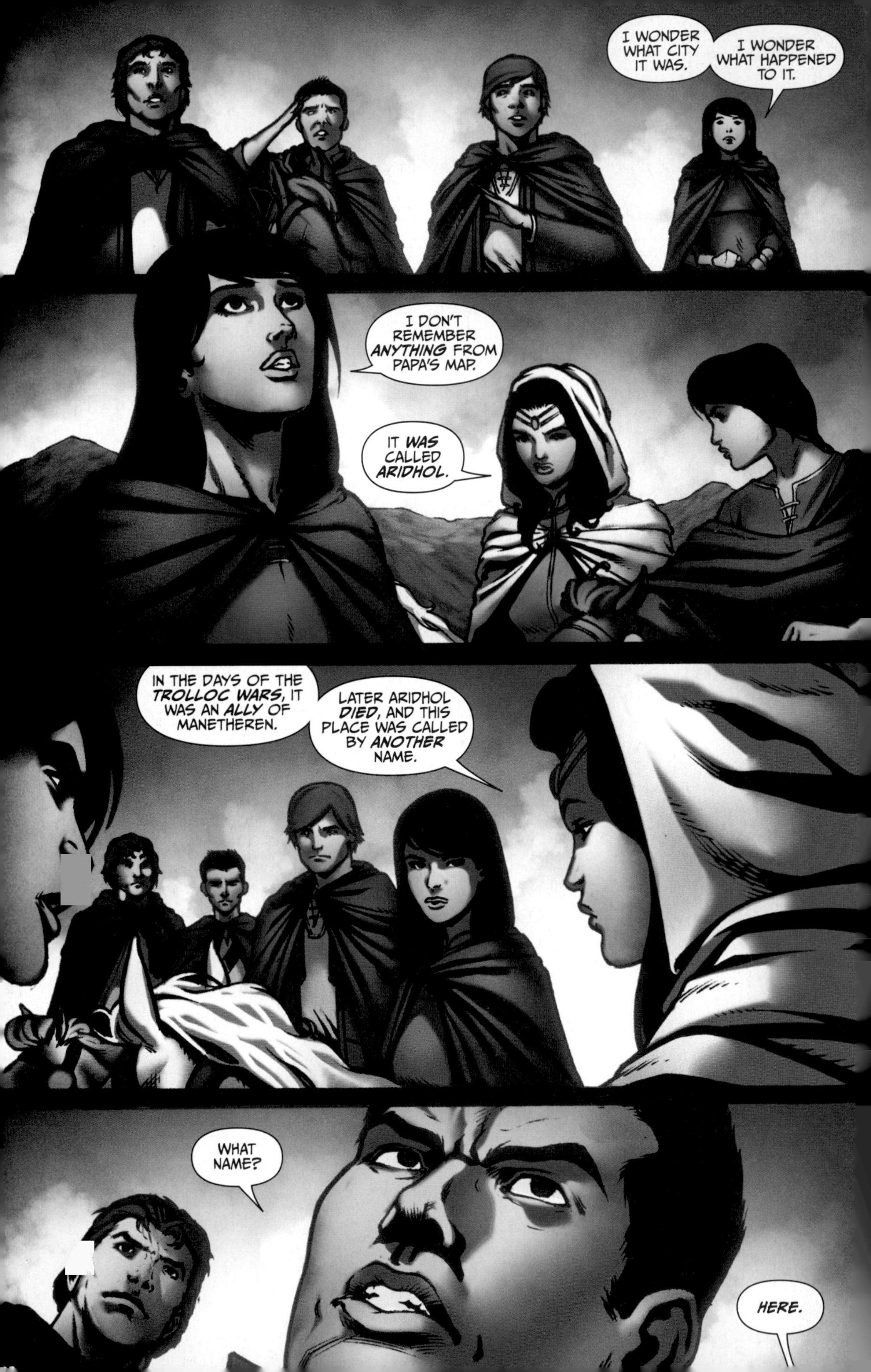
I WONDER WHAT CITY IT WAS.
I WONDER WHAT HAPPENED TO IT.
I DON'T REMEMBER *ANYTHING* FROM PAPA'S MAP.
IT *WAS* CALLED *ARIDHOL.*
IN THE DAYS OF THE *TROLLOC WARS,* IT WAS AN *ALLY* OF MANETHEREN.
LATER ARIDHOL *DIED,* AND THIS PLACE WAS CALLED BY *ANOTHER* NAME.
WHAT NAME?
HERE.

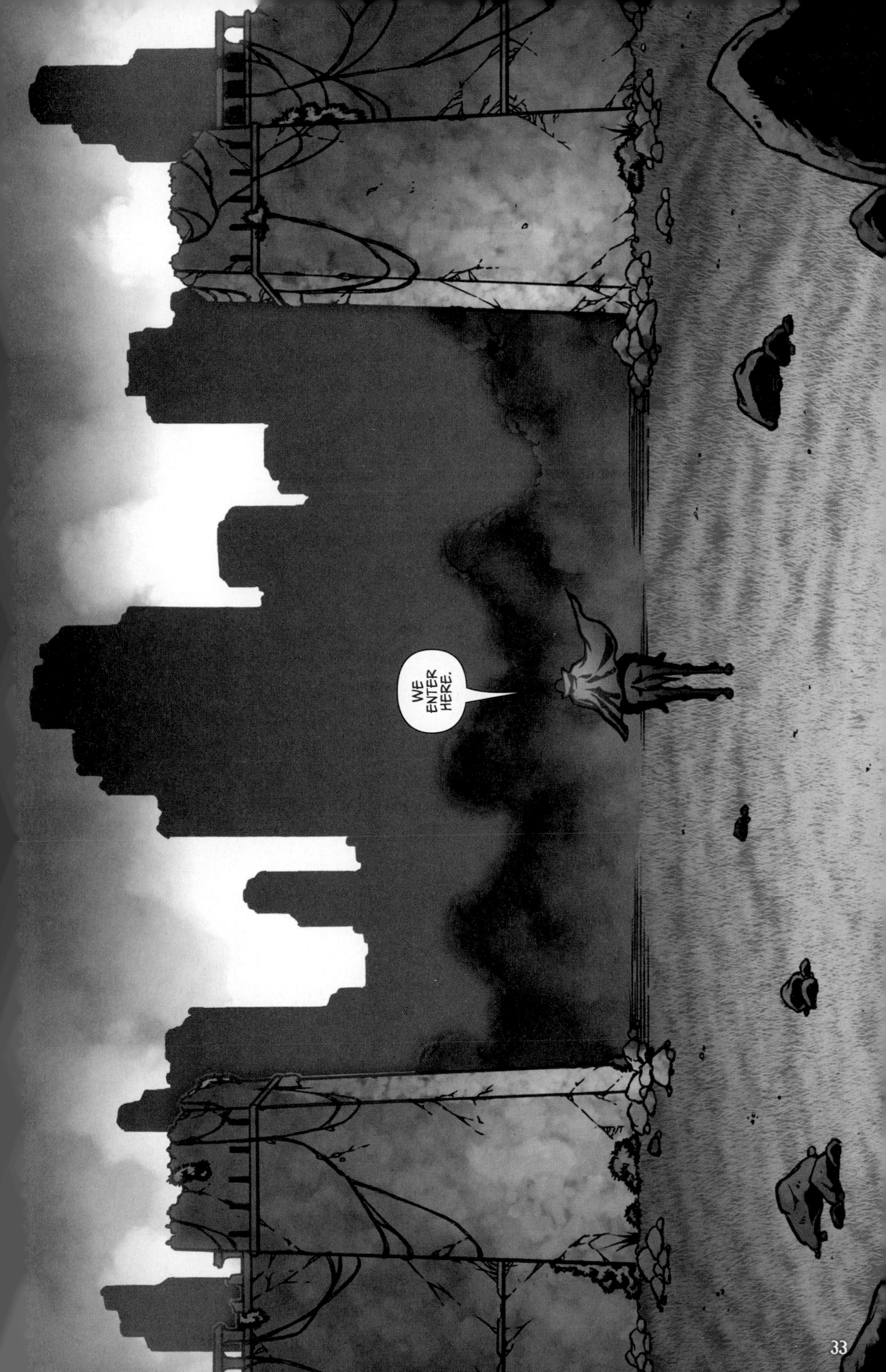
WE ENTER HERE.

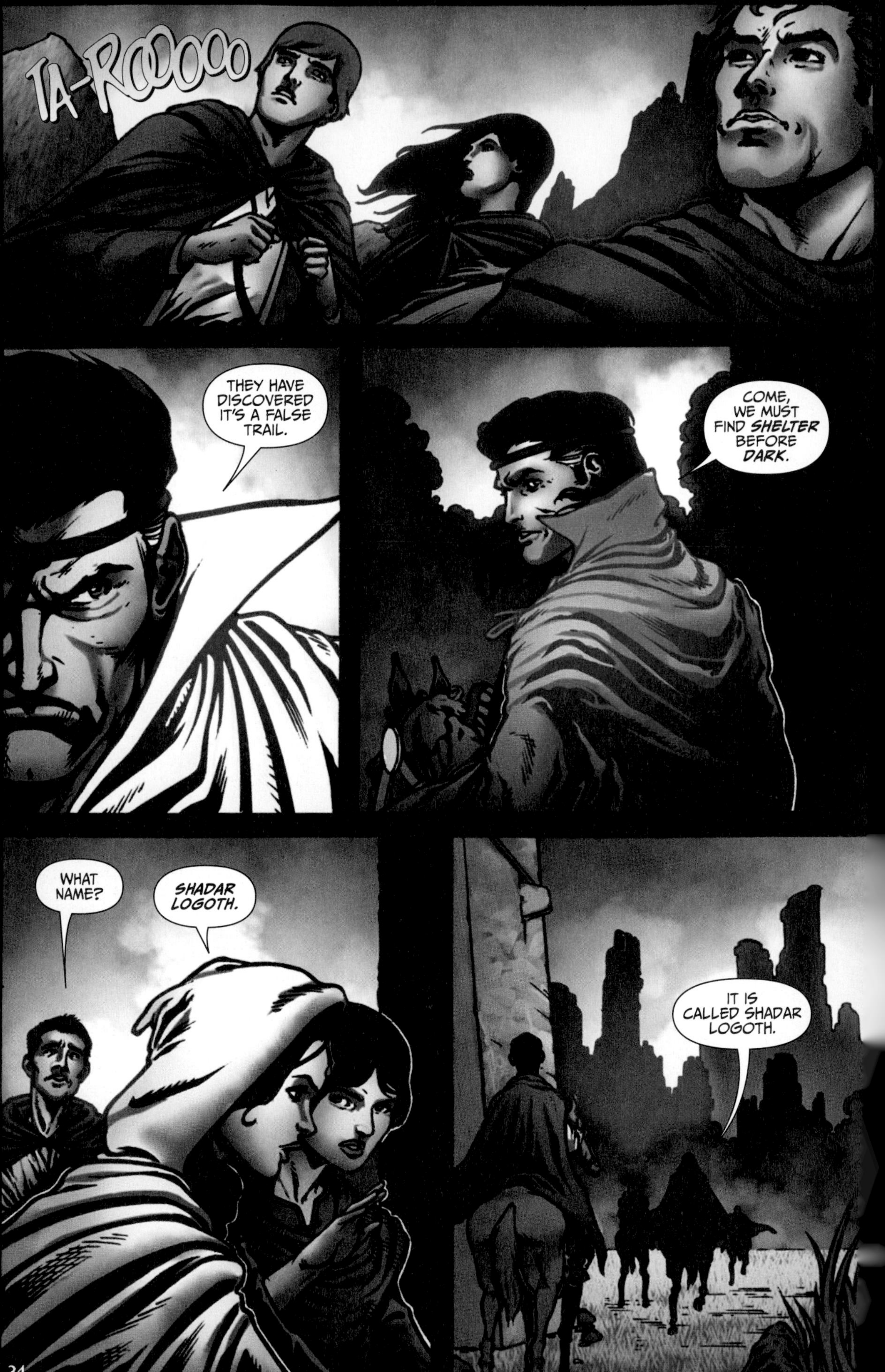
TA-ROOOOO
THEY HAVE DISCOVERED IT'S A FALSE TRAIL.
COME, WE MUST FIND SHELTER BEFORE DARK.
WHAT NAME?
SHADAR LOGOTH.
IT IS CALLED SHADAR LOGOTH.

chapter two

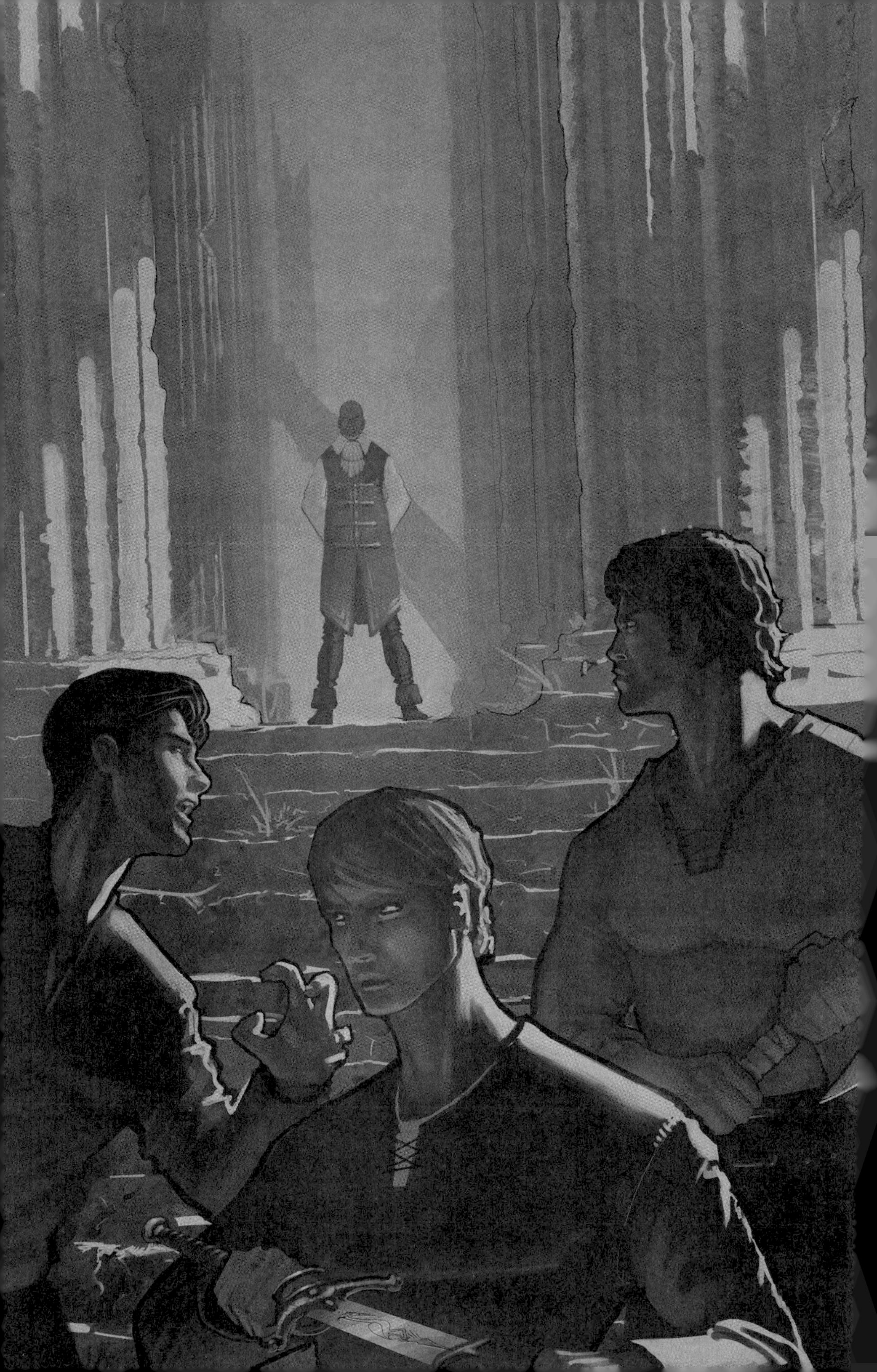

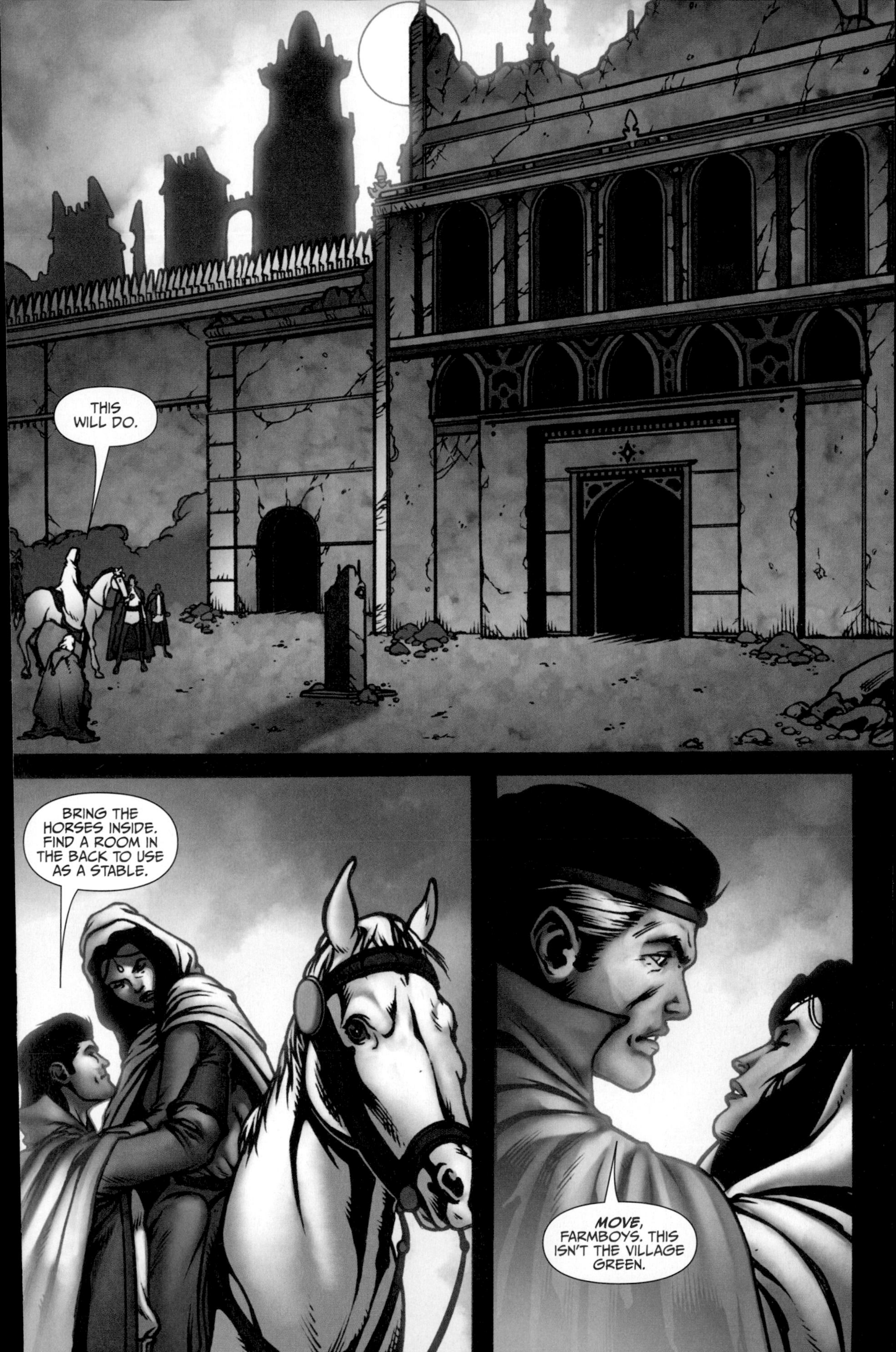

THIS WILL DO.
BRING THE HORSES INSIDE. FIND A ROOM IN THE BACK TO USE AS A STABLE.
MOVE, FARMBOYS. THIS ISN'T THE VILLAGE GREEN.

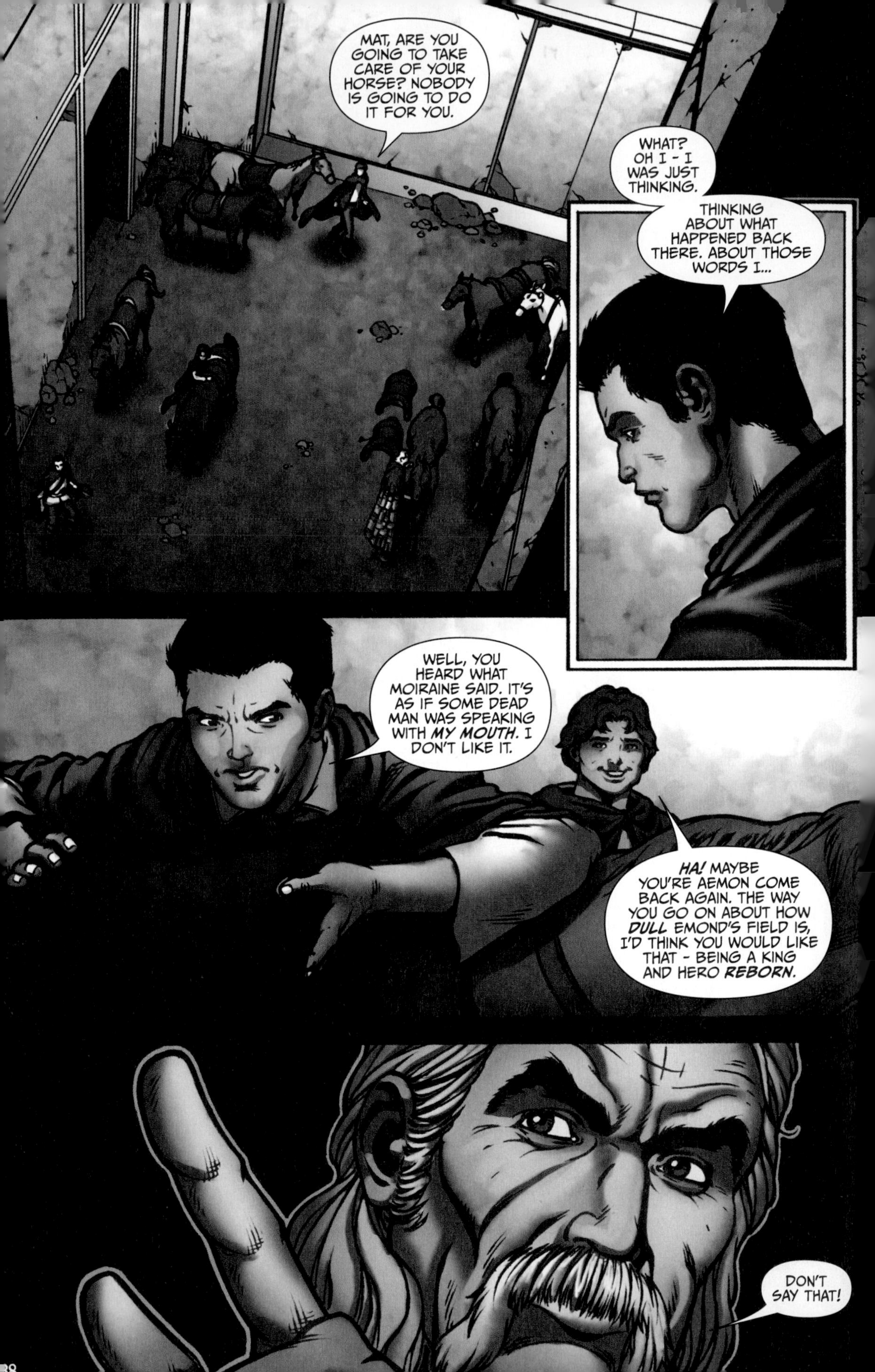
MAT, ARE YOU GOING TO TAKE CARE OF YOUR HORSE? NOBODY IS GOING TO DO IT FOR YOU.
WHAT? OH I - I WAS JUST THINKING.
THINKING ABOUT WHAT HAPPENED BACK THERE. ABOUT THOSE WORDS I...
WELL, YOU HEARD WHAT MOIRAINE SAID. IT'S AS IF SOME DEAD MAN WAS SPEAKING WITH MY MOUTH. I DON'T LIKE IT.
HA! MAYBE YOU'RE AEMON COME BACK AGAIN. THE WAY YOU GO ON ABOUT HOW DULL EMOND'S FIELD IS, I'D THINK YOU WOULD LIKE THAT - BEING A KING AND HERO REBORN.
DON'T SAY THAT!

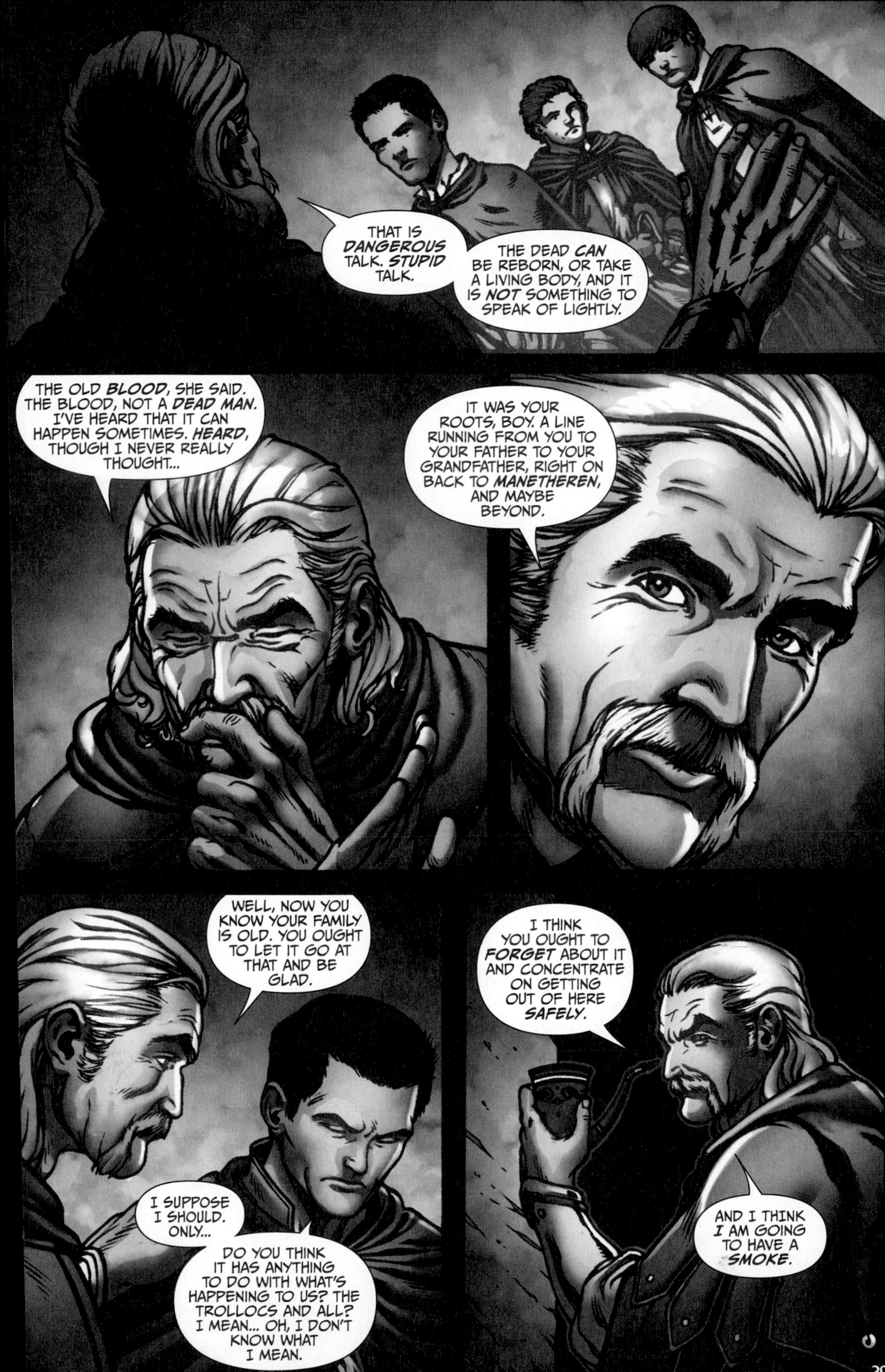

THAT IS DANGEROUS TALK. STUPID TALK.
THE DEAD CAN BE REBORN, OR TAKE A LIVING BODY, AND IT IS NOT SOMETHING TO SPEAK OF LIGHTLY.
THE OLD BLOOD, SHE SAID. THE BLOOD, NOT A DEAD MAN. I'VE HEARD THAT IT CAN HAPPEN SOMETIMES. HEARD, THOUGH I NEVER REALLY THOUGHT...
IT WAS YOUR ROOTS, BOY. A LINE RUNNING FROM YOU TO YOUR FATHER TO YOUR GRANDFATHER, RIGHT ON BACK TO MANETHEREN, AND MAYBE BEYOND.
WELL, NOW YOU KNOW YOUR FAMILY IS OLD. YOU OUGHT TO LET IT GO AT THAT AND BE GLAD.
I SUPPOSE I SHOULD. ONLY...
DO YOU THINK IT HAS ANYTHING TO DO WITH WHAT'S HAPPENING TO US? THE TROLLOCS AND ALL? I MEAN... OH, I DON'T KNOW WHAT I MEAN.
I THINK YOU OUGHT TO FORGET ABOUT IT AND CONCENTRATE ON GETTING OUT OF HERE SAFELY.
AND I THINK I AM GOING TO HAVE A SMOKE.

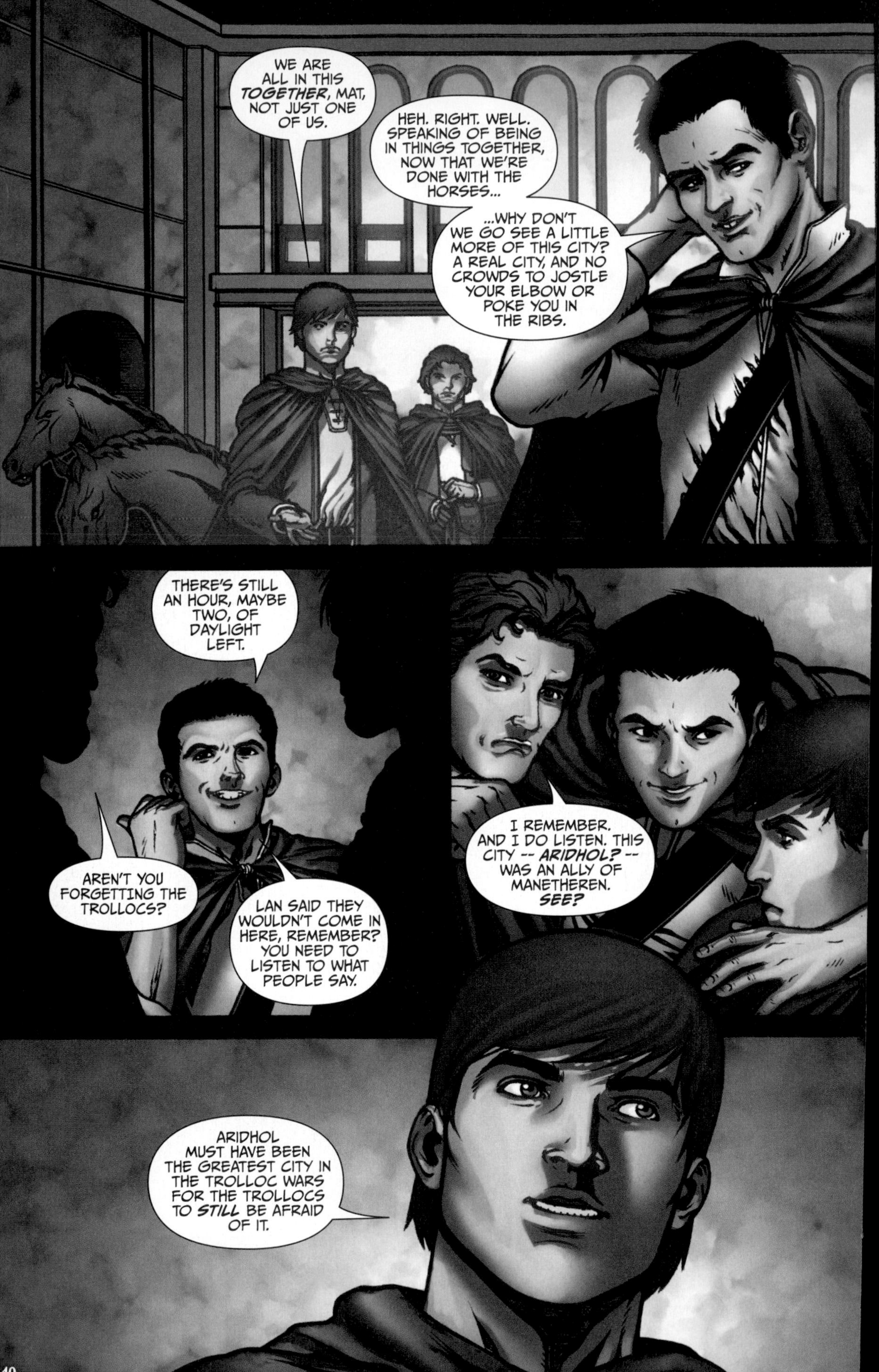

WE ARE ALL IN THIS TOGETHER, MAT, NOT JUST ONE OF US.
HEH. RIGHT. WELL. SPEAKING OF BEING IN THINGS TOGETHER, NOW THAT WE'RE DONE WITH THE HORSES...
...WHY DON'T WE GO SEE A LITTLE MORE OF THIS CITY? A REAL CITY, AND NO CROWDS TO JOSTLE YOUR ELBOW OR POKE YOU IN THE RIBS.
THERE'S STILL AN HOUR, MAYBE TWO, OF DAYLIGHT LEFT.
AREN'T YOU FORGETTING THE TROLLOCS?
LAN SAID THEY WOULDN'T COME IN HERE, REMEMBER? YOU NEED TO LISTEN TO WHAT PEOPLE SAY.
I REMEMBER. AND I DO LISTEN. THIS CITY -- ARIDHOL? -- WAS AN ALLY OF MANETHEREN. SEE?
ARIDHOL MUST HAVE BEEN THE GREATEST CITY IN THE TROLLOC WARS FOR THE TROLLOCS TO STILL BE AFRAID OF IT.

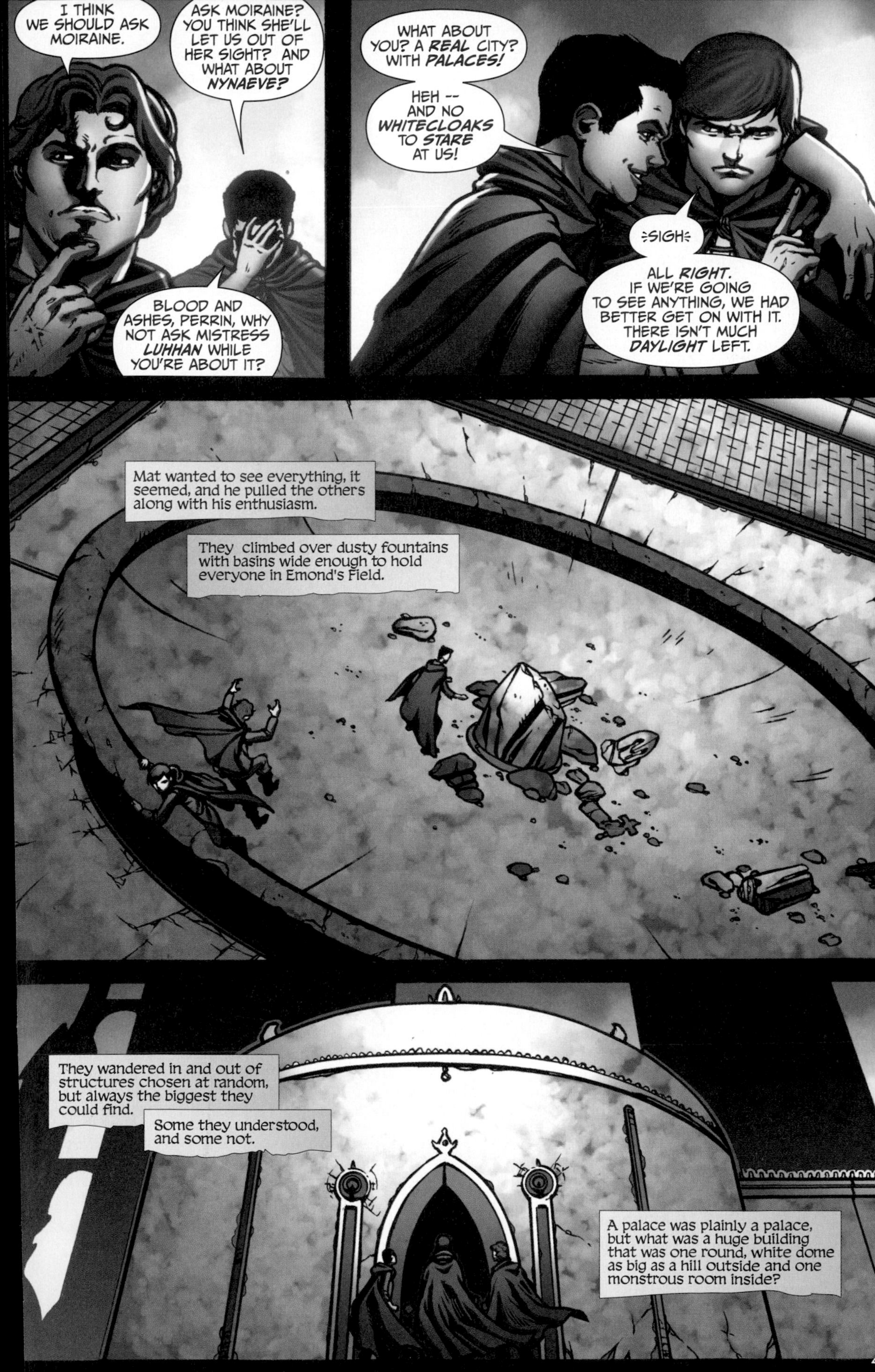
I THINK WE SHOULD ASK MOIRAINE.
ASK MOIRAINE? YOU THINK SHE'LL LET US OUT OF HER SIGHT? AND WHAT ABOUT NYNAEVE?
BLOOD AND ASHES, PERRIN, WHY NOT ASK MISTRESS LUHHAN WHILE YOU'RE ABOUT IT?
WHAT ABOUT YOU? A REAL CITY? WITH PALACES!
HEH -- AND NO WHITECLOAKS TO STARE AT US!
SIGH
ALL RIGHT. IF WE'RE GOING TO SEE ANYTHING, WE HAD BETTER GET ON WITH IT. THERE ISN'T MUCH DAYLIGHT LEFT.
Mat wanted to see everything, it seemed, and he pulled the others along with his enthusiasm.
They climbed over dusty fountains with basins wide enough to hold everyone in Emond's Field.
They wandered in and out of structures chosen at random, but always the biggest they could find.
Some they understood, and some not.
A palace was plainly a palace, but what was a huge building that was one round, white dome as big as a hill outside and one monstrous room inside?

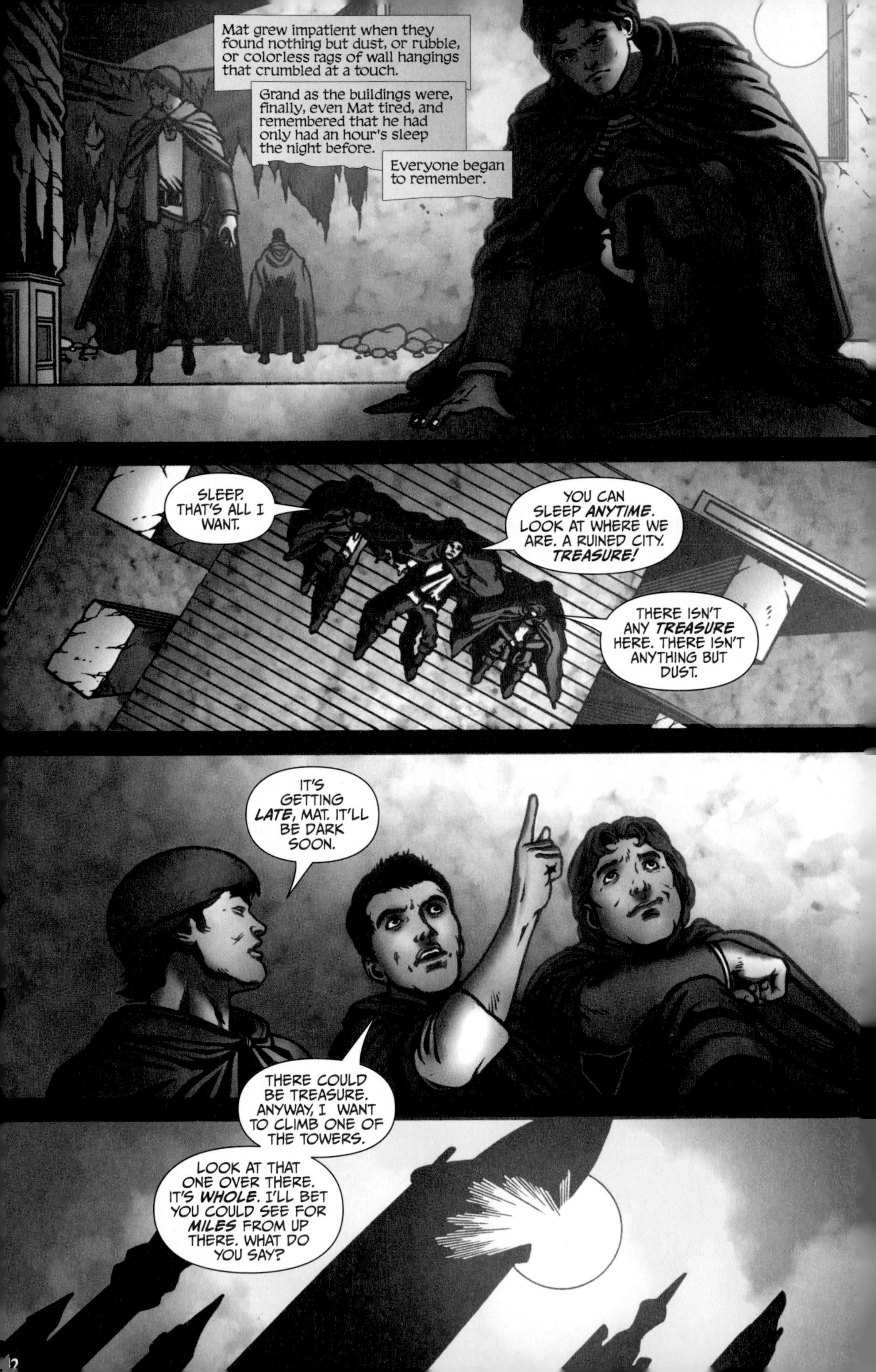
Mat grew impatient when they found nothing but dust, or rubble, or colorless rags of wall hangings that crumbled at a touch.
Grand as the buildings were, finally, even Mat tired, and remembered that he had only had an hour's sleep the night before.
Everyone began to remember.
SLEEP. THAT'S ALL I WANT.
YOU CAN SLEEP ANYTIME. LOOK AT WHERE WE ARE. A RUINED CITY. TREASURE!
THERE ISN'T ANY TREASURE HERE. THERE ISN'T ANYTHING BUT DUST.
IT'S GETTING LATE, MAT. IT'LL BE DARK SOON.
THERE COULD BE TREASURE. ANYWAY, I WANT TO CLIMB ONE OF THE TOWERS.
LOOK AT THAT ONE OVER THERE. IT'S WHOLE. I'LL BET YOU COULD SEE FOR MILES FROM UP THERE. WHAT DO YOU SAY?

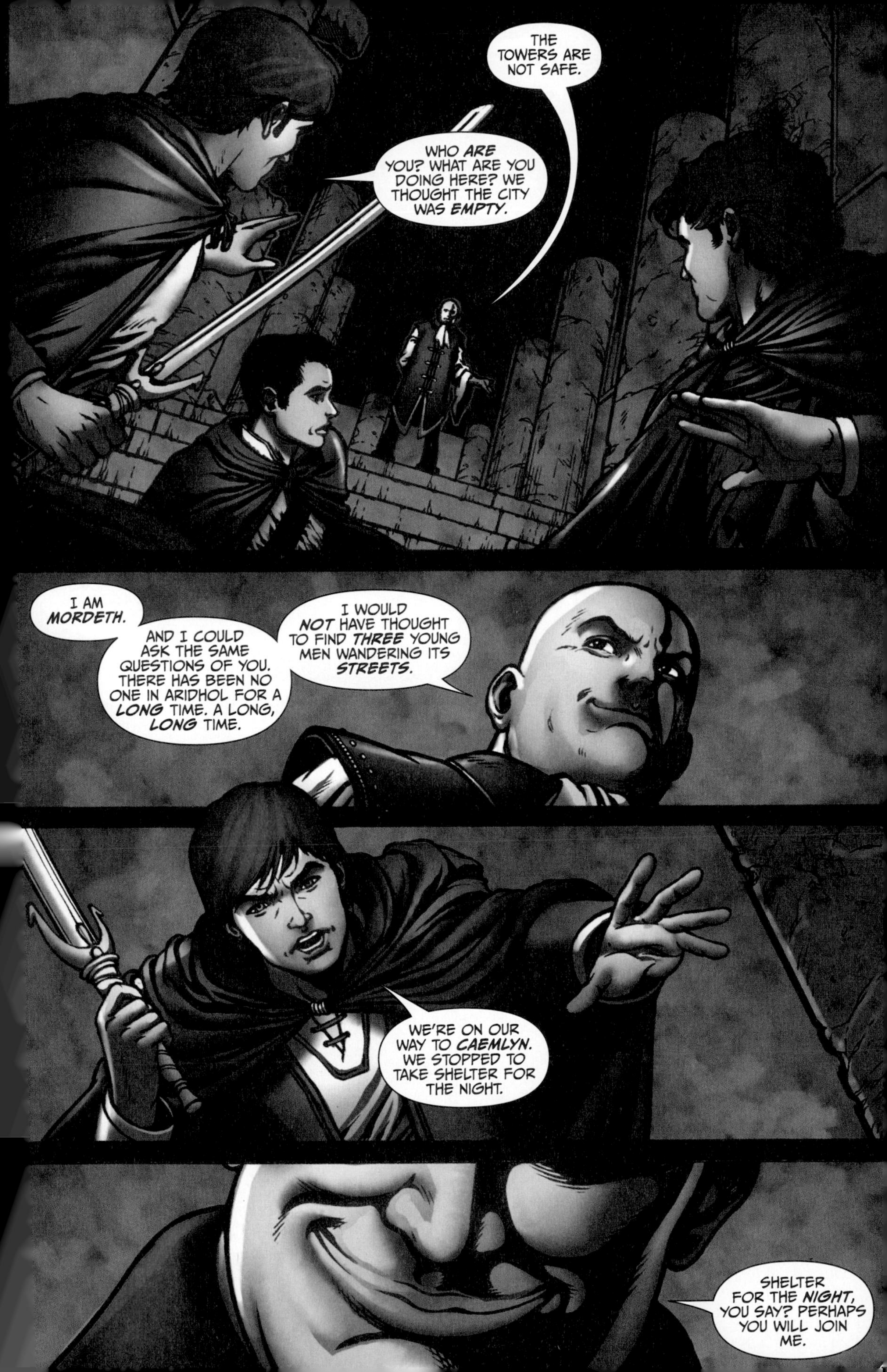

WHO ARE YOU? WHAT ARE YOU DOING HERE? WE THOUGHT THE CITY WAS EMPTY.
THE TOWERS ARE NOT SAFE.
I AM MORDETH.
AND I COULD ASK THE SAME QUESTIONS OF YOU. THERE HAS BEEN NO ONE IN ARIDHOL FOR A LONG TIME. A LONG, LONG TIME.
I WOULD NOT HAVE THOUGHT TO FIND THREE YOUNG MEN WANDERING ITS STREETS.
WE'RE ON OUR WAY TO CAEMLYN. WE STOPPED TO TAKE SHELTER FOR THE NIGHT.
SHELTER FOR THE NIGHT, YOU SAY? PERHAPS YOU WILL JOIN ME.

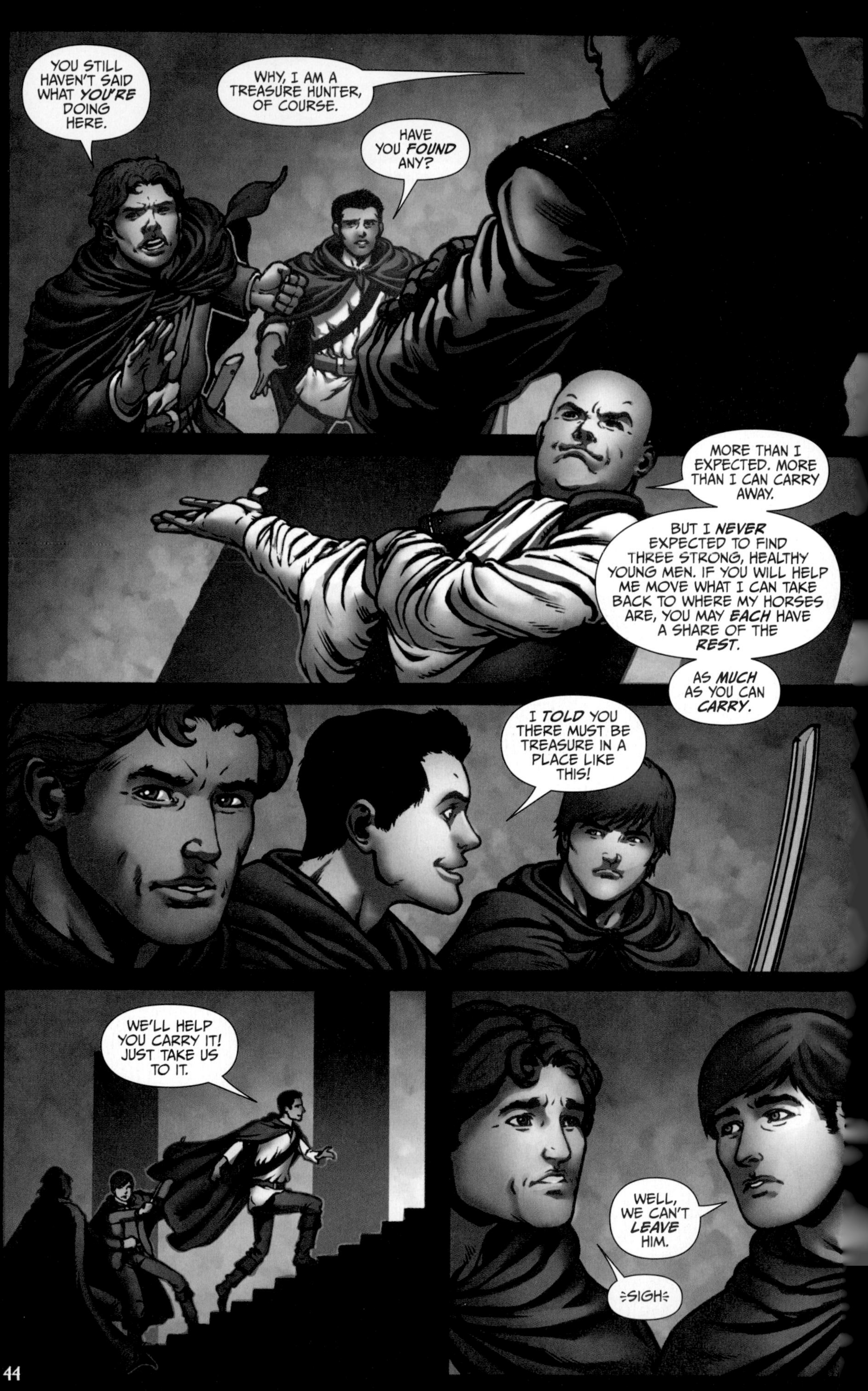
YOU STILL HAVEN'T SAID WHAT *YOU'RE* DOING HERE.
WHY, I AM A TREASURE HUNTER, OF COURSE.
HAVE YOU *FOUND* ANY?
MORE THAN I EXPECTED. MORE THAN I CAN CARRY AWAY.
BUT I *NEVER* EXPECTED TO FIND THREE STRONG, HEALTHY YOUNG MEN. IF YOU WILL HELP ME MOVE WHAT I CAN TAKE BACK TO WHERE MY HORSES ARE, YOU MAY *EACH* HAVE A SHARE OF THE *REST*.
AS *MUCH* AS YOU CAN *CARRY*.
I *TOLD* YOU THERE MUST BE TREASURE IN A PLACE LIKE THIS!
WE'LL HELP YOU CARRY IT! JUST TAKE US TO IT.
WELL, WE CAN'T *LEAVE* HIM.
SIGH

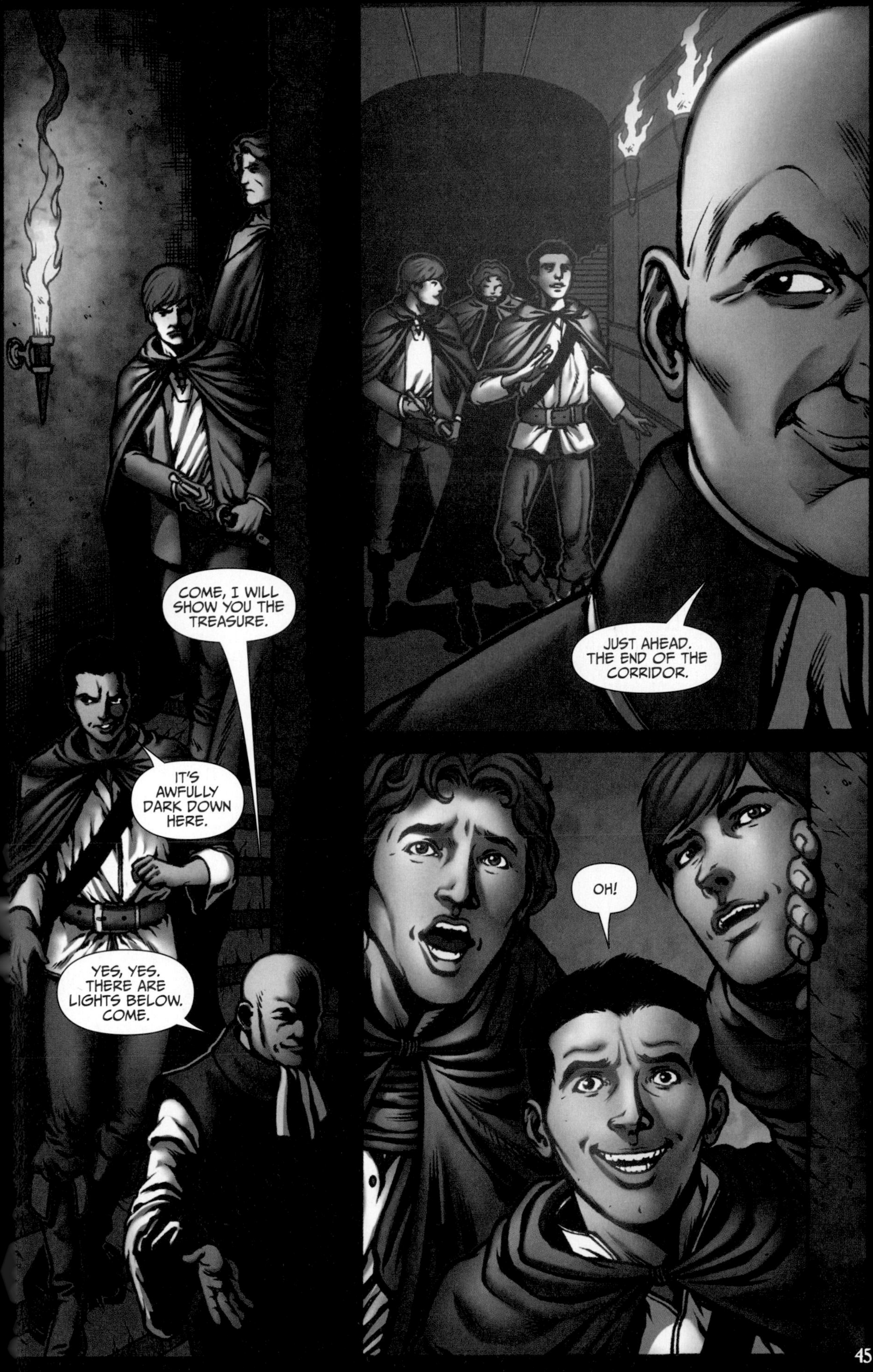
COME, I WILL SHOW YOU THE TREASURE.
IT'S AWFULLY DARK DOWN HERE.
YES, YES. THERE ARE LIGHTS BELOW. COME.
JUST AHEAD. THE END OF THE CORRIDOR.
OH!

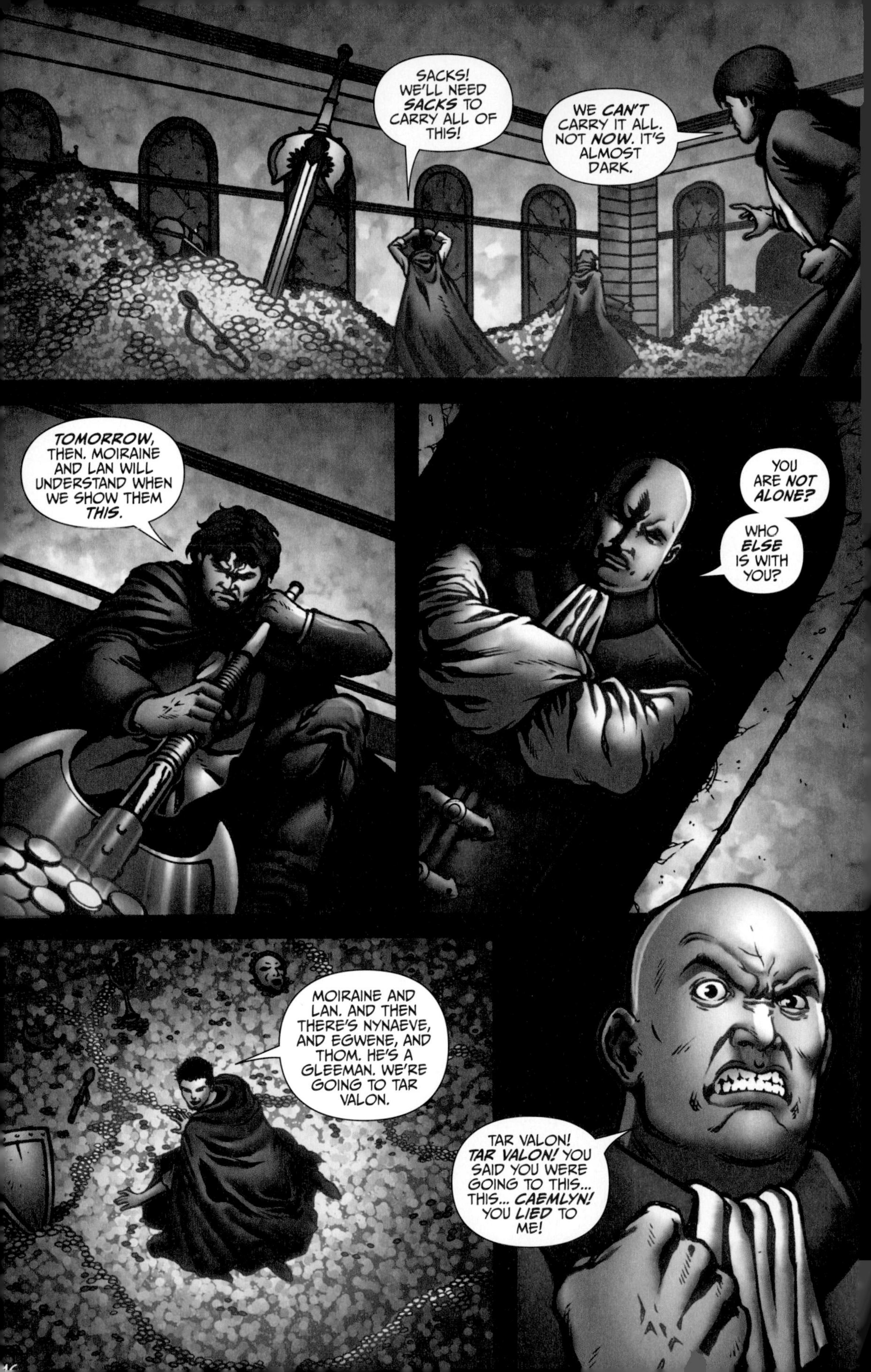
SACKS! WE'LL NEED SACKS TO CARRY ALL OF THIS!
WE CAN'T CARRY IT ALL. NOT NOW. IT'S ALMOST DARK.
TOMORROW, THEN. MOIRAINE AND LAN WILL UNDERSTAND WHEN WE SHOW THEM THIS.
YOU ARE NOT ALONE?
WHO ELSE IS WITH YOU?
MOIRAINE AND LAN. AND THEN THERE'S NYNAEVE, AND EGWENE, AND THOM. HE'S A GLEEMAN. WE'RE GOING TO TAR VALON.
TAR VALON! TAR VALON! YOU SAID YOU WERE GOING TO THIS... THIS... CAEMLYN! YOU LIED TO ME!

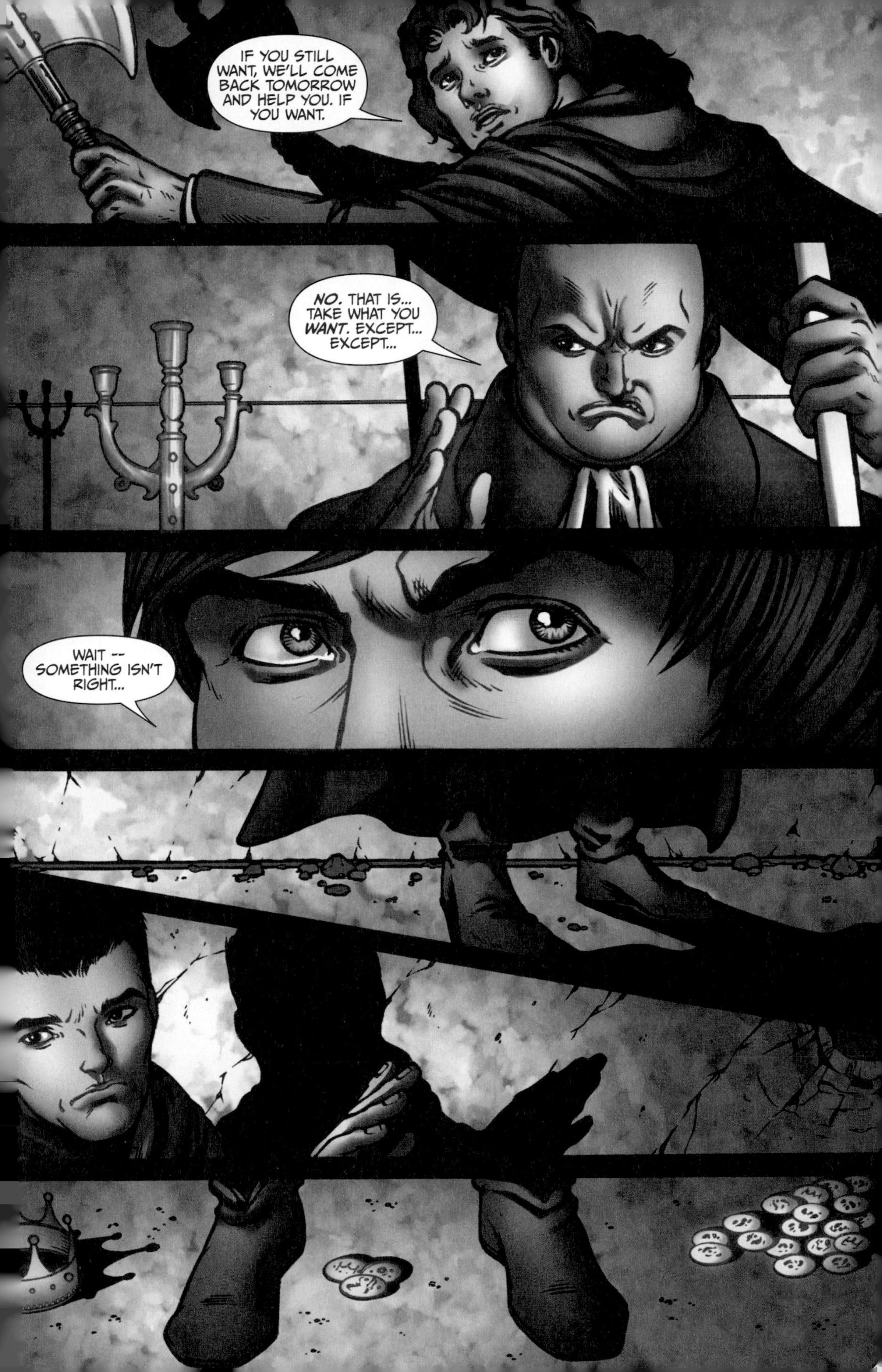
IF YOU STILL WANT, WE'LL COME BACK TOMORROW AND HELP YOU. IF YOU WANT.
NO. THAT IS... TAKE WHAT YOU WANT. EXCEPT... EXCEPT...
WAIT -- SOMETHING ISN'T RIGHT...

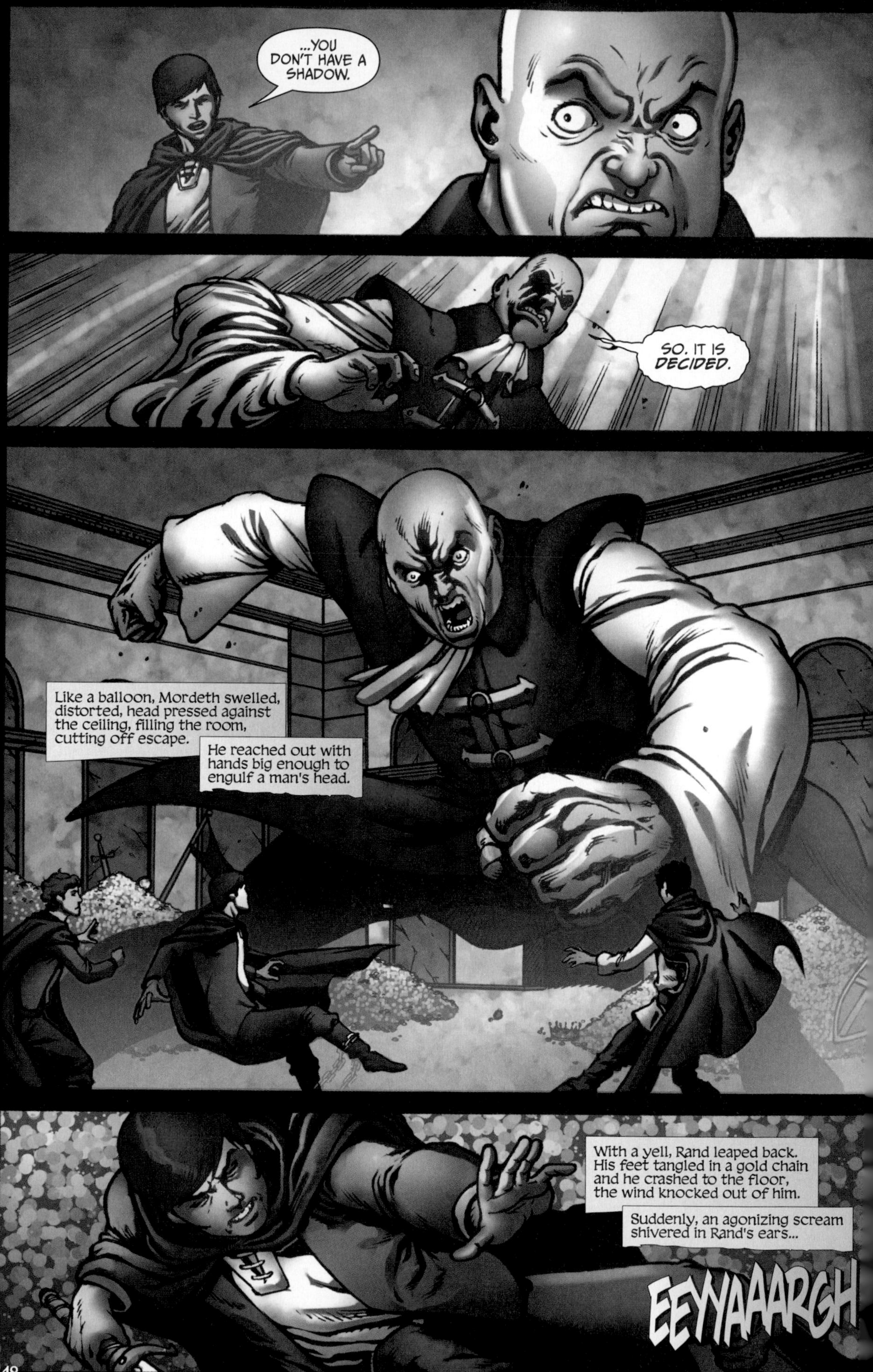
...YOU DON'T HAVE A SHADOW.
SO. IT IS *DECIDED*.
Like a balloon, Mordeth swelled, distorted, head pressed against the ceiling, filling the room, cutting off escape.
He reached out with hands big enough to engulf a man's head.
With a yell, Rand leaped back. His feet tangled in a gold chain and he crashed to the floor, the wind knocked out of him.
Suddenly, an agonizing scream shivered in Rand's ears...
EEYYAAARGH

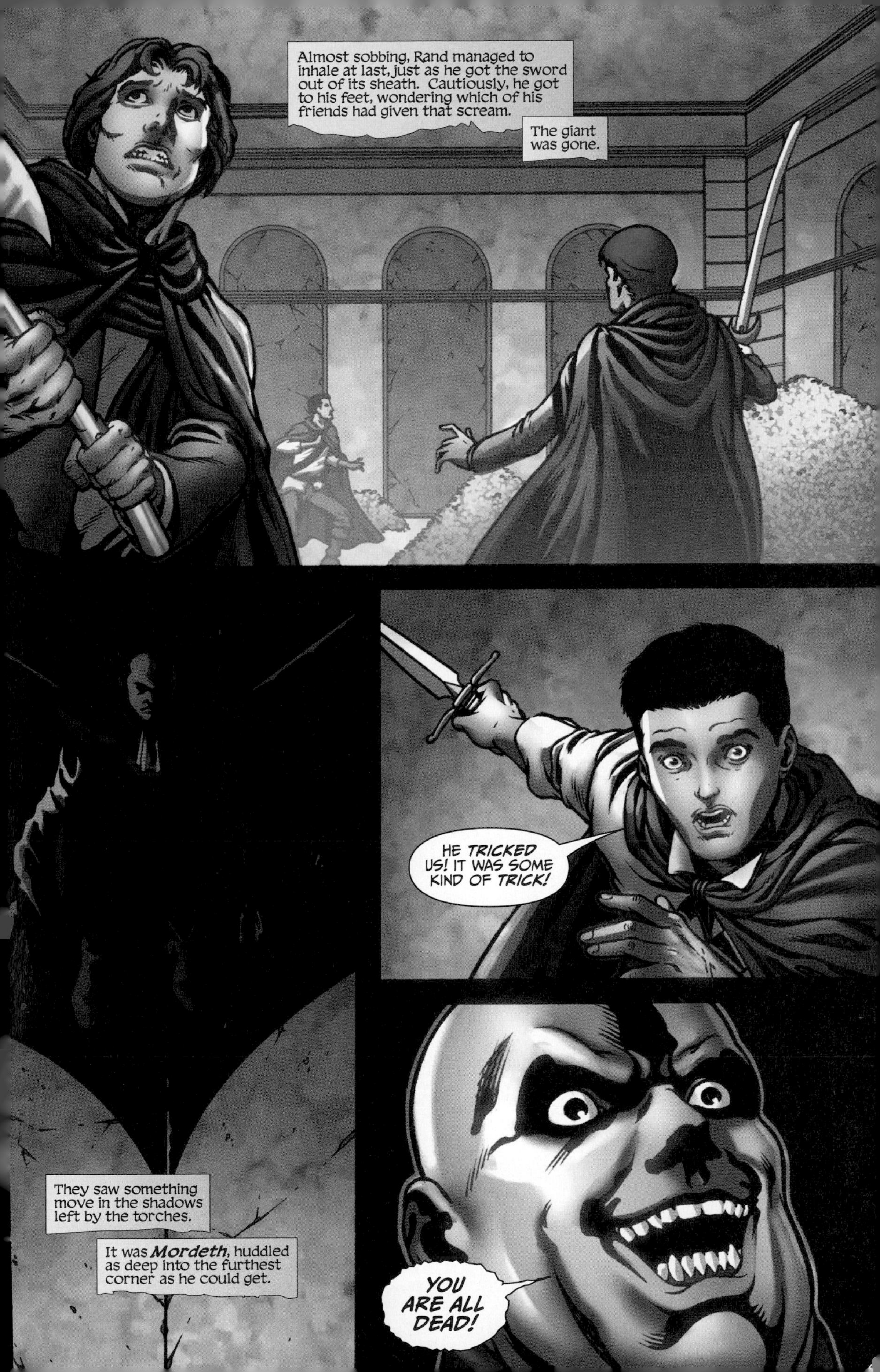
Almost sobbing, Rand managed to inhale at last, just as he got the sword out of its sheath. Cautiously, he got to his feet, wondering which of his friends had given that scream.
The giant was gone.
HE TRICKED US! IT WAS SOME KIND OF TRICK!
They saw something move in the shadows left by the torches.
It was Mordeth, huddled as deep into the furthest corner as he could get.
YOU ARE ALL DEAD!

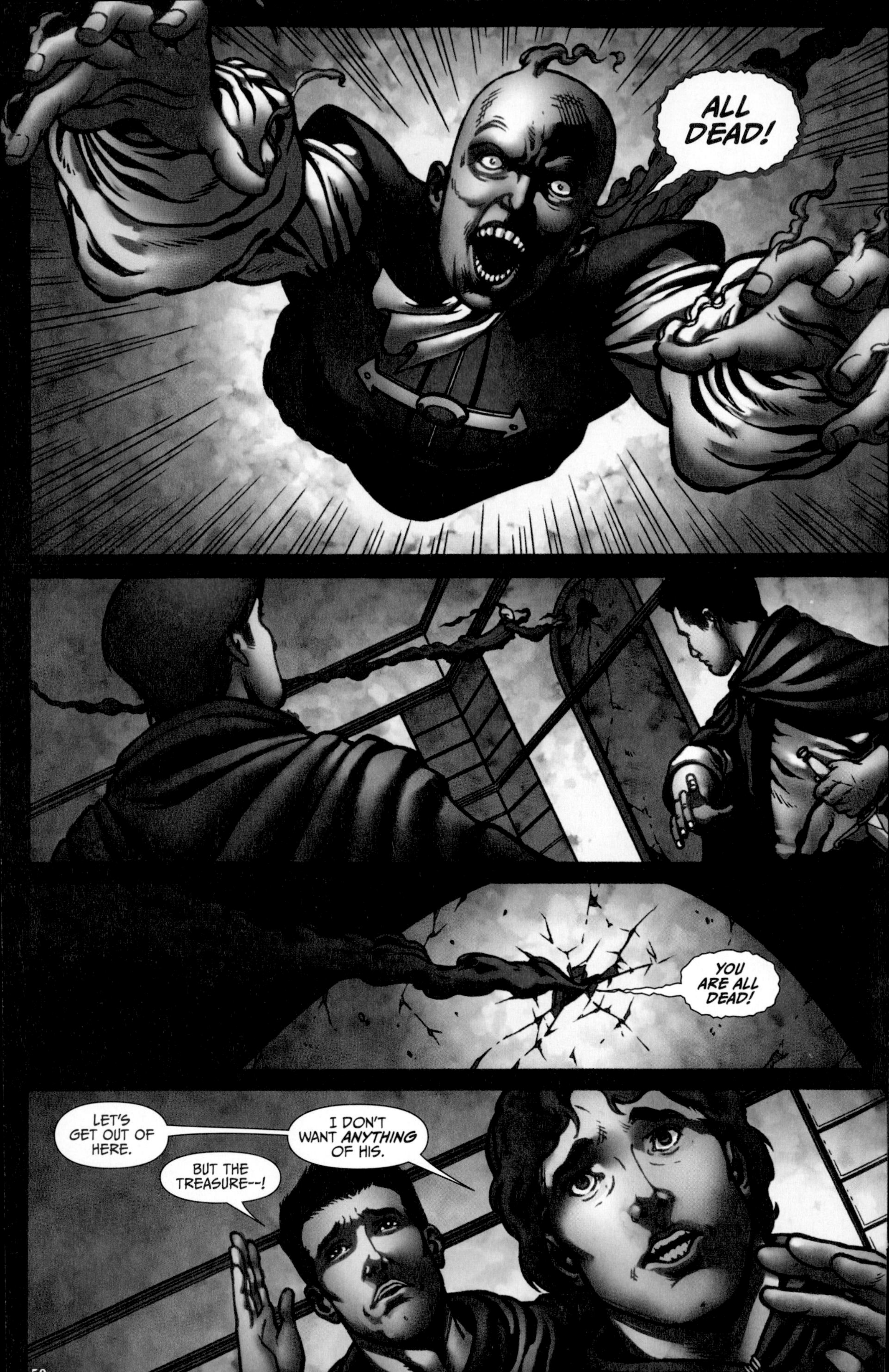
ALL DEAD!
YOU ARE ALL DEAD!
LET'S GET OUT OF HERE.
BUT THE TREASURE--!
I DON'T WANT ANYTHING OF HIS.

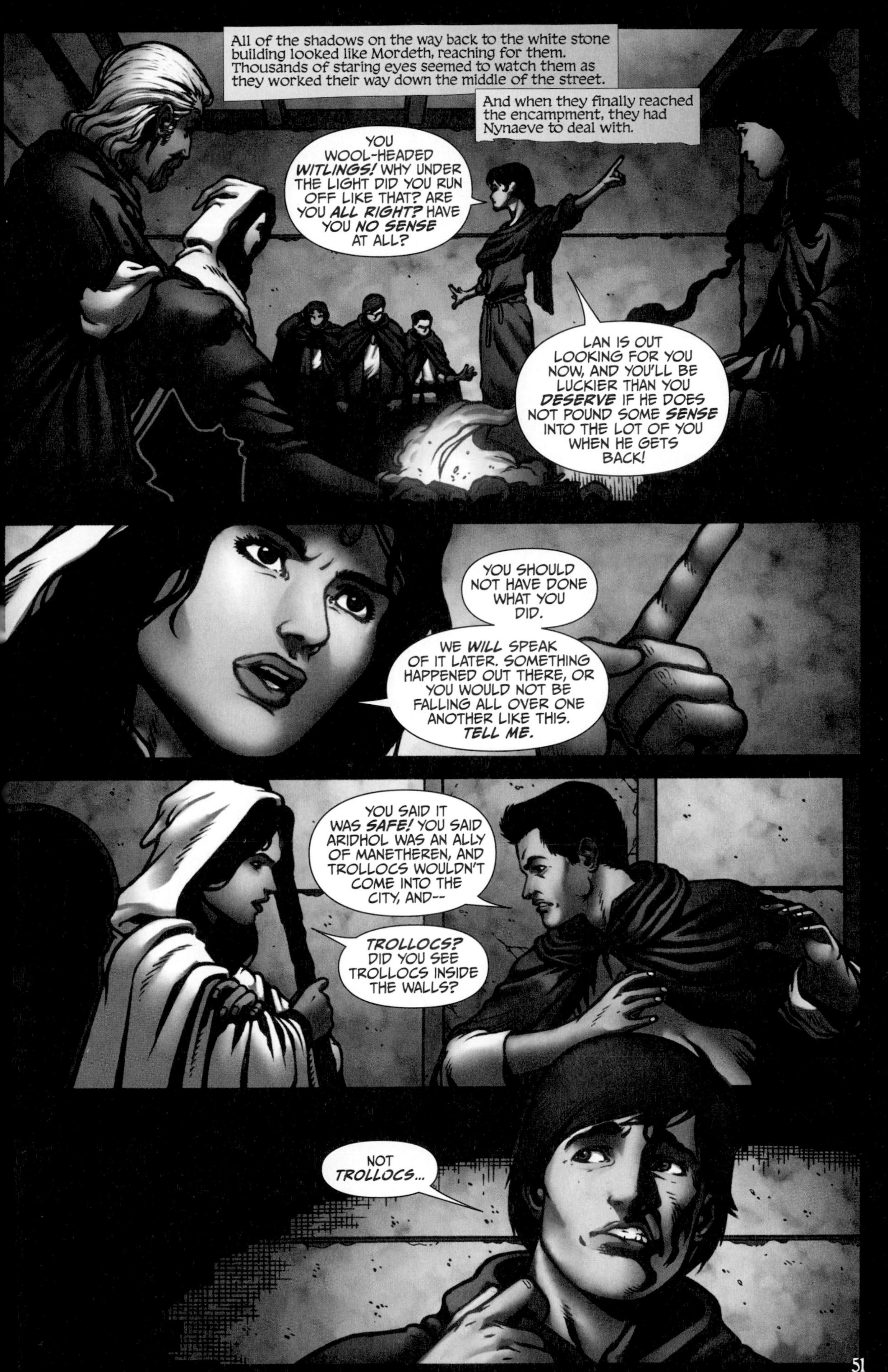
All of the shadows on the way back to the white stone building looked like Mordeth, reaching for them. Thousands of staring eyes seemed to watch them as they worked their way down the middle of the street.
And when they finally reached the encampment, they had Nynaeve to deal with.
YOU WOOL-HEADED WITLINGS! WHY UNDER THE LIGHT DID YOU RUN OFF LIKE THAT? ARE YOU ALL RIGHT? HAVE YOU NO SENSE AT ALL?
LAN IS OUT LOOKING FOR YOU NOW, AND YOU'LL BE LUCKIER THAN YOU DESERVE IF HE DOES NOT POUND SOME SENSE INTO THE LOT OF YOU WHEN HE GETS BACK!
YOU SHOULD NOT HAVE DONE WHAT YOU DID.
WE WILL SPEAK OF IT LATER. SOMETHING HAPPENED OUT THERE, OR YOU WOULD NOT BE FALLING ALL OVER ONE ANOTHER LIKE THIS. TELL ME.
YOU SAID IT WAS SAFE! YOU SAID ARIDHOL WAS AN ALLY OF MANETHEREN, AND TROLLOCS WOULDN'T COME INTO THE CITY, AND--
TROLLOCS? DID YOU SEE TROLLOCS INSIDE THE WALLS?
NOT TROLLOCS...

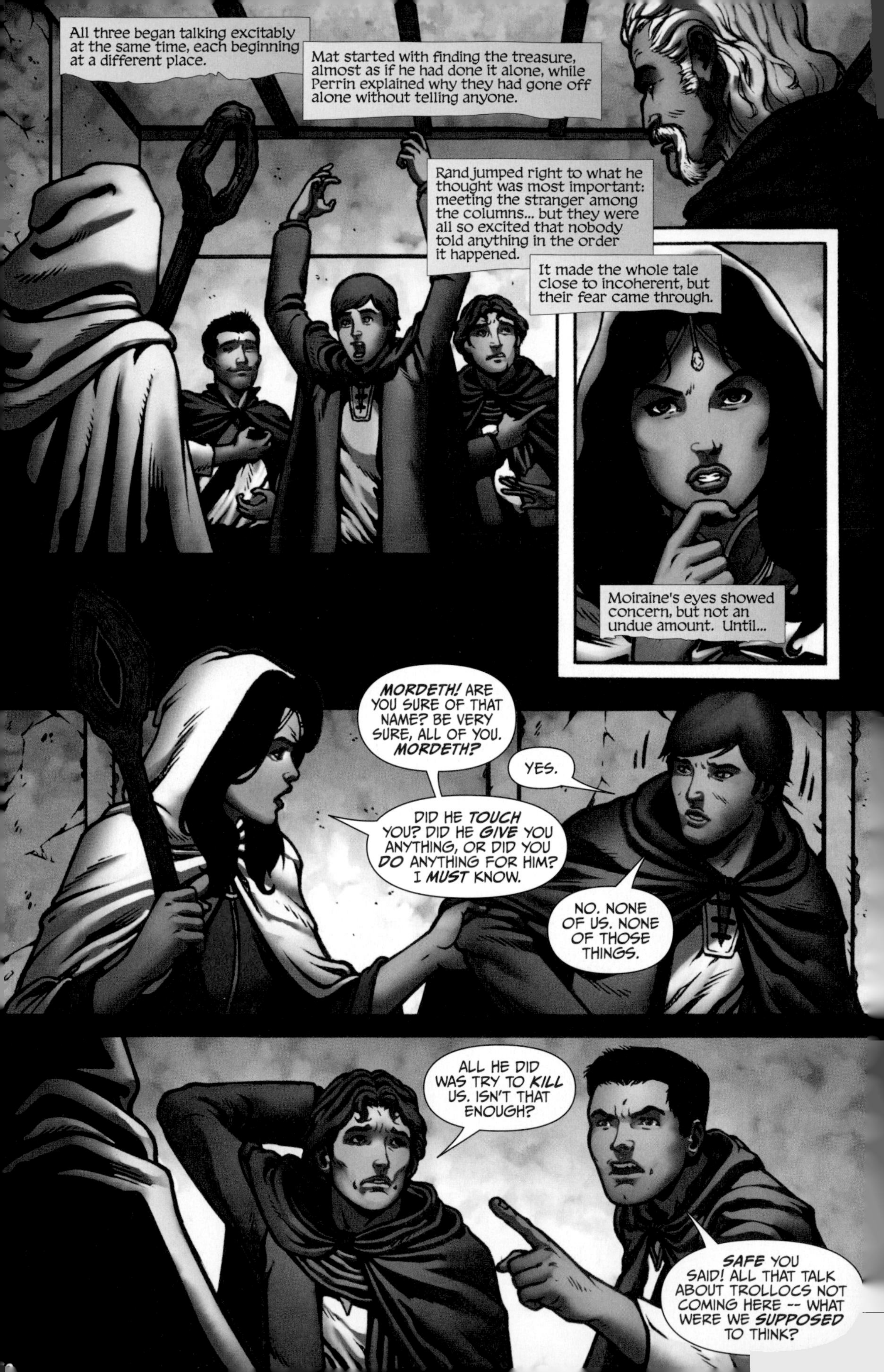
All three began talking excitably at the same time, each beginning at a different place.
Mat started with finding the treasure, almost as if he had done it alone, while Perrin explained why they had gone off alone without telling anyone.
Rand jumped right to what he thought was most important: meeting the stranger among the columns... but they were all so excited that nobody told anything in the order it happened.
It made the whole tale close to incoherent, but their fear came through.
Moiraine's eyes showed concern, but not an undue amount. Until...
MORDETH! ARE YOU SURE OF THAT NAME? BE VERY SURE, ALL OF YOU. MORDETH?
YES.
DID HE TOUCH YOU? DID HE GIVE YOU ANYTHING, OR DID YOU DO ANYTHING FOR HIM? I MUST KNOW.
NO. NONE OF US. NONE OF THOSE THINGS.
ALL HE DID WAS TRY TO KILL US. ISN'T THAT ENOUGH?
SAFE YOU SAID! ALL THAT TALK ABOUT TROLLOCS NOT COMING HERE -- WHAT WERE WE SUPPOSED TO THINK?

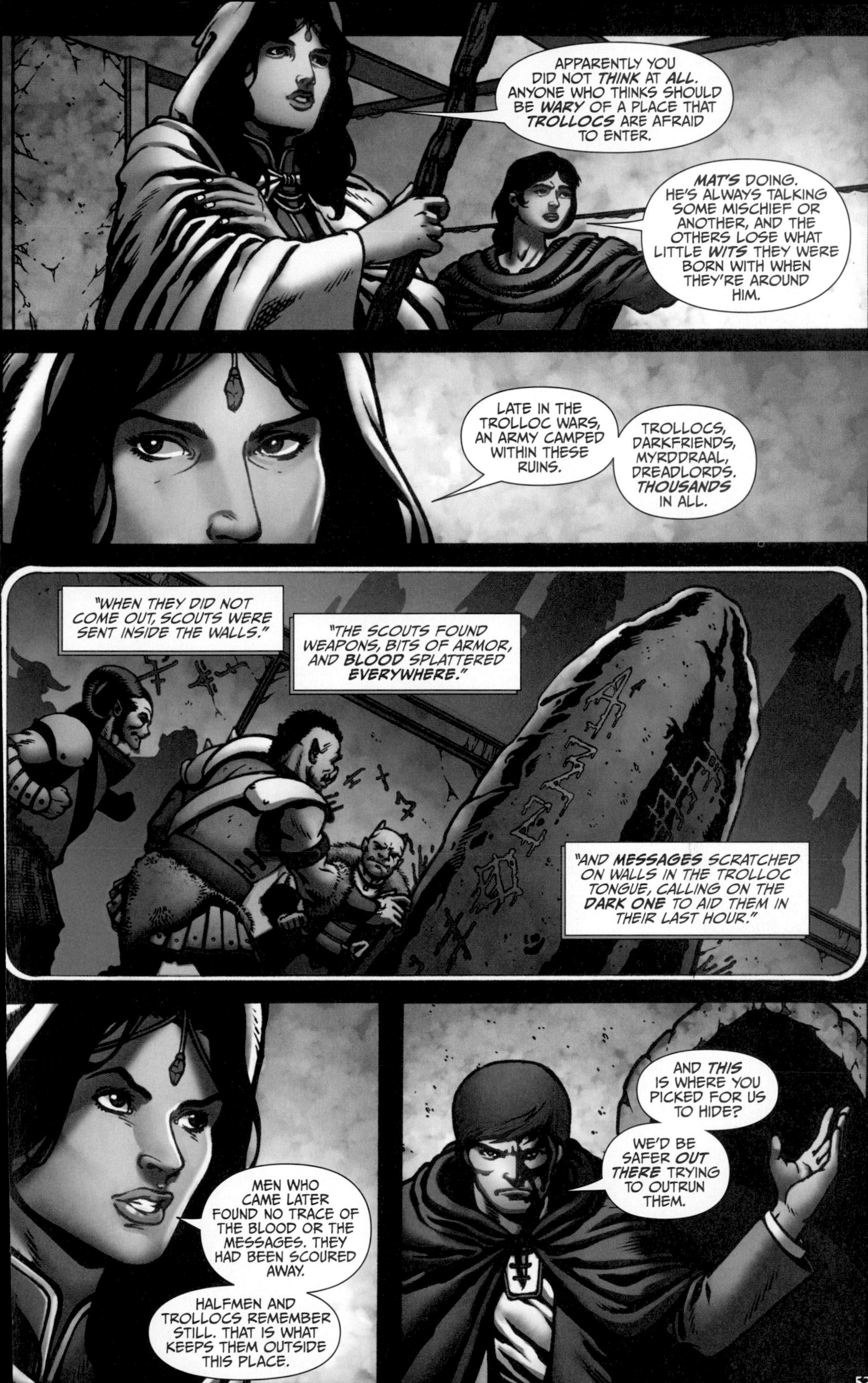
APPARENTLY YOU DID NOT THINK AT ALL. ANYONE WHO THINKS SHOULD BE WARY OF A PLACE THAT TROLLOCS ARE AFRAID TO ENTER.
MAT'S DOING. HE'S ALWAYS TALKING SOME MISCHIEF OR ANOTHER, AND THE OTHERS LOSE WHAT LITTLE WITS THEY WERE BORN WITH WHEN THEY'RE AROUND HIM.
LATE IN THE TROLLOC WARS, AN ARMY CAMPED WITHIN THESE RUINS.
TROLLOCS, DARKFRIENDS, MYRDDRAAL, DREADLORDS. THOUSANDS IN ALL.
"WHEN THEY DID NOT COME OUT, SCOUTS WERE SENT INSIDE THE WALLS."
"THE SCOUTS FOUND WEAPONS, BITS OF ARMOR, AND BLOOD SPLATTERED EVERYWHERE."
"AND MESSAGES SCRATCHED ON WALLS IN THE TROLLOC TONGUE, CALLING ON THE DARK ONE TO AID THEM IN THEIR LAST HOUR."
MEN WHO CAME LATER FOUND NO TRACE OF THE BLOOD OR THE MESSAGES. THEY HAD BEEN SCOURED AWAY.
HALFMEN AND TROLLOCS REMEMBER STILL. THAT IS WHAT KEEPS THEM OUTSIDE THIS PLACE.
AND THIS IS WHERE YOU PICKED FOR US TO HIDE?
WE'D BE SAFER OUT THERE TRYING TO OUTRUN THEM.

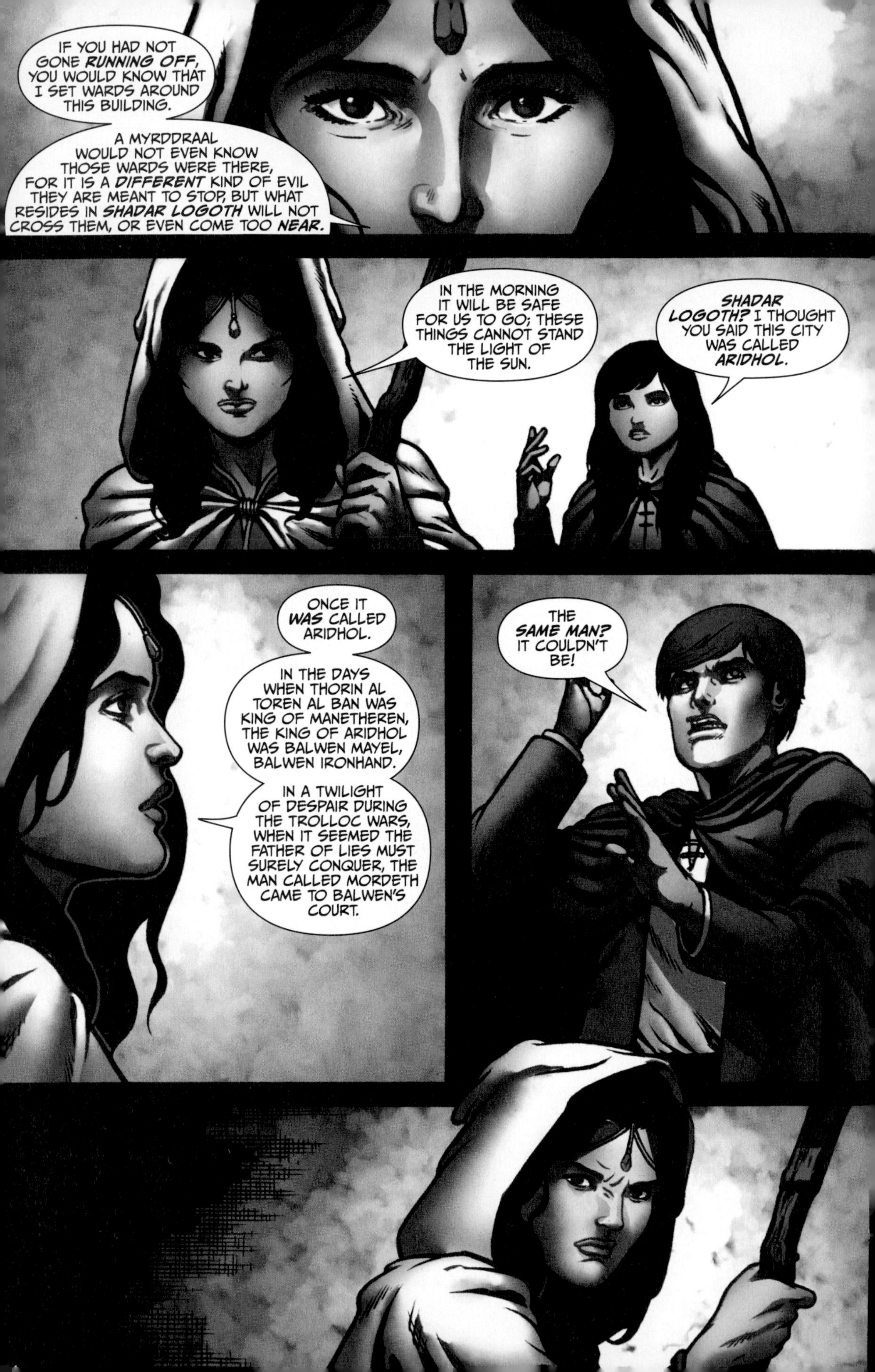
IF YOU HAD NOT GONE RUNNING OFF, YOU WOULD KNOW THAT I SET WARDS AROUND THIS BUILDING.
A MYRDDRAAL WOULD NOT EVEN KNOW THOSE WARDS WERE THERE, FOR IT IS A DIFFERENT KIND OF EVIL THEY ARE MEANT TO STOP, BUT WHAT RESIDES IN SHADAR LOGOTH WILL NOT CROSS THEM, OR EVEN COME TOO NEAR.
IN THE MORNING IT WILL BE SAFE FOR US TO GO; THESE THINGS CANNOT STAND THE LIGHT OF THE SUN.
SHADAR LOGOTH? I THOUGHT YOU SAID THIS CITY WAS CALLED ARIDHOL.
ONCE IT WAS CALLED ARIDHOL.
IN THE DAYS WHEN THORIN AL TOREN AL BAN WAS KING OF MANETHEREN, THE KING OF ARIDHOL WAS BALWEN MAYEL, BALWEN IRONHAND.
IN A TWILIGHT OF DESPAIR DURING THE TROLLOC WARS, WHEN IT SEEMED THE FATHER OF LIES MUST SURELY CONQUER, THE MAN CALLED MORDETH CAME TO BALWEN'S COURT.
THE SAME MAN? IT COULDN'T BE!

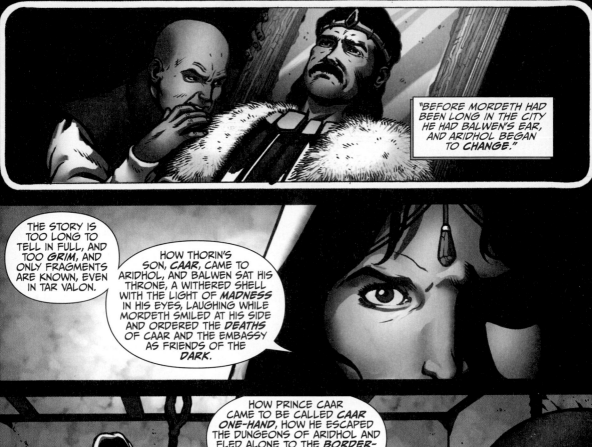

"BEFORE MORDETH HAD BEEN LONG IN THE CITY HE HAD BALWEN'S EAR, AND ARIDHOL BEGAN TO *CHANGE*."

THE STORY IS TOO LONG TO TELL IN FULL, AND TOO *GRIM*, AND ONLY FRAGMENTS ARE KNOWN, EVEN IN TAR VALON.

HOW THORIN'S SON, *CAAR*, CAME TO ARIDHOL, AND BALWEN SAT HIS THRONE, A WITHERED SHELL WITH THE LIGHT OF *MADNESS* IN HIS EYES, LAUGHING WHILE MORDETH SMILED AT HIS SIDE AND ORDERED THE *DEATHS* OF CAAR AND THE EMBASSY AS FRIENDS OF THE *DARK*.

HOW PRINCE CAAR CAME TO BE CALLED *CAAR ONE-HAND*, HOW HE ESCAPED THE DUNGEONS OF ARIDHOL AND FLED ALONE TO THE *BORDER-LANDS* WITH MORDETH'S *UNNATURAL* ASSASSINS AT HIS HEELS.

HOW THERE HE MET *RHEA*, WHO DID NOT KNOW WHO HE WAS, AND MARRIED HER, AND SET THE SKEIN IN THE PATTERN THAT LED TO HIS *DEATH* AT HER HANDS, AND HERS BY HER OWN HAND BEFORE HIS TOMB, AND THE FALL OF ALETH-LORIEL.

HOW THE ARMIES OF MANETHEREN CAME TO AVENGE CAAR AND FOUND THE GATES OF ARIDHOL TORN DOWN, NO *LIVING THING* INSIDE THE WALLS, BUT SOMETHING *WORSE* THAN *DEATH*.

NO ENEMY HAD COME TO ARIDHOL BUT ARIDHOL. SUSPICION AND HATE HAD GIVEN BIRTH TO SOMETHING THAT FED ON THAT WHICH HAD CREATED IT, SOMETHING LOCKED IN THE BEDROCK ON WHICH THE CITY STOOD.

MASHADAR WAITS STILL, HUNGERING. MEN SPOKE OF ARIDHOL NO MORE. THEY NAMED IT *SHADAR LOGOTH*, THE PLACE WHERE THE SHADOW WAITS.

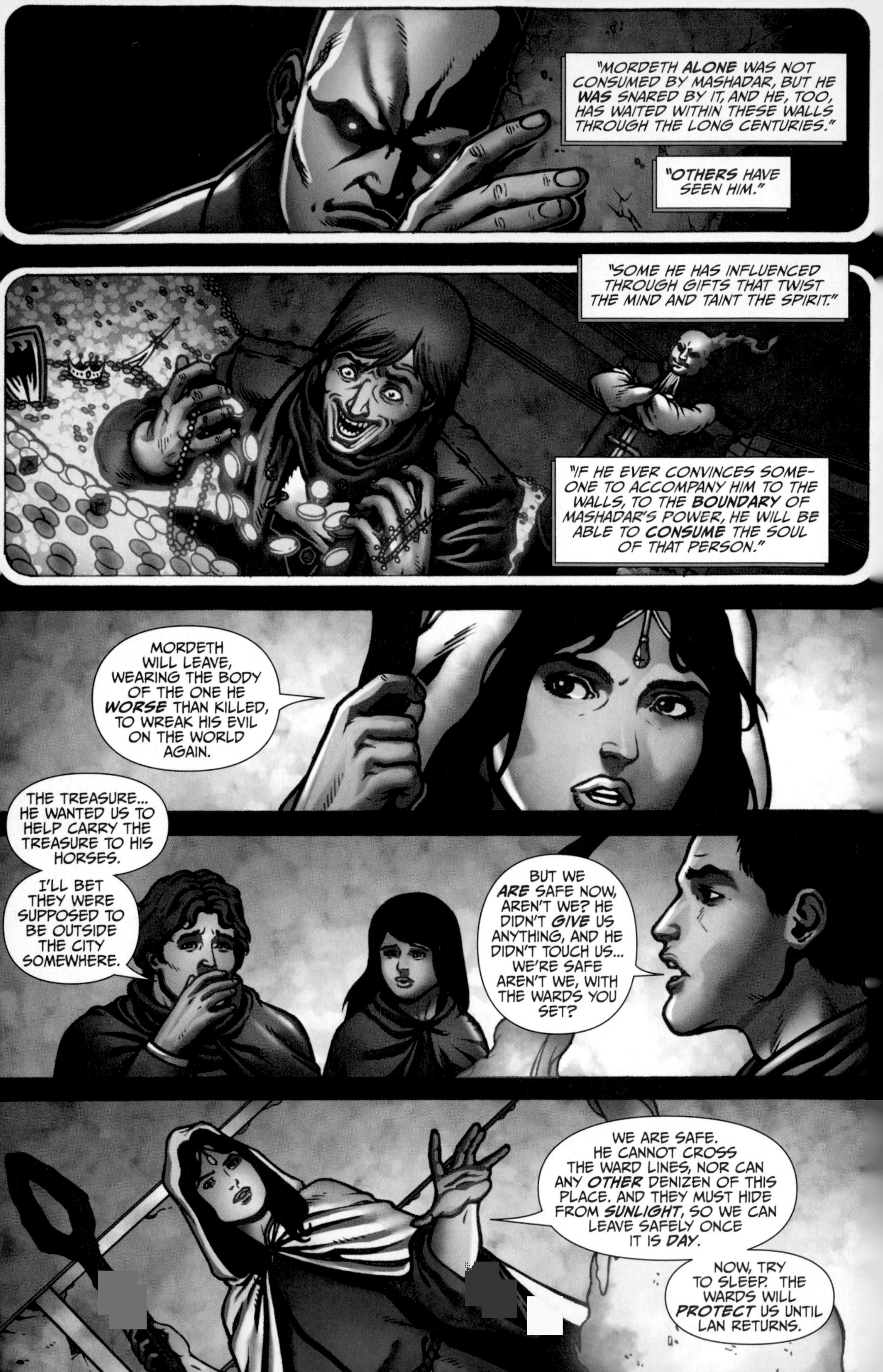
"MORDETH ALONE WAS NOT CONSUMED BY MASHADAR, BUT HE WAS SNARED BY IT, AND HE, TOO, HAS WAITED WITHIN THESE WALLS THROUGH THE LONG CENTURIES."
"OTHERS HAVE SEEN HIM."
"SOME HE HAS INFLUENCED THROUGH GIFTS THAT TWIST THE MIND AND TAINT THE SPIRIT."
"IF HE EVER CONVINCES SOME-ONE TO ACCOMPANY HIM TO THE WALLS, TO THE BOUNDARY OF MASHADAR'S POWER, HE WILL BE ABLE TO CONSUME THE SOUL OF THAT PERSON."
MORDETH WILL LEAVE, WEARING THE BODY OF THE ONE HE WORSE THAN KILLED, TO WREAK HIS EVIL ON THE WORLD AGAIN.
THE TREASURE... HE WANTED US TO HELP CARRY THE TREASURE TO HIS HORSES.
I'LL BET THEY WERE SUPPOSED TO BE OUTSIDE THE CITY SOMEWHERE.
BUT WE ARE SAFE NOW, AREN'T WE? HE DIDN'T GIVE US ANYTHING, AND HE DIDN'T TOUCH US... WE'RE SAFE AREN'T WE, WITH THE WARDS YOU SET?
WE ARE SAFE. HE CANNOT CROSS THE WARD LINES, NOR CAN ANY OTHER DENIZEN OF THIS PLACE. AND THEY MUST HIDE FROM SUNLIGHT, SO WE CAN LEAVE SAFELY ONCE IT IS DAY.
NOW, TRY TO SLEEP. THE WARDS WILL PROTECT US UNTIL LAN RETURNS.

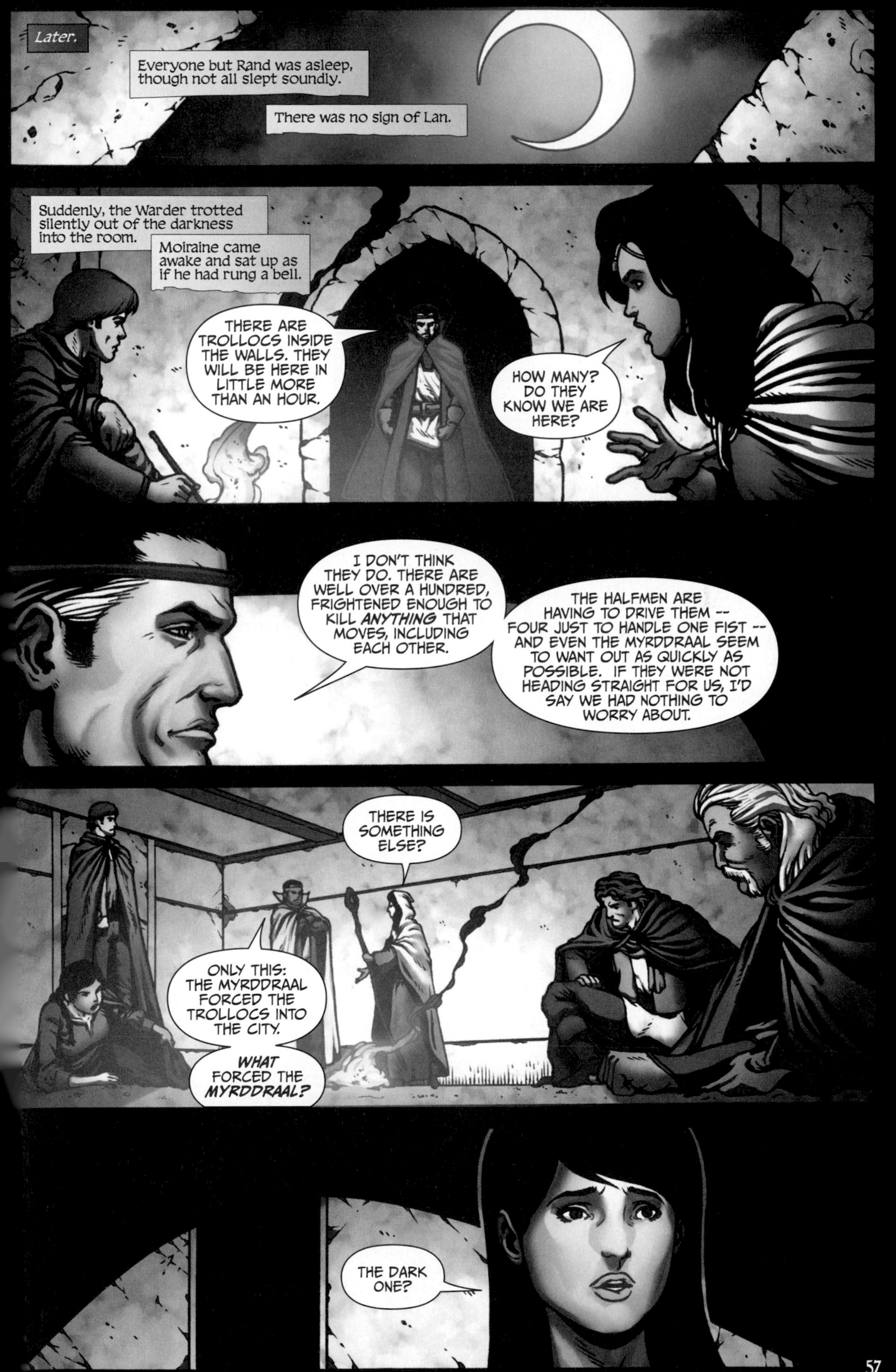
Later.
Everyone but Rand was asleep, though not all slept soundly.
There was no sign of Lan.
Suddenly, the Warder trotted silently out of the darkness into the room.
Moiraine came awake and sat up as if he had rung a bell.
THERE ARE TROLLOCS INSIDE THE WALLS. THEY WILL BE HERE IN LITTLE MORE THAN AN HOUR.
HOW MANY? DO THEY KNOW WE ARE HERE?
I DON'T THINK THEY DO. THERE ARE WELL OVER A HUNDRED, FRIGHTENED ENOUGH TO KILL ANYTHING THAT MOVES, INCLUDING EACH OTHER.
THE HALFMEN ARE HAVING TO DRIVE THEM -- FOUR JUST TO HANDLE ONE FIST -- AND EVEN THE MYRDDRAAL SEEM TO WANT OUT AS QUICKLY AS POSSIBLE. IF THEY WERE NOT HEADING STRAIGHT FOR US, I'D SAY WE HAD NOTHING TO WORRY ABOUT.
THERE IS SOMETHING ELSE?
ONLY THIS: THE MYRDDRAAL FORCED THE TROLLOCS INTO THE CITY.
WHAT FORCED THE MYRDDRAAL?
THE DARK ONE?

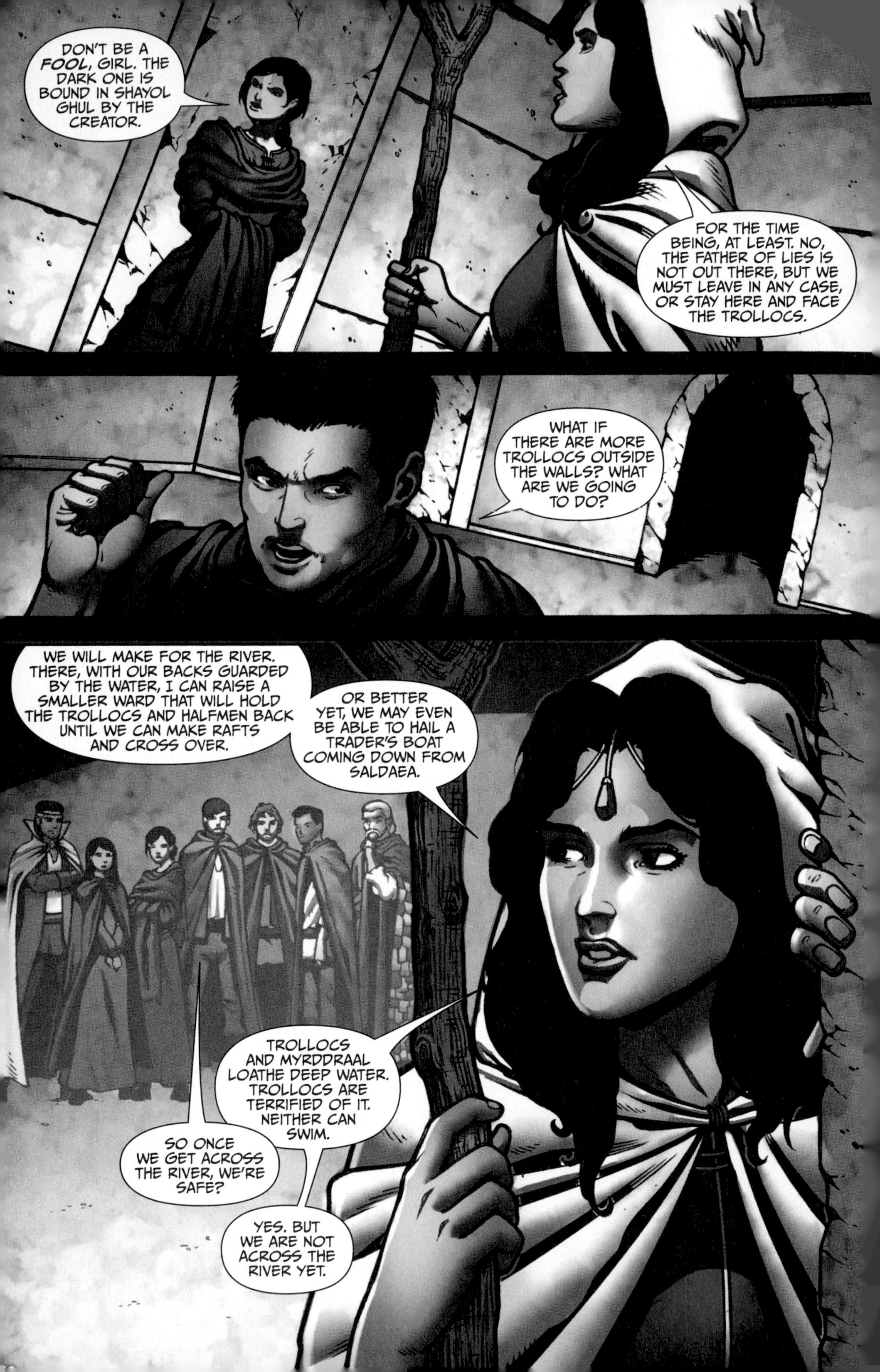
DON'T BE A *FOOL*, GIRL. THE DARK ONE IS BOUND IN SHAYOL GHUL BY THE CREATOR.
FOR THE TIME BEING, AT LEAST. NO, THE FATHER OF LIES IS NOT OUT THERE, BUT WE MUST LEAVE IN ANY CASE, OR STAY HERE AND FACE THE TROLLOCS.
WHAT IF THERE ARE MORE TROLLOCS OUTSIDE THE WALLS? WHAT ARE WE GOING TO DO?
WE WILL MAKE FOR THE RIVER. THERE, WITH OUR BACKS GUARDED BY THE WATER, I CAN RAISE A SMALLER WARD THAT WILL HOLD THE TROLLOCS AND HALFMEN BACK UNTIL WE CAN MAKE RAFTS AND CROSS OVER.
OR BETTER YET, WE MAY EVEN BE ABLE TO HAIL A TRADER'S BOAT COMING DOWN FROM SALDAEA.
TROLLOCS AND MYRDDRAAL LOATHE DEEP WATER. TROLLOCS ARE TERRIFIED OF IT. NEITHER CAN SWIM.
SO ONCE WE GET ACROSS THE RIVER, WE'RE SAFE?
YES. BUT WE ARE NOT ACROSS THE RIVER YET.

chapter three

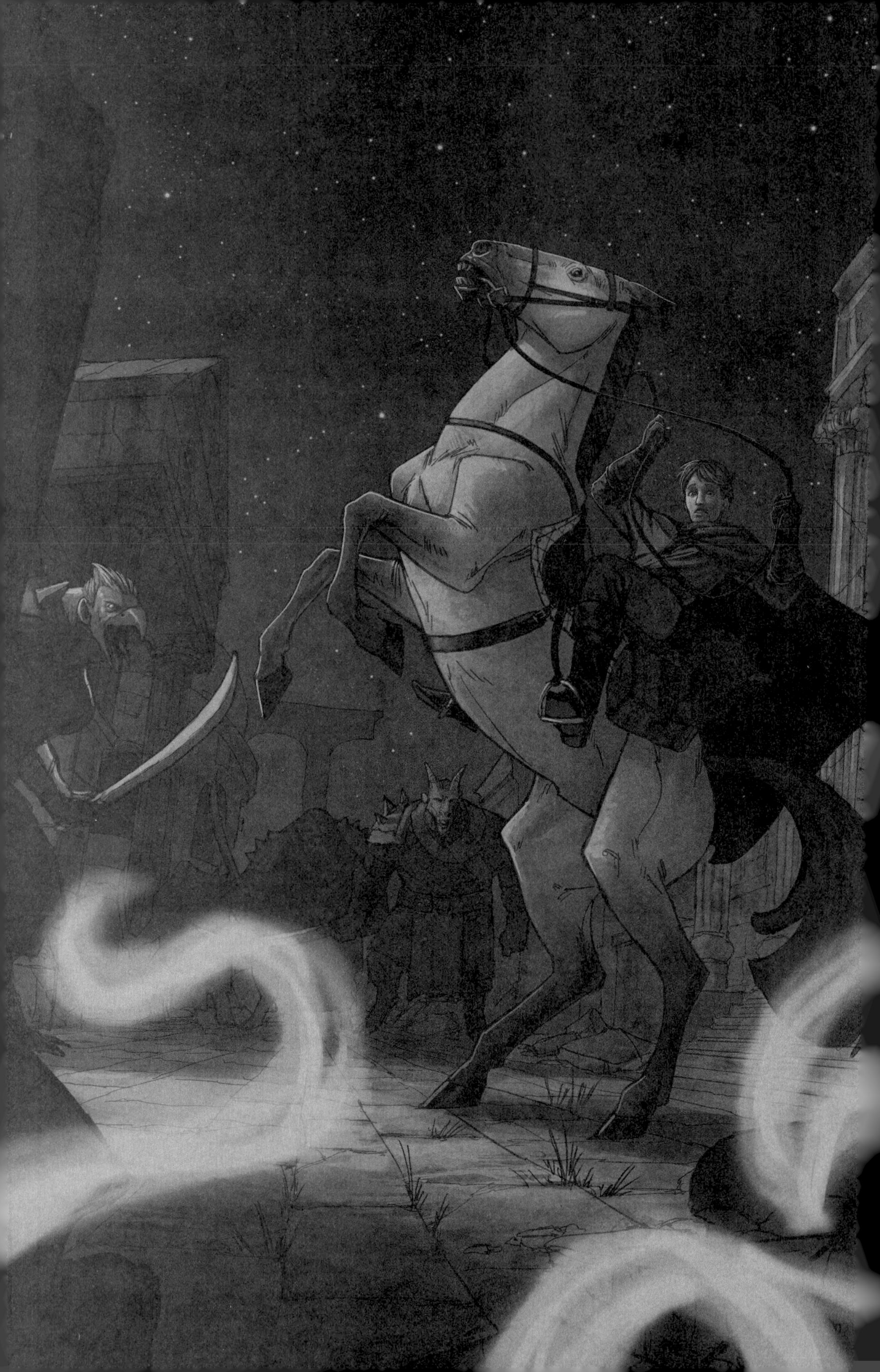

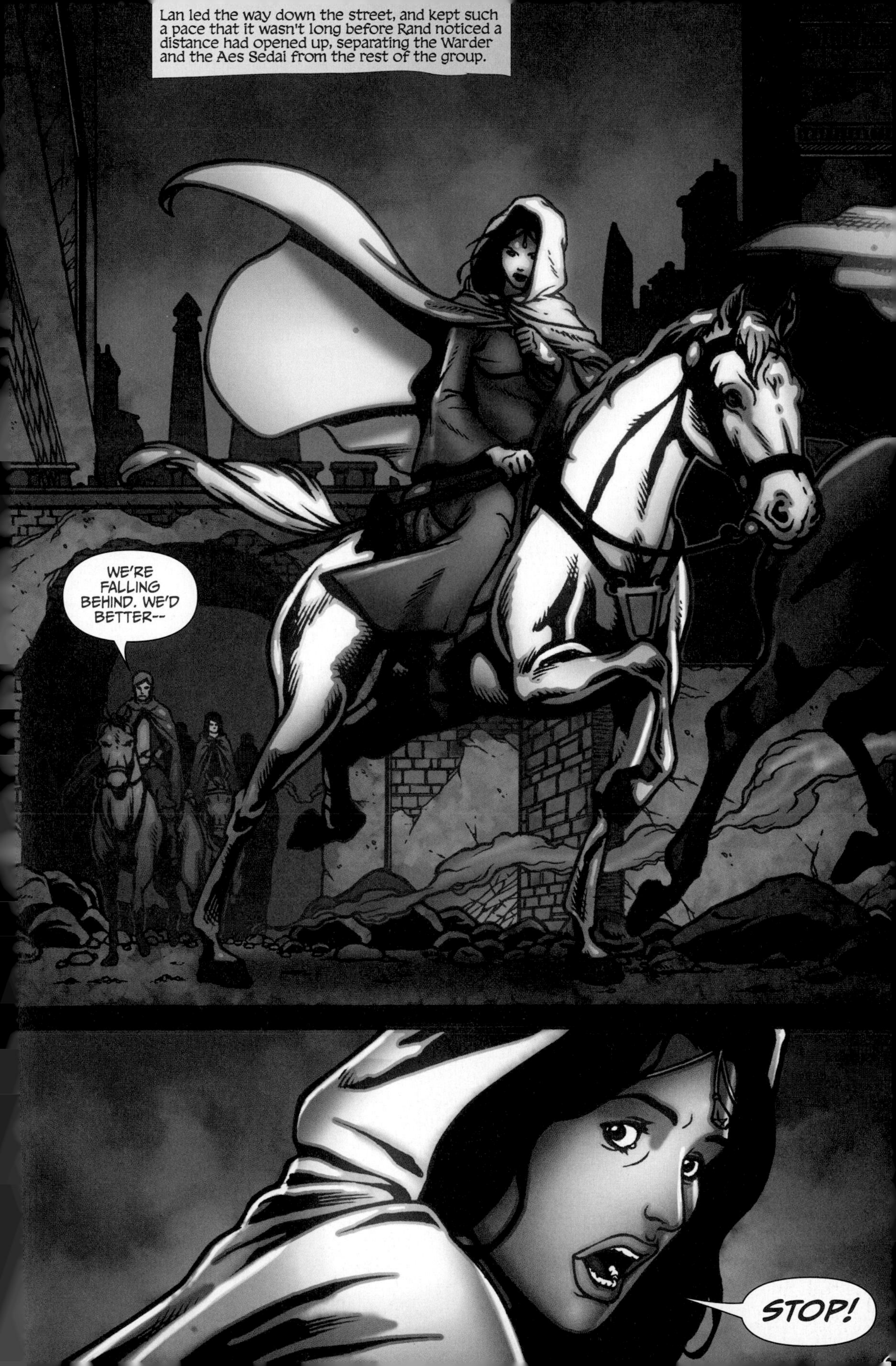
Lan led the way down the street, and kept such a pace that it wasn't long before Rand noticed a distance had opened up, separating the Warder and the Aes Sedai from the rest of the group.
WE'RE FALLING BEHIND. WE'D BETTER--
STOP!

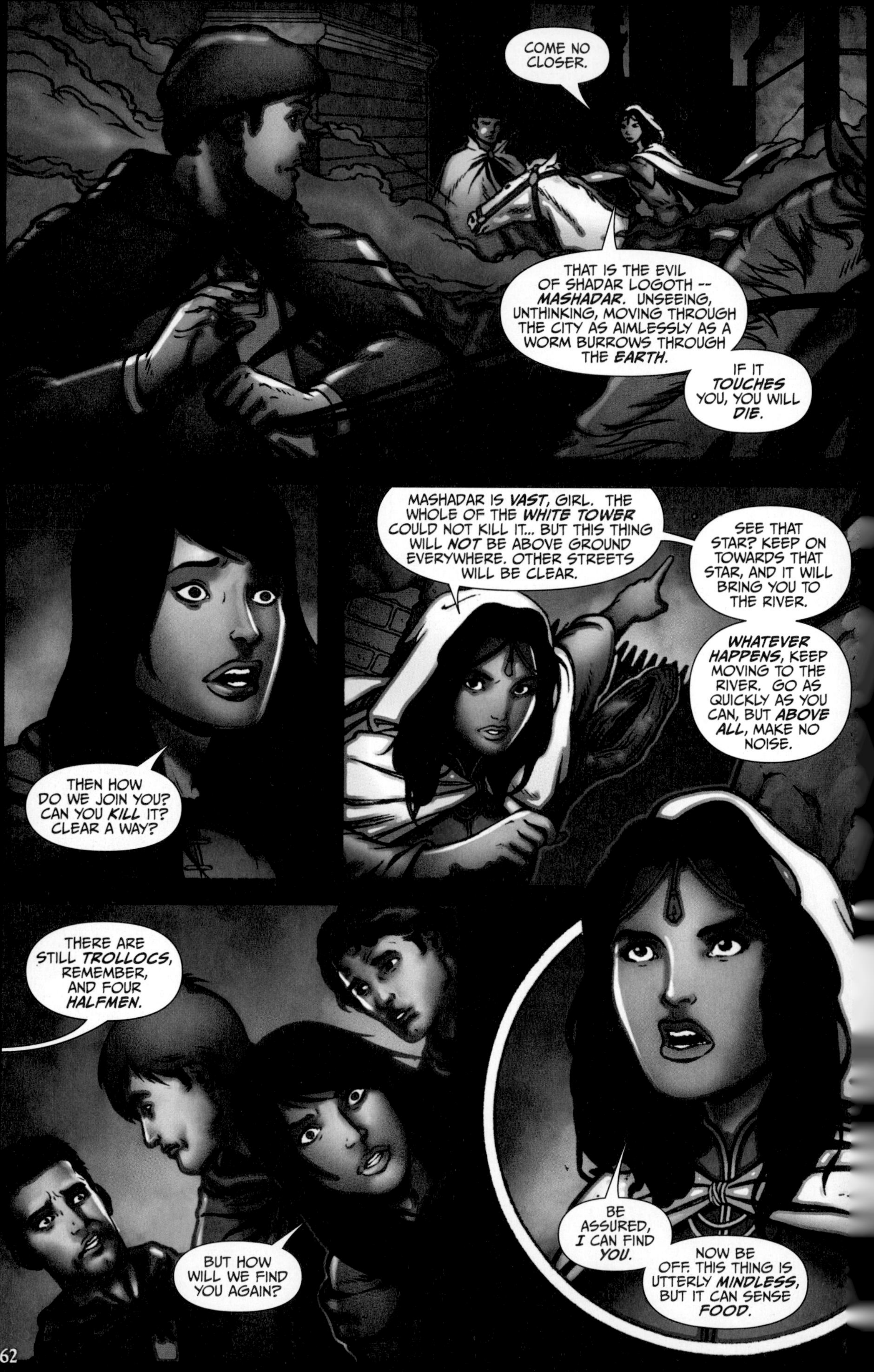
COME NO CLOSER.
THAT IS THE EVIL OF SHADAR LOGOTH -- MASHADAR. UNSEEING, UNTHINKING, MOVING THROUGH THE CITY AS AIMLESSLY AS A WORM BURROWS THROUGH THE EARTH.
IF IT TOUCHES YOU, YOU WILL DIE.
THEN HOW DO WE JOIN YOU? CAN YOU KILL IT? CLEAR A WAY?
MASHADAR IS VAST, GIRL. THE WHOLE OF THE WHITE TOWER COULD NOT KILL IT... BUT THIS THING WILL NOT BE ABOVE GROUND EVERYWHERE. OTHER STREETS WILL BE CLEAR.
SEE THAT STAR? KEEP ON TOWARDS THAT STAR, AND IT WILL BRING YOU TO THE RIVER.
WHATEVER HAPPENS, KEEP MOVING TO THE RIVER. GO AS QUICKLY AS YOU CAN, BUT ABOVE ALL, MAKE NO NOISE.
THERE ARE STILL TROLLOCS, REMEMBER, AND FOUR HALFMEN.
BUT HOW WILL WE FIND YOU AGAIN?
BE ASSURED, I CAN FIND YOU.
NOW BE OFF. THIS THING IS UTTERLY MINDLESS, BUT IT CAN SENSE FOOD.

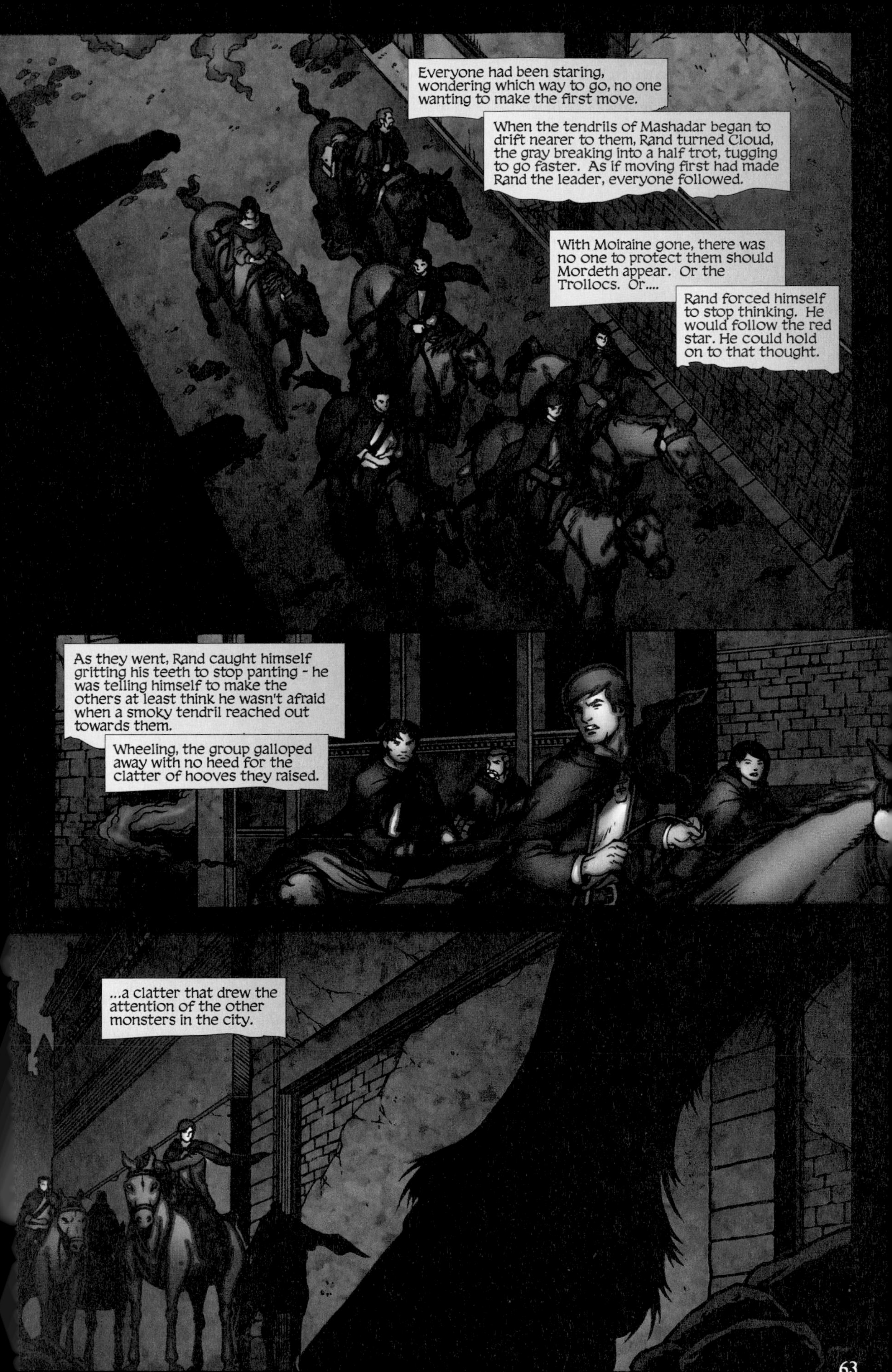
Everyone had been staring, wondering which way to go, no one wanting to make the first move.
When the tendrils of Mashadar began to drift nearer to them, Rand turned Cloud, the gray breaking into a half trot, tugging to go faster. As if moving first had made Rand the leader, everyone followed.
With Moiraine gone, there was no one to protect them should Mordeth appear. Or the Trollocs. Or....
Rand forced himself to stop thinking. He would follow the red star. He could hold on to that thought.
As they went, Rand caught himself gritting his teeth to stop panting - he was telling himself to make the others at least think he wasn't afraid when a smoky tendril reached out towards them.
Wheeling, the group galloped away with no heed for the clatter of hooves they raised.
...a clatter that drew the attention of the other monsters in the city.

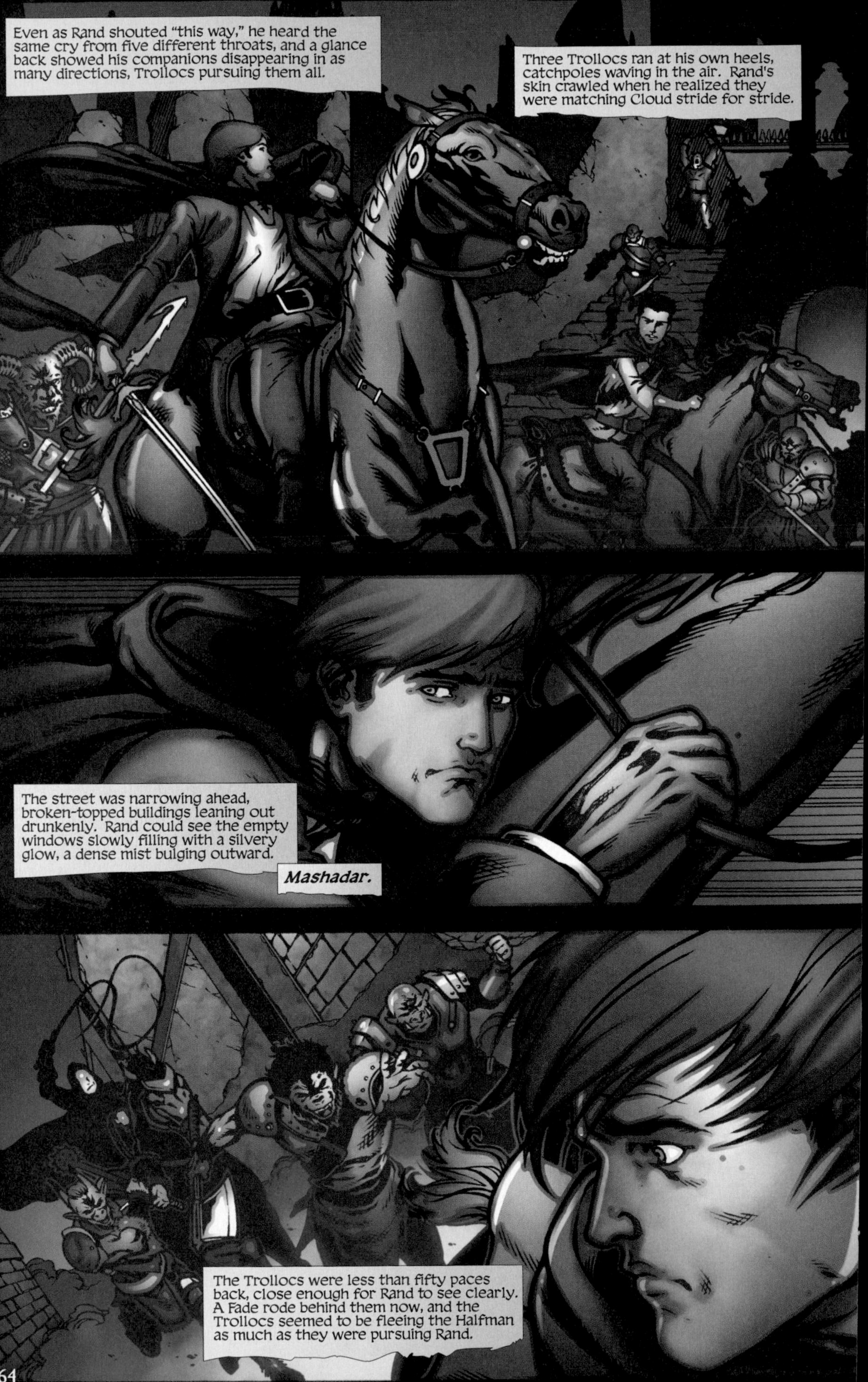
Even as Rand shouted "this way," he heard the same cry from five different throats, and a glance back showed his companions disappearing in as many directions, Trollocs pursuing them all.
Three Trollocs ran at his own heels, catchpoles waving in the air. Rand's skin crawled when he realized they were matching Cloud stride for stride.
The street was narrowing ahead, broken-topped buildings leaning out drunkenly. Rand could see the empty windows slowly filling with a silvery glow, a dense mist bulging outward.
Mashadar.
The Trollocs were less than fifty paces back, close enough for Rand to see clearly. A Fade rode behind them now, and the Trollocs seemed to be fleeing the Halfman as much as they were pursuing Rand.

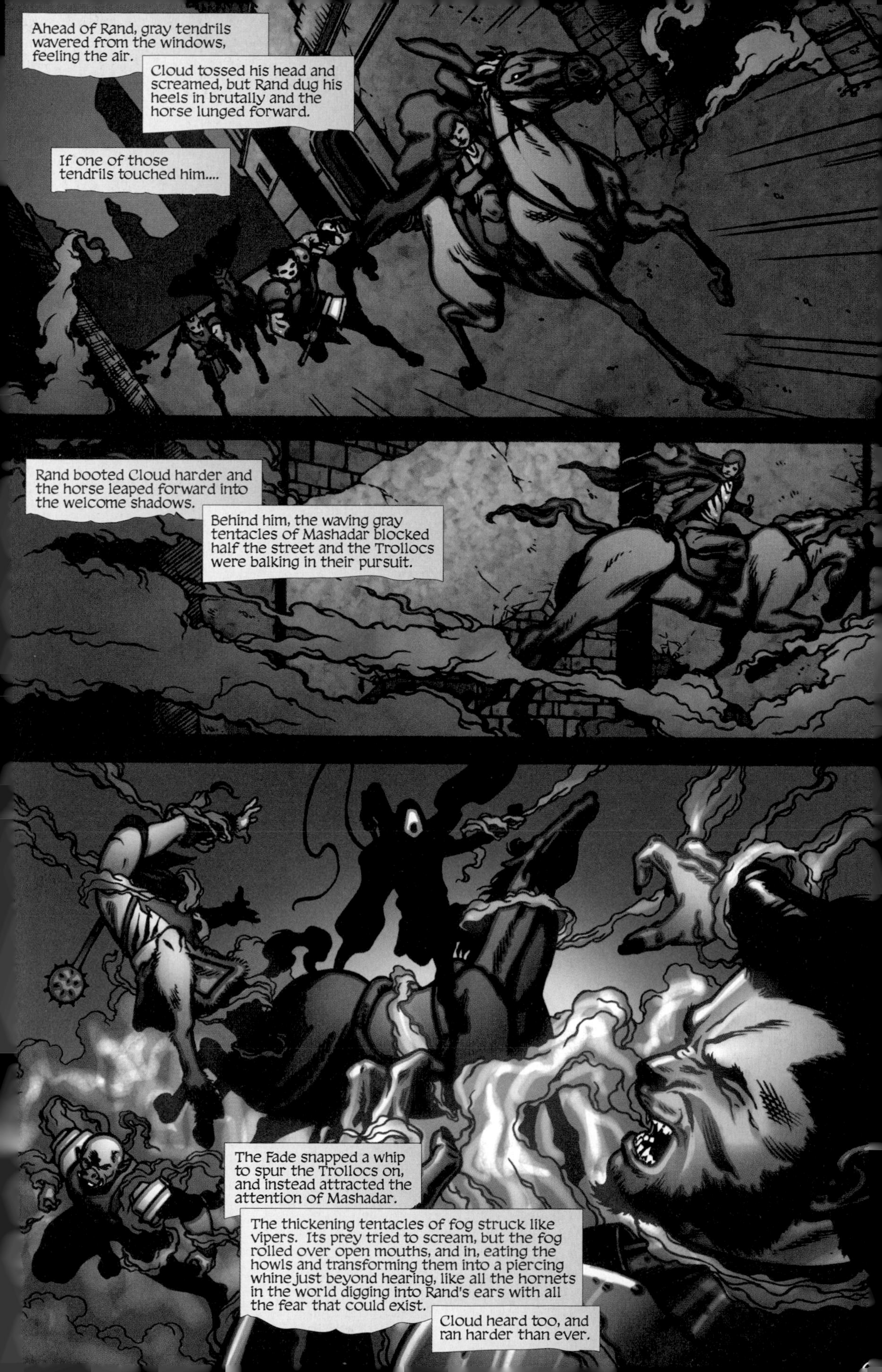
Ahead of Rand, gray tendrils wavered from the windows, feeling the air.
Cloud tossed his head and screamed, but Rand dug his heels in brutally and the horse lunged forward.
If one of those tendrils touched him....
Rand booted Cloud harder and the horse leaped forward into the welcome shadows.
Behind him, the waving gray tentacles of Mashadar blocked half the street and the Trollocs were balking in their pursuit.
The Fade snapped a whip to spur the Trollocs on, and instead attracted the attention of Mashadar.
The thickening tentacles of fog struck like vipers. Its prey tried to scream, but the fog rolled over open mouths, and in, eating the howls and transforming them into a piercing whine just beyond hearing, like all the hornets in the world digging into Rand's ears with all the fear that could exist.
Cloud heard too, and ran harder than ever.

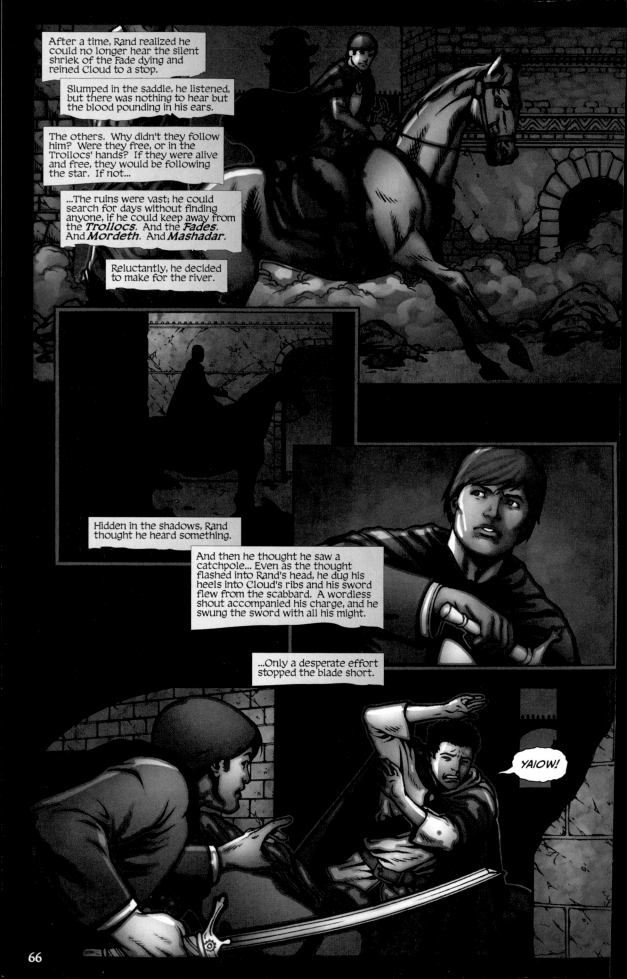

After a time, Rand realized he could no longer hear the silent shriek of the Fade dying and reined Cloud to a stop.

Slumped in the saddle, he listened, but there was nothing to hear but the blood pounding in his ears.

The others. Why didn't they follow him? Were they free, or in the Trollocs' hands? If they were alive and free, they would be following the star. If not...

...The ruins were vast; he could search for days without finding anyone, if he could keep away from the *Trollocs*. And the *Fades*. And *Mordeth*. And *Mashadar*.

Reluctantly, he decided to make for the river.

Hidden in the shadows, Rand thought he heard something.

And then he thought he saw a catchpole... Even as the thought flashed into Rand's head, he dug his heels into Cloud's ribs and his sword flew from the scabbard. A wordless shout accompanied his charge, and he swung the sword with all his might.

...Only a desperate effort stopped the blade short.

YAIOW!

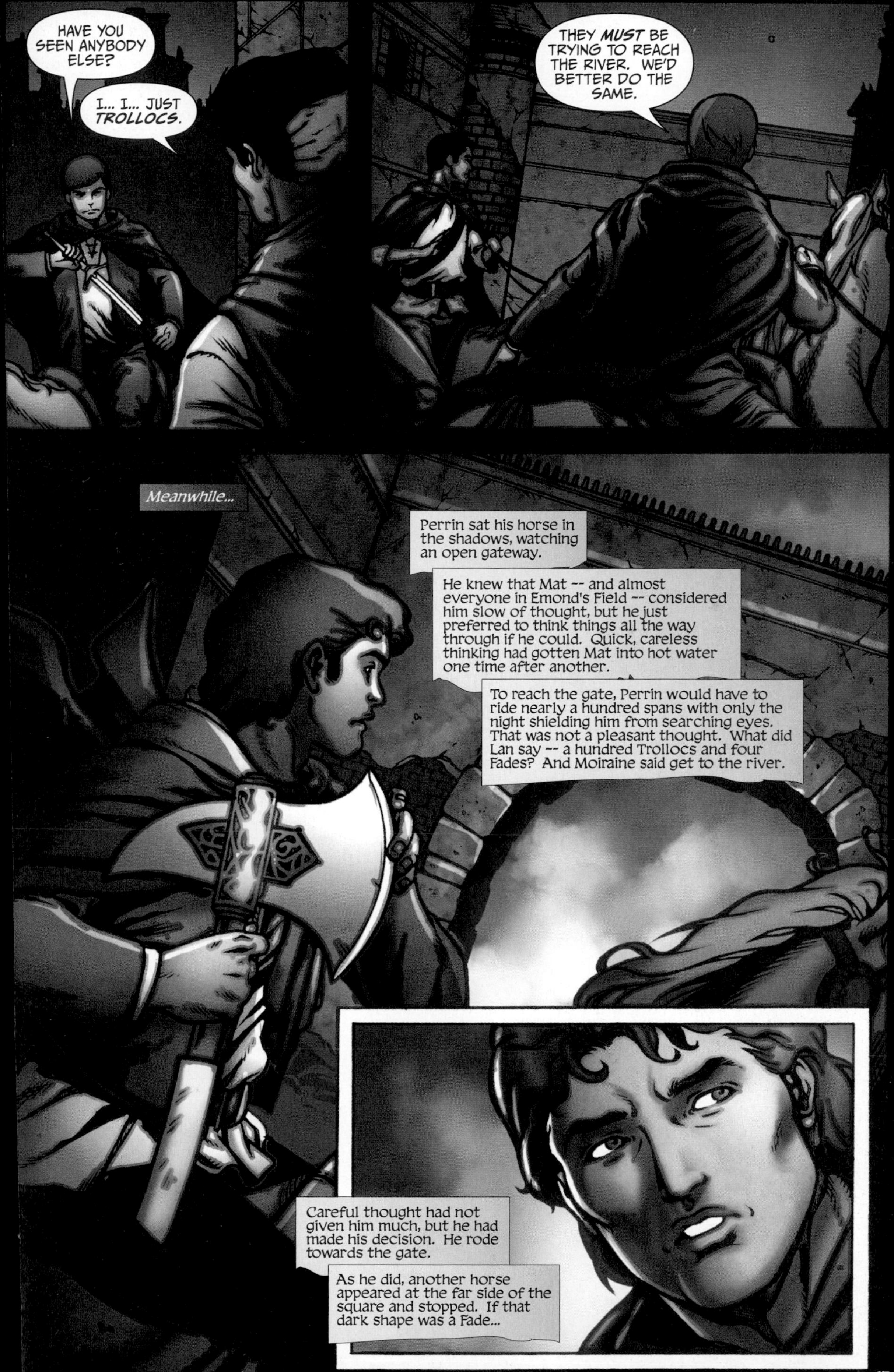
HAVE YOU SEEN ANYBODY ELSE?
I... I... JUST TROLLOCS.
THEY MUST BE TRYING TO REACH THE RIVER. WE'D BETTER DO THE SAME.
Meanwhile...
Perrin sat his horse in the shadows, watching an open gateway.
He knew that Mat -- and almost everyone in Emond's Field -- considered him slow of thought, but he just preferred to think things all the way through if he could. Quick, careless thinking had gotten Mat into hot water one time after another.
To reach the gate, Perrin would have to ride nearly a hundred spans with only the night shielding him from searching eyes. That was not a pleasant thought. What did Lan say -- a hundred Trollocs and four Fades? And Moiraine said get to the river.
Careful thought had not given him much, but he had made his decision. He rode towards the gate.
As he did, another horse appeared at the far side of the square and stopped. If that dark shape was a Fade...

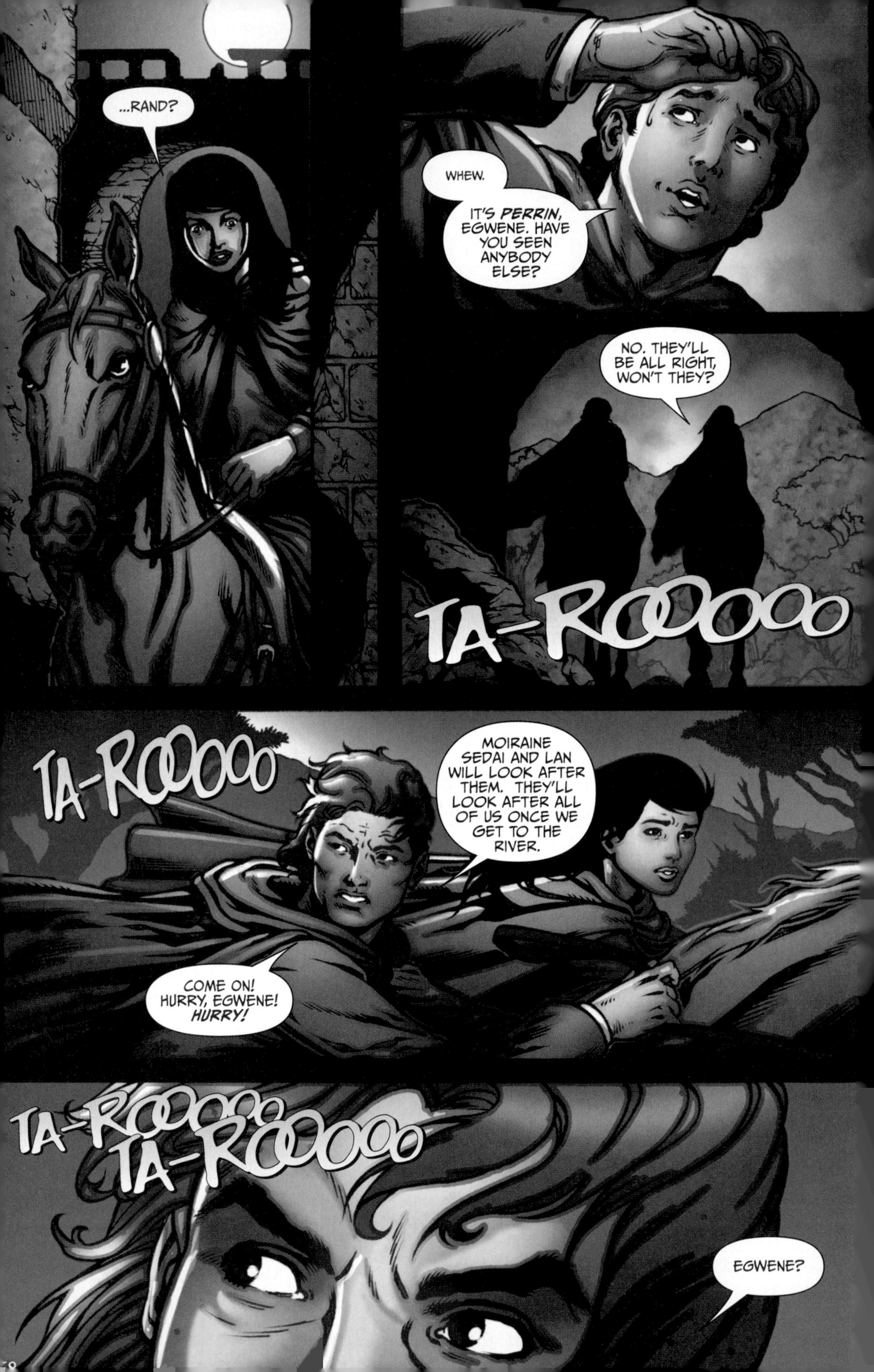
...RAND?
WHEW.
IT'S *PERRIN*, EGWENE. HAVE YOU SEEN ANYBODY ELSE?
NO. THEY'LL BE ALL RIGHT, WON'T THEY?
TA-ROOOOO
TA-ROOOOO
MOIRAINE SEDAI AND LAN WILL LOOK AFTER THEM. THEY'LL LOOK AFTER ALL OF US ONCE WE GET TO THE RIVER.
COME ON! HURRY, EGWENE! *HURRY!*
TA-ROOOOO
TA-ROOOOO
EGWENE?

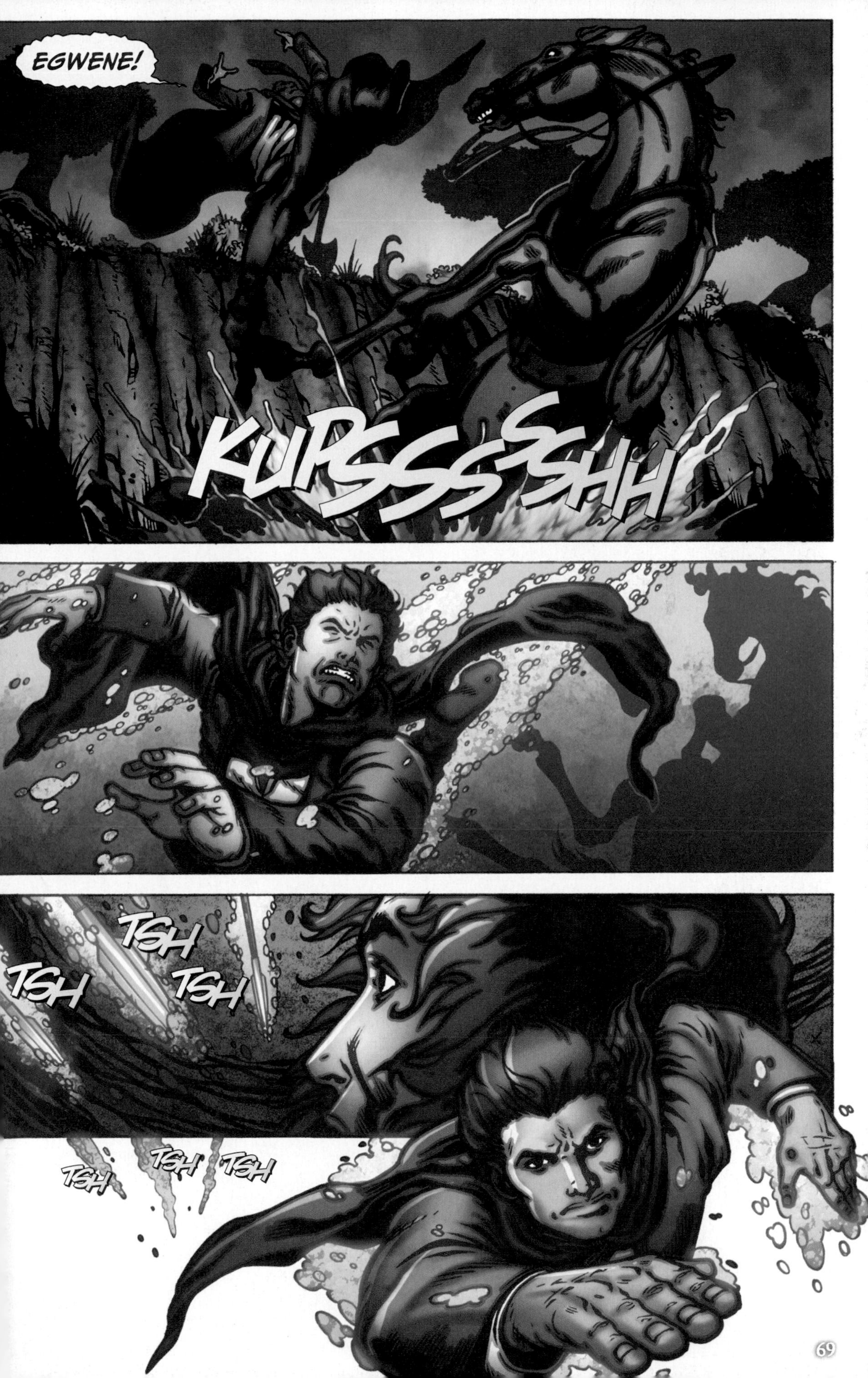
EGWENE!
KUPSSSSSHH
TSH
TSH
TSH
TSH
TSH
TSH

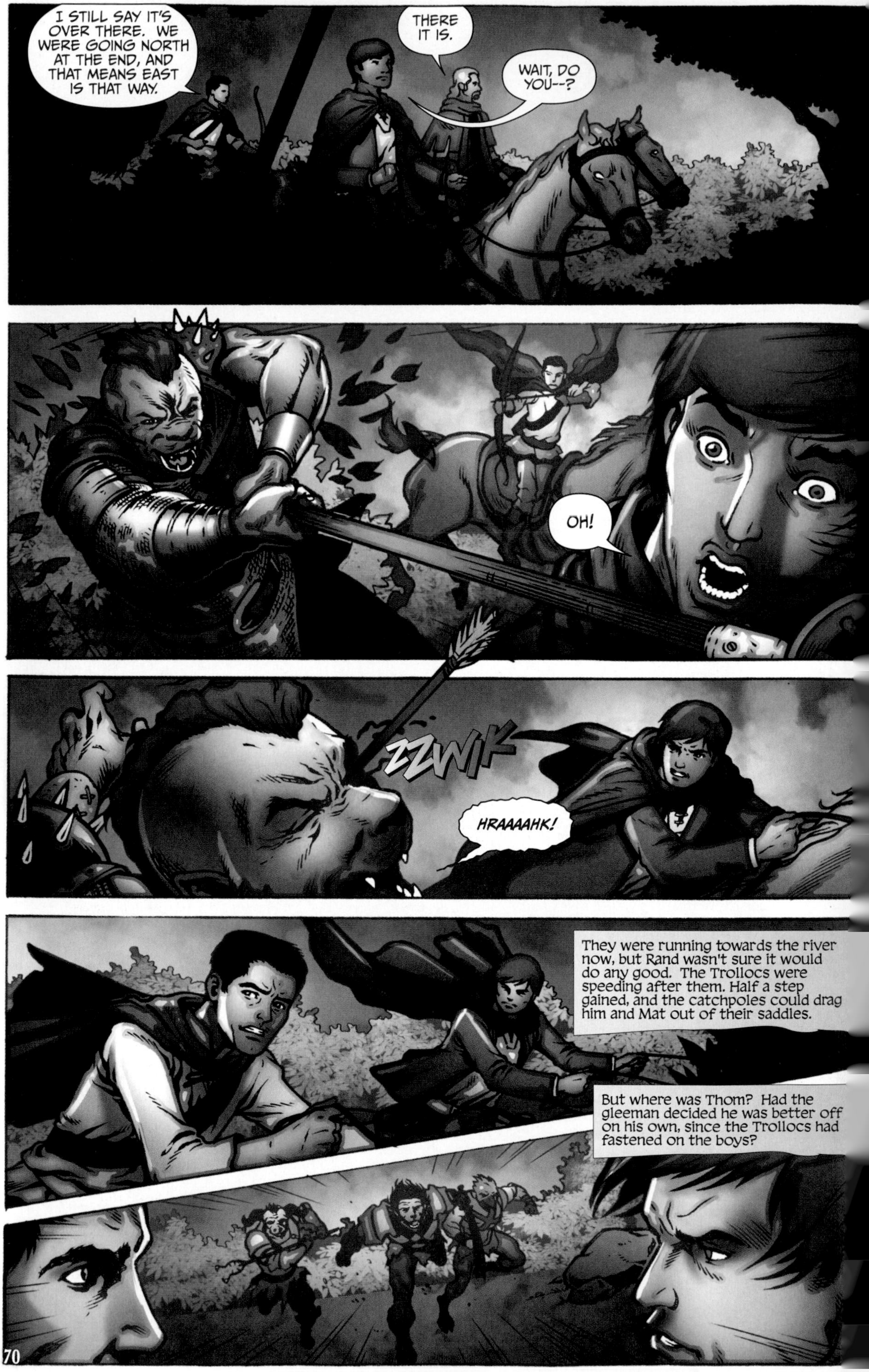
I STILL SAY IT'S OVER THERE. WE WERE GOING NORTH AT THE END, AND THAT MEANS EAST IS THAT WAY.
THERE IT IS.
WAIT, DO YOU--?
OH!
ZZWIK
HRAAAAHK!
They were running towards the river now, but Rand wasn't sure it would do any good. The Trollocs were speeding after them. Half a step gained, and the catchpoles could drag him and Mat out of their saddles.
But where was Thom? Had the gleeman decided he was better off on his own, since the Trollocs had fastened on the boys?

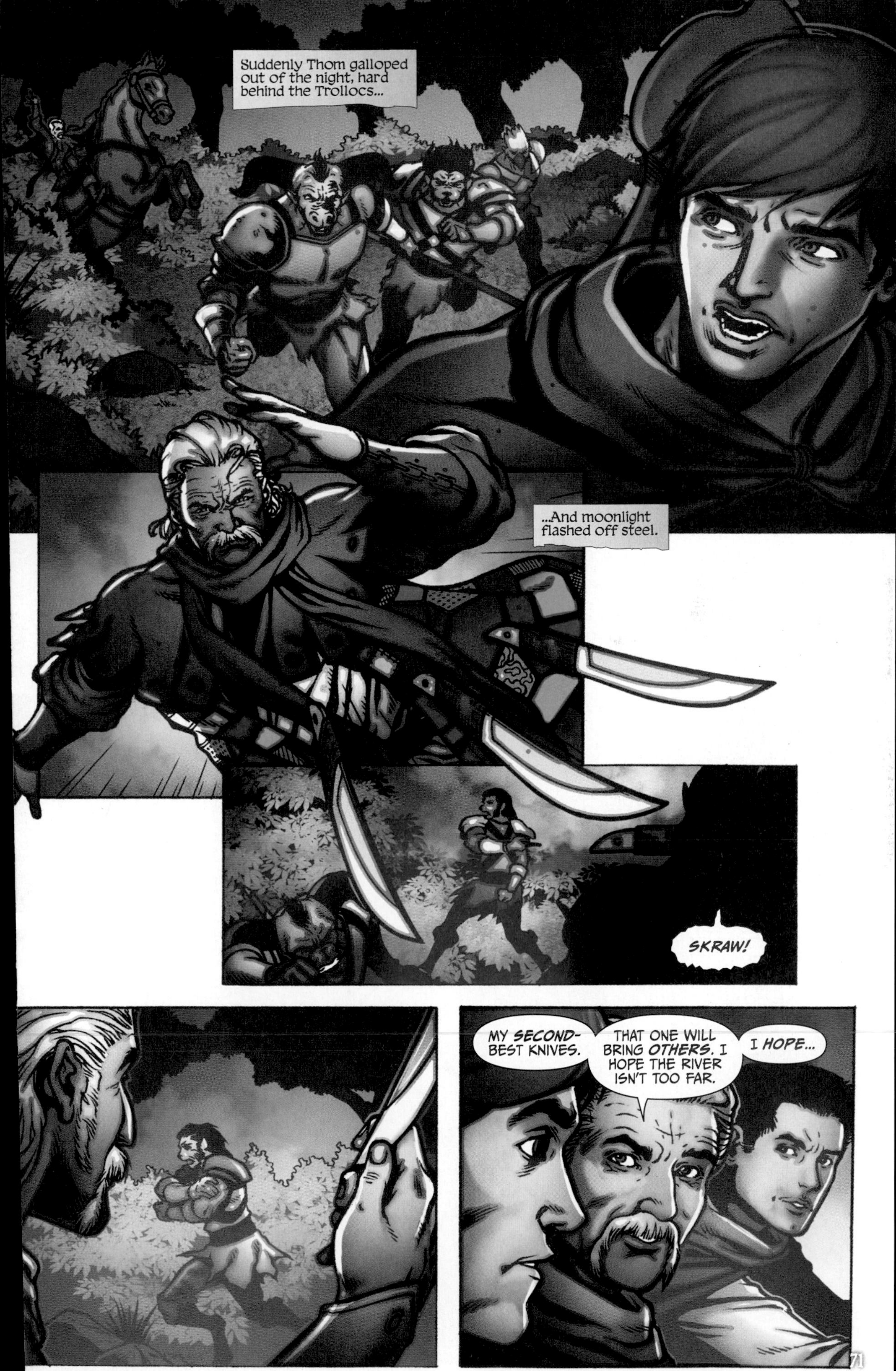

Suddenly Thom galloped out of the night, hard behind the Trollocs...
...And moonlight flashed off steel.
SKRAW!
MY SECOND-BEST KNIVES.
THAT ONE WILL BRING OTHERS. I HOPE THE RIVER ISN'T TOO FAR.
I HOPE...

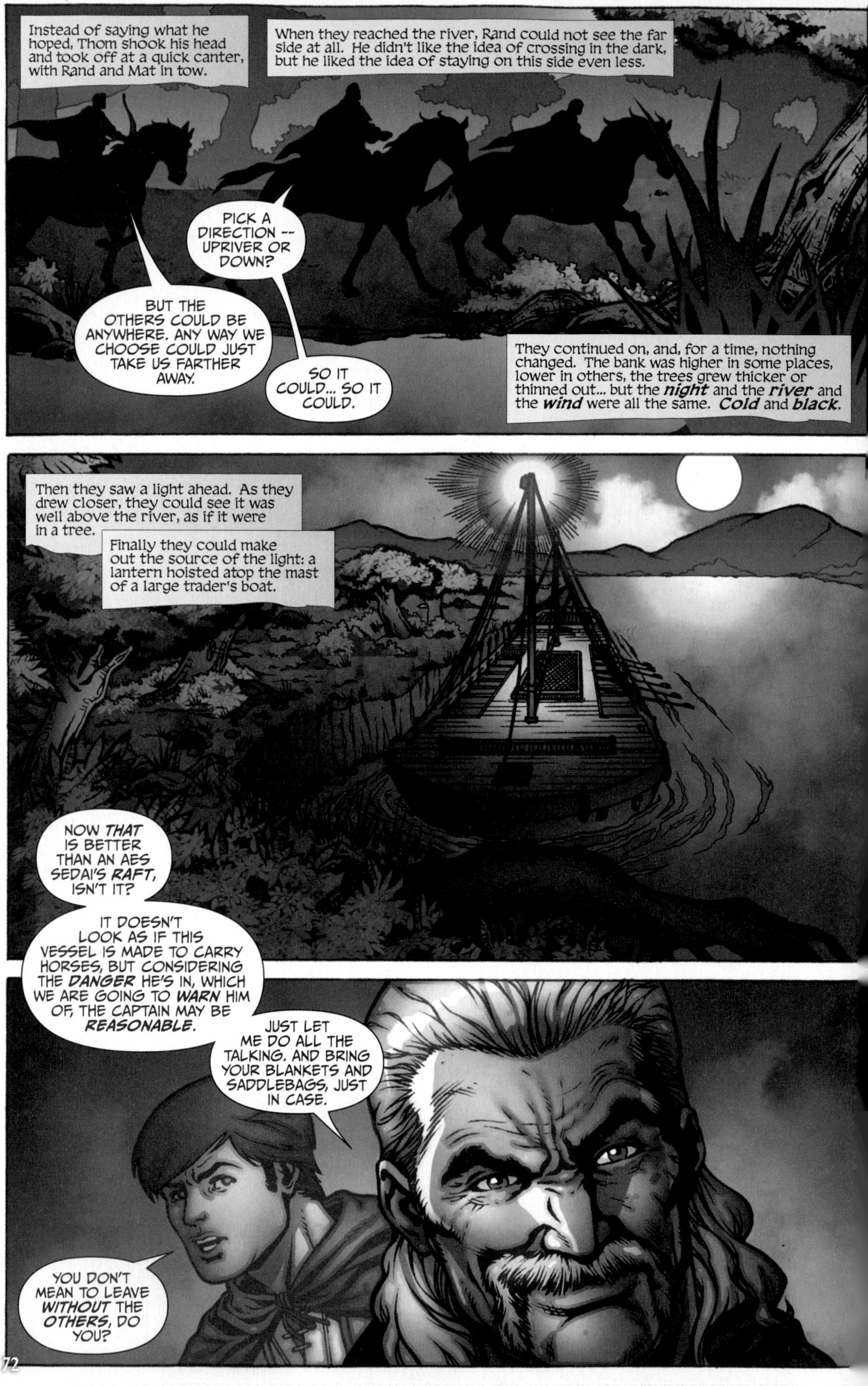

Instead of saying what he hoped, Thom shook his head and took off at a quick canter, with Rand and Mat in tow.
When they reached the river, Rand could not see the far side at all. He didn't like the idea of crossing in the dark, but he liked the idea of staying on this side even less.
PICK A DIRECTION -- UPRIVER OR DOWN?
BUT THE OTHERS COULD BE ANYWHERE. ANY WAY WE CHOOSE COULD JUST TAKE US FARTHER AWAY.
SO IT COULD... SO IT COULD.
They continued on, and, for a time, nothing changed. The bank was higher in some places, lower in others, the trees grew thicker or thinned out... but the *night* and the *river* and the *wind* were all the same. *Cold* and *black*.
Then they saw a light ahead. As they drew closer, they could see it was well above the river, as if it were in a tree.
Finally they could make out the source of the light: a lantern hoisted atop the mast of a large trader's boat.
NOW *THAT* IS BETTER THAN AN AES SEDAI'S *RAFT*, ISN'T IT?
IT DOESN'T LOOK AS IF THIS VESSEL IS MADE TO CARRY HORSES, BUT CONSIDERING THE *DANGER* HE'S IN, WHICH WE ARE GOING TO *WARN* HIM OF, THE CAPTAIN MAY BE *REASONABLE*.
JUST LET ME DO ALL THE TALKING. AND BRING YOUR BLANKETS AND SADDLEBAGS, JUST IN CASE.
YOU DON'T MEAN TO LEAVE *WITHOUT* THE *OTHERS*, DO YOU?

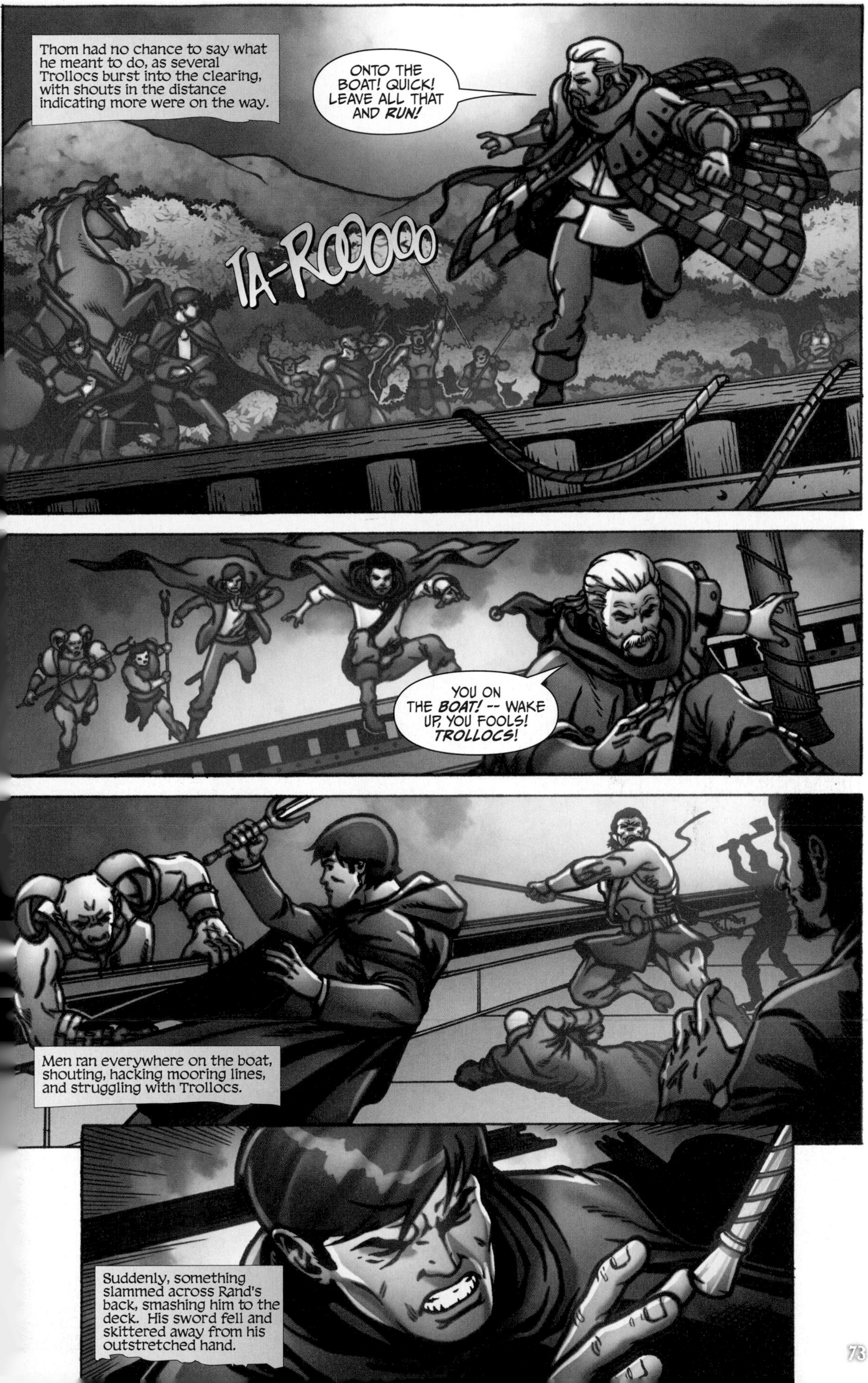
Thom had no chance to say what he meant to do, as several Trollocs burst into the clearing, with shouts in the distance indicating more were on the way.
ONTO THE BOAT! QUICK! LEAVE ALL THAT AND RUN!
TA-ROOOOO
YOU ON THE BOAT! -- WAKE UP, YOU FOOLS! TROLLOCS!
Men ran everywhere on the boat, shouting, hacking mooring lines, and struggling with Trollocs.
Suddenly, something slammed across Rand's back, smashing him to the deck. His sword fell and skittered away from his outstretched hand.

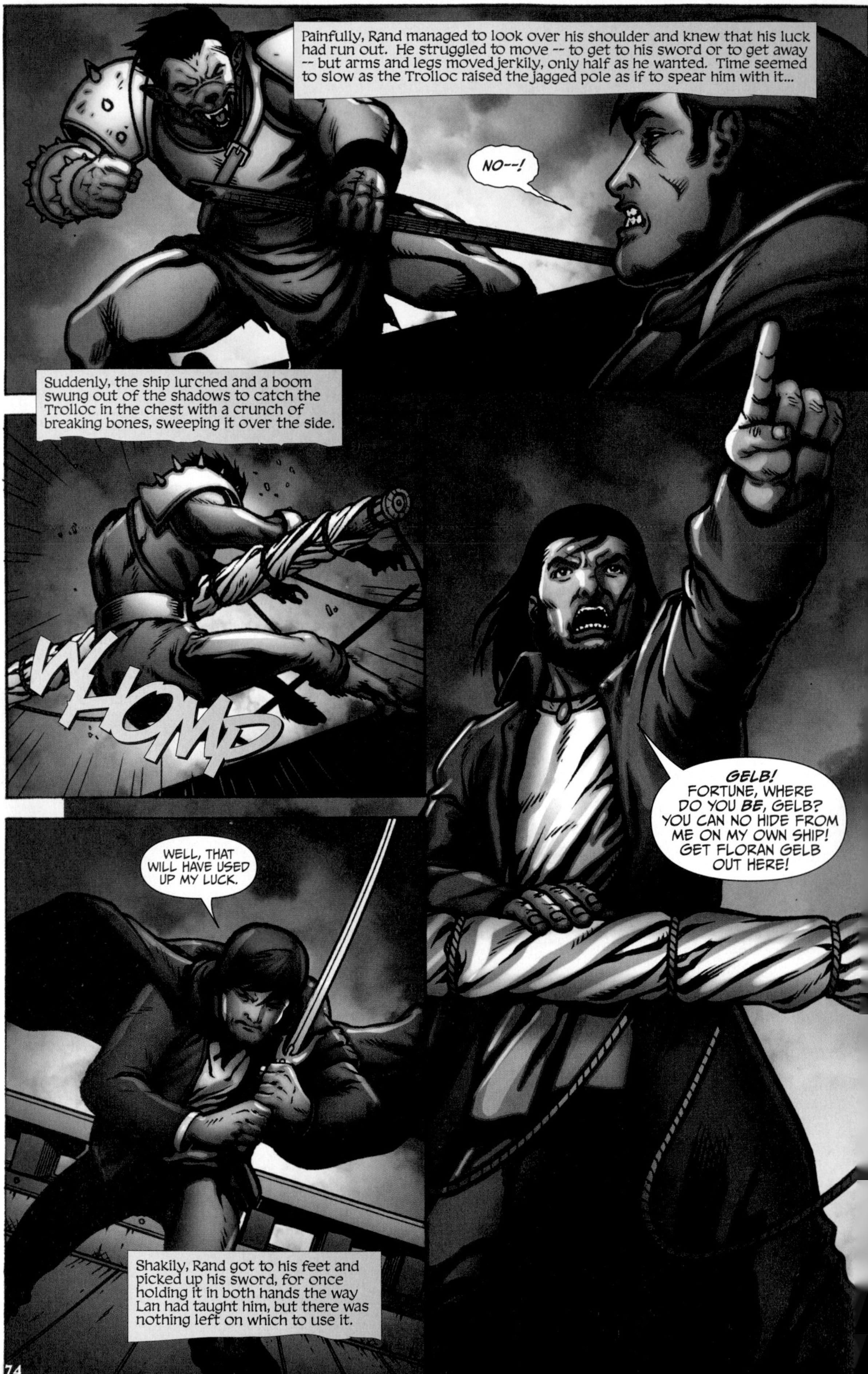
Painfully, Rand managed to look over his shoulder and knew that his luck had run out. He struggled to move -- to get to his sword or to get away -- but arms and legs moved jerkily, only half as he wanted. Time seemed to slow as the Trolloc raised the jagged pole as if to spear him with it...
NO--!
Suddenly, the ship lurched and a boom swung out of the shadows to catch the Trolloc in the chest with a crunch of breaking bones, sweeping it over the side.
WHOMP
GELB! FORTUNE, WHERE DO YOU BE, GELB? YOU CAN NO HIDE FROM ME ON MY OWN SHIP! GET FLORAN GELB OUT HERE!
WELL, THAT WILL HAVE USED UP MY LUCK.
Shakily, Rand got to his feet and picked up his sword, for once holding it in both hands the way Lan had taught him, but there was nothing left on which to use it.

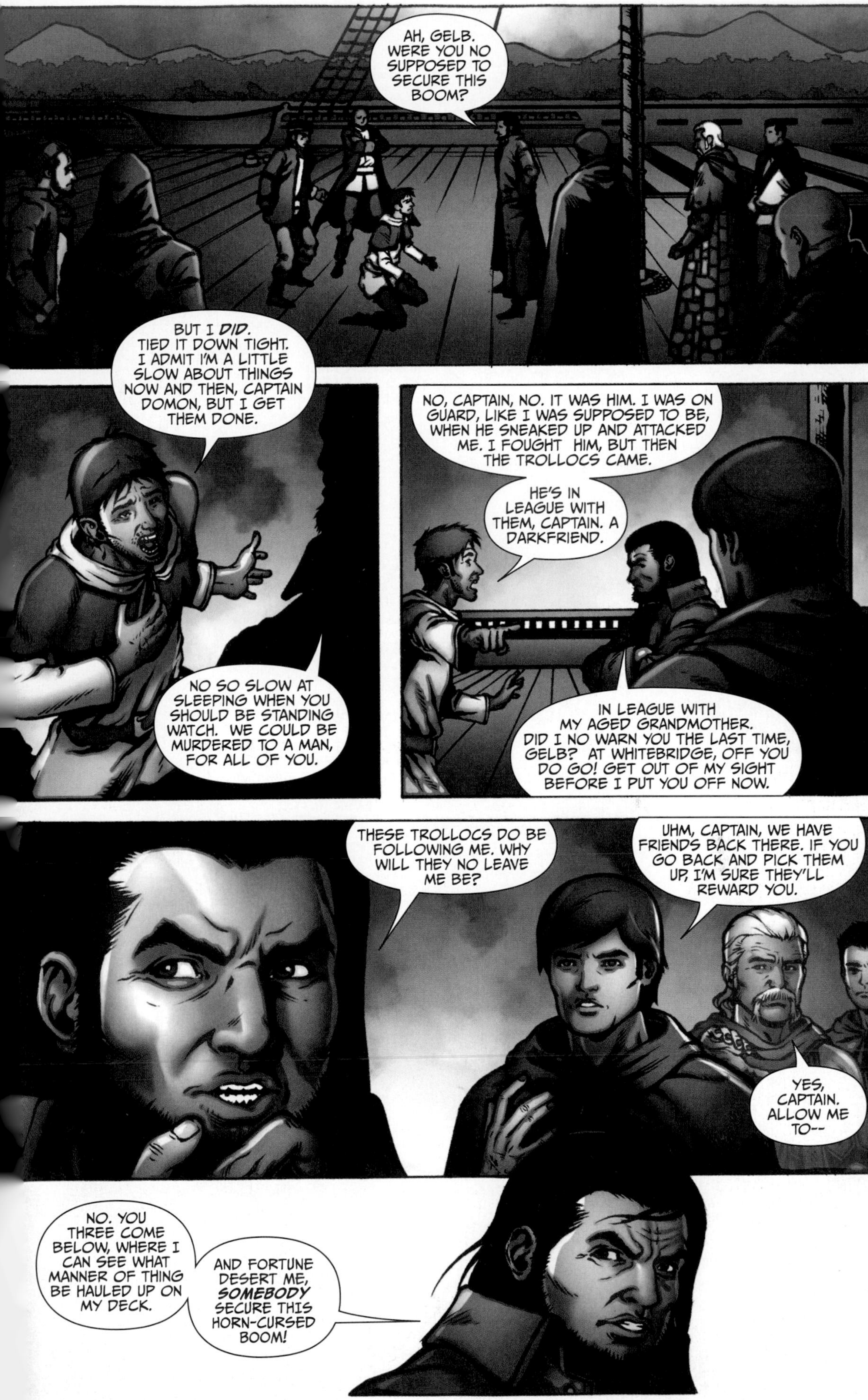
AH, GELB. WERE YOU NO SUPPOSED TO SECURE THIS BOOM?
BUT I *DID*. TIED IT DOWN TIGHT. I ADMIT I'M A LITTLE SLOW ABOUT THINGS NOW AND THEN, CAPTAIN DOMON, BUT I GET THEM DONE.
NO SO SLOW AT SLEEPING WHEN YOU SHOULD BE STANDING WATCH. WE COULD BE MURDERED TO A MAN, FOR ALL OF YOU.
NO, CAPTAIN, NO. IT WAS HIM. I WAS ON GUARD, LIKE I WAS SUPPOSED TO BE, WHEN HE SNEAKED UP AND ATTACKED ME. I FOUGHT HIM, BUT THEN THE TROLLOCS CAME.
HE'S IN LEAGUE WITH THEM, CAPTAIN. A DARKFRIEND.
IN LEAGUE WITH MY AGED GRANDMOTHER. DID I NO WARN YOU THE LAST TIME, GELB? AT WHITEBRIDGE, OFF YOU DO GO! GET OUT OF MY SIGHT BEFORE I PUT YOU OFF NOW.
THESE TROLLOCS DO BE FOLLOWING ME. WHY WILL THEY NO LEAVE ME BE?
UHM, CAPTAIN, WE HAVE FRIENDS BACK THERE. IF YOU GO BACK AND PICK THEM UP, I'M SURE THEY'LL REWARD YOU.
YES, CAPTAIN. ALLOW ME TO--
NO. YOU THREE COME BELOW, WHERE I CAN SEE WHAT MANNER OF THING BE HAULED UP ON MY DECK.
AND FORTUNE DESERT ME, ***SOMEBODY*** SECURE THIS HORN-CURSED BOOM!

NOW MY NAME BE BAYLE DOMON, CAPTAIN AND OWNER OF THE SPRAY, WHICH BE THIS SHIP.

NOW WHO BE YOU, AND WHY SHOULD I NO THROW YOU OVER THE SIDE FOR THE TROUBLE YOU'VE BROUGHT ME?

WE DIDN'T *MEAN* TO CAUSE YOU TROUBLE. WE'RE ON OUR WAY TO CAEMLYN, AND THEN TO--

AND THEN WHERE THE WIND TAKES US. THAT'S HOW GLEEMEN TRAVEL, LIKE DUST ON THE WIND. I AM A GLEEMAN, YOU UNDERSTAND, THOM MERRILIN BY NAME.

THESE TWO COUNTRY LOUTS WANT TO BECOME MY APPRENTICES, THOUGH I AM NOT YET SURE THAT I WANT THEM.

THAT BE ALL VERY WELL, MAN, BUT IT TELLS ME *NOTHING*. FORTUNE PRICK ME, THAT PLACE BE ON NO ROAD TO CAEMLYN FROM ANYWHERE I EVER HEARD TELL OF.

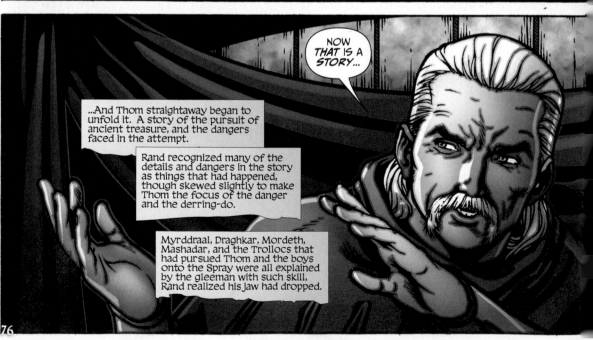

NOW *THAT* IS A STORY...

...And Thom straightaway began to unfold it. A story of the pursuit of ancient treasure, and the dangers faced in the attempt.

Rand recognized many of the details and dangers in the story as things that had happened, though skewed slightly to make Thom the focus of the danger and the derring-do.

Myrddraal, Draghkar, Mordeth, Mashadar, and the Trollocs that had pursued Thom and the boys onto the Spray were all explained by the gleeman with such skill, Rand realized his jaw had dropped.

THAT BE A TALE MANY FOLK WOULD NO BELIEVE. OF COURSE, I DID SEE THE TROLLOCS, DID I NO.

NOW, HAPPEN YOU TO HAVE SOME OF THIS *TREASURE* YOU MENTIONED WITH YOU?

ALAS, WHAT LITTLE WE MANAGED TO CARRY AWAY WAS LOST WITH OUR HORSES, WHICH BOLTED WHEN THOSE LAST TROLLOCS APPEARED. ALL I HAVE LEFT ARE MY FLUTE AND MY HARP, A FEW COPPERS, AND THE CLOTHES ON MY BACK.

BUT BELIEVE ME, YOU WANT NO PART OF THAT TREASURE. IT HAS THE TAINT OF THE DARK ONE. BEST TO LEAVE IT TO THE RUINS AND THE TROLLOCS.

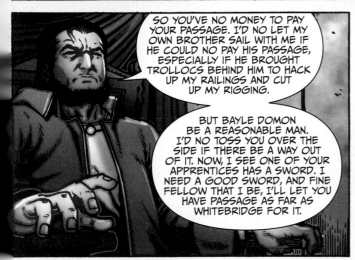

SO YOU'VE NO MONEY TO PAY YOUR PASSAGE. I'D NO LET MY OWN BROTHER SAIL WITH ME IF HE COULD NO PAY HIS PASSAGE, ESPECIALLY IF HE BROUGHT TROLLOCS BEHIND HIM TO HACK UP MY RAILINGS AND CUT UP MY RIGGING.

BUT BAYLE DOMON BE A REASONABLE MAN. I'D NO TOSS YOU OVER THE SIDE IF THERE BE A WAY OUT OF IT. NOW, I SEE ONE OF YOUR APPRENTICES HAS A SWORD. I NEED A GOOD SWORD, AND FINE FELLOW THAT I BE, I'LL LET YOU HAVE PASSAGE AS FAR AS WHITEBRIDGE FOR IT.

MY-- NO!

WELL, IF IT BE NO, IT BE NO. BUT BAYLE DOMON NO GIVE FREE PASSAGE, NOT TO HIS OWN MOTHER.

WELL, I-- HOLD ON...

Reluctantly, Rand emptied his pocket. There was not much -- a few coppers and the silver coin Moiraine had given him. He held it out to the captain, and, after a second, Mat sighed and did the same.

77

HMM. YES. AS FAR AS WHITEBRIDGE.

THAT'S A DEAR PASSAGE JUST TO WHITEBRIDGE.

PLUS DAMAGES TO MY VESSEL. PLUS A BIT FOR BRINGING TROLLOCS DOWN ON ME SO I MUST RUN DOWNRIVER IN THE NIGHT.

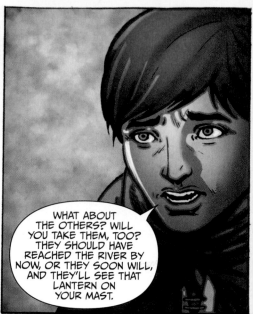

WHAT ABOUT THE OTHERS? WILL YOU TAKE THEM, TOO? THEY SHOULD HAVE REACHED THE RIVER BY NOW, OR THEY SOON WILL, AND THEY'LL SEE THAT LANTERN ON YOUR MAST.

HAPPEN YOU THINK WE BE STANDING STILL, MAN? FORTUNE PRICK ME, WE BE THREE, FOUR MILES DOWNRIVER FROM WHERE YOU CAME ABOARD. TROLLOCS MAKE THESE FELLOWS PUT THEIR BACKS INTO THEIR OARS, AND THE CURRENT HELPS, TOO.

BUT IT MAKES NO NEVERMIND. I'D NO PUT IN AGAIN TONIGHT IF MY OLD GRAND-MOTHER WAS ON THE RIVERBANK.

I MAY NO PUT IN AGAIN *AT ALL* UNTIL I REACH WHITEBRIDGE.

NO...

THERE ISN'T ANYTHING YOU CAN DO, LAD. BESIDES, THEY'RE LIKELY SAFE WITH THE... WITH MOIRAINE AND LAN BY THIS TIME. CAN YOU THINK OF ANY BETTER THAN THOSE TWO FOR GETTING THE LOT OF THEM IN THE CLEAR?

I TRIED TO TALK HER OUT OF COMING.

YOU DID WHAT YOU COULD, LAD. NO ONE COULD ASK MORE.

I SHOULD HAVE TRIED *HARDER.*

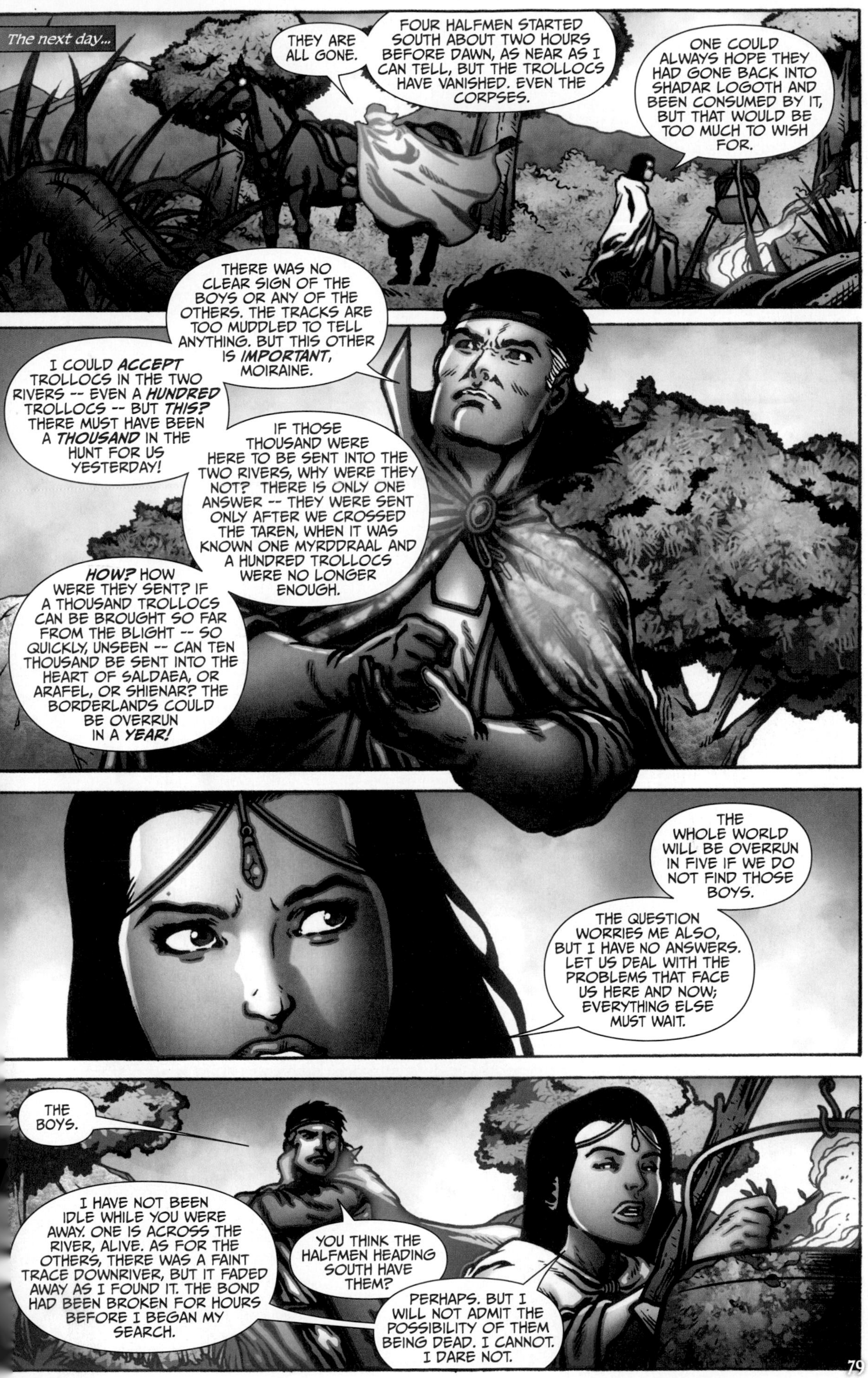

The next day...
THEY ARE ALL GONE.
FOUR HALFMEN STARTED SOUTH ABOUT TWO HOURS BEFORE DAWN, AS NEAR AS I CAN TELL, BUT THE TROLLOCS HAVE VANISHED. EVEN THE CORPSES.
ONE COULD ALWAYS HOPE THEY HAD GONE BACK INTO SHADAR LOGOTH AND BEEN CONSUMED BY IT, BUT THAT WOULD BE TOO MUCH TO WISH FOR.
THERE WAS NO CLEAR SIGN OF THE BOYS OR ANY OF THE OTHERS. THE TRACKS ARE TOO MUDDLED TO TELL ANYTHING. BUT THIS OTHER IS *IMPORTANT*, MOIRAINE.
I COULD *ACCEPT* TROLLOCS IN THE TWO RIVERS -- EVEN A *HUNDRED* TROLLOCS -- BUT *THIS?* THERE MUST HAVE BEEN A *THOUSAND* IN THE HUNT FOR US YESTERDAY!
IF THOSE THOUSAND WERE HERE TO BE SENT INTO THE TWO RIVERS, WHY WERE THEY NOT? THERE IS ONLY ONE ANSWER -- THEY WERE SENT ONLY AFTER WE CROSSED THE TAREN, WHEN IT WAS KNOWN ONE MYRDDRAAL AND A HUNDRED TROLLOCS WERE NO LONGER ENOUGH.
HOW? HOW WERE THEY SENT? IF A THOUSAND TROLLOCS CAN BE BROUGHT SO FAR FROM THE BLIGHT -- SO QUICKLY, UNSEEN -- CAN TEN THOUSAND BE SENT INTO THE HEART OF SALDAEA, OR ARAFEL, OR SHIENAR? THE BORDERLANDS COULD BE OVERRUN IN A *YEAR!*
THE WHOLE WORLD WILL BE OVERRUN IN FIVE IF WE DO NOT FIND THOSE BOYS.
THE QUESTION WORRIES ME ALSO, BUT I HAVE NO ANSWERS. LET US DEAL WITH THE PROBLEMS THAT FACE US HERE AND NOW; EVERYTHING ELSE MUST WAIT.
THE BOYS.
I HAVE NOT BEEN IDLE WHILE YOU WERE AWAY. ONE IS ACROSS THE RIVER, ALIVE. AS FOR THE OTHERS, THERE WAS A FAINT TRACE DOWNRIVER, BUT IT FADED AWAY AS I FOUND IT. THE BOND HAD BEEN BROKEN FOR HOURS BEFORE I BEGAN MY SEARCH.
YOU THINK THE HALFMEN HEADING SOUTH HAVE THEM?
PERHAPS. BUT I WILL NOT ADMIT THE POSSIBILITY OF THEM BEING DEAD. I CANNOT. I DARE NOT.

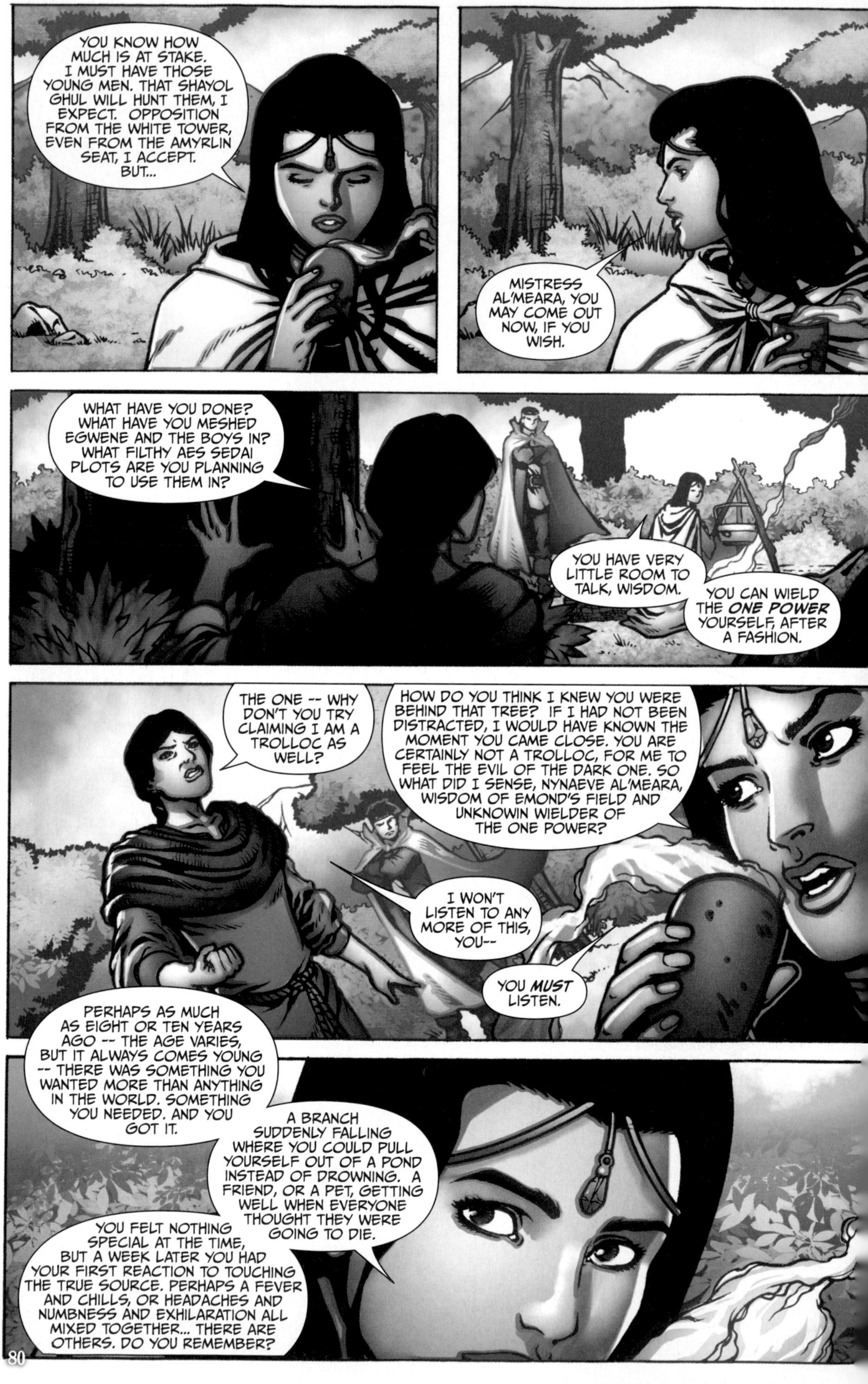
YOU KNOW HOW MUCH IS AT STAKE. I MUST HAVE THOSE YOUNG MEN. THAT SHAYOL GHUL WILL HUNT THEM, I EXPECT. OPPOSITION FROM THE WHITE TOWER, EVEN FROM THE AMYRLIN SEAT, I ACCEPT. BUT...
MISTRESS AL'MEARA, YOU MAY COME OUT NOW, IF YOU WISH.
WHAT HAVE YOU DONE? WHAT HAVE YOU MESHED EGWENE AND THE BOYS IN? WHAT FILTHY AES SEDAI PLOTS ARE YOU PLANNING TO USE THEM IN?
YOU HAVE VERY LITTLE ROOM TO TALK, WISDOM.
YOU CAN WIELD THE ***ONE POWER*** YOURSELF, AFTER A FASHION.
THE ONE -- WHY DON'T YOU TRY CLAIMING I AM A TROLLOC AS WELL?
HOW DO YOU THINK I KNEW YOU WERE BEHIND THAT TREE? IF I HAD NOT BEEN DISTRACTED, I WOULD HAVE KNOWN THE MOMENT YOU CAME CLOSE. YOU ARE CERTAINLY NOT A TROLLOC, FOR ME TO FEEL THE EVIL OF THE DARK ONE. SO WHAT DID I SENSE, NYNAEVE AL'MEARA, WISDOM OF EMOND'S FIELD AND UNKNOWIN WIELDER OF THE ONE POWER?
I WON'T LISTEN TO ANY MORE OF THIS, YOU--
YOU ***MUST*** LISTEN.
PERHAPS AS MUCH AS EIGHT OR TEN YEARS AGO -- THE AGE VARIES, BUT IT ALWAYS COMES YOUNG -- THERE WAS SOMETHING YOU WANTED MORE THAN ANYTHING IN THE WORLD. SOMETHING YOU NEEDED. AND YOU GOT IT.
A BRANCH SUDDENLY FALLING WHERE YOU COULD PULL YOURSELF OUT OF A POND INSTEAD OF DROWNING. A FRIEND, OR A PET, GETTING WELL WHEN EVERYONE THOUGHT THEY WERE GOING TO DIE.
YOU FELT NOTHING SPECIAL AT THE TIME, BUT A WEEK LATER YOU HAD YOUR FIRST REACTION TO TOUCHING THE TRUE SOURCE. PERHAPS A FEVER AND CHILLS, OR HEADACHES AND NUMBNESS AND EXHILARATION ALL MIXED TOGETHER... THERE ARE OTHERS. DO YOU REMEMBER?

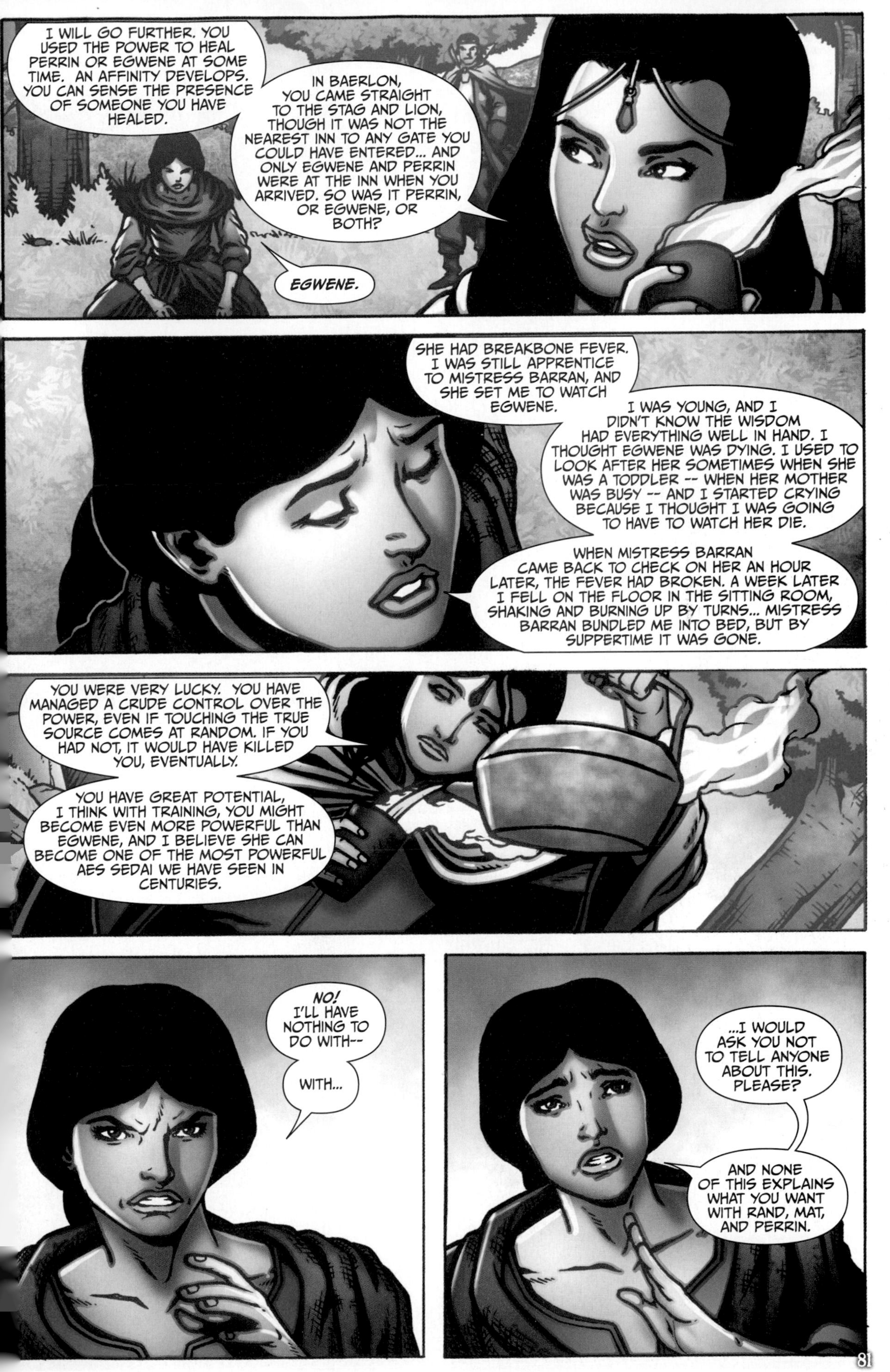
I WILL GO FURTHER. YOU USED THE POWER TO HEAL PERRIN OR EGWENE AT SOME TIME. AN AFFINITY DEVELOPS. YOU CAN SENSE THE PRESENCE OF SOMEONE YOU HAVE HEALED.
IN BAERLON, YOU CAME STRAIGHT TO THE STAG AND LION, THOUGH IT WAS NOT THE NEAREST INN TO ANY GATE YOU COULD HAVE ENTERED... AND ONLY EGWENE AND PERRIN WERE AT THE INN WHEN YOU ARRIVED. SO WAS IT PERRIN, OR EGWENE, OR BOTH?
EGWENE.
SHE HAD BREAKBONE FEVER. I WAS STILL APPRENTICE TO MISTRESS BARRAN, AND SHE SET ME TO WATCH EGWENE.
I WAS YOUNG, AND I DIDN'T KNOW THE WISDOM HAD EVERYTHING WELL IN HAND. I THOUGHT EGWENE WAS DYING. I USED TO LOOK AFTER HER SOMETIMES WHEN SHE WAS A TODDLER -- WHEN HER MOTHER WAS BUSY -- AND I STARTED CRYING BECAUSE I THOUGHT I WAS GOING TO HAVE TO WATCH HER DIE.
WHEN MISTRESS BARRAN CAME BACK TO CHECK ON HER AN HOUR LATER, THE FEVER HAD BROKEN. A WEEK LATER I FELL ON THE FLOOR IN THE SITTING ROOM, SHAKING AND BURNING UP BY TURNS... MISTRESS BARRAN BUNDLED ME INTO BED, BUT BY SUPPERTIME IT WAS GONE.
YOU WERE VERY LUCKY. YOU HAVE MANAGED A CRUDE CONTROL OVER THE POWER, EVEN IF TOUCHING THE TRUE SOURCE COMES AT RANDOM. IF YOU HAD NOT, IT WOULD HAVE KILLED YOU, EVENTUALLY.
YOU HAVE GREAT POTENTIAL, I THINK WITH TRAINING, YOU MIGHT BECOME EVEN MORE POWERFUL THAN EGWENE, AND I BELIEVE SHE CAN BECOME ONE OF THE MOST POWERFUL AES SEDAI WE HAVE SEEN IN CENTURIES.
NO! I'LL HAVE NOTHING TO DO WITH--
WITH...
...I WOULD ASK YOU NOT TO TELL ANYONE ABOUT THIS. PLEASE?
AND NONE OF THIS EXPLAINS WHAT YOU WANT WITH RAND, MAT, AND PERRIN.

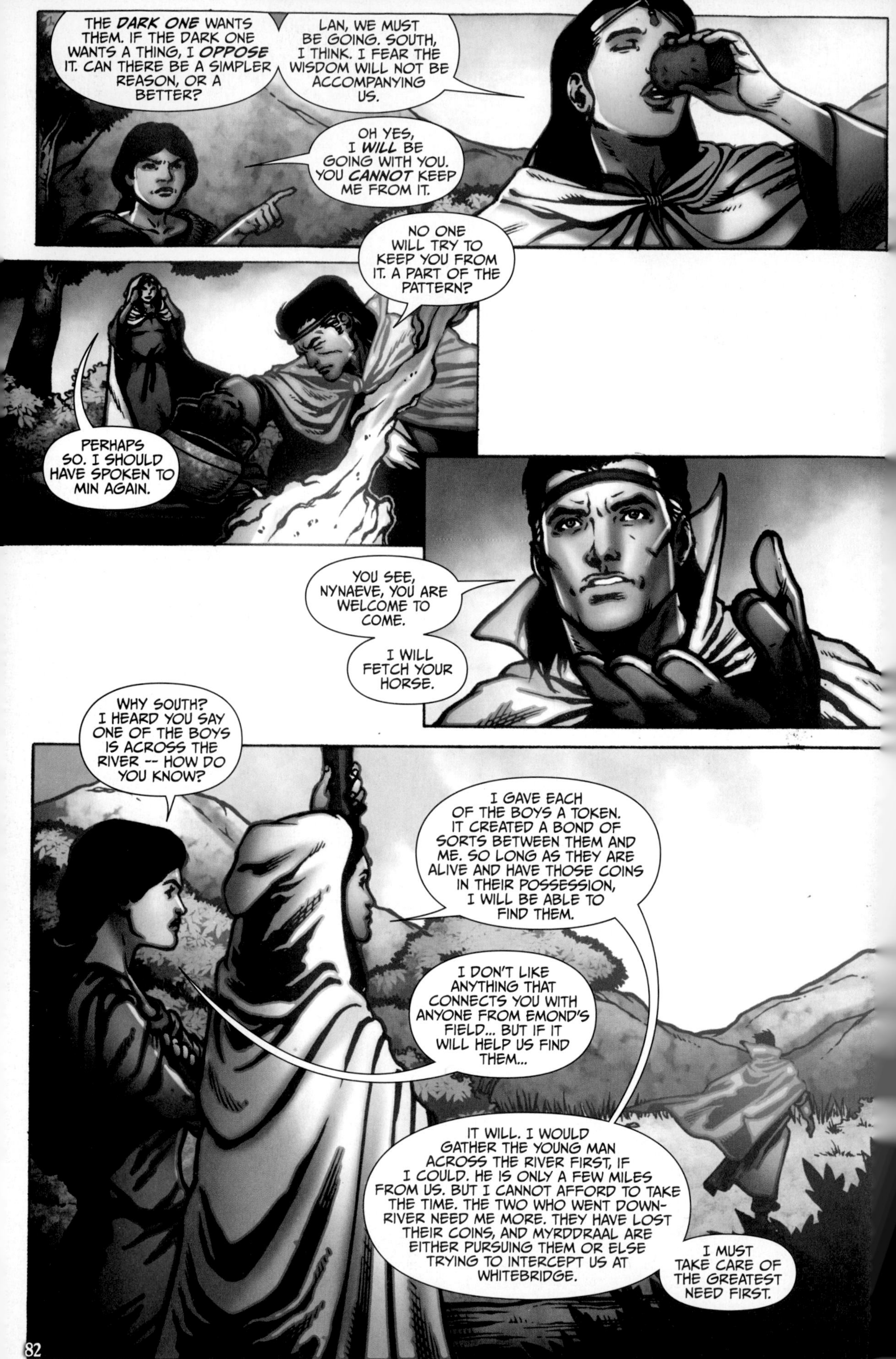
THE DARK ONE WANTS THEM. IF THE DARK ONE WANTS A THING, I OPPOSE IT. CAN THERE BE A SIMPLER REASON, OR A BETTER?
LAN, WE MUST BE GOING. SOUTH, I THINK. I FEAR THE WISDOM WILL NOT BE ACCOMPANYING US.
OH YES, I WILL BE GOING WITH YOU. YOU CANNOT KEEP ME FROM IT.
NO ONE WILL TRY TO KEEP YOU FROM IT. A PART OF THE PATTERN?
PERHAPS SO. I SHOULD HAVE SPOKEN TO MIN AGAIN.
YOU SEE, NYNAEVE, YOU ARE WELCOME TO COME.
I WILL FETCH YOUR HORSE.
WHY SOUTH? I HEARD YOU SAY ONE OF THE BOYS IS ACROSS THE RIVER -- HOW DO YOU KNOW?
I GAVE EACH OF THE BOYS A TOKEN. IT CREATED A BOND OF SORTS BETWEEN THEM AND ME. SO LONG AS THEY ARE ALIVE AND HAVE THOSE COINS IN THEIR POSSESSION, I WILL BE ABLE TO FIND THEM.
I DON'T LIKE ANYTHING THAT CONNECTS YOU WITH ANYONE FROM EMOND'S FIELD... BUT IF IT WILL HELP US FIND THEM...
IT WILL. I WOULD GATHER THE YOUNG MAN ACROSS THE RIVER FIRST, IF I COULD. HE IS ONLY A FEW MILES FROM US. BUT I CANNOT AFFORD TO TAKE THE TIME. THE TWO WHO WENT DOWN-RIVER NEED ME MORE. THEY HAVE LOST THEIR COINS, AND MYRDDRAAL ARE EITHER PURSUING THEM OR ELSE TRYING TO INTERCEPT US AT WHITEBRIDGE.
I MUST TAKE CARE OF THE GREATEST NEED FIRST.

chapter four

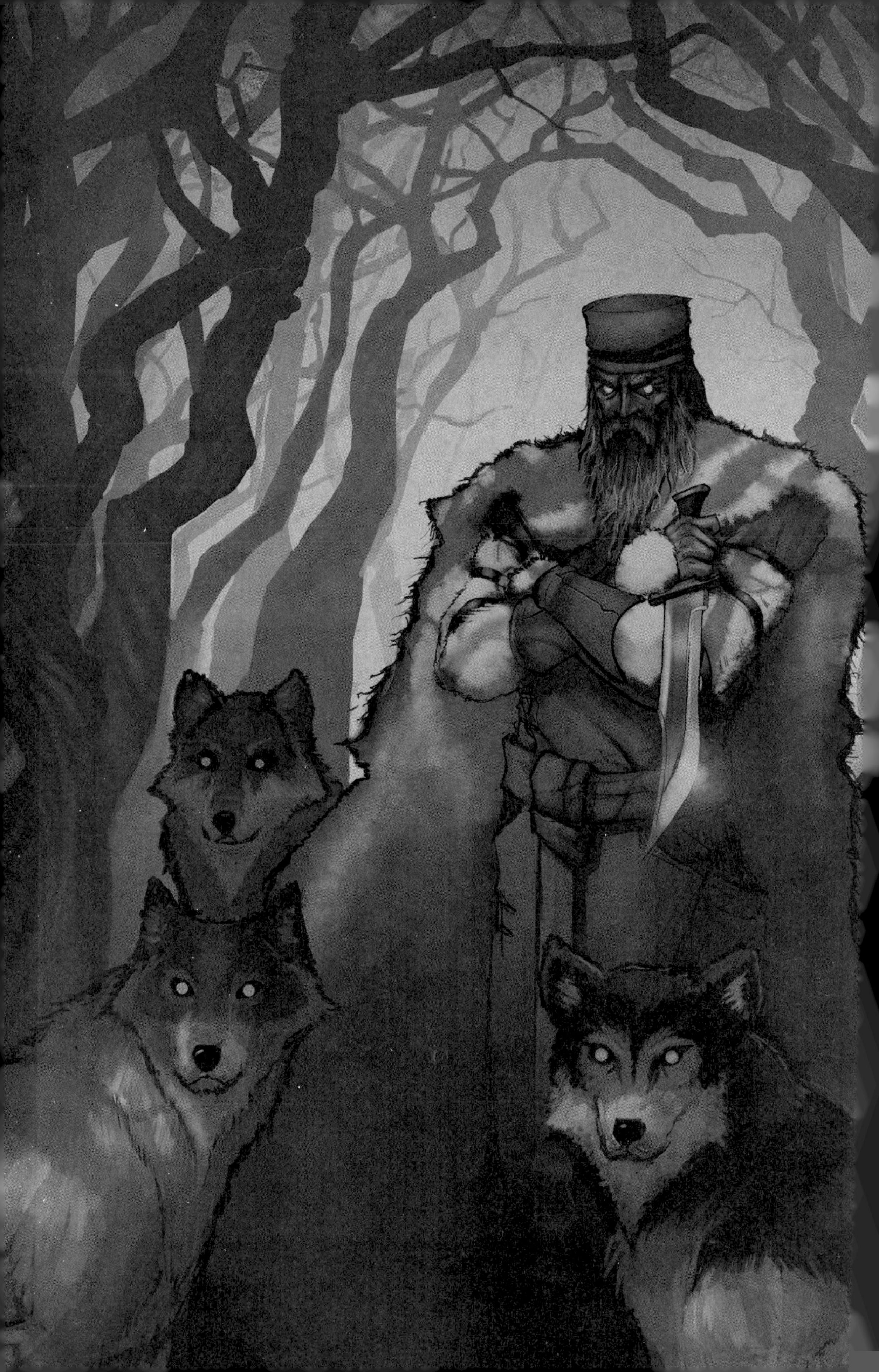

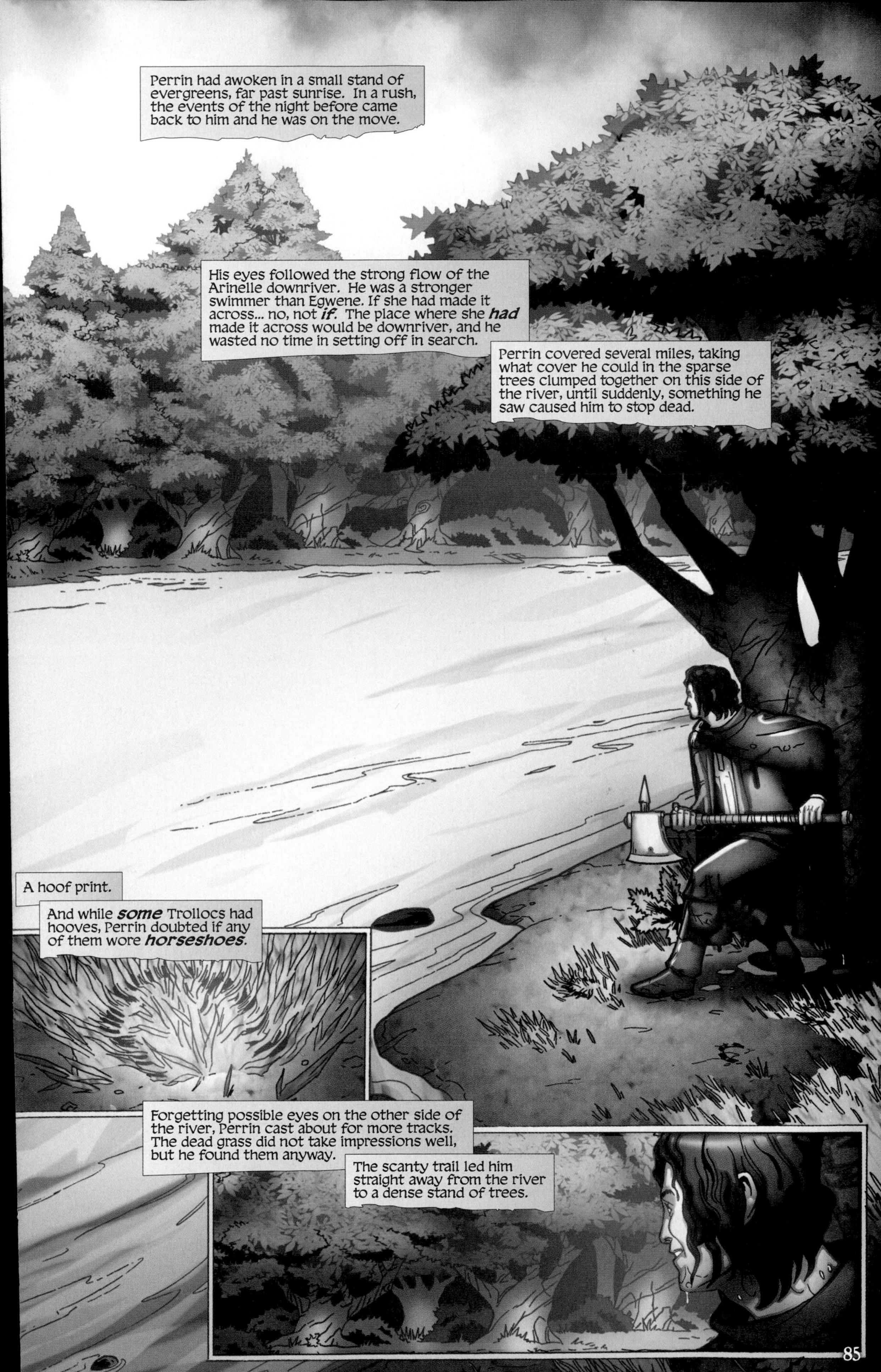
Perrin had awoken in a small stand of evergreens, far past sunrise. In a rush, the events of the night before came back to him and he was on the move.
His eyes followed the strong flow of the Arinelle downriver. He was a stronger swimmer than Egwene. If she had made it across... no, not *if*. The place where she *had* made it across would be downriver, and he wasted no time in setting off in search.
Perrin covered several miles, taking what cover he could in the sparse trees clumped together on this side of the river, until suddenly, something he saw caused him to stop dead.
A hoof print.
And while *some* Trollocs had hooves, Perrin doubted if any of them wore *horseshoes*.
Forgetting possible eyes on the other side of the river, Perrin cast about for more tracks. The dead grass did not take impressions well, but he found them anyway.
The scanty trail led him straight away from the river to a dense stand of trees.

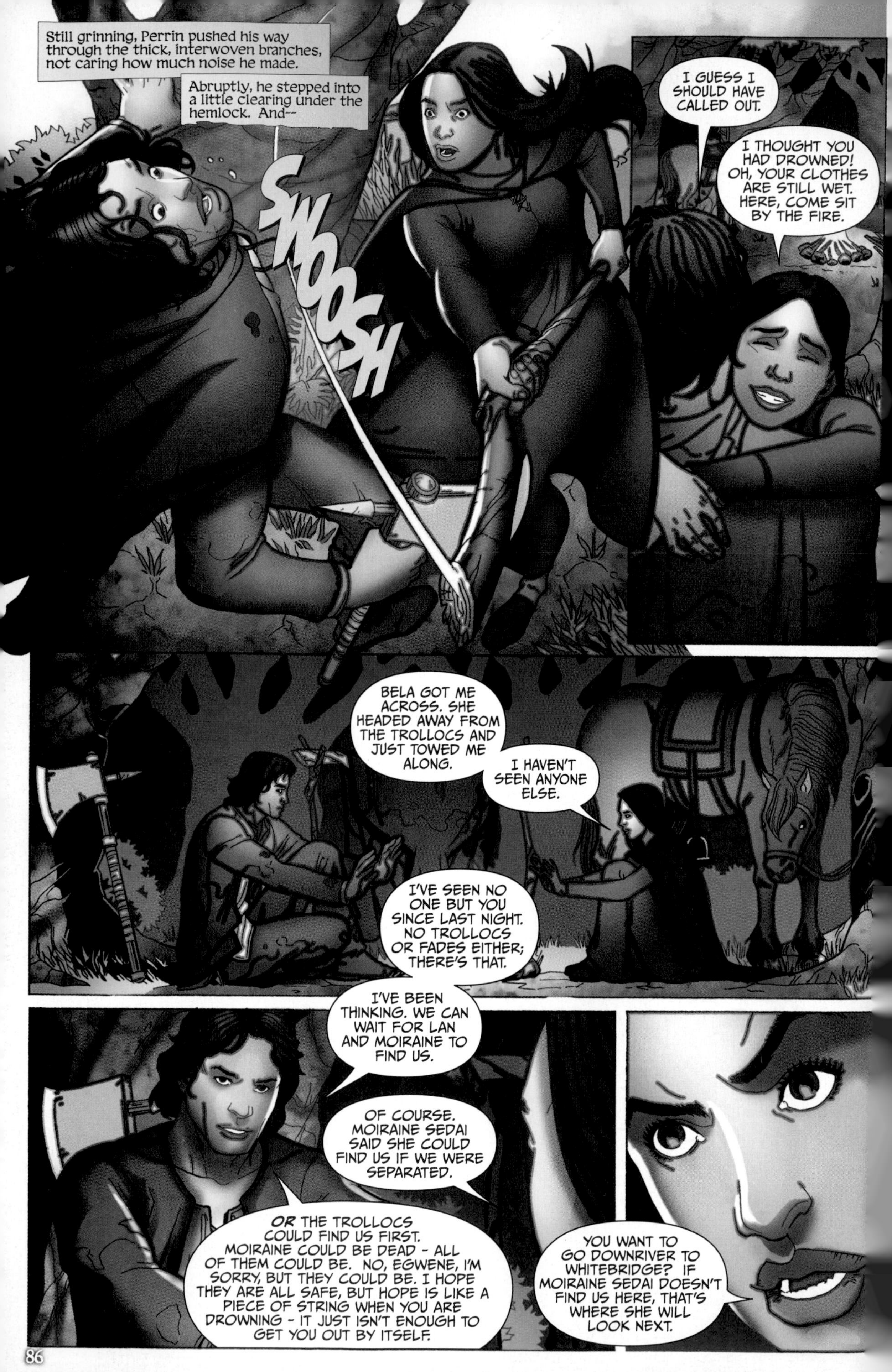
Still grinning, Perrin pushed his way through the thick, interwoven branches, not caring how much noise he made.
Abruptly, he stepped into a little clearing under the hemlock. And--
SWOOSH
I GUESS I SHOULD HAVE CALLED OUT.
I THOUGHT YOU HAD DROWNED! OH, YOUR CLOTHES ARE STILL WET. HERE, COME SIT BY THE FIRE.
BELA GOT ME ACROSS. SHE HEADED AWAY FROM THE TROLLOCS AND JUST TOWED ME ALONG.
I HAVEN'T SEEN ANYONE ELSE.
I'VE SEEN NO ONE BUT YOU SINCE LAST NIGHT. NO TROLLOCS OR FADES EITHER; THERE'S THAT.
I'VE BEEN THINKING. WE CAN WAIT FOR LAN AND MOIRAINE TO FIND US.
OF COURSE. MOIRAINE SEDAI SAID SHE COULD FIND US IF WE WERE SEPARATED.
OR THE TROLLOCS COULD FIND US FIRST. MOIRAINE COULD BE DEAD - ALL OF THEM COULD BE. NO, EGWENE, I'M SORRY, BUT THEY COULD BE. I HOPE THEY ARE ALL SAFE, BUT HOPE IS LIKE A PIECE OF STRING WHEN YOU ARE DROWNING - IT JUST ISN'T ENOUGH TO GET YOU OUT BY ITSELF.
YOU WANT TO GO DOWNRIVER TO WHITEBRIDGE? IF MOIRAINE SEDAI DOESN'T FIND US HERE, THAT'S WHERE SHE WILL LOOK NEXT.

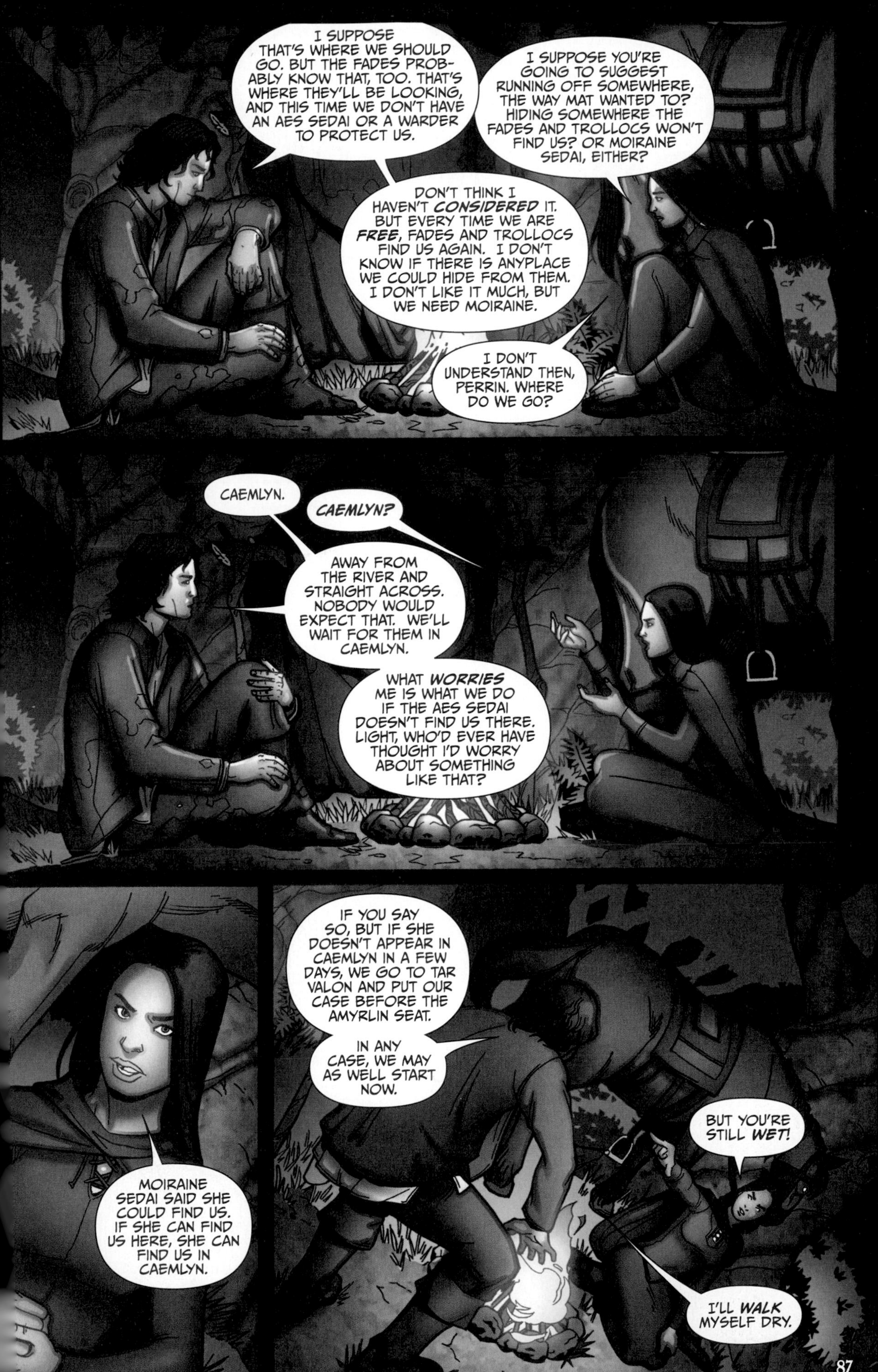
I SUPPOSE THAT'S WHERE WE SHOULD GO. BUT THE FADES PROB-ABLY KNOW THAT, TOO. THAT'S WHERE THEY'LL BE LOOKING, AND THIS TIME WE DON'T HAVE AN AES SEDAI OR A WARDER TO PROTECT US.
I SUPPOSE YOU'RE GOING TO SUGGEST RUNNING OFF SOMEWHERE, THE WAY MAT WANTED TO? HIDING SOMEWHERE THE FADES AND TROLLOCS WON'T FIND US? OR MOIRAINE SEDAI, EITHER?
DON'T THINK I HAVEN'T CONSIDERED IT. BUT EVERY TIME WE ARE FREE, FADES AND TROLLOCS FIND US AGAIN. I DON'T KNOW IF THERE IS ANYPLACE WE COULD HIDE FROM THEM. I DON'T LIKE IT MUCH, BUT WE NEED MOIRAINE.
I DON'T UNDERSTAND THEN, PERRIN. WHERE DO WE GO?
CAEMLYN.
CAEMLYN?
AWAY FROM THE RIVER AND STRAIGHT ACROSS. NOBODY WOULD EXPECT THAT. WE'LL WAIT FOR THEM IN CAEMLYN.
WHAT WORRIES ME IS WHAT WE DO IF THE AES SEDAI DOESN'T FIND US THERE. LIGHT, WHO'D EVER HAVE THOUGHT I'D WORRY ABOUT SOMETHING LIKE THAT?
MOIRAINE SEDAI SAID SHE COULD FIND US. IF SHE CAN FIND US HERE, SHE CAN FIND US IN CAEMLYN.
IF YOU SAY SO, BUT IF SHE DOESN'T APPEAR IN CAEMLYN IN A FEW DAYS, WE GO TO TAR VALON AND PUT OUR CASE BEFORE THE AMYRLIN SEAT.
IN ANY CASE, WE MAY AS WELL START NOW.
BUT YOU'RE STILL WET!
I'LL WALK MYSELF DRY.

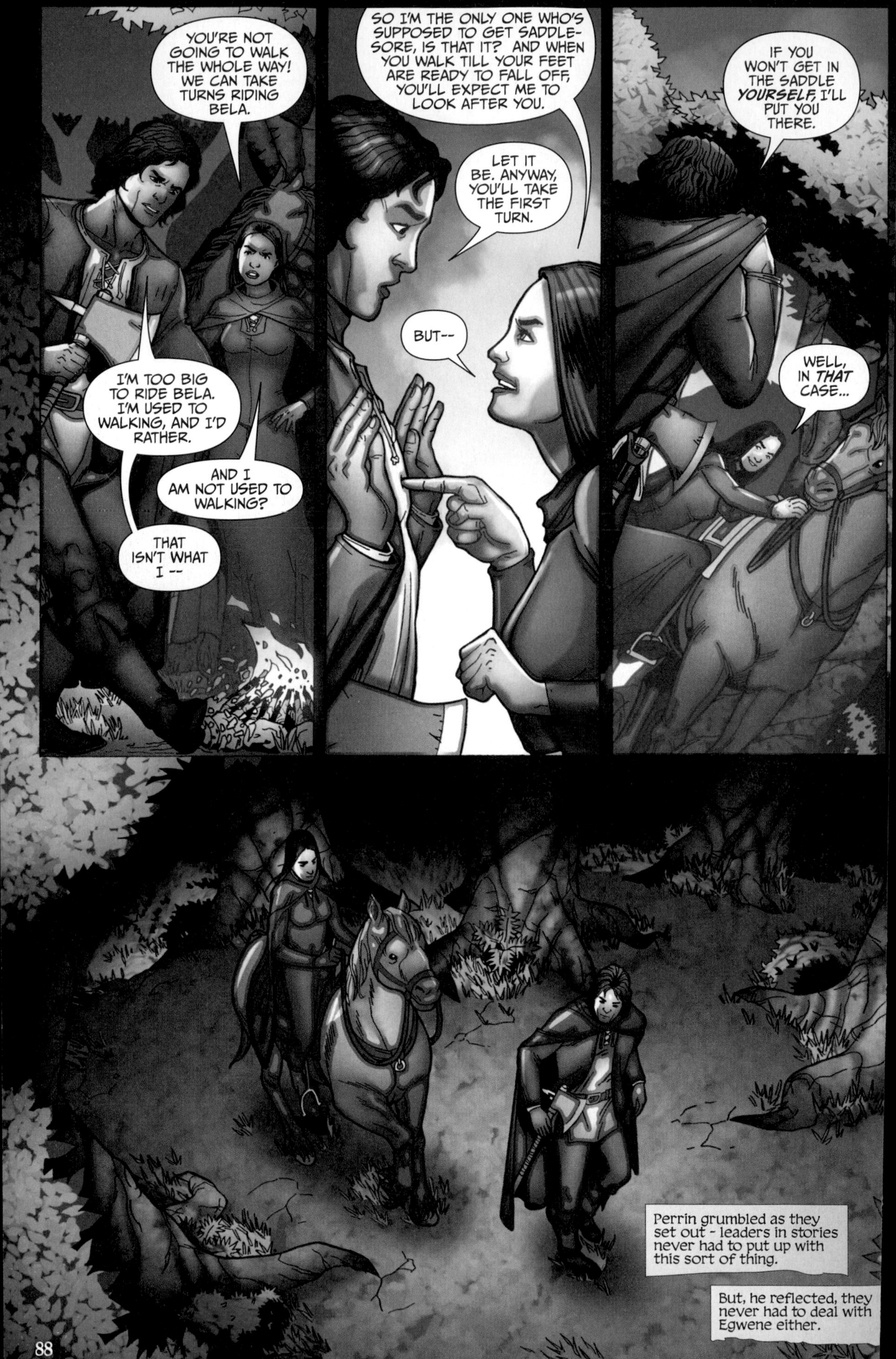
YOU'RE NOT GOING TO WALK THE WHOLE WAY! WE CAN TAKE TURNS RIDING BELA.
I'M TOO BIG TO RIDE BELA. I'M USED TO WALKING, AND I'D RATHER.
AND I AM NOT USED TO WALKING?
THAT ISN'T WHAT I --
SO I'M THE ONLY ONE WHO'S SUPPOSED TO GET SADDLE-SORE, IS THAT IT? AND WHEN YOU WALK TILL YOUR FEET ARE READY TO FALL OFF, YOU'LL EXPECT ME TO LOOK AFTER YOU.
LET IT BE. ANYWAY, YOU'LL TAKE THE FIRST TURN.
BUT--
IF YOU WON'T GET IN THE SADDLE YOURSELF, I'LL PUT YOU THERE.
WELL, IN THAT CASE...
Perrin grumbled as they set out - leaders in stories never had to put up with this sort of thing.
But, he reflected, they never had to deal with Egwene either.

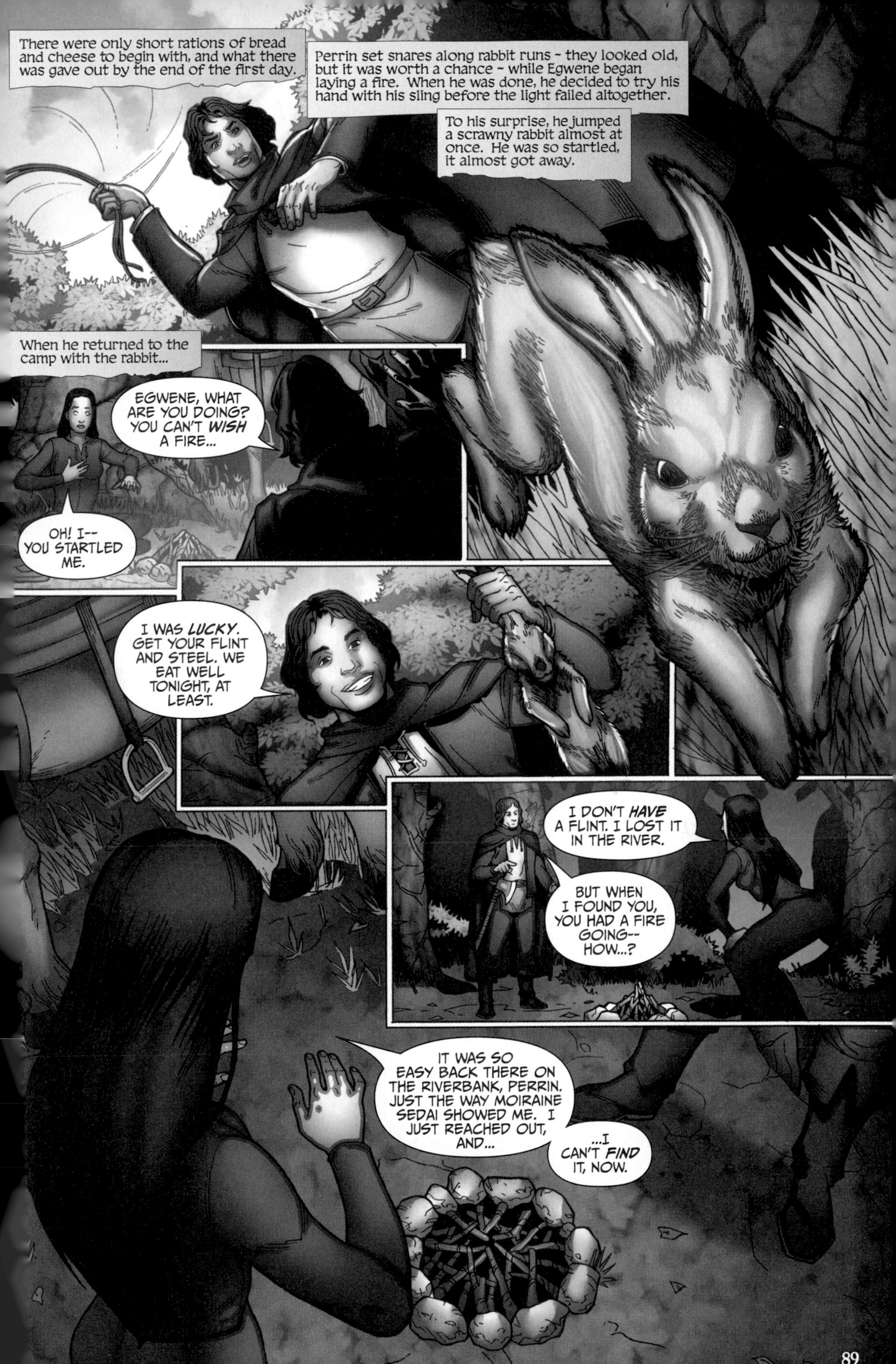
There were only short rations of bread and cheese to begin with, and what there was gave out by the end of the first day.
Perrin set snares along rabbit runs ~ they looked old, but it was worth a chance ~ while Egwene began laying a fire. When he was done, he decided to try his hand with his sling before the light failed altogether.
To his surprise, he jumped a scrawny rabbit almost at once. He was so startled, it almost got away.
When he returned to the camp with the rabbit...
EGWENE, WHAT ARE YOU DOING? YOU CAN'T *WISH* A FIRE...
OH! I-- YOU STARTLED ME.
I WAS *LUCKY*. GET YOUR FLINT AND STEEL. WE EAT WELL TONIGHT, AT LEAST.
I DON'T *HAVE* A FLINT. I LOST IT IN THE RIVER.
BUT WHEN I FOUND YOU, YOU HAD A FIRE GOING-- HOW...?
IT WAS SO EASY BACK THERE ON THE RIVERBANK, PERRIN. JUST THE WAY MOIRAINE SEDAI SHOWED ME. I JUST REACHED OUT, AND...
...I CAN'T *FIND* IT, NOW.

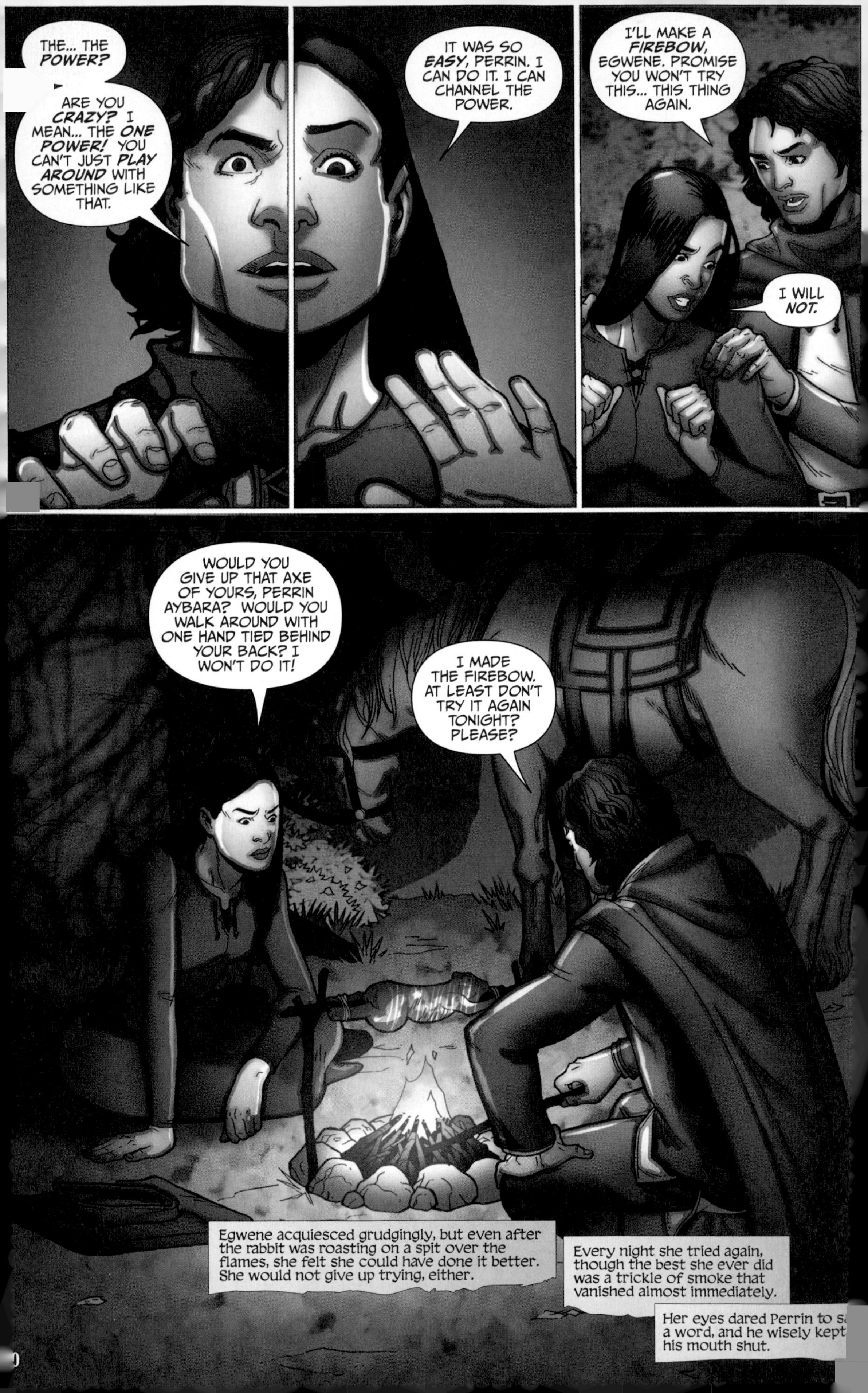
THE... THE POWER?
ARE YOU CRAZY? I MEAN... THE ONE POWER! YOU CAN'T JUST PLAY AROUND WITH SOMETHING LIKE THAT.
IT WAS SO EASY, PERRIN. I CAN DO IT. I CAN CHANNEL THE POWER.
I'LL MAKE A FIREBOW, EGWENE. PROMISE YOU WON'T TRY THIS... THIS THING AGAIN.
I WILL NOT.
WOULD YOU GIVE UP THAT AXE OF YOURS, PERRIN AYBARA? WOULD YOU WALK AROUND WITH ONE HAND TIED BEHIND YOUR BACK? I WON'T DO IT!
I MADE THE FIREBOW. AT LEAST DON'T TRY IT AGAIN TONIGHT? PLEASE?
Egwene acquiesced grudgingly, but even after the rabbit was roasting on a spit over the flames, she felt she could have done it better. She would not give up trying, either.
Every night she tried again, though the best she ever did was a trickle of smoke that vanished almost immediately.
Her eyes dared Perrin to sa a word, and he wisely kept his mouth shut.

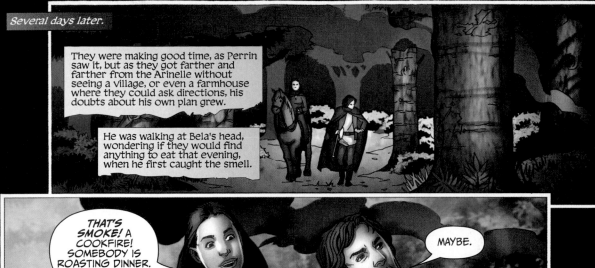

They were making good time, as Perrin saw it, but as they got farther and farther from the Arinelle without seeing a village, or even a farmhouse where they could ask directions, his doubts about his own plan grew.

He was walking at Bela's head, wondering if they would find anything to eat that evening, when he first caught the smell.

THAT'S SMOKE! A COOKFIRE! SOMEBODY IS ROASTING DINNER. MMM--RABBIT.

MAYBE.

WAIT HERE.

AND BE QUIET! WE DON'T KNOW WHO IT IS, YET.

Perrin had not spent as much time in the forests around Emond's Field as Rand or Mat, but still he had done his share of hunting rabbits.

He crept from tree to tree without so much as snapping a twig.

It was not long before he was peering around the bole of a tall oak at the source of the cookfire.

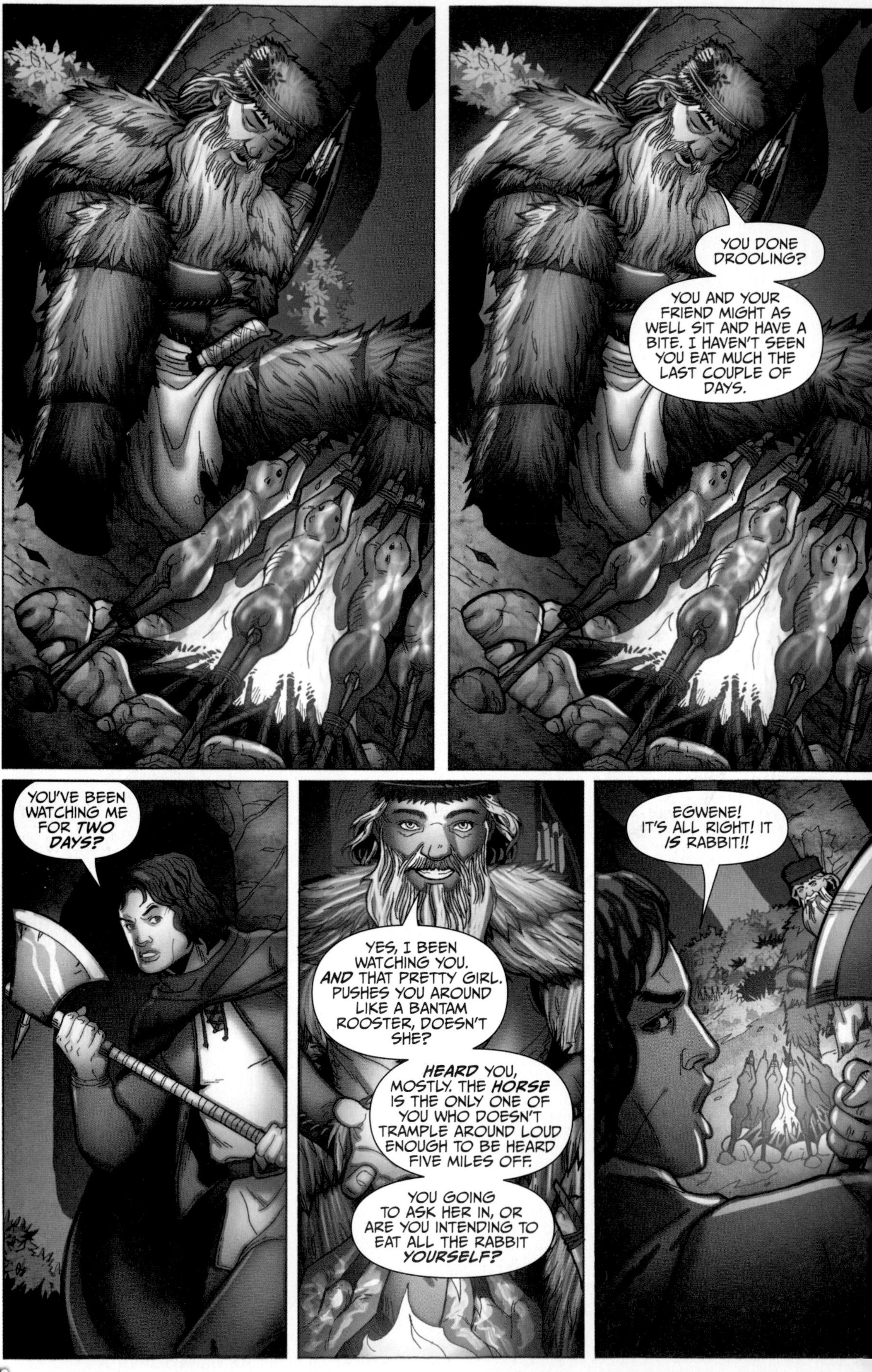
YOU DONE DROOLING?
YOU AND YOUR FRIEND MIGHT AS WELL SIT AND HAVE A BITE. I HAVEN'T SEEN YOU EAT MUCH THE LAST COUPLE OF DAYS.
YOU'VE BEEN WATCHING ME FOR *TWO DAYS?*
YES, I BEEN WATCHING YOU. ***AND*** THAT PRETTY GIRL. PUSHES YOU AROUND LIKE A BANTAM ROOSTER, DOESN'T SHE?
HEARD YOU, MOSTLY. THE ***HORSE*** IS THE ONLY ONE OF YOU WHO DOESN'T TRAMPLE AROUND LOUD ENOUGH TO BE HEARD FIVE MILES OFF.
YOU GOING TO ASK HER IN, OR ARE YOU INTENDING TO EAT ALL THE RABBIT ***YOURSELF?***
EGWENE! IT'S ALL RIGHT! IT ***IS*** RABBIT!!

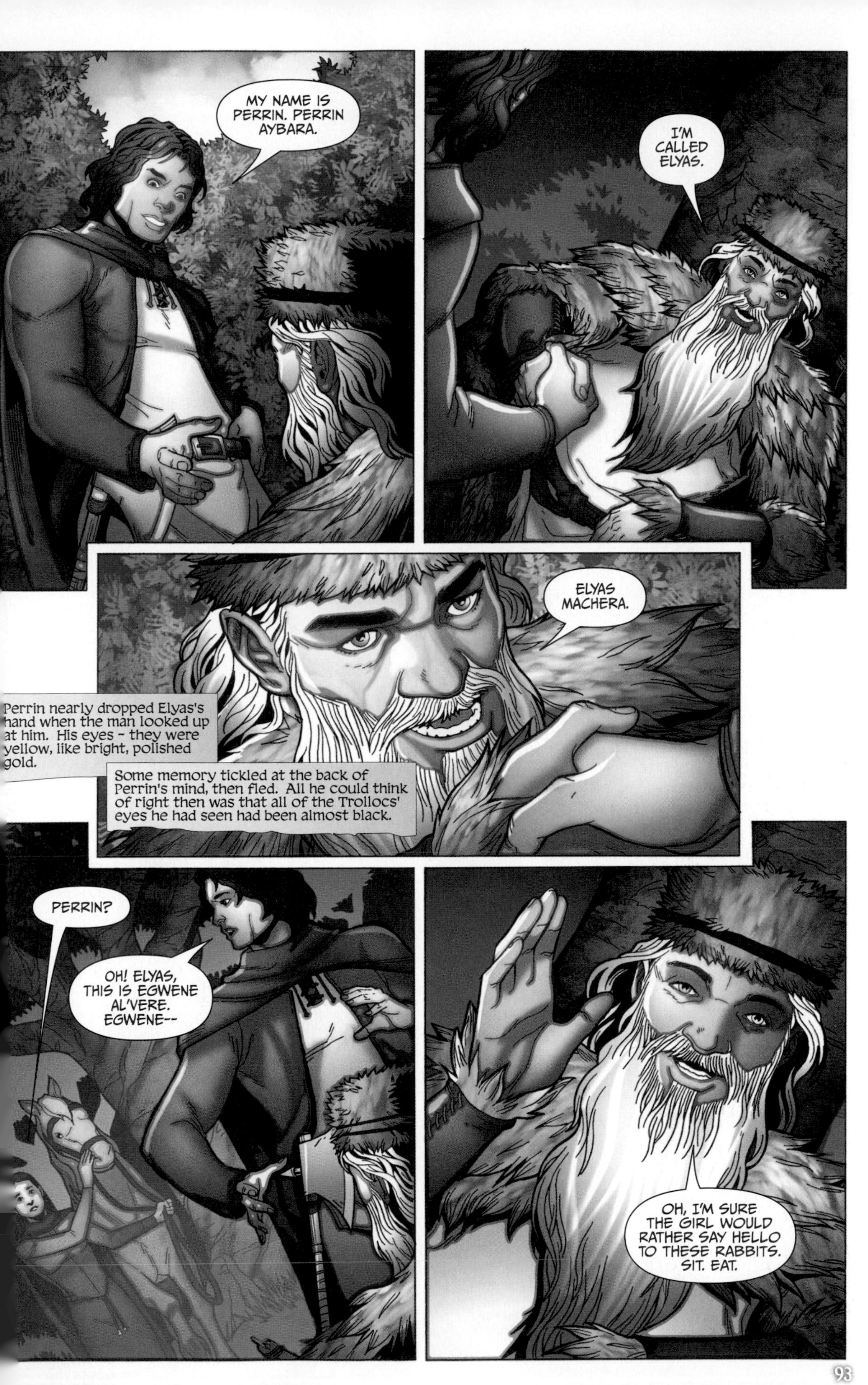
MY NAME IS PERRIN. PERRIN AYBARA.
I'M CALLED ELYAS.
ELYAS MACHERA.
Perrin nearly dropped Elyas's hand when the man looked up at him. His eyes - they were yellow, like bright, polished gold.
Some memory tickled at the back of Perrin's mind, then fled. All he could think of right then was that all of the Trollocs' eyes he had seen had been almost black.
PERRIN?
OH! ELYAS, THIS IS EGWENE AL'VERE. EGWENE--
OH, I'M SURE THE GIRL WOULD RATHER SAY HELLO TO THESE RABBITS. SIT. EAT.

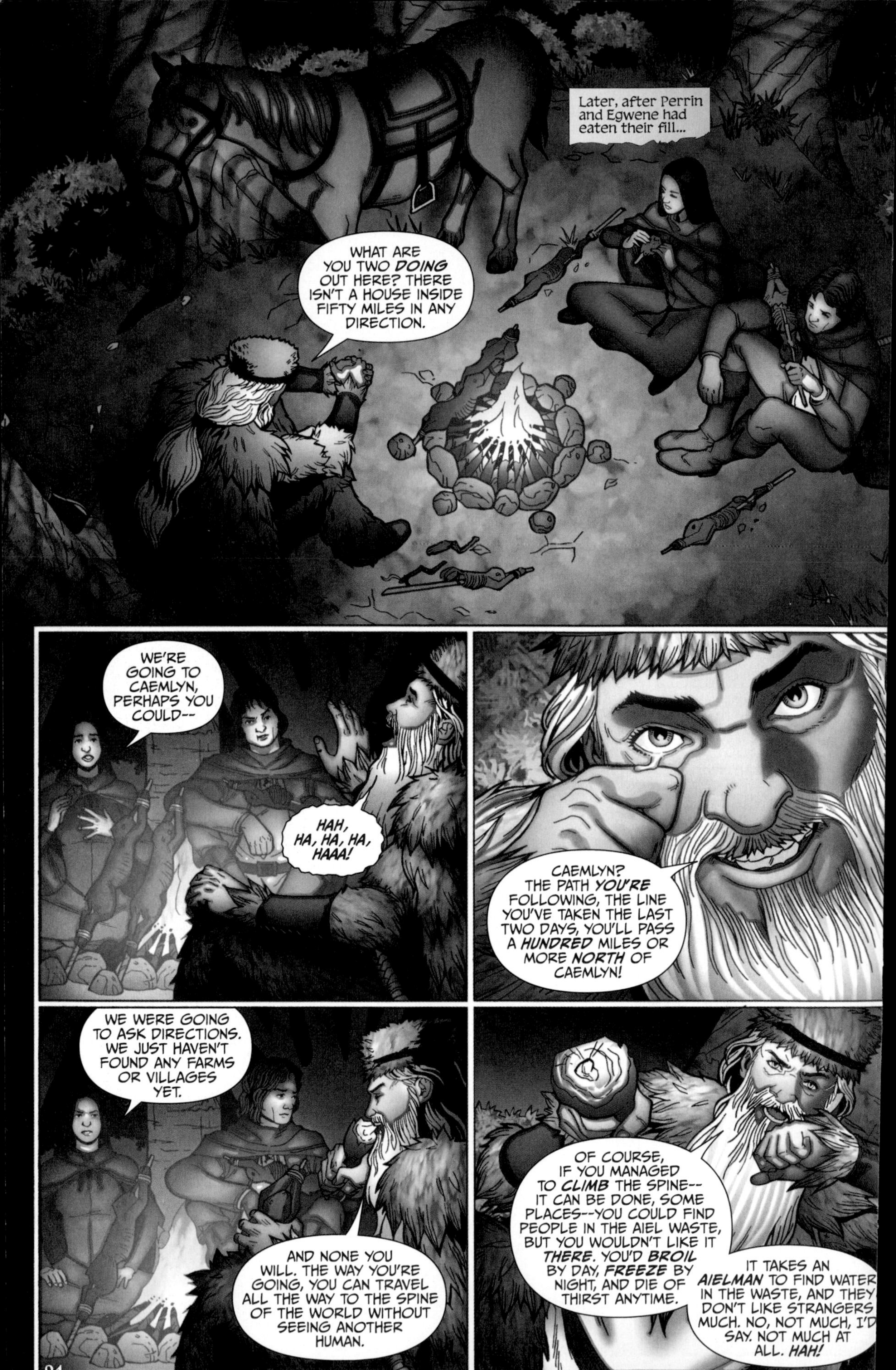
Later, after Perrin and Egwene had eaten their fill...
WHAT ARE YOU TWO *DOING* OUT HERE? THERE ISN'T A HOUSE INSIDE FIFTY MILES IN ANY DIRECTION.
WE'RE GOING TO CAEMLYN, PERHAPS YOU COULD--
HAH, HA, HA, HA, HAAA!
CAEMLYN? THE PATH *YOU'RE* FOLLOWING, THE LINE YOU'VE TAKEN THE LAST TWO DAYS, YOU'LL PASS A *HUNDRED* MILES OR MORE *NORTH* OF CAEMLYN!
WE WERE GOING TO ASK DIRECTIONS. WE JUST HAVEN'T FOUND ANY FARMS OR VILLAGES YET.
AND NONE YOU WILL. THE WAY YOU'RE GOING, YOU CAN TRAVEL ALL THE WAY TO THE SPINE OF THE WORLD WITHOUT SEEING ANOTHER HUMAN.
OF COURSE, IF YOU MANAGED TO *CLIMB* THE SPINE-- IT CAN BE DONE, SOME PLACES--YOU COULD FIND PEOPLE IN THE AIEL WASTE, BUT YOU WOULDN'T LIKE IT *THERE*. YOU'D *BROIL* BY DAY, *FREEZE* BY NIGHT, AND DIE OF THIRST ANYTIME.
IT TAKES AN *AIELMAN* TO FIND WATER IN THE WASTE, AND THEY DON'T LIKE STRANGERS MUCH. NO, NOT MUCH, I'D SAY. NOT MUCH AT ALL. *HAH!*

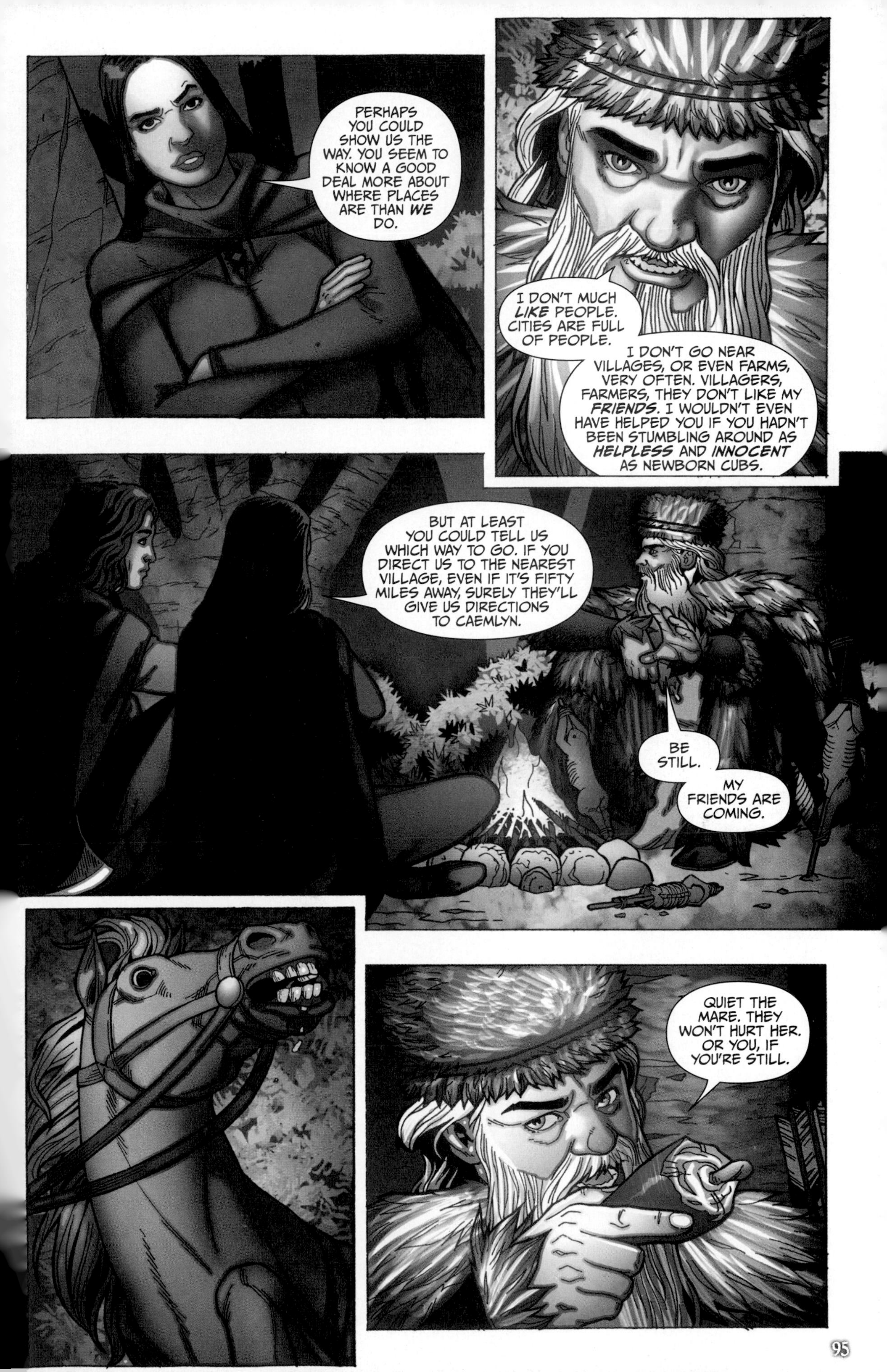
PERHAPS YOU COULD SHOW US THE WAY. YOU SEEM TO KNOW A GOOD DEAL MORE ABOUT WHERE PLACES ARE THAN *WE* DO.
I DON'T MUCH *LIKE* PEOPLE. CITIES ARE FULL OF PEOPLE.
I DON'T GO NEAR VILLAGES, OR EVEN FARMS, VERY OFTEN. VILLAGERS, FARMERS, THEY DON'T LIKE MY *FRIENDS*. I WOULDN'T EVEN HAVE HELPED YOU IF YOU HADN'T BEEN STUMBLING AROUND AS *HELPLESS* AND *INNOCENT* AS NEWBORN CUBS.
BUT AT LEAST YOU COULD TELL US WHICH WAY TO GO. IF YOU DIRECT US TO THE NEAREST VILLAGE, EVEN IF IT'S FIFTY MILES AWAY, SURELY THEY'LL GIVE US DIRECTIONS TO CAEMLYN.
BE STILL.
MY FRIENDS ARE COMING.
QUIET THE MARE. THEY WON'T HURT HER. OR YOU, IF YOU'RE STILL.

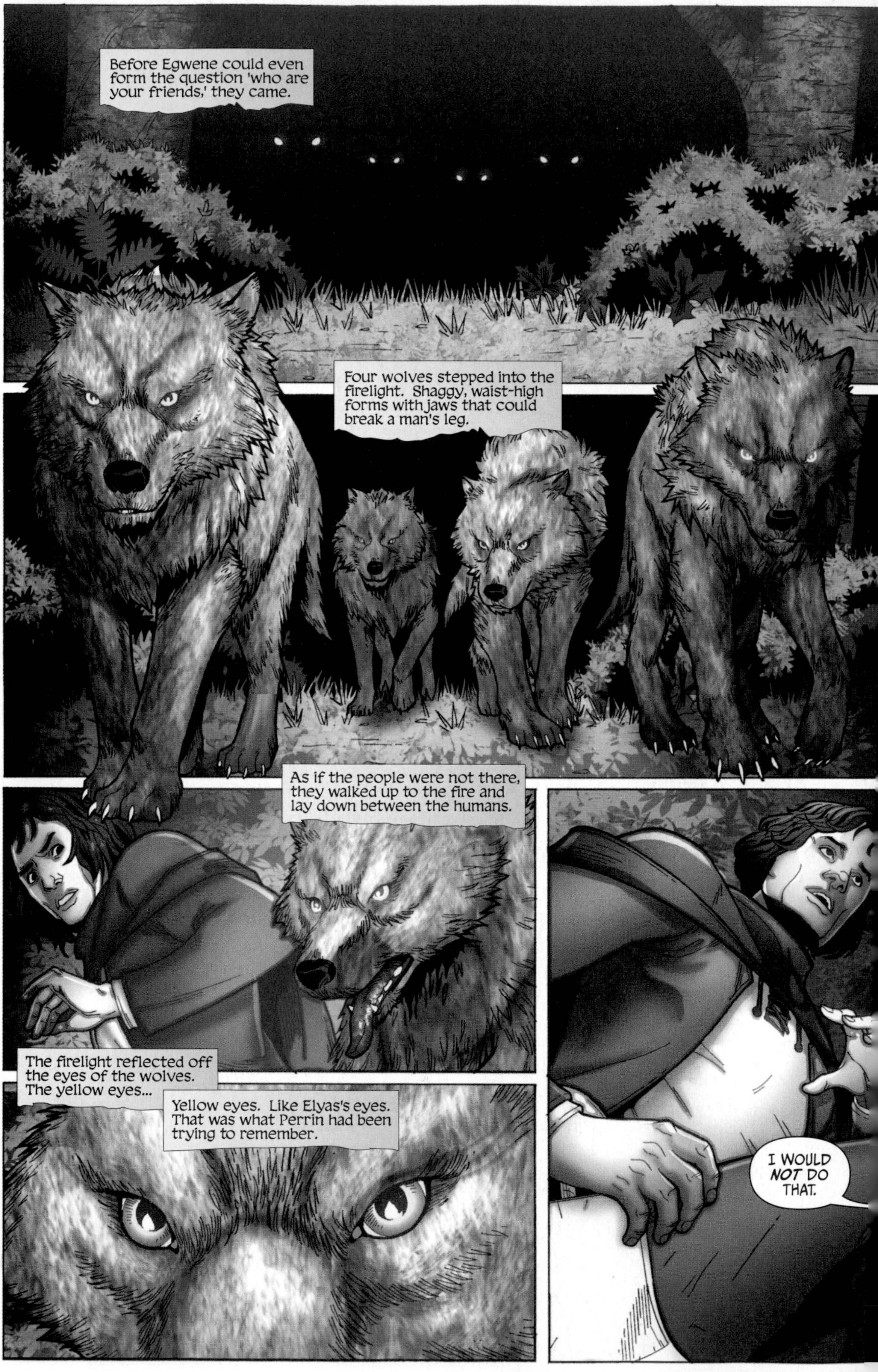
Before Egwene could even form the question 'who are your friends,' they came.
Four wolves stepped into the firelight. Shaggy, waist-high forms with jaws that could break a man's leg.
As if the people were not there, they walked up to the fire and lay down between the humans.
The firelight reflected off the eyes of the wolves. The yellow eyes...
Yellow eyes. Like Elyas's eyes. That was what Perrin had been trying to remember.
I WOULD *NOT* DO THAT.

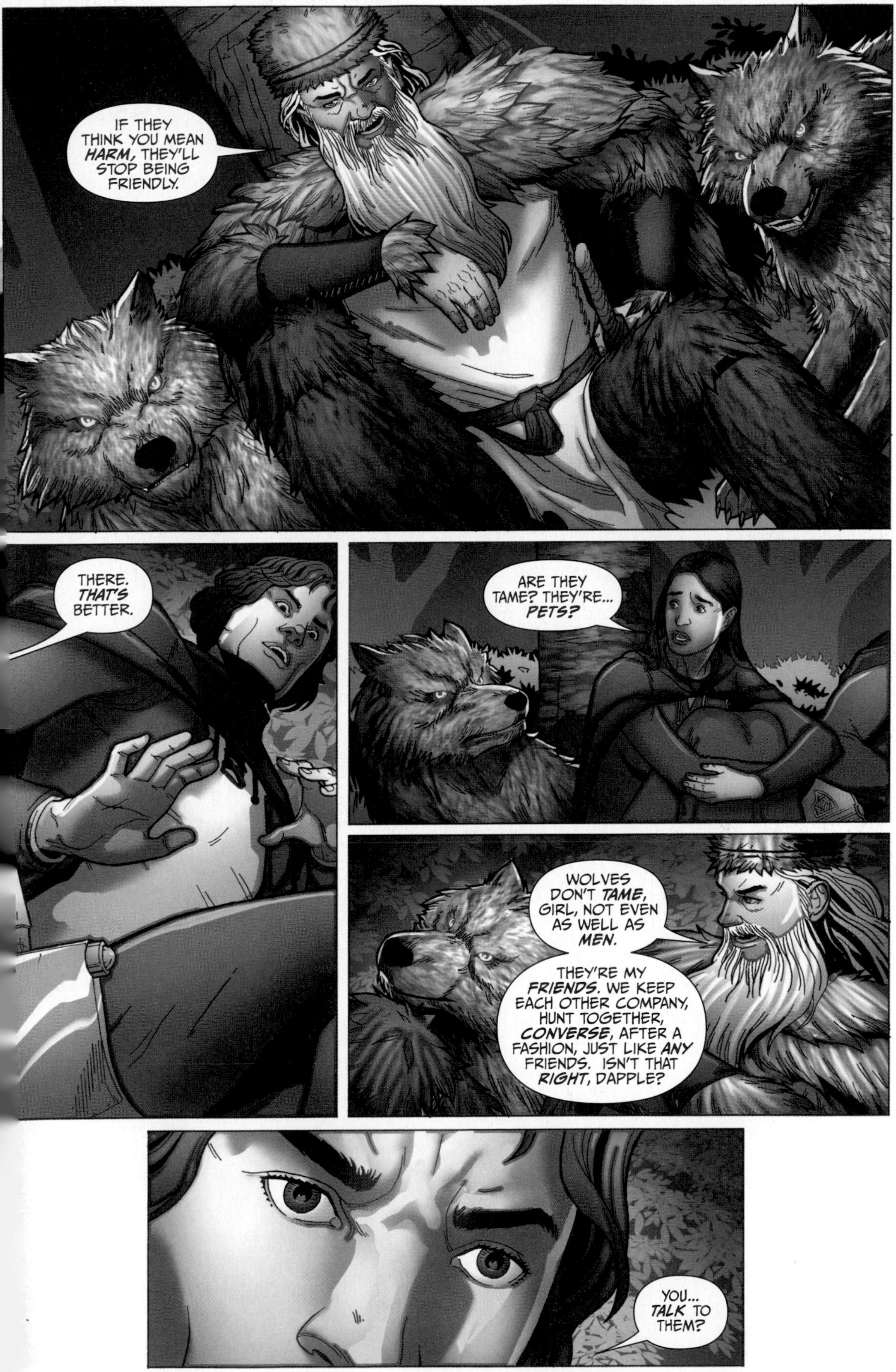
IF THEY THINK YOU MEAN HARM, THEY'LL STOP BEING FRIENDLY.
THERE. THAT'S BETTER.
ARE THEY TAME? THEY'RE... PETS?
WOLVES DON'T TAME, GIRL, NOT EVEN AS WELL AS MEN.
THEY'RE MY FRIENDS. WE KEEP EACH OTHER COMPANY, HUNT TOGETHER, CONVERSE, AFTER A FASHION, JUST LIKE ANY FRIENDS. ISN'T THAT RIGHT, DAPPLE?
YOU... TALK TO THEM?

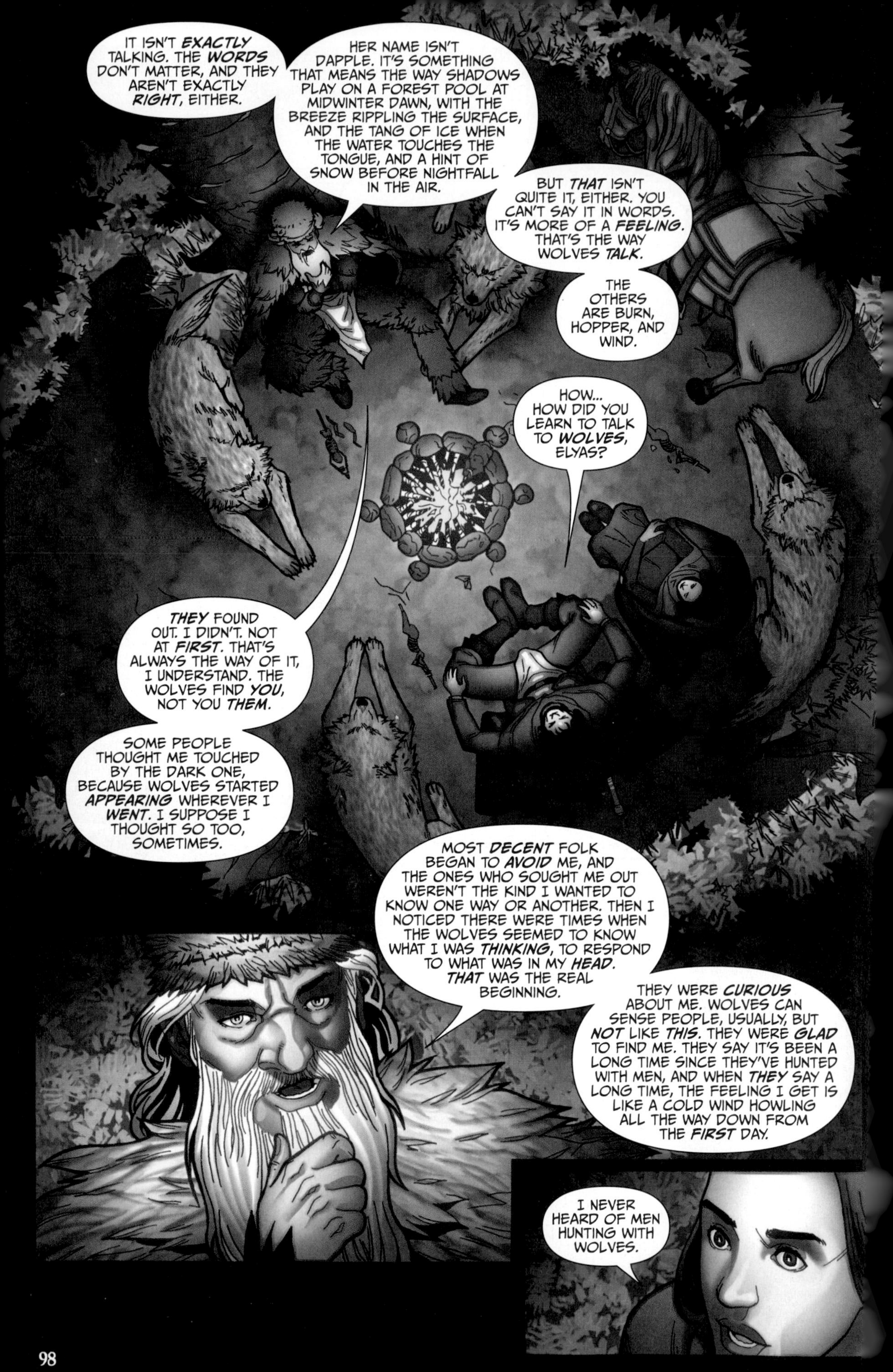
IT ISN'T EXACTLY TALKING. THE WORDS DON'T MATTER, AND THEY AREN'T EXACTLY RIGHT, EITHER.
HER NAME ISN'T DAPPLE. IT'S SOMETHING THAT MEANS THE WAY SHADOWS PLAY ON A FOREST POOL AT MIDWINTER DAWN, WITH THE BREEZE RIPPLING THE SURFACE, AND THE TANG OF ICE WHEN THE WATER TOUCHES THE TONGUE, AND A HINT OF SNOW BEFORE NIGHTFALL IN THE AIR.
BUT THAT ISN'T QUITE IT, EITHER. YOU CAN'T SAY IT IN WORDS. IT'S MORE OF A FEELING. THAT'S THE WAY WOLVES TALK.
THE OTHERS ARE BURN, HOPPER, AND WIND.
HOW... HOW DID YOU LEARN TO TALK TO WOLVES, ELYAS?
THEY FOUND OUT. I DIDN'T. NOT AT FIRST. THAT'S ALWAYS THE WAY OF IT, I UNDERSTAND. THE WOLVES FIND YOU, NOT YOU THEM.
SOME PEOPLE THOUGHT ME TOUCHED BY THE DARK ONE, BECAUSE WOLVES STARTED APPEARING WHEREVER I WENT. I SUPPOSE I THOUGHT SO TOO, SOMETIMES.
MOST DECENT FOLK BEGAN TO AVOID ME, AND THE ONES WHO SOUGHT ME OUT WEREN'T THE KIND I WANTED TO KNOW ONE WAY OR ANOTHER. THEN I NOTICED THERE WERE TIMES WHEN THE WOLVES SEEMED TO KNOW WHAT I WAS THINKING, TO RESPOND TO WHAT WAS IN MY HEAD. THAT WAS THE REAL BEGINNING.
THEY WERE CURIOUS ABOUT ME. WOLVES CAN SENSE PEOPLE, USUALLY, BUT NOT LIKE THIS. THEY WERE GLAD TO FIND ME. THEY SAY IT'S BEEN A LONG TIME SINCE THEY'VE HUNTED WITH MEN, AND WHEN THEY SAY A LONG TIME, THE FEELING I GET IS LIKE A COLD WIND HOWLING ALL THE WAY DOWN FROM THE FIRST DAY.
I NEVER HEARD OF MEN HUNTING WITH WOLVES.

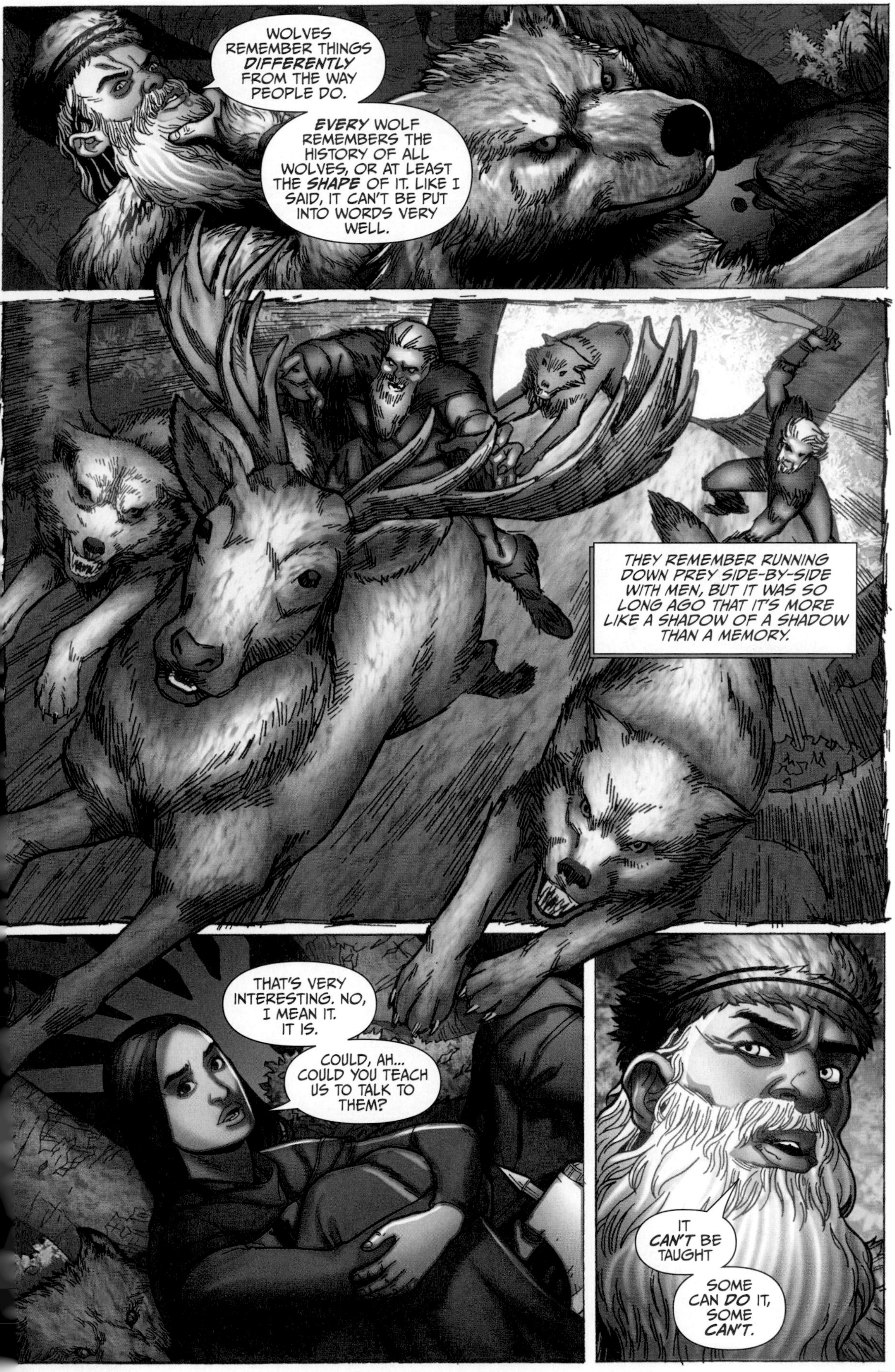
WOLVES REMEMBER THINGS DIFFERENTLY FROM THE WAY PEOPLE DO.
EVERY WOLF REMEMBERS THE HISTORY OF ALL WOLVES, OR AT LEAST THE SHAPE OF IT. LIKE I SAID, IT CAN'T BE PUT INTO WORDS VERY WELL.
THEY REMEMBER RUNNING DOWN PREY SIDE-BY-SIDE WITH MEN, BUT IT WAS SO LONG AGO THAT IT'S MORE LIKE A SHADOW OF A SHADOW THAN A MEMORY.
THAT'S VERY INTERESTING. NO, I MEAN IT. IT IS.
COULD, AH... COULD YOU TEACH US TO TALK TO THEM?
IT CAN'T BE TAUGHT
SOME CAN DO IT, SOME CAN'T.

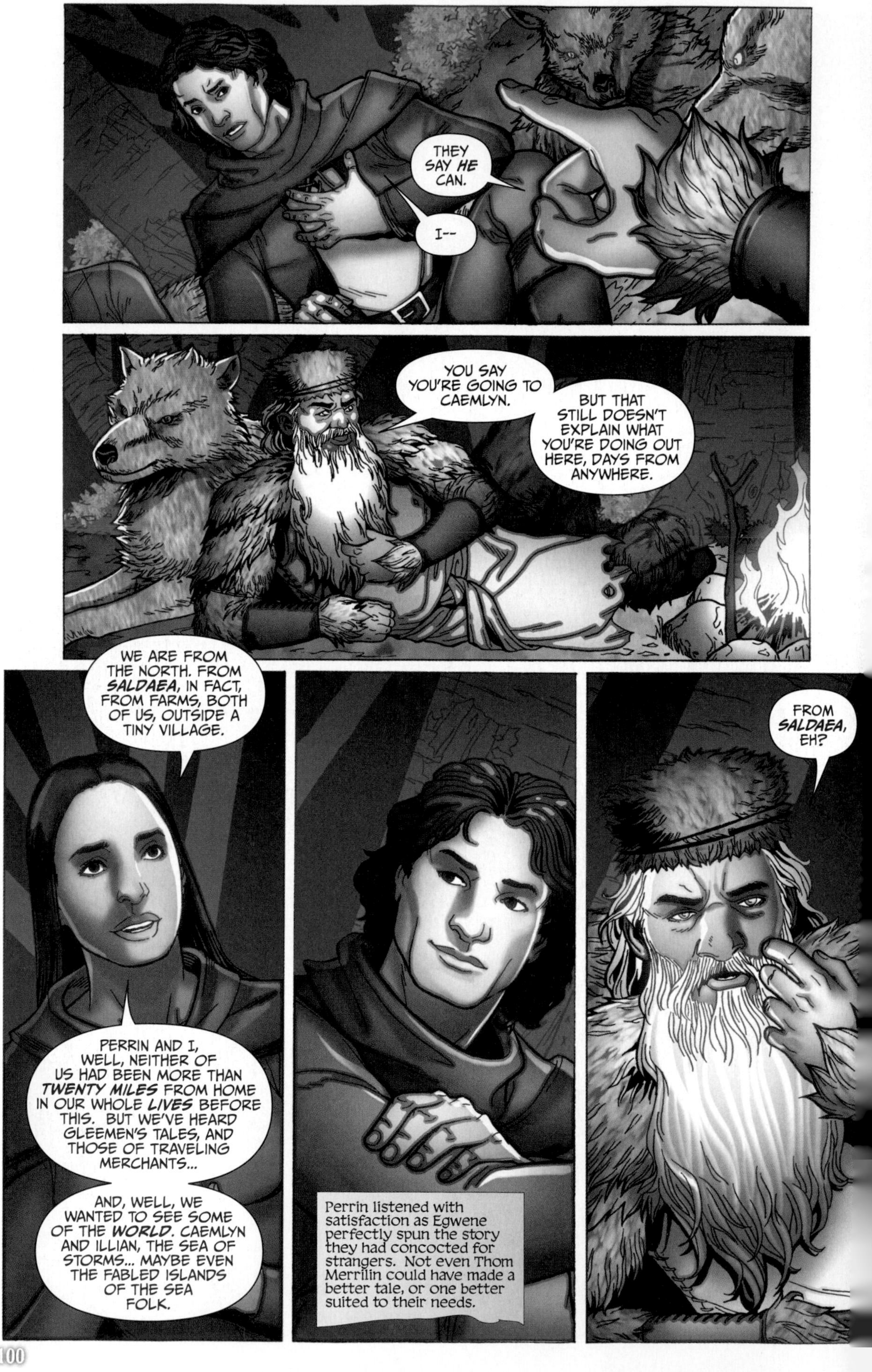

THEY SAY *HE* CAN.
I--
YOU SAY YOU'RE GOING TO CAEMLYN.
BUT THAT STILL DOESN'T EXPLAIN WHAT YOU'RE DOING OUT HERE, DAYS FROM ANYWHERE.
WE ARE FROM THE NORTH. FROM *SALDAEA*, IN FACT, FROM FARMS, BOTH OF US, OUTSIDE A TINY VILLAGE.
PERRIN AND I, WELL, NEITHER OF US HAD BEEN MORE THAN *TWENTY MILES* FROM HOME IN OUR WHOLE *LIVES* BEFORE THIS. BUT WE'VE HEARD GLEEMEN'S TALES, AND THOSE OF TRAVELING MERCHANTS...
AND, WELL, WE WANTED TO SEE SOME OF THE *WORLD*. CAEMLYN AND ILLIAN, THE SEA OF STORMS... MAYBE EVEN THE FABLED ISLANDS OF THE SEA FOLK.
Perrin listened with satisfaction as Egwene perfectly spun the story they had concocted for strangers. Not even Thom Merrilin could have made a better tale, or one better suited to their needs.
FROM *SALDAEA*, EH?

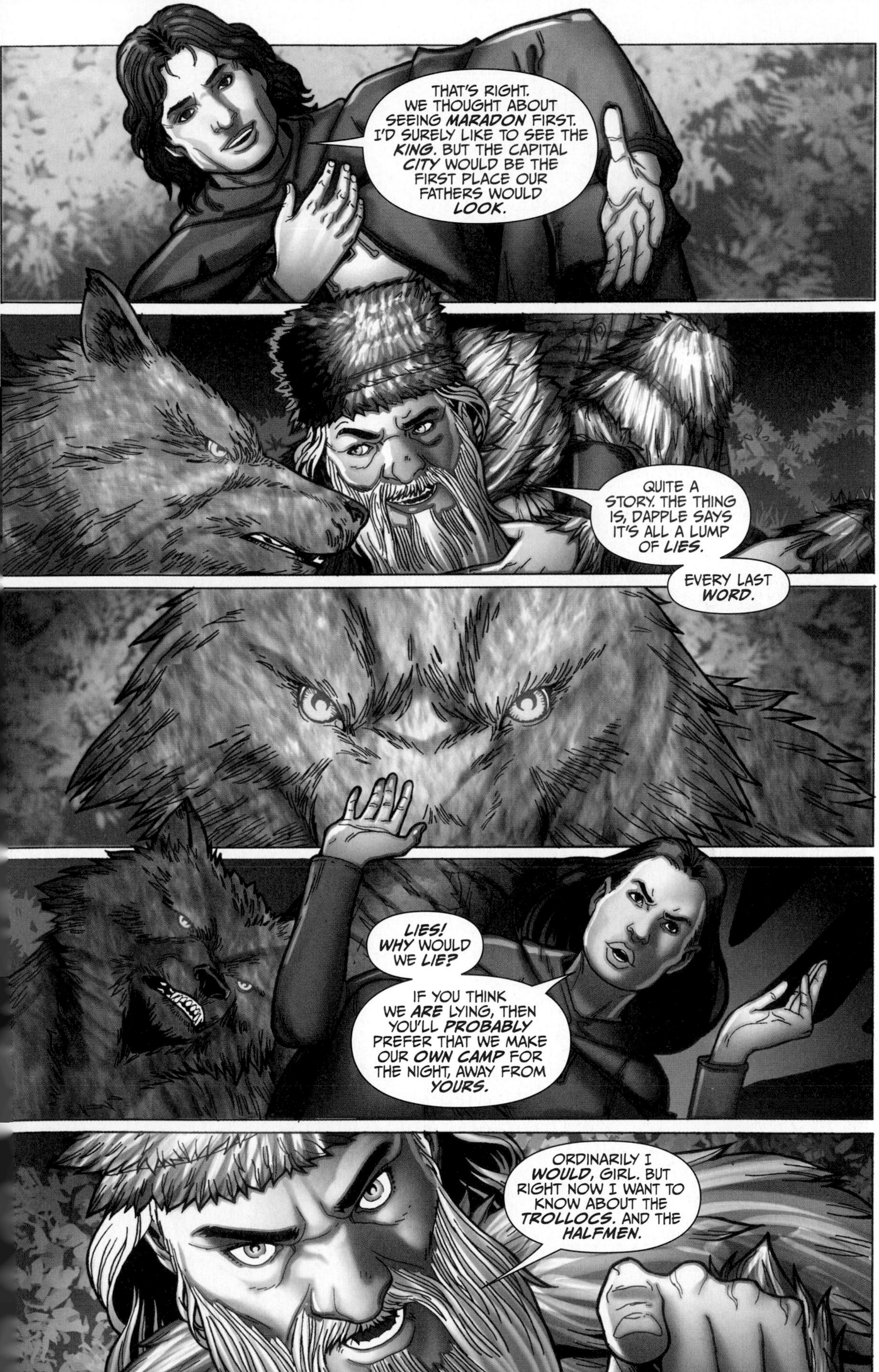
THAT'S RIGHT. WE THOUGHT ABOUT SEEING MARADON FIRST. I'D SURELY LIKE TO SEE THE KING. BUT THE CAPITAL CITY WOULD BE THE FIRST PLACE OUR FATHERS WOULD LOOK.
QUITE A STORY. THE THING IS, DAPPLE SAYS IT'S ALL A LUMP OF LIES.
EVERY LAST WORD.
LIES! WHY WOULD WE LIE?
IF YOU THINK WE ARE LYING, THEN YOU'LL PROBABLY PREFER THAT WE MAKE OUR OWN CAMP FOR THE NIGHT, AWAY FROM YOURS.
ORDINARILY I WOULD, GIRL. BUT RIGHT NOW I WANT TO KNOW ABOUT THE TROLLOCS. AND THE HALFMEN.

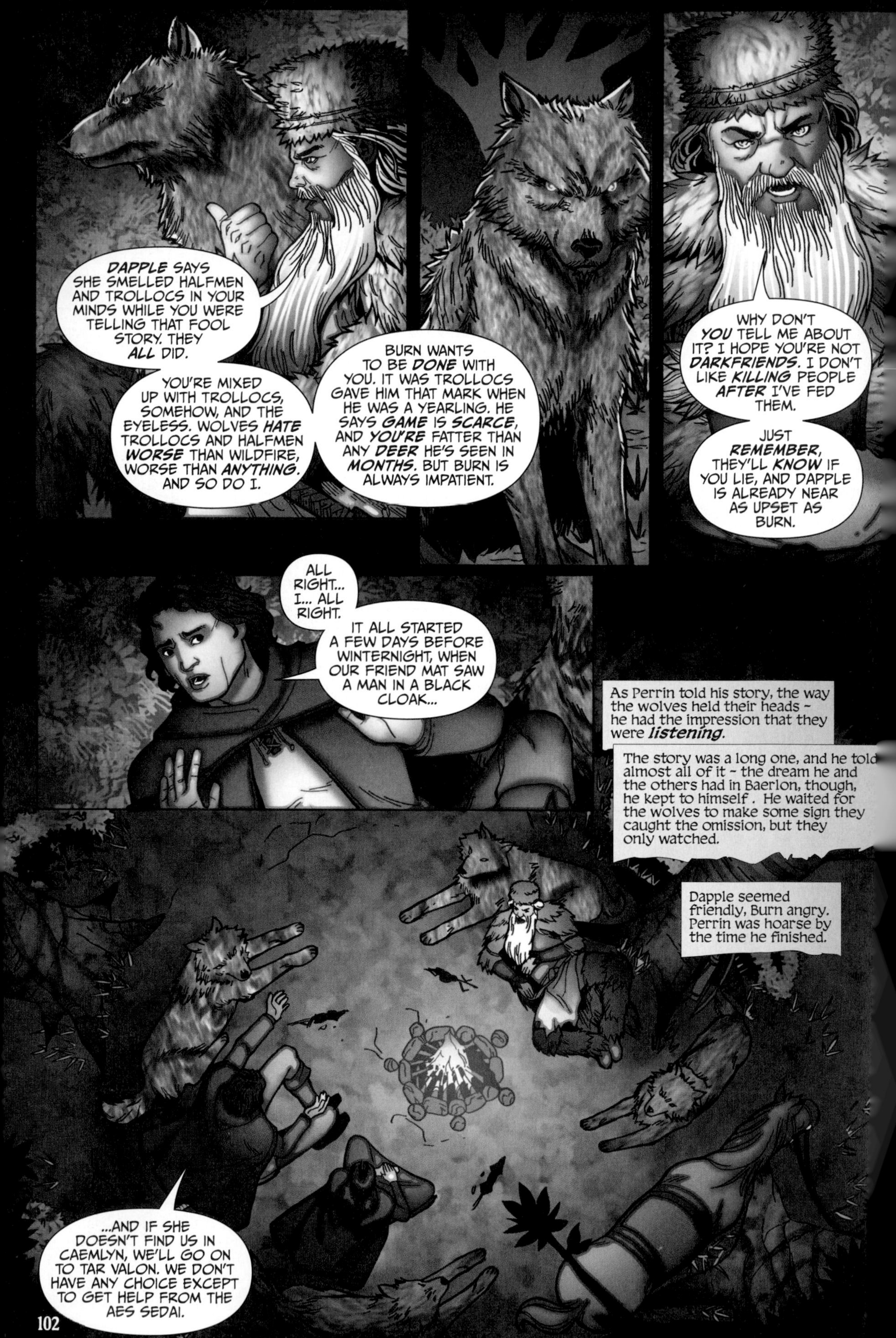
DAPPLE SAYS SHE SMELLED HALFMEN AND TROLLOCS IN YOUR MINDS WHILE YOU WERE TELLING THAT FOOL STORY. THEY ALL DID.
YOU'RE MIXED UP WITH TROLLOCS, SOMEHOW, AND THE EYELESS. WOLVES HATE TROLLOCS AND HALFMEN WORSE THAN WILDFIRE, WORSE THAN ANYTHING. AND SO DO I.
BURN WANTS TO BE DONE WITH YOU. IT WAS TROLLOCS GAVE HIM THAT MARK WHEN HE WAS A YEARLING. HE SAYS GAME IS SCARCE, AND YOU'RE FATTER THAN ANY DEER HE'S SEEN IN MONTHS. BUT BURN IS ALWAYS IMPATIENT.
WHY DON'T YOU TELL ME ABOUT IT? I HOPE YOU'RE NOT DARKFRIENDS. I DON'T LIKE KILLING PEOPLE AFTER I'VE FED THEM.
JUST REMEMBER, THEY'LL KNOW IF YOU LIE, AND DAPPLE IS ALREADY NEAR AS UPSET AS BURN.
ALL RIGHT... I... ALL RIGHT.
IT ALL STARTED A FEW DAYS BEFORE WINTERNIGHT, WHEN OUR FRIEND MAT SAW A MAN IN A BLACK CLOAK...
As Perrin told his story, the way the wolves held their heads ~ he had the impression that they were listening.
The story was a long one, and he told almost all of it ~ the dream he and the others had in Baerlon, though, he kept to himself . He waited for the wolves to make some sign they caught the omission, but they only watched.
Dapple seemed friendly, Burn angry. Perrin was hoarse by the time he finished.
...AND IF SHE DOESN'T FIND US IN CAEMLYN, WE'LL GO ON TO TAR VALON. WE DON'T HAVE ANY CHOICE EXCEPT TO GET HELP FROM THE AES SEDAI.

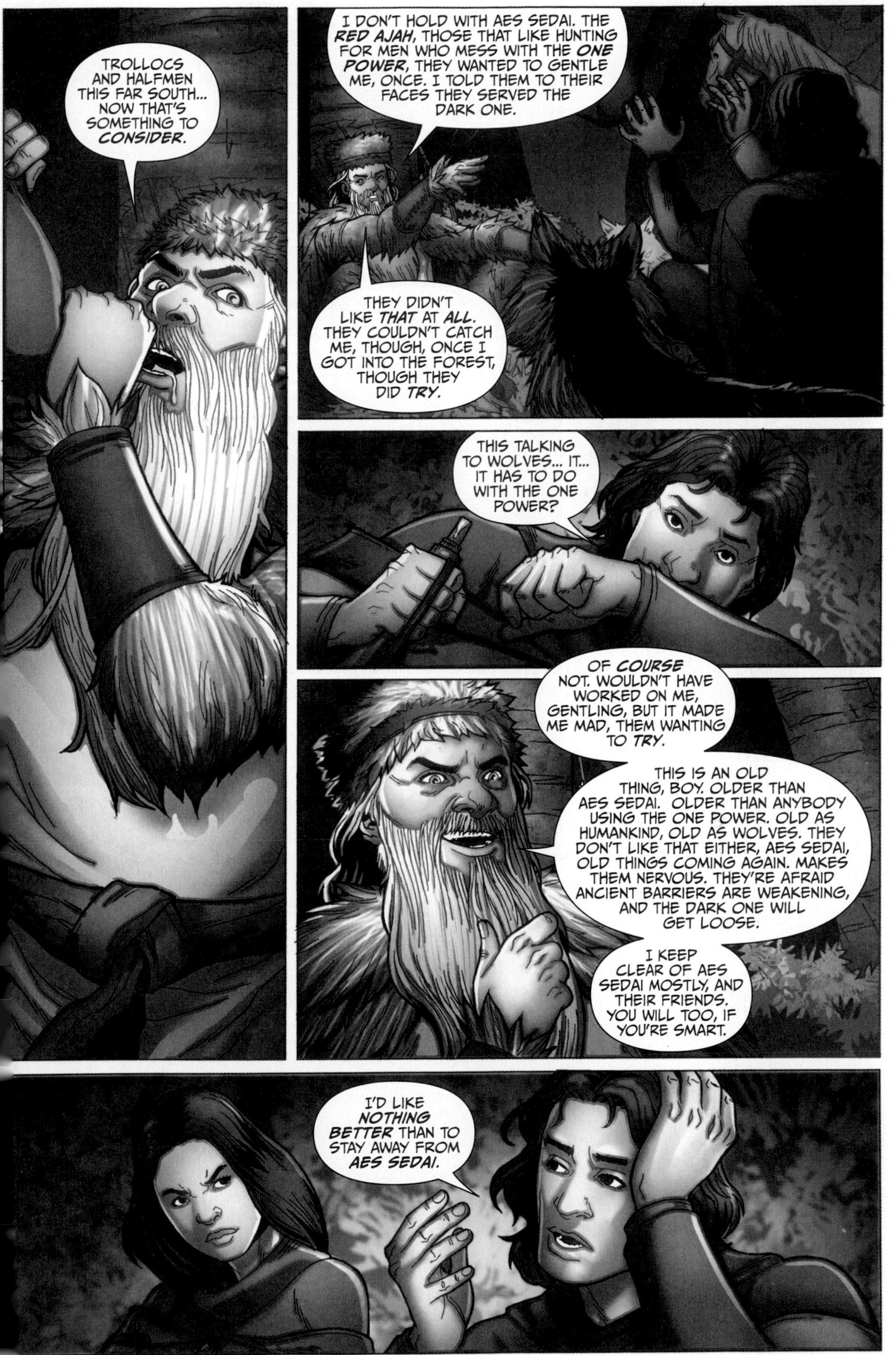
TROLLOCS AND HALFMEN THIS FAR SOUTH... NOW THAT'S SOMETHING TO CONSIDER.
I DON'T HOLD WITH AES SEDAI. THE RED AJAH, THOSE THAT LIKE HUNTING FOR MEN WHO MESS WITH THE ONE POWER, THEY WANTED TO GENTLE ME, ONCE. I TOLD THEM TO THEIR FACES THEY SERVED THE DARK ONE.
THEY DIDN'T LIKE THAT AT ALL. THEY COULDN'T CATCH ME, THOUGH, ONCE I GOT INTO THE FOREST, THOUGH THEY DID TRY.
THIS TALKING TO WOLVES... IT... IT HAS TO DO WITH THE ONE POWER?
OF COURSE NOT. WOULDN'T HAVE WORKED ON ME, GENTLING, BUT IT MADE ME MAD, THEM WANTING TO TRY.
THIS IS AN OLD THING, BOY. OLDER THAN AES SEDAI. OLDER THAN ANYBODY USING THE ONE POWER. OLD AS HUMANKIND, OLD AS WOLVES. THEY DON'T LIKE THAT EITHER, AES SEDAI, OLD THINGS COMING AGAIN. MAKES THEM NERVOUS. THEY'RE AFRAID ANCIENT BARRIERS ARE WEAKENING, AND THE DARK ONE WILL GET LOOSE.
I KEEP CLEAR OF AES SEDAI MOSTLY, AND THEIR FRIENDS. YOU WILL TOO, IF YOU'RE SMART.
I'D LIKE NOTHING BETTER THAN TO STAY AWAY FROM AES SEDAI.

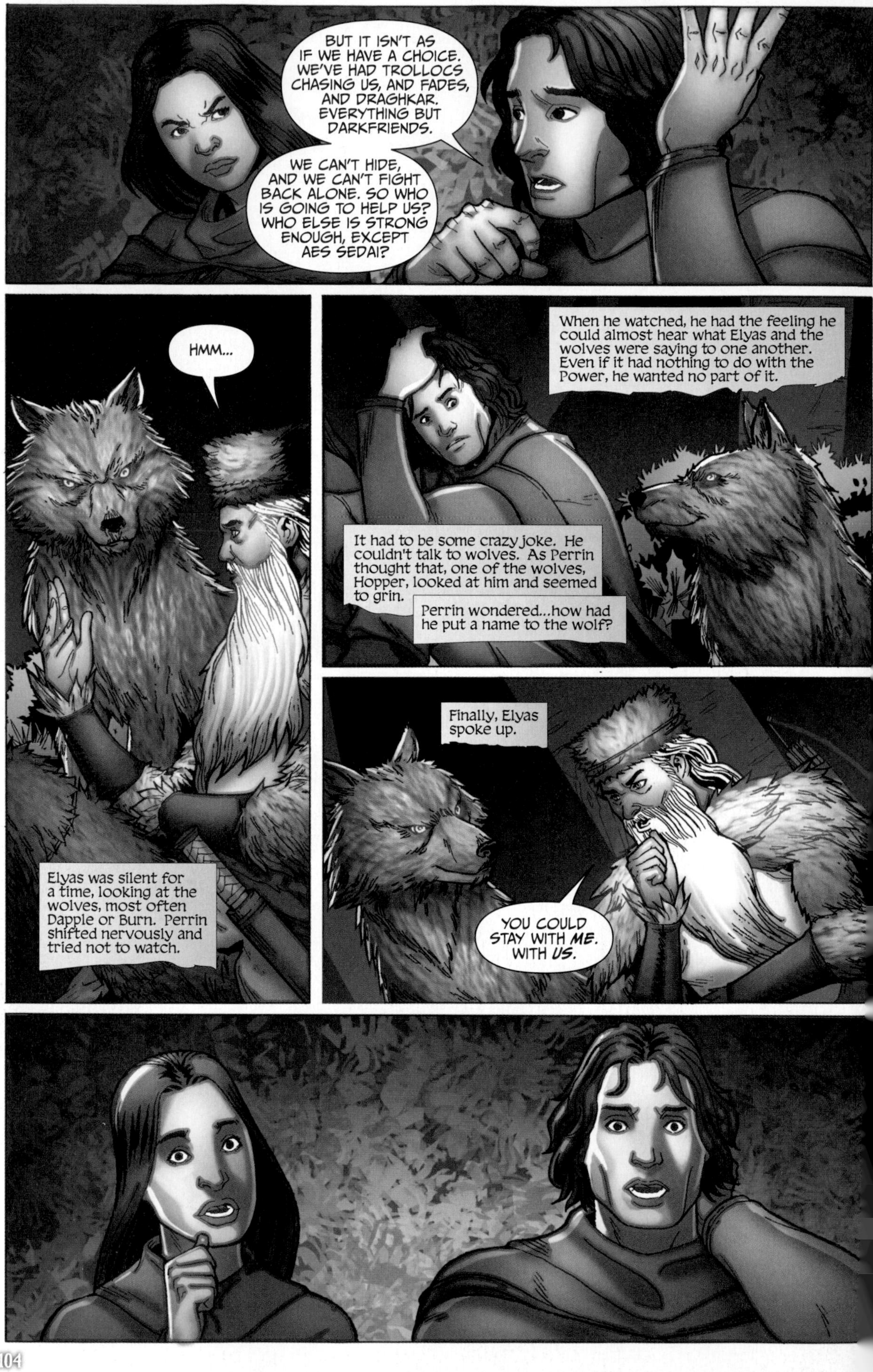
BUT IT ISN'T AS IF WE HAVE A CHOICE. WE'VE HAD TROLLOCS CHASING US, AND FADES, AND DRAGHKAR. EVERYTHING BUT DARKFRIENDS.
WE CAN'T HIDE, AND WE CAN'T FIGHT BACK ALONE. SO WHO IS GOING TO HELP US? WHO ELSE IS STRONG ENOUGH, EXCEPT AES SEDAI?
HMM...
Elyas was silent for a time, looking at the wolves, most often Dapple or Burn. Perrin shifted nervously and tried not to watch.
When he watched, he had the feeling he could almost hear what Elyas and the wolves were saying to one another. Even if it had nothing to do with the Power, he wanted no part of it.
It had to be some crazy joke. He couldn't talk to wolves. As Perrin thought that, one of the wolves, Hopper, looked at him and seemed to grin.
Perrin wondered...how had he put a name to the wolf?
Finally, Elyas spoke up.
YOU COULD STAY WITH *ME*. WITH *US*.

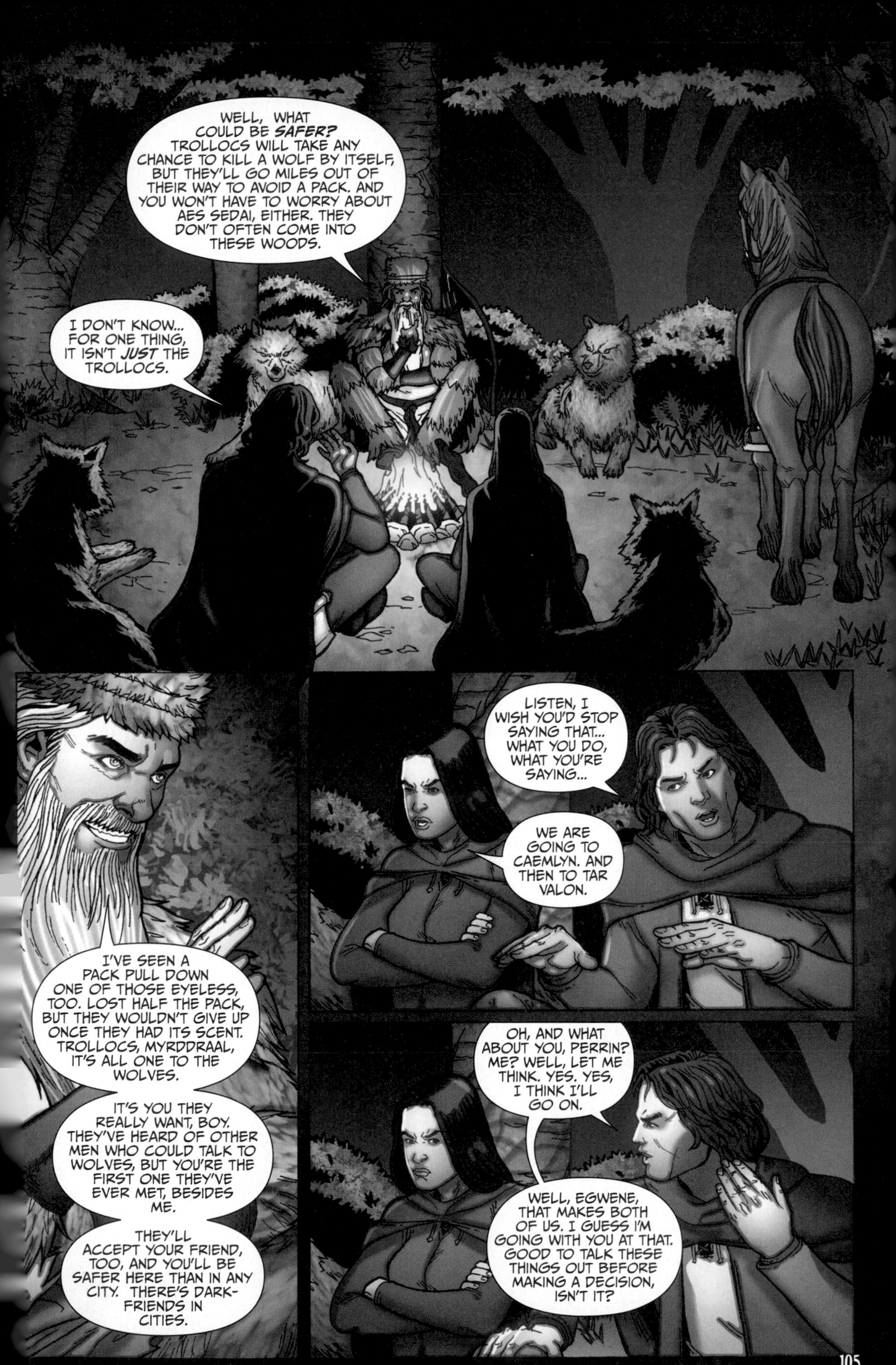
WELL, WHAT COULD BE SAFER? TROLLOCS WILL TAKE ANY CHANCE TO KILL A WOLF BY ITSELF, BUT THEY'LL GO MILES OUT OF THEIR WAY TO AVOID A PACK. AND YOU WON'T HAVE TO WORRY ABOUT AES SEDAI, EITHER. THEY DON'T OFTEN COME INTO THESE WOODS.
I DON'T KNOW... FOR ONE THING, IT ISN'T JUST THE TROLLOCS.
I'VE SEEN A PACK PULL DOWN ONE OF THOSE EYELESS, TOO. LOST HALF THE PACK, BUT THEY WOULDN'T GIVE UP ONCE THEY HAD ITS SCENT. TROLLOCS, MYRDDRAAL, IT'S ALL ONE TO THE WOLVES.
IT'S YOU THEY REALLY WANT, BOY. THEY'VE HEARD OF OTHER MEN WHO COULD TALK TO WOLVES, BUT YOU'RE THE FIRST ONE THEY'VE EVER MET, BESIDES ME.
THEY'LL ACCEPT YOUR FRIEND, TOO, AND YOU'LL BE SAFER HERE THAN IN ANY CITY. THERE'S DARK-FRIENDS IN CITIES.
LISTEN, I WISH YOU'D STOP SAYING THAT... WHAT YOU DO, WHAT YOU'RE SAYING...
WE ARE GOING TO CAEMLYN. AND THEN TO TAR VALON.
OH, AND WHAT ABOUT YOU, PERRIN? ME? WELL, LET ME THINK. YES. YES, I THINK I'LL GO ON.
WELL, EGWENE, THAT MAKES BOTH OF US. I GUESS I'M GOING WITH YOU AT THAT. GOOD TO TALK THESE THINGS OUT BEFORE MAKING A DECISION, ISN'T IT?

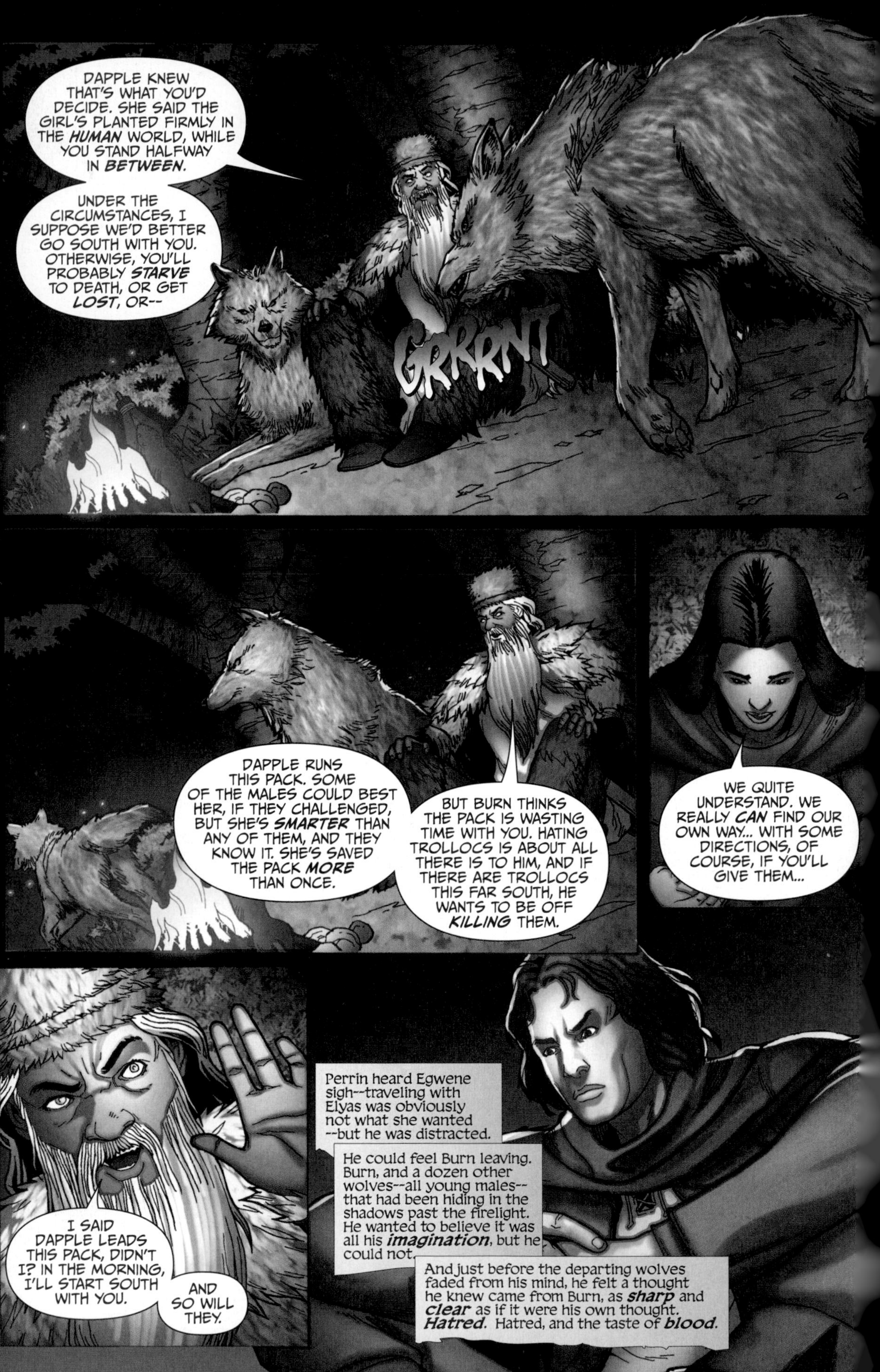

DAPPLE KNEW THAT'S WHAT YOU'D DECIDE. SHE SAID THE GIRL'S PLANTED FIRMLY IN THE *HUMAN* WORLD, WHILE YOU STAND HALFWAY IN *BETWEEN*.
UNDER THE CIRCUMSTANCES, I SUPPOSE WE'D BETTER GO SOUTH WITH YOU. OTHERWISE, YOU'LL PROBABLY *STARVE* TO DEATH, OR GET *LOST*, OR--
GRRRNT
DAPPLE RUNS THIS PACK. SOME OF THE MALES COULD BEST HER, IF THEY CHALLENGED, BUT SHE'S *SMARTER* THAN ANY OF THEM, AND THEY KNOW IT. SHE'S SAVED THE PACK *MORE* THAN ONCE.
BUT BURN THINKS THE PACK IS WASTING TIME WITH YOU. HATING TROLLOCS IS ABOUT ALL THERE IS TO HIM, AND IF THERE ARE TROLLOCS THIS FAR SOUTH, HE WANTS TO BE OFF *KILLING* THEM.
WE QUITE UNDERSTAND. WE REALLY *CAN* FIND OUR OWN WAY... WITH SOME DIRECTIONS, OF COURSE, IF YOU'LL GIVE THEM...
Perrin heard Egwene sigh--traveling with Elyas was obviously not what she wanted --but he was distracted.
He could feel Burn leaving. Burn, and a dozen other wolves--all young males--that had been hiding in the shadows past the firelight. He wanted to believe it was all his *imagination*, but he could not.
I SAID DAPPLE LEADS THIS PACK, DIDN'T I? IN THE MORNING, I'LL START SOUTH WITH YOU.
AND SO WILL THEY.
And just before the departing wolves faded from his mind, he felt a thought he knew came from Burn, as *sharp* and *clear* as if it were his own thought. *Hatred*. Hatred, and the taste of *blood*.

chapter five

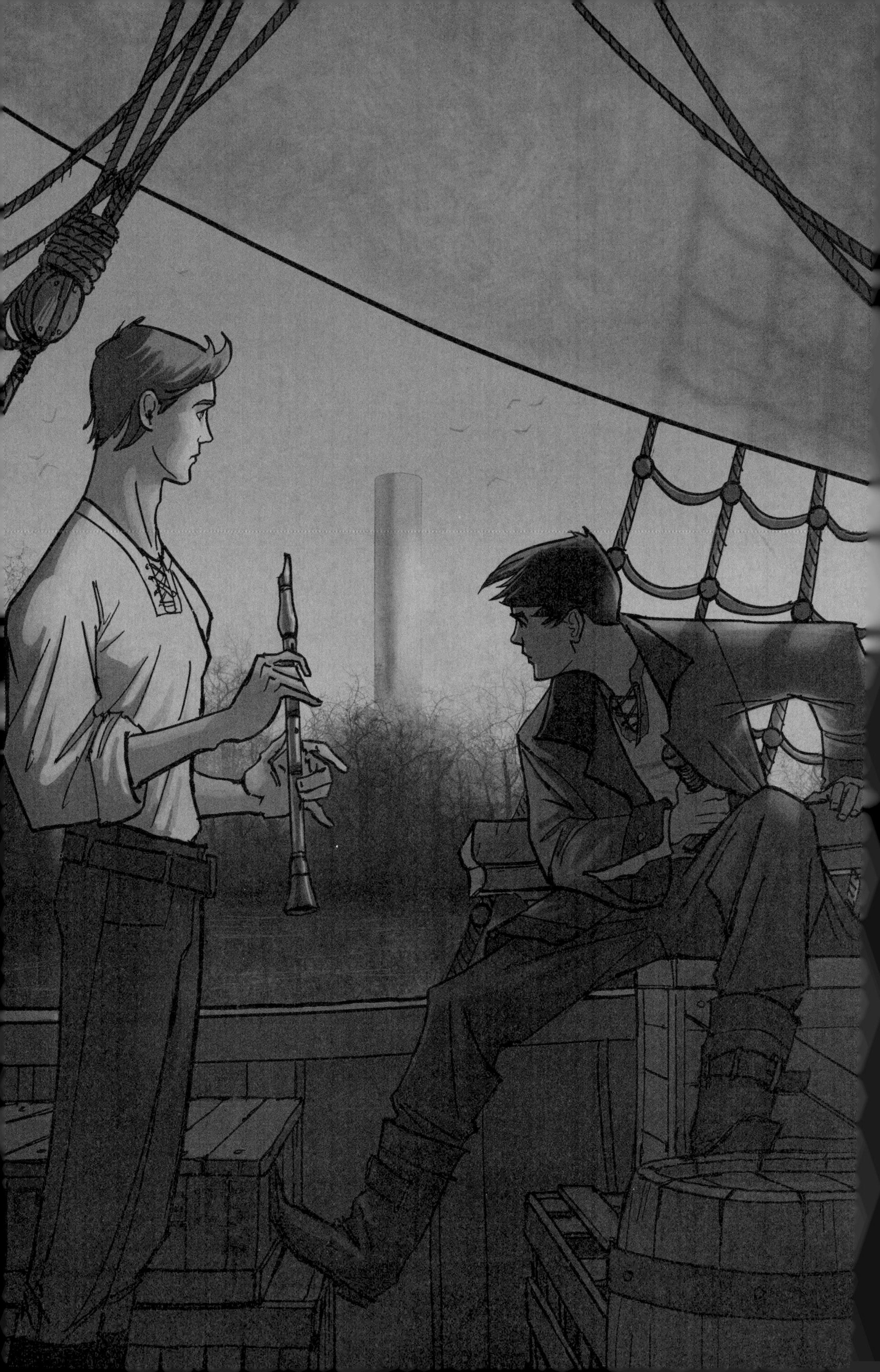

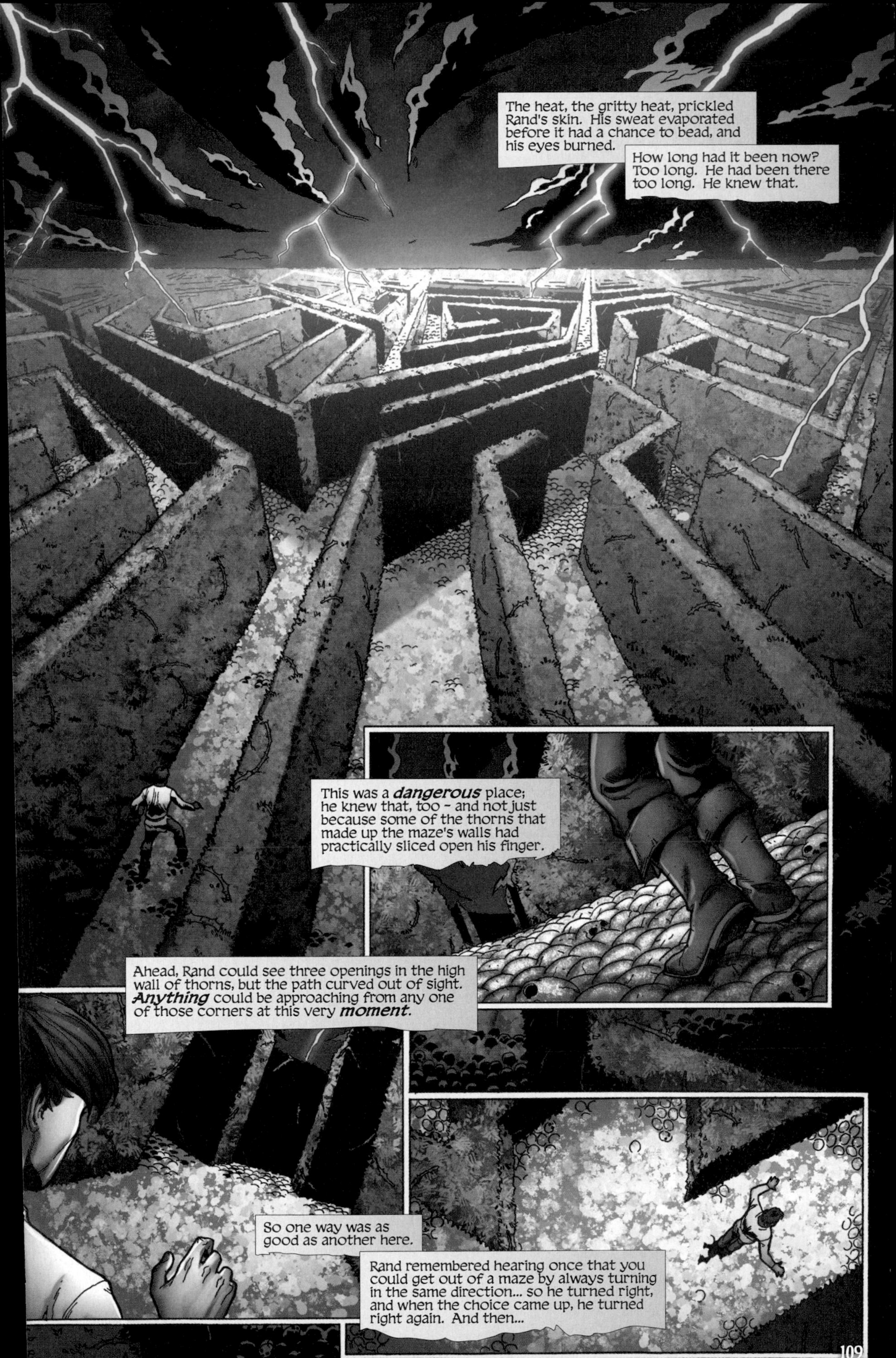
The heat, the gritty heat, prickled Rand's skin. His sweat evaporated before it had a chance to bead, and his eyes burned.
How long had it been now? Too long. He had been there too long. He knew that.
This was a ***dangerous*** place; he knew that, too - and not just because some of the thorns that made up the maze's walls had practically sliced open his finger.
Ahead, Rand could see three openings in the high wall of thorns, but the path curved out of sight. ***Anything*** could be approaching from any one of those corners at this very ***moment***.
So one way was as good as another here.
Rand remembered hearing once that you could get out of a maze by always turning in the same direction... so he turned right, and when the choice came up, he turned right again. And then...

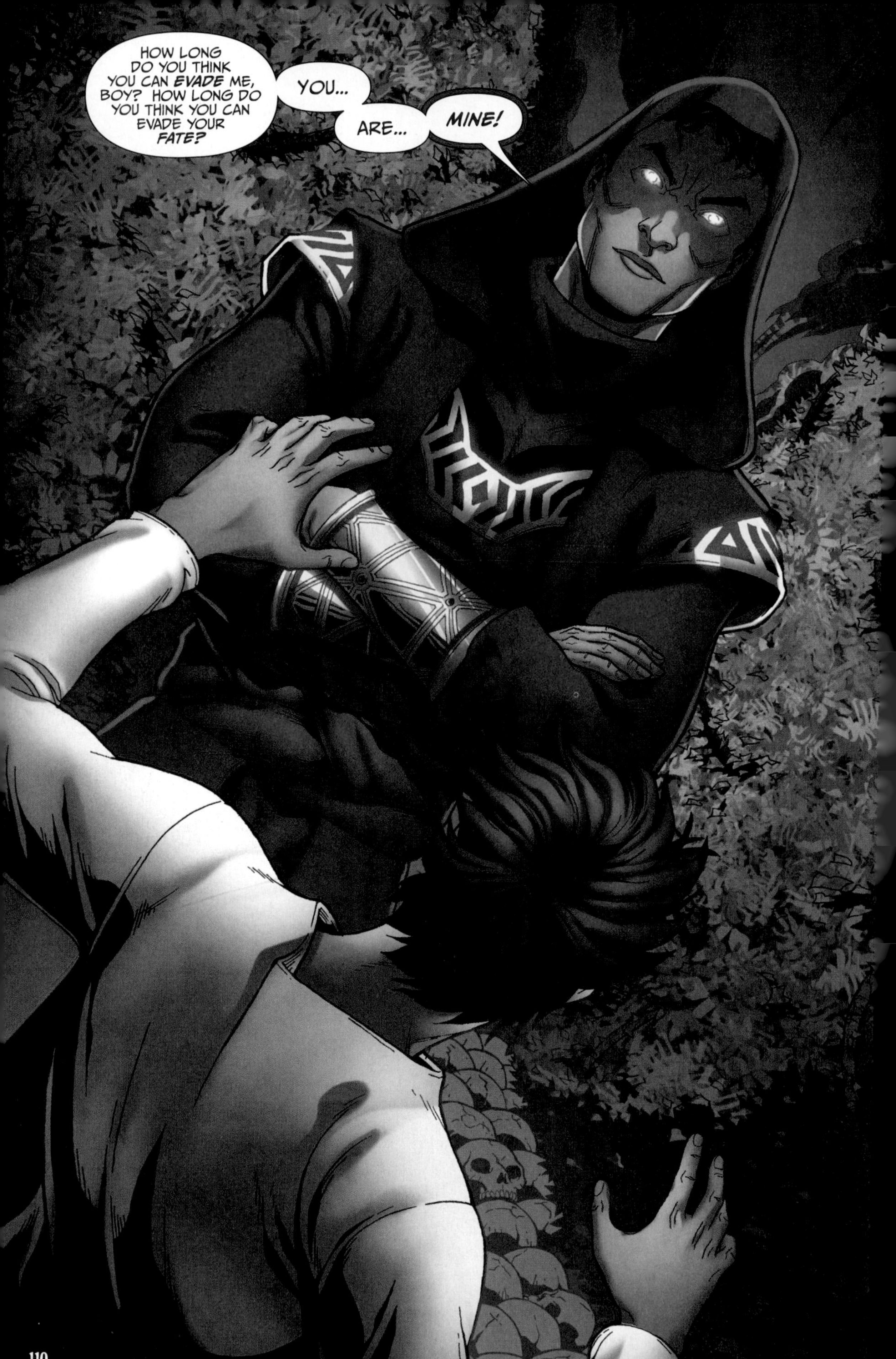
HOW LONG DO YOU THINK YOU CAN EVADE ME, BOY? HOW LONG DO YOU THINK YOU CAN EVADE YOUR FATE?
YOU...
ARE...
MINE!

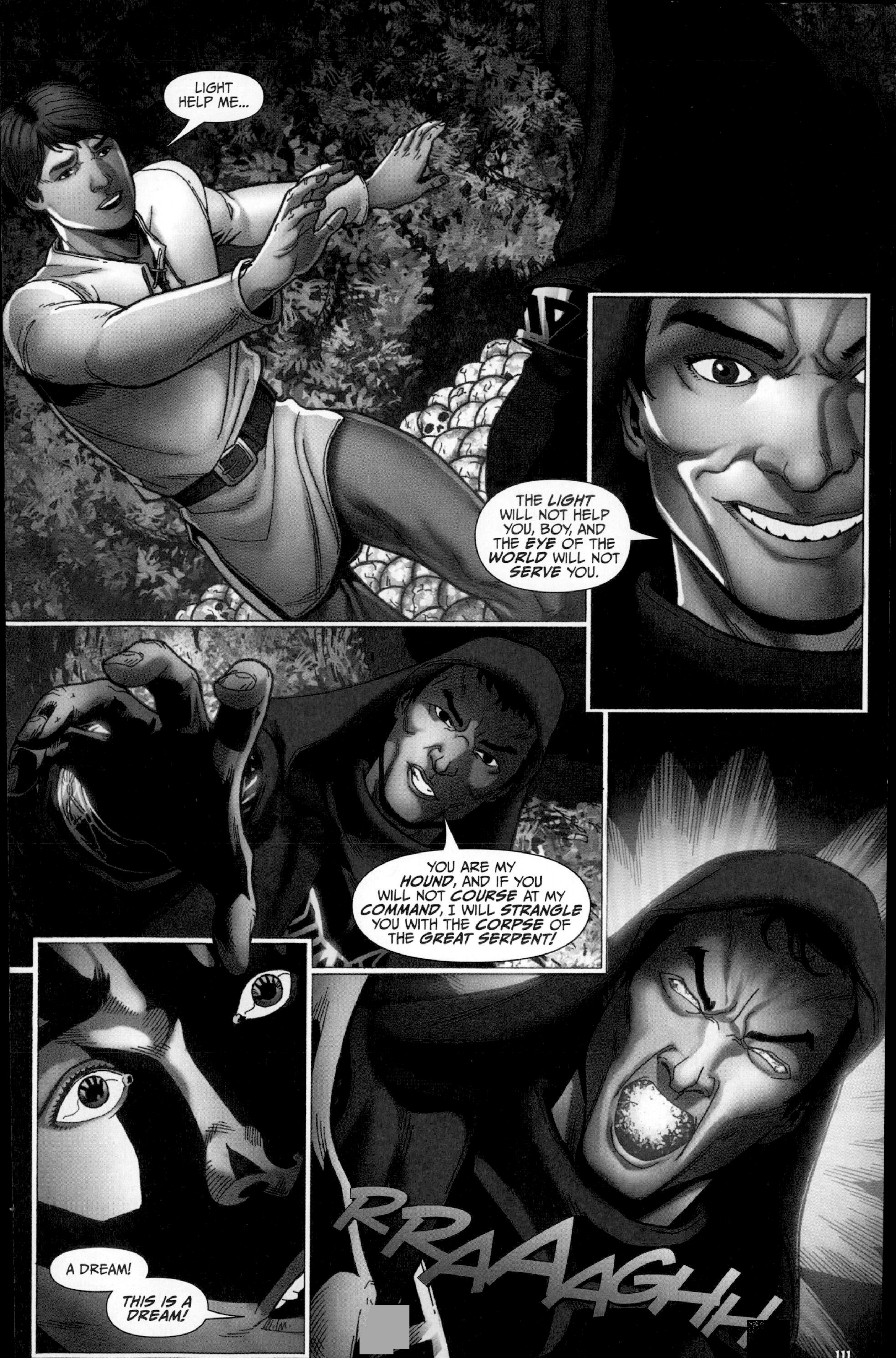
LIGHT HELP ME...
THE LIGHT WILL NOT HELP YOU, BOY, AND THE EYE OF THE WORLD WILL NOT SERVE YOU.
YOU ARE MY HOUND, AND IF YOU WILL NOT COURSE AT MY COMMAND, I WILL STRANGLE YOU WITH THE CORPSE OF THE GREAT SERPENT!
A DREAM!
THIS IS A DREAM!
RRAAAGHH!

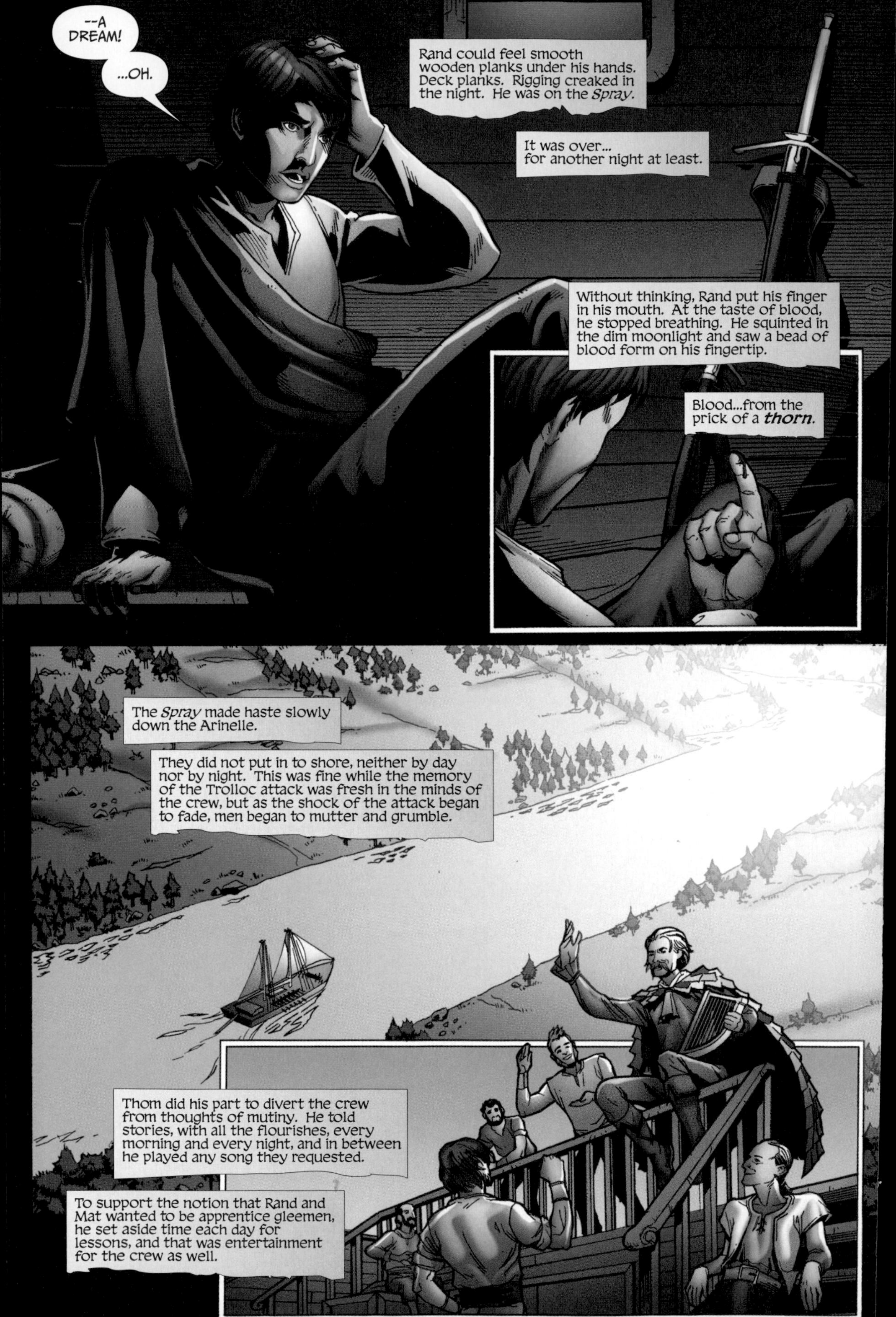
--A DREAM!
...OH.
Rand could feel smooth wooden planks under his hands. Deck planks. Rigging creaked in the night. He was on the *Spray*.
It was over... for another night at least.
Without thinking, Rand put his finger in his mouth. At the taste of blood, he stopped breathing. He squinted in the dim moonlight and saw a bead of blood form on his fingertip.
Blood...from the prick of a ***thorn***.
The *Spray* made haste slowly down the Arinelle.
They did not put in to shore, neither by day nor by night. This was fine while the memory of the Trolloc attack was fresh in the minds of the crew, but as the shock of the attack began to fade, men began to mutter and grumble.
Thom did his part to divert the crew from thoughts of mutiny. He told stories, with all the flourishes, every morning and every night, and in between he played any song they requested.
To support the notion that Rand and Mat wanted to be apprentice gleemen, he set aside time each day for lessons, and that was entertainment for the crew as well.

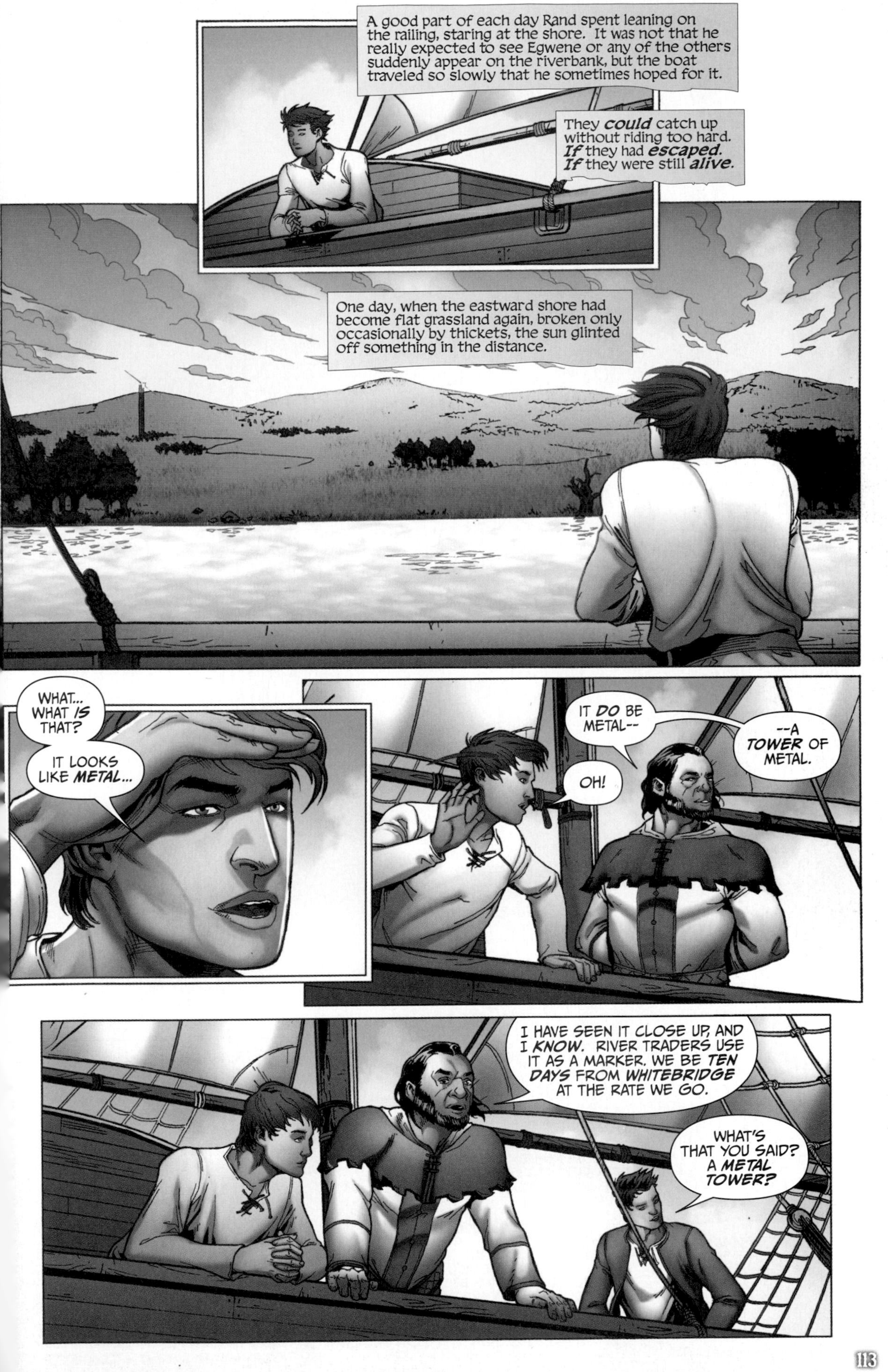
A good part of each day Rand spent leaning on the railing, staring at the shore. It was not that he really expected to see Egwene or any of the others suddenly appear on the riverbank, but the boat traveled so slowly that he sometimes hoped for it.
They could catch up without riding too hard. If they had escaped. If they were still alive.
One day, when the eastward shore had become flat grassland again, broken only occasionally by thickets, the sun glinted off something in the distance.
WHAT... WHAT IS THAT?
IT LOOKS LIKE METAL...
IT DO BE METAL--
--A TOWER OF METAL.
OH!
I HAVE SEEN IT CLOSE UP, AND I KNOW. RIVER TRADERS USE IT AS A MARKER. WE BE TEN DAYS FROM WHITEBRIDGE AT THE RATE WE GO.
WHAT'S THAT YOU SAID? A METAL TOWER?

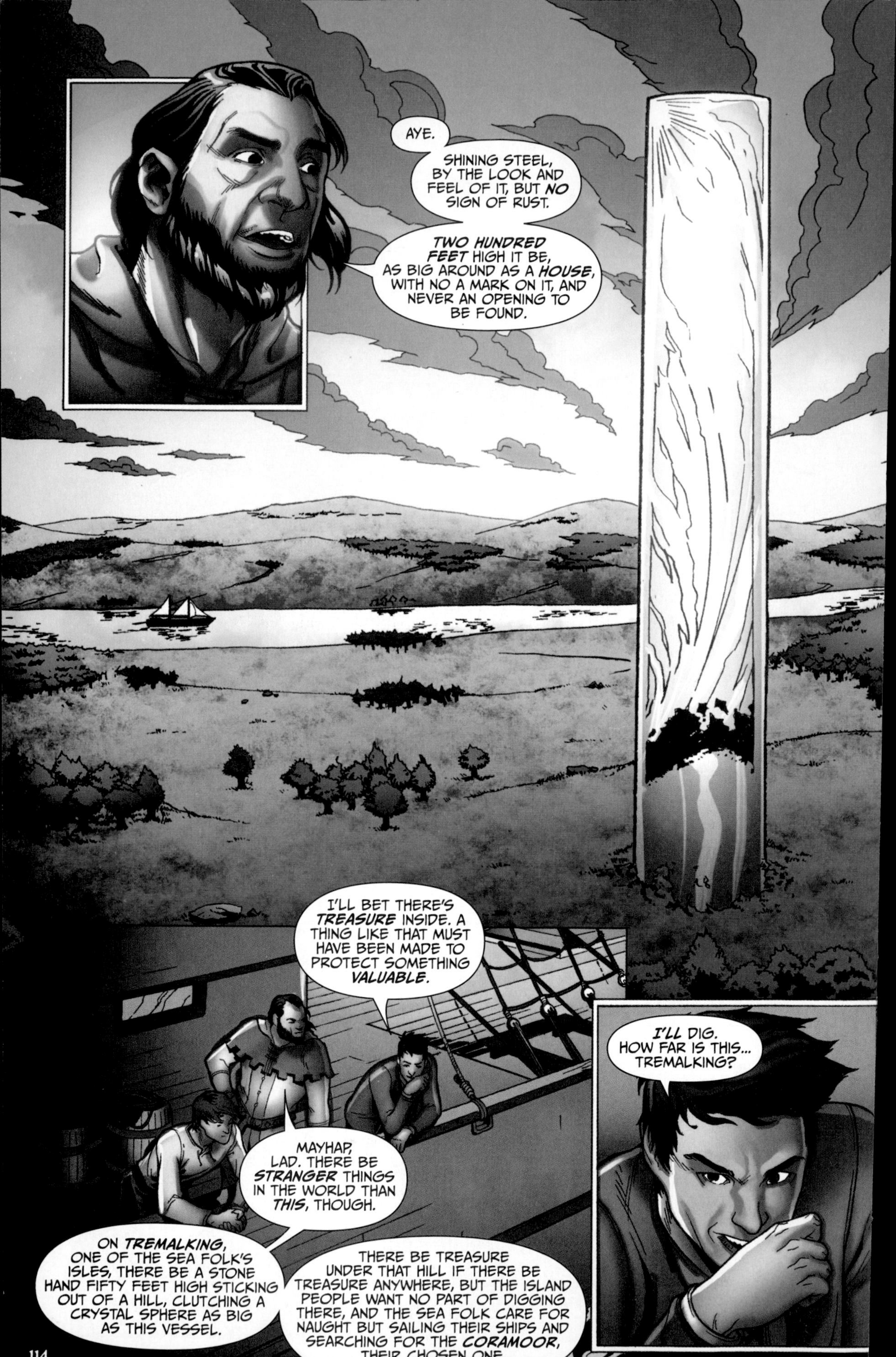
AYE.
SHINING STEEL, BY THE LOOK AND FEEL OF IT, BUT NO SIGN OF RUST.
TWO HUNDRED FEET HIGH IT BE, AS BIG AROUND AS A HOUSE, WITH NO A MARK ON IT, AND NEVER AN OPENING TO BE FOUND.
I'LL BET THERE'S TREASURE INSIDE. A THING LIKE THAT MUST HAVE BEEN MADE TO PROTECT SOMETHING VALUABLE.
MAYHAP, LAD. THERE BE STRANGER THINGS IN THE WORLD THAN THIS, THOUGH.
ON TREMALKING, ONE OF THE SEA FOLK'S ISLES, THERE BE A STONE HAND FIFTY FEET HIGH STICKING OUT OF A HILL, CLUTCHING A CRYSTAL SPHERE AS BIG AS THIS VESSEL.
THERE BE TREASURE UNDER THAT HILL IF THERE BE TREASURE ANYWHERE, BUT THE ISLAND PEOPLE WANT NO PART OF DIGGING THERE, AND THE SEA FOLK CARE FOR NAUGHT BUT SAILING THEIR SHIPS AND SEARCHING FOR THE CORAMOOR, THEIR CHOSEN ONE.
I'LL DIG. HOW FAR IS THIS... TREMALKING?

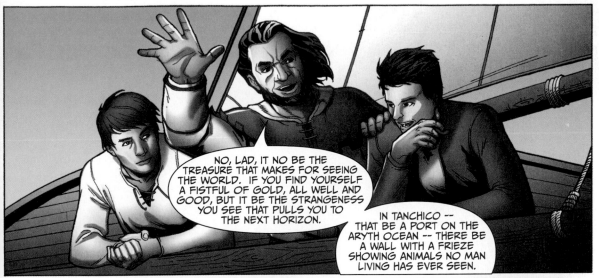

NO, LAD, IT NO BE THE TREASURE THAT MAKES FOR SEEING THE WORLD. IF YOU FIND YOURSELF A FISTFUL OF GOLD, ALL WELL AND GOOD, BUT IT BE THE STRANGENESS YOU SEE THAT PULLS YOU TO THE NEXT HORIZON.

IN TANCHICO -- THAT BE A PORT ON THE ARYTH OCEAN -- THERE BE A WALL WITH A FRIEZE SHOWING ANIMALS NO MAN LIVING HAS EVER SEEN.

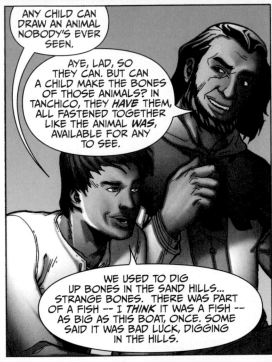

ANY CHILD CAN DRAW AN ANIMAL NOBODY'S EVER SEEN.

AYE, LAD, SO THEY CAN. BUT CAN A CHILD MAKE THE BONES OF THOSE ANIMALS? IN TANCHICO, THEY *HAVE* THEM, ALL FASTENED TOGETHER LIKE THE ANIMAL *WAS*, AVAILABLE FOR ANY TO SEE.

WE USED TO DIG UP BONES IN THE SAND HILLS... STRANGE BONES. THERE WAS PART OF A FISH -- I *THINK* IT WAS A FISH -- AS BIG AS THIS BOAT, ONCE. SOME SAID IT WAS BAD LUCK, DIGGING IN THE HILLS.

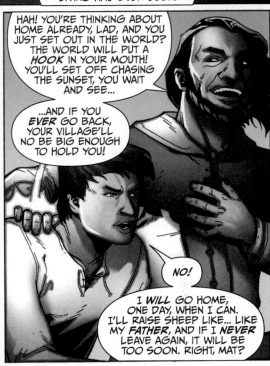

HAH! YOU'RE THINKING ABOUT HOME ALREADY, LAD, AND YOU JUST SET OUT IN THE WORLD? THE WORLD WILL PUT A *HOOK* IN YOUR MOUTH! YOU'LL SET OFF CHASING THE SUNSET, YOU WAIT AND SEE...

...AND IF YOU *EVER* GO BACK, YOUR VILLAGE'LL NO BE BIG ENOUGH TO HOLD YOU!

NO!

I *WILL* GO HOME, ONE DAY, WHEN I CAN. I'LL RAISE SHEEP LIKE... LIKE MY *FATHER*, AND IF I *NEVER* LEAVE AGAIN, IT WILL BE TOO SOON. RIGHT, MAT?

AS SOON AS WE CAN, WE'LL GO HOME AND FORGET ALL OF THIS EVEN *EXISTS*.

WHAT? OH.

YES, OF COURSE. WE'LL GO HOME. OF COURSE.

I'LL BET HE JUST DOESN'T WANT ANYBODY ELSE GOING AFTER THE TREASURE.

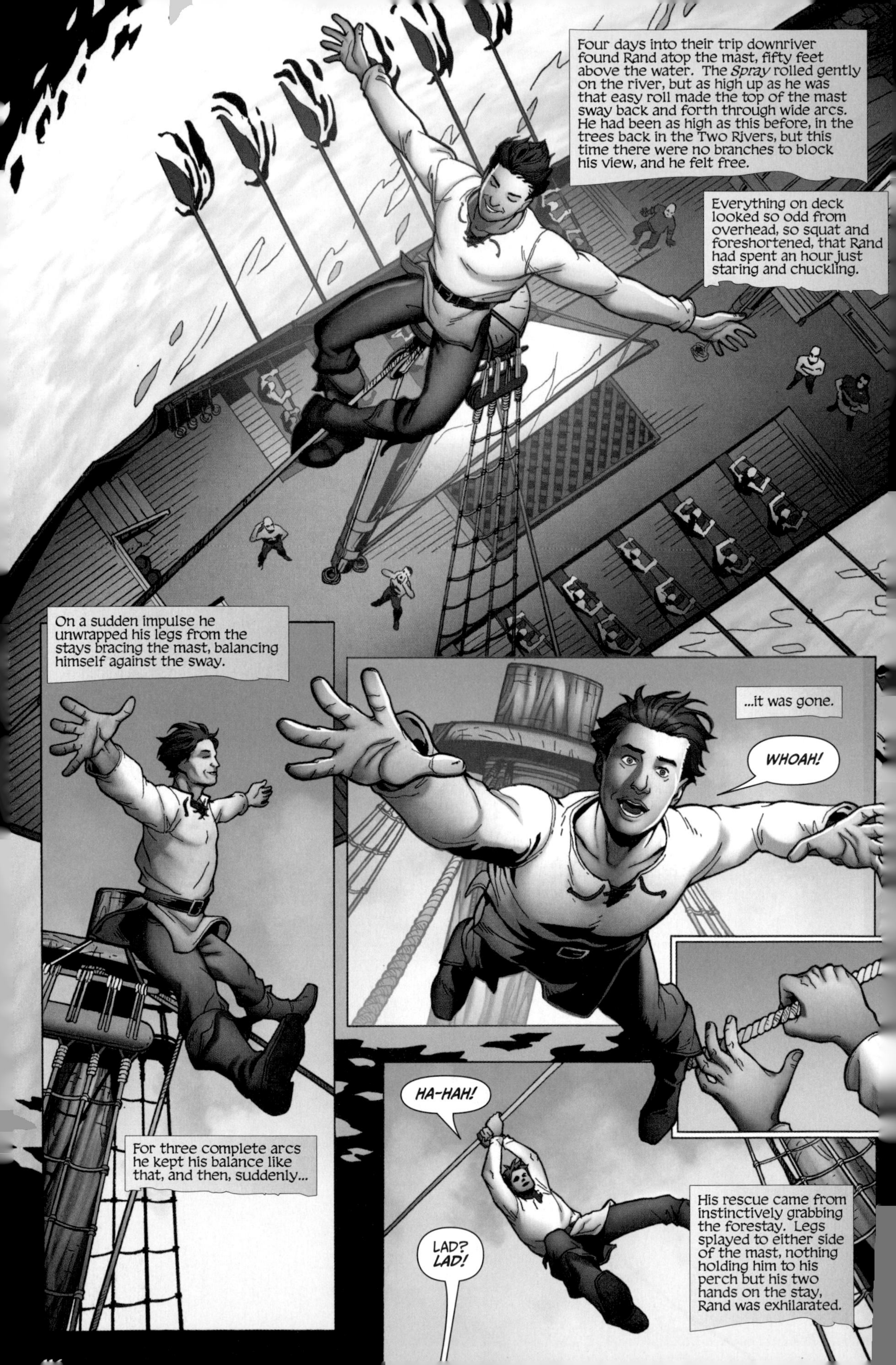

Four days into their trip downriver found Rand atop the mast, fifty feet above the water. The *Spray* rolled gently on the river, but as high up as he was that easy roll made the top of the mast sway back and forth through wide arcs. He had been as high as this before, in the trees back in the Two Rivers, but this time there were no branches to block his view, and he felt free.
Everything on deck looked so odd from overhead, so squat and foreshortened, that Rand had spent an hour just staring and chuckling.
On a sudden impulse he unwrapped his legs from the stays bracing the mast, balancing himself against the sway.
For three complete arcs he kept his balance like that, and then, suddenly...
...it was gone.
WHOAH!
HA-HAH!
His rescue came from instinctively grabbing the forestay. Legs splayed to either side of the mast, nothing holding him to his perch but his two hands on the stay, Rand was exhilarated.
LAD? LAD!

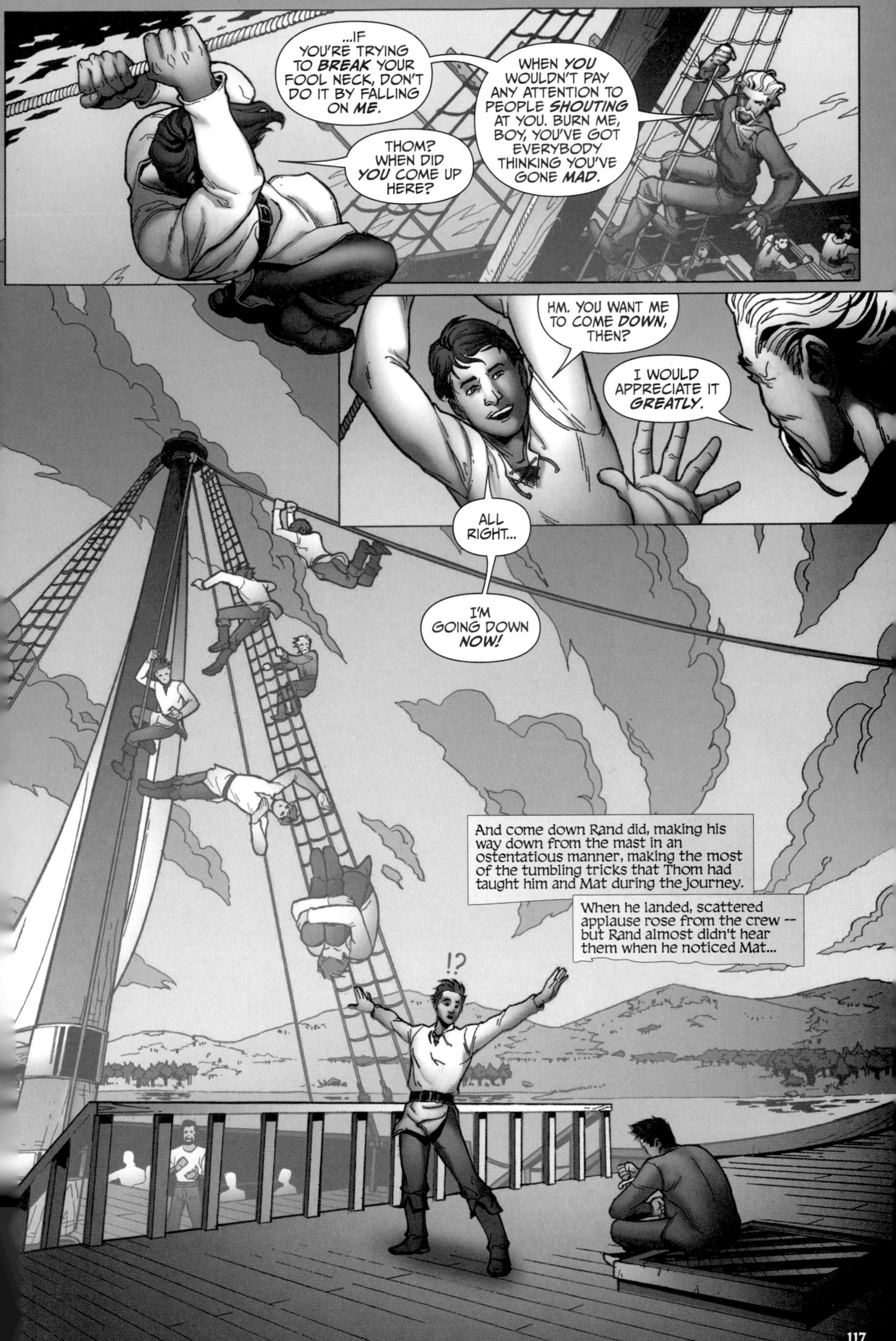

THOM? WHEN DID *YOU* COME UP HERE?
...IF YOU'RE TRYING TO *BREAK* YOUR FOOL NECK, DON'T DO IT BY FALLING ON *ME*.
WHEN *YOU* WOULDN'T PAY ANY ATTENTION TO PEOPLE *SHOUTING* AT YOU. BURN ME, BOY, YOU'VE GOT EVERYBODY THINKING YOU'VE GONE *MAD*.
HM. YOU WANT ME TO COME *DOWN*, THEN?
I WOULD APPRECIATE IT *GREATLY*.
ALL RIGHT...
I'M GOING DOWN *NOW!*
And come down Rand did, making his way down from the mast in an ostentatious manner, making the most of the tumbling tricks that Thom had taught him and Mat during the journey.
When he landed, scattered applause rose from the crew -- but Rand almost didn't hear them when he noticed Mat...
!?

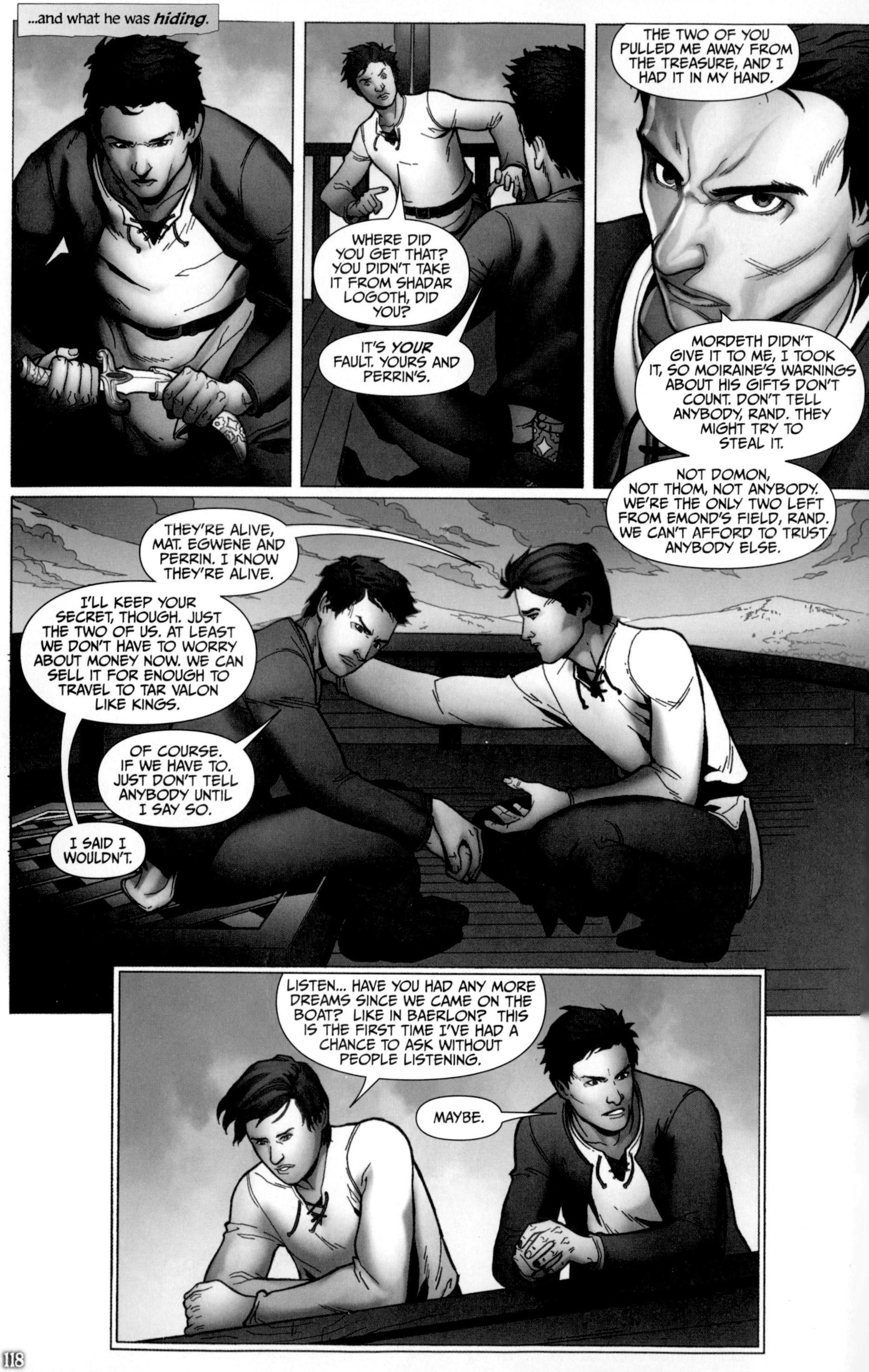
...and what he was *hiding*.
WHERE DID YOU GET THAT? YOU DIDN'T TAKE IT FROM SHADAR LOGOTH, DID YOU?
IT'S *YOUR* FAULT. YOURS AND PERRIN'S.
THE TWO OF YOU PULLED ME AWAY FROM THE TREASURE, AND I HAD IT IN MY HAND.
MORDETH DIDN'T GIVE IT TO ME, I TOOK IT, SO MOIRAINE'S WARNINGS ABOUT HIS GIFTS DON'T COUNT. DON'T TELL ANYBODY, RAND. THEY MIGHT TRY TO STEAL IT.
NOT DOMON, NOT THOM, NOT ANYBODY. WE'RE THE ONLY TWO LEFT FROM EMOND'S FIELD, RAND. WE CAN'T AFFORD TO TRUST ANYBODY ELSE.
THEY'RE ALIVE, MAT. EGWENE AND PERRIN. I KNOW THEY'RE ALIVE.
I'LL KEEP YOUR SECRET, THOUGH. JUST THE TWO OF US. AT LEAST WE DON'T HAVE TO WORRY ABOUT MONEY NOW. WE CAN SELL IT FOR ENOUGH TO TRAVEL TO TAR VALON LIKE KINGS.
OF COURSE. IF WE HAVE TO. JUST DON'T TELL ANYBODY UNTIL I SAY SO.
I SAID I WOULDN'T.
LISTEN... HAVE YOU HAD ANY MORE DREAMS SINCE WE CAME ON THE BOAT? LIKE IN BAERLON? THIS IS THE FIRST TIME I'VE HAD A CHANCE TO ASK WITHOUT PEOPLE LISTENING.
MAYBE.

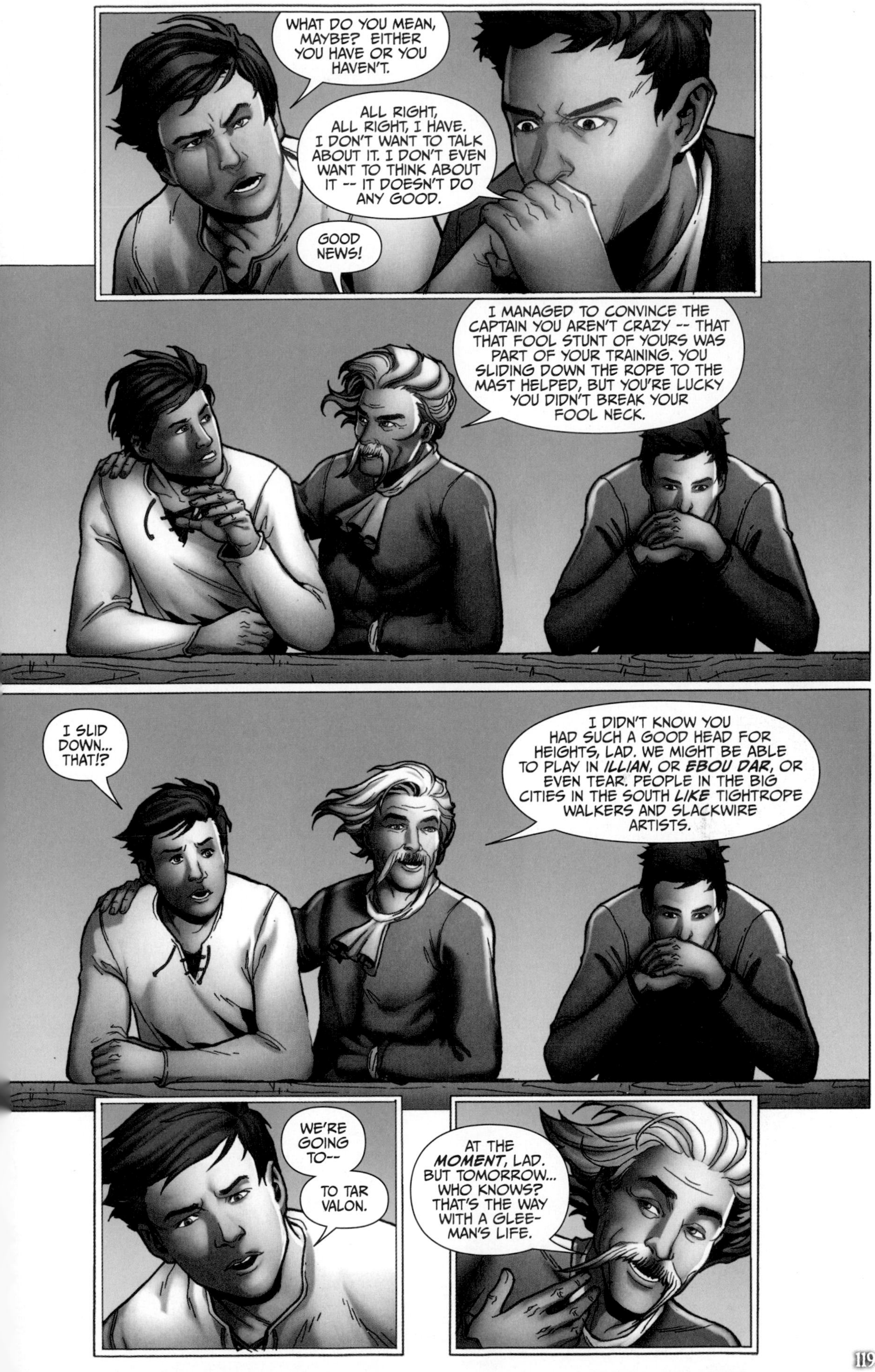
WHAT DO YOU MEAN, MAYBE? EITHER YOU HAVE OR YOU HAVEN'T.
ALL RIGHT, ALL RIGHT, I HAVE. I DON'T WANT TO TALK ABOUT IT. I DON'T EVEN WANT TO THINK ABOUT IT -- IT DOESN'T DO ANY GOOD.
GOOD NEWS!
I MANAGED TO CONVINCE THE CAPTAIN YOU AREN'T CRAZY -- THAT THAT FOOL STUNT OF YOURS WAS PART OF YOUR TRAINING. YOU SLIDING DOWN THE ROPE TO THE MAST HELPED, BUT YOU'RE LUCKY YOU DIDN'T BREAK YOUR FOOL NECK.
I SLID DOWN... THAT!?
I DIDN'T KNOW YOU HAD SUCH A GOOD HEAD FOR HEIGHTS, LAD. WE MIGHT BE ABLE TO PLAY IN *ILLIAN*, OR *EBOU DAR*, OR EVEN TEAR. PEOPLE IN THE BIG CITIES IN THE SOUTH *LIKE* TIGHTROPE WALKERS AND SLACKWIRE ARTISTS.
WE'RE GOING TO--
TO TAR VALON.
AT THE *MOMENT*, LAD. BUT TOMORROW... WHO KNOWS? THAT'S THE WAY WITH A GLEE-MAN'S LIFE.

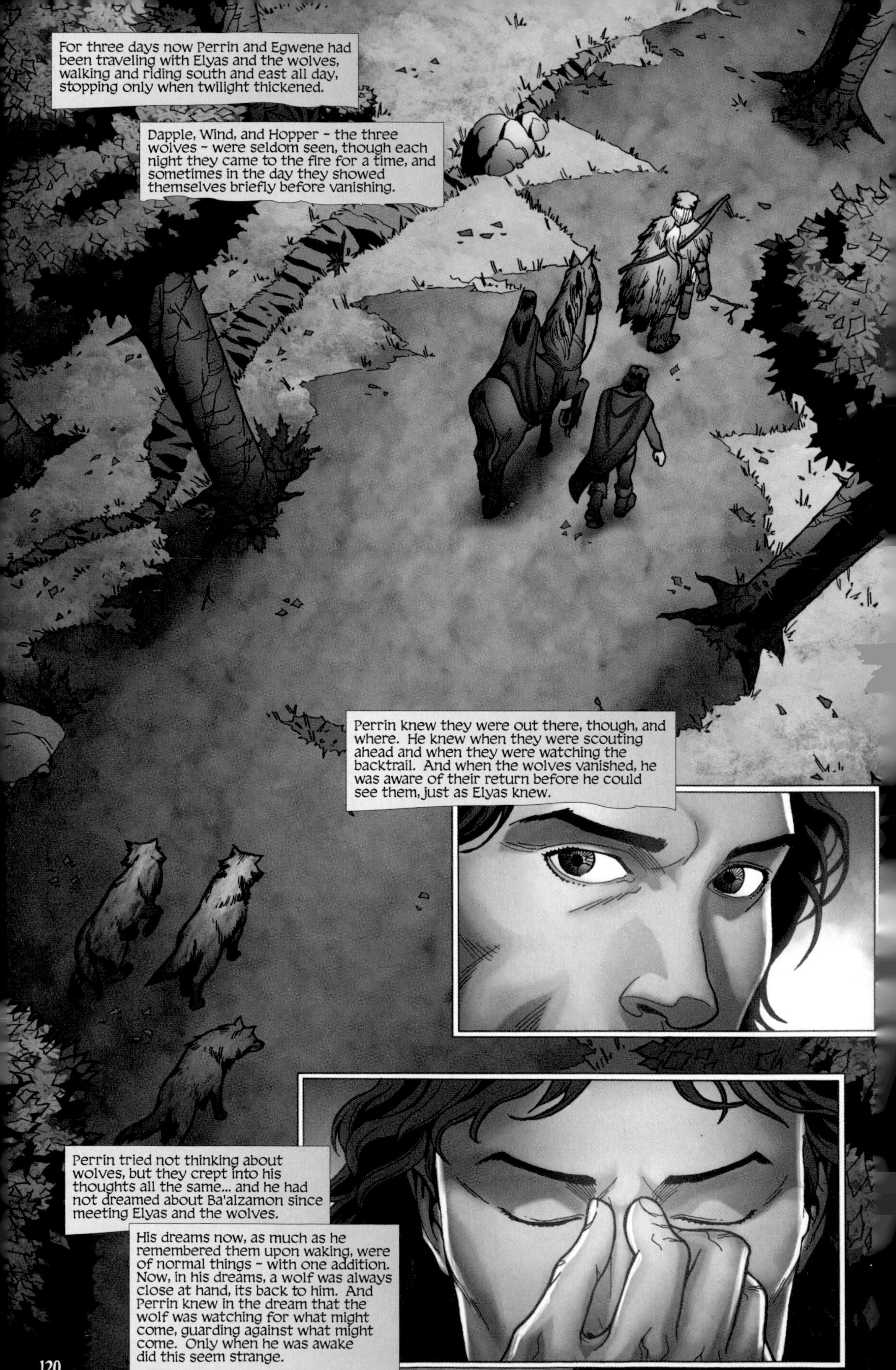
For three days now Perrin and Egwene had been traveling with Elyas and the wolves, walking and riding south and east all day, stopping only when twilight thickened.
Dapple, Wind, and Hopper ~ the three wolves ~ were seldom seen, though each night they came to the fire for a time, and sometimes in the day they showed themselves briefly before vanishing.
Perrin knew they were out there, though, and where. He knew when they were scouting ahead and when they were watching the backtrail. And when the wolves vanished, he was aware of their return before he could see them, just as Elyas knew.
Perrin tried not thinking about wolves, but they crept into his thoughts all the same... and he had not dreamed about Ba'alzamon since meeting Elyas and the wolves.
His dreams now, as much as he remembered them upon waking, were of normal things ~ with one addition. Now, in his dreams, a wolf was always close at hand, its back to him. And Perrin knew in the dream that the wolf was watching for what might come, guarding against what might come. Only when he was awake did this seem strange.

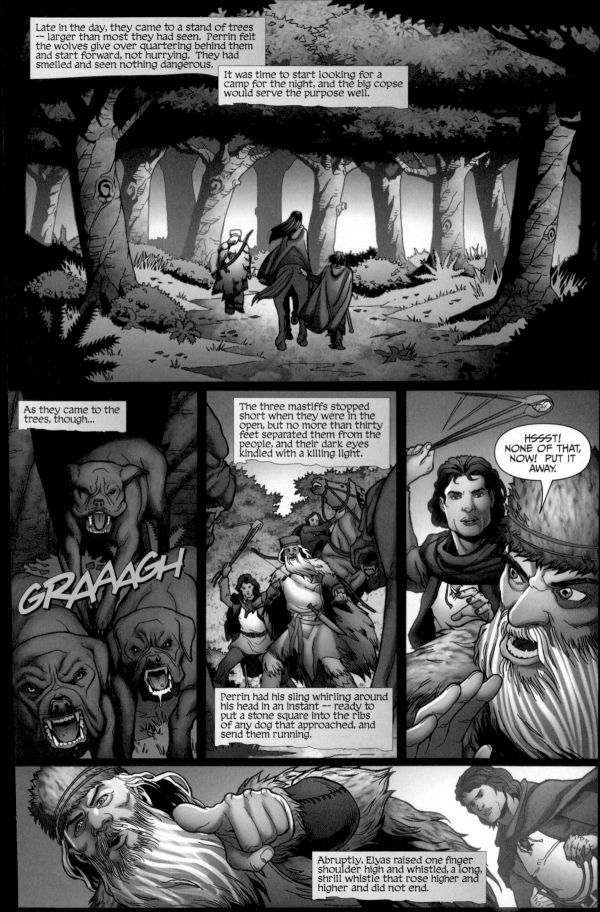

Late in the day, they came to a stand of trees -- larger than most they had seen. Perrin felt the wolves give over quartering behind them and start forward, not hurrying. They had smelled and seen nothing dangerous.

It was time to start looking for a camp for the night, and the big copse would serve the purpose well.

As they came to the trees, though...

GRAAAGH

The three mastiffs stopped short when they were in the open, but no more than thirty feet separated them from the people, and their dark eyes kindled with a killing light.

HSSST! NONE OF THAT, NOW! PUT IT AWAY.

Perrin had his sling whirling around his head in an instant -- ready to put a stone square into the ribs of any dog that approached, and send them running.

Abruptly, Elyas raised one finger shoulder high and whistled, a long, shrill whistle that rose higher and higher and did not end.

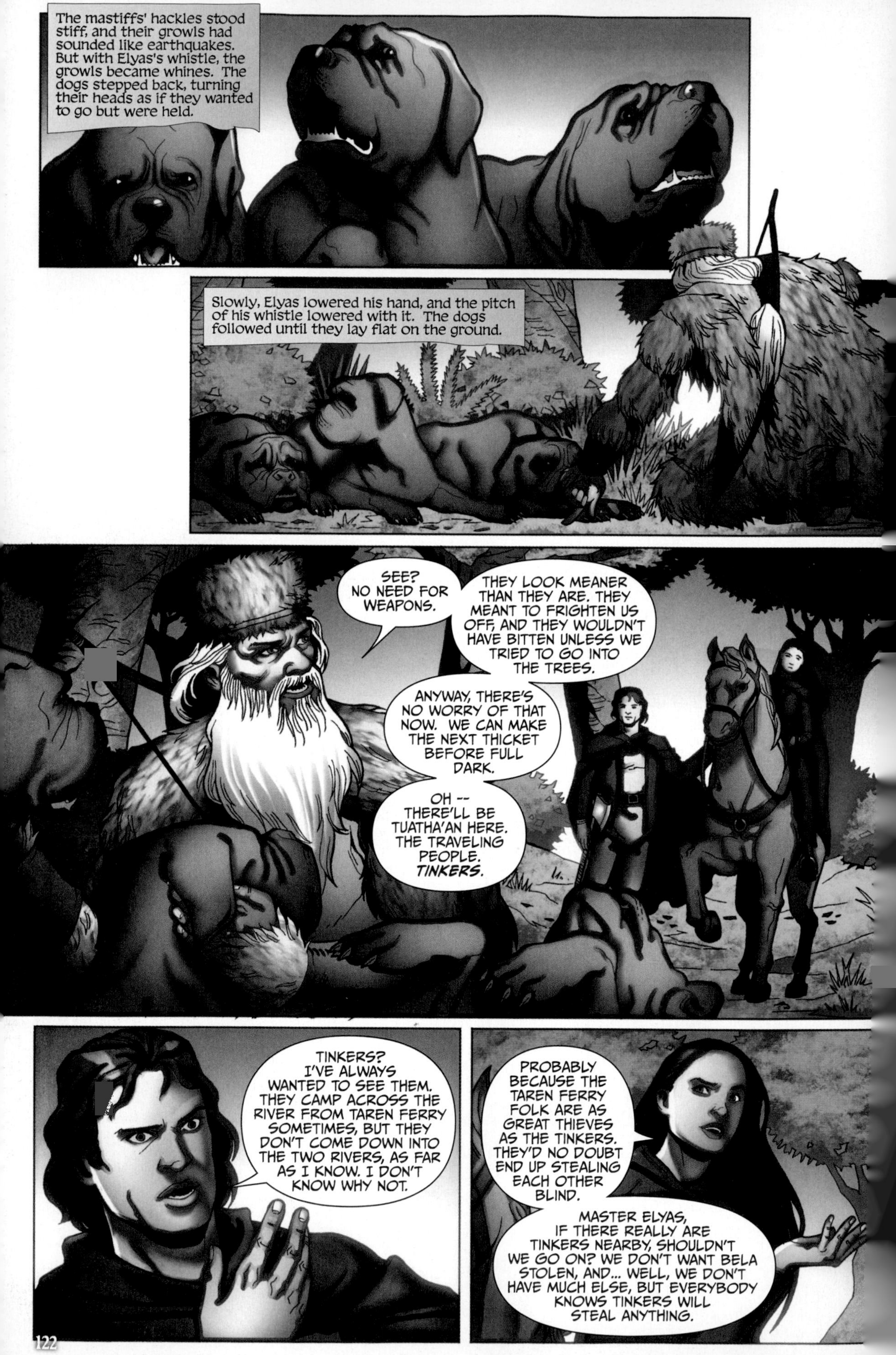
The mastiffs' hackles stood stiff, and their growls had sounded like earthquakes. But with Elyas's whistle, the growls became whines. The dogs stepped back, turning their heads as if they wanted to go but were held.
Slowly, Elyas lowered his hand, and the pitch of his whistle lowered with it. The dogs followed until they lay flat on the ground.
SEE? NO NEED FOR WEAPONS.
THEY LOOK MEANER THAN THEY ARE. THEY MEANT TO FRIGHTEN US OFF, AND THEY WOULDN'T HAVE BITTEN UNLESS WE TRIED TO GO INTO THE TREES.
ANYWAY, THERE'S NO WORRY OF THAT NOW. WE CAN MAKE THE NEXT THICKET BEFORE FULL DARK.
OH -- THERE'LL BE TUATHA'AN HERE. THE TRAVELING PEOPLE. *TINKERS*.
TINKERS? I'VE ALWAYS WANTED TO SEE THEM. THEY CAMP ACROSS THE RIVER FROM TAREN FERRY SOMETIMES, BUT THEY DON'T COME DOWN INTO THE TWO RIVERS, AS FAR AS I KNOW. I DON'T KNOW WHY NOT.
PROBABLY BECAUSE THE TAREN FERRY FOLK ARE AS GREAT THIEVES AS THE TINKERS. THEY'D NO DOUBT END UP STEALING EACH OTHER BLIND.
MASTER ELYAS, IF THERE REALLY ARE TINKERS NEARBY, SHOULDN'T WE GO ON? WE DON'T WANT BELA STOLEN, AND... WELL, WE DON'T HAVE MUCH ELSE, BUT EVERYBODY KNOWS TINKERS WILL STEAL ANYTHING.

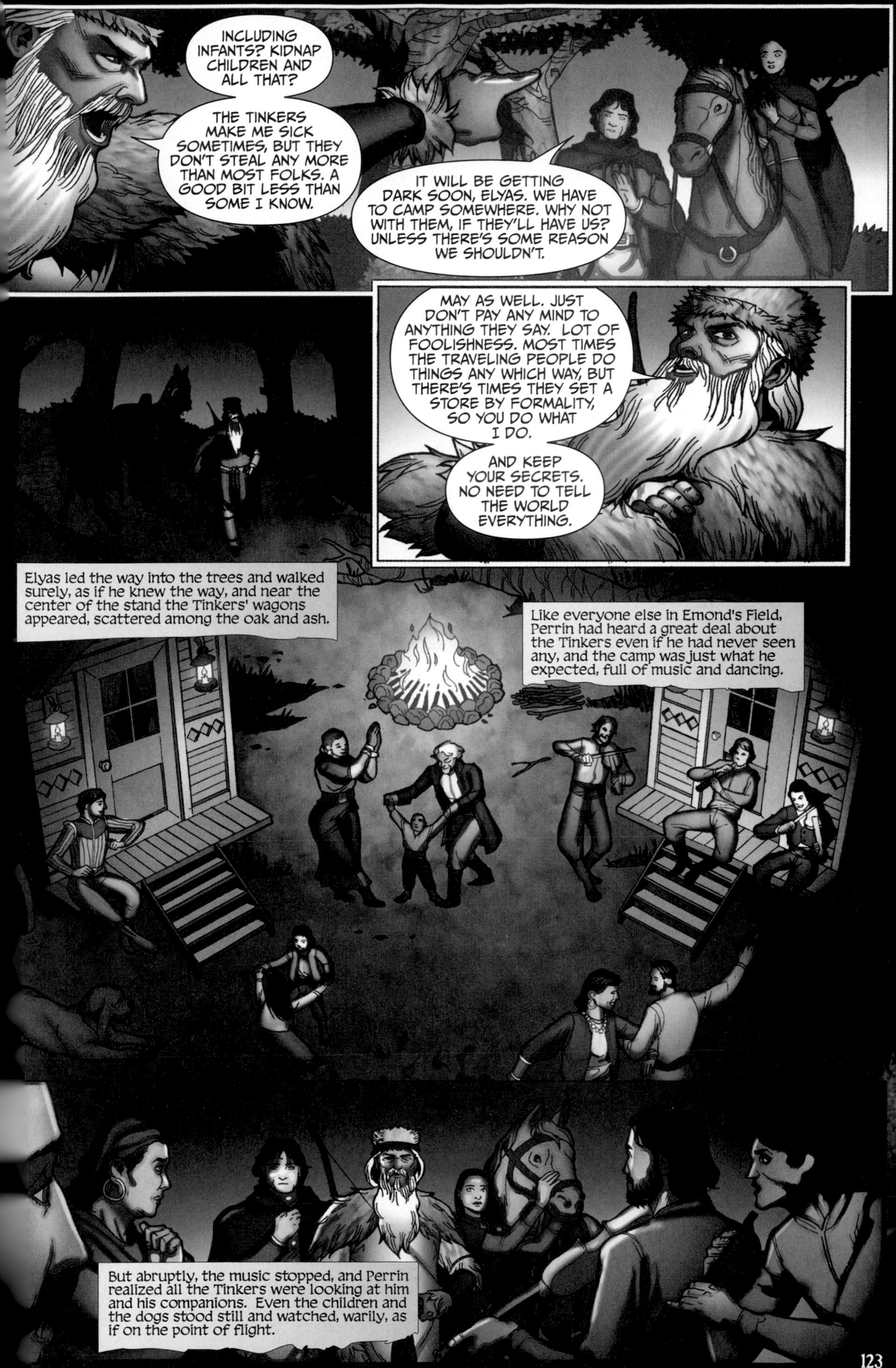
INCLUDING INFANTS? KIDNAP CHILDREN AND ALL THAT?
THE TINKERS MAKE ME SICK SOMETIMES, BUT THEY DON'T STEAL ANY MORE THAN MOST FOLKS. A GOOD BIT LESS THAN SOME I KNOW.
IT WILL BE GETTING DARK SOON, ELYAS. WE HAVE TO CAMP SOMEWHERE. WHY NOT WITH THEM, IF THEY'LL HAVE US? UNLESS THERE'S SOME REASON WE SHOULDN'T.
MAY AS WELL. JUST DON'T PAY ANY MIND TO ANYTHING THEY SAY. LOT OF FOOLISHNESS. MOST TIMES THE TRAVELING PEOPLE DO THINGS ANY WHICH WAY, BUT THERE'S TIMES THEY SET A STORE BY FORMALITY, SO YOU DO WHAT I DO.
AND KEEP YOUR SECRETS. NO NEED TO TELL THE WORLD EVERYTHING.
Elyas led the way into the trees and walked surely, as if he knew the way, and near the center of the stand the Tinkers' wagons appeared, scattered among the oak and ash.
Like everyone else in Emond's Field, Perrin had heard a great deal about the Tinkers even if he had never seen any, and the camp was just what he expected, full of music and dancing.
But abruptly, the music stopped, and Perrin realized all the Tinkers were looking at him and his companions. Even the children and the dogs stood still and watched, warily, as if on the point of flight.

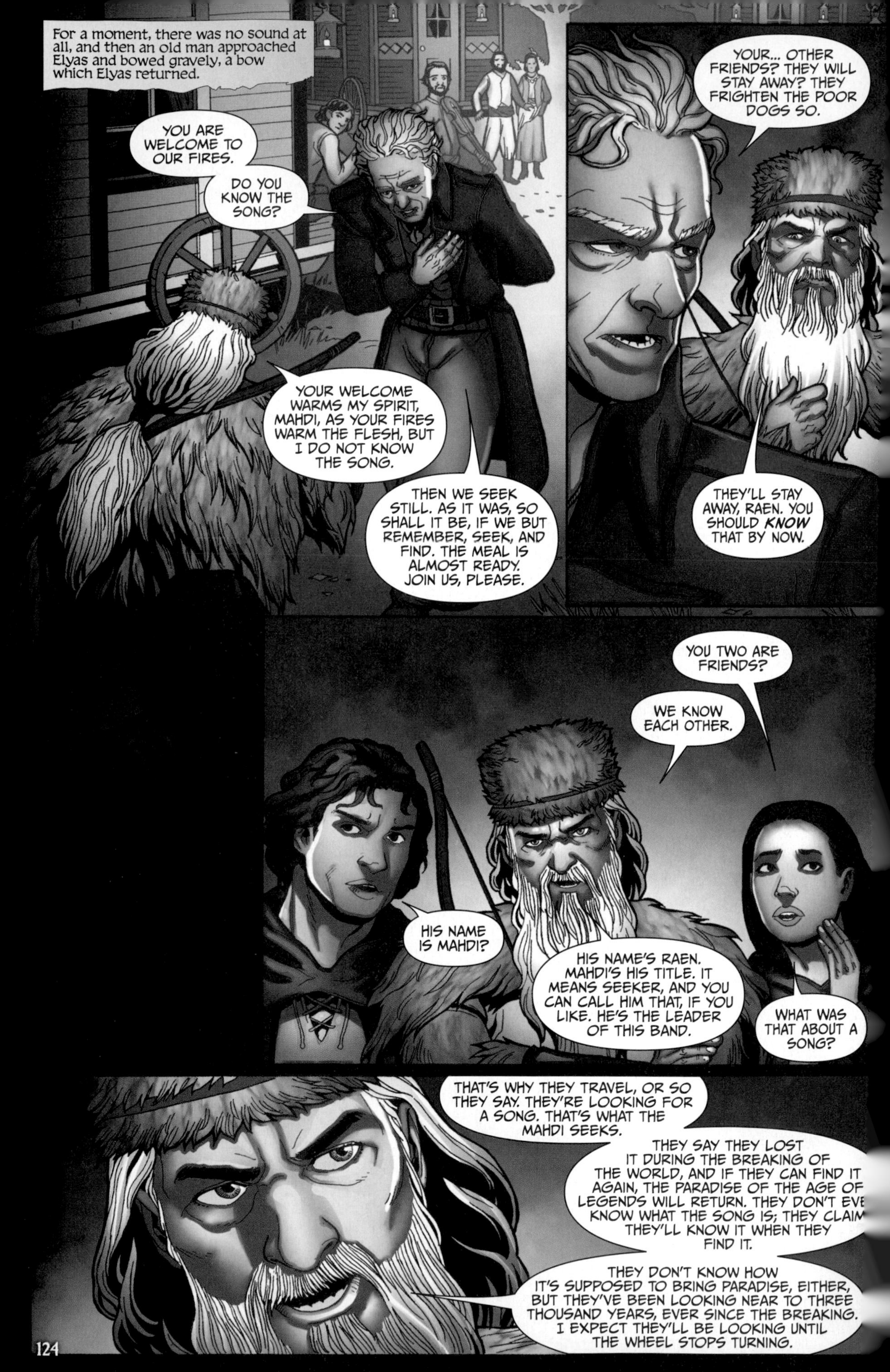

For a moment, there was no sound at all, and then an old man approached Elyas and bowed gravely, a bow which Elyas returned.
YOU ARE WELCOME TO OUR FIRES.
DO YOU KNOW THE SONG?
YOUR WELCOME WARMS MY SPIRIT, MAHDI, AS YOUR FIRES WARM THE FLESH, BUT I DO NOT KNOW THE SONG.
THEN WE SEEK STILL. AS IT WAS, SO SHALL IT BE, IF WE BUT REMEMBER, SEEK, AND FIND. THE MEAL IS ALMOST READY. JOIN US, PLEASE.
YOUR... OTHER FRIENDS? THEY WILL STAY AWAY? THEY FRIGHTEN THE POOR DOGS SO.
THEY'LL STAY AWAY, RAEN. YOU SHOULD *KNOW* THAT BY NOW.
YOU TWO ARE FRIENDS?
WE KNOW EACH OTHER.
HIS NAME IS MAHDI?
HIS NAME'S RAEN. MAHDI'S HIS TITLE. IT MEANS SEEKER, AND YOU CAN CALL HIM THAT, IF YOU LIKE. HE'S THE LEADER OF THIS BAND.
WHAT WAS THAT ABOUT A SONG?
THAT'S WHY THEY TRAVEL, OR SO THEY SAY. THEY'RE LOOKING FOR A SONG. THAT'S WHAT THE MAHDI SEEKS.
THEY SAY THEY LOST IT DURING THE BREAKING OF THE WORLD, AND IF THEY CAN FIND IT AGAIN, THE PARADISE OF THE AGE OF LEGENDS WILL RETURN. THEY DON'T EVE KNOW WHAT THE SONG IS; THEY CLAIM THEY'LL KNOW IT WHEN THEY FIND IT.
THEY DON'T KNOW HOW IT'S SUPPOSED TO BRING PARADISE, EITHER, BUT THEY'VE BEEN LOOKING NEAR TO THREE THOUSAND YEARS, EVER SINCE THE BREAKING. I EXPECT THEY'LL BE LOOKING UNTIL THE WHEEL STOPS TURNING.

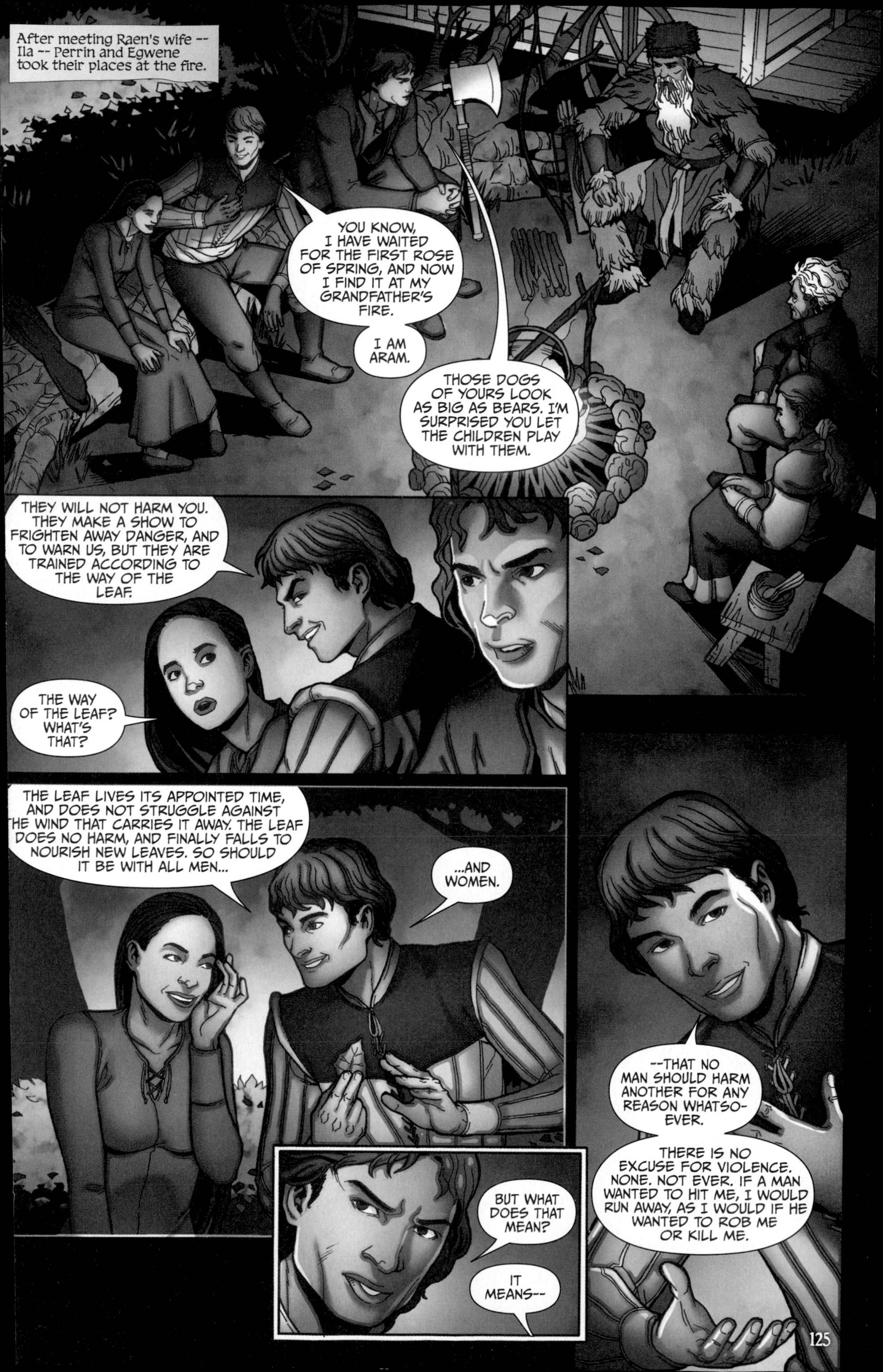
After meeting Raen's wife -- Ila -- Perrin and Egwene took their places at the fire.
YOU KNOW, I HAVE WAITED FOR THE FIRST ROSE OF SPRING, AND NOW I FIND IT AT MY GRANDFATHER'S FIRE.
I AM ARAM.
THOSE DOGS OF YOURS LOOK AS BIG AS BEARS. I'M SURPRISED YOU LET THE CHILDREN PLAY WITH THEM.
THEY WILL NOT HARM YOU. THEY MAKE A SHOW TO FRIGHTEN AWAY DANGER, AND TO WARN US, BUT THEY ARE TRAINED ACCORDING TO THE WAY OF THE LEAF.
THE WAY OF THE LEAF? WHAT'S THAT?
THE LEAF LIVES ITS APPOINTED TIME, AND DOES NOT STRUGGLE AGAINST THE WIND THAT CARRIES IT AWAY. THE LEAF DOES NO HARM, AND FINALLY FALLS TO NOURISH NEW LEAVES. SO SHOULD IT BE WITH ALL MEN...
...AND WOMEN.
BUT WHAT DOES THAT MEAN?
IT MEANS--
--THAT NO MAN SHOULD HARM ANOTHER FOR ANY REASON WHATSO-EVER.
THERE IS NO EXCUSE FOR VIOLENCE. NONE. NOT EVER. IF A MAN WANTED TO HIT ME, I WOULD RUN AWAY, AS I WOULD IF HE WANTED TO ROB ME OR KILL ME.

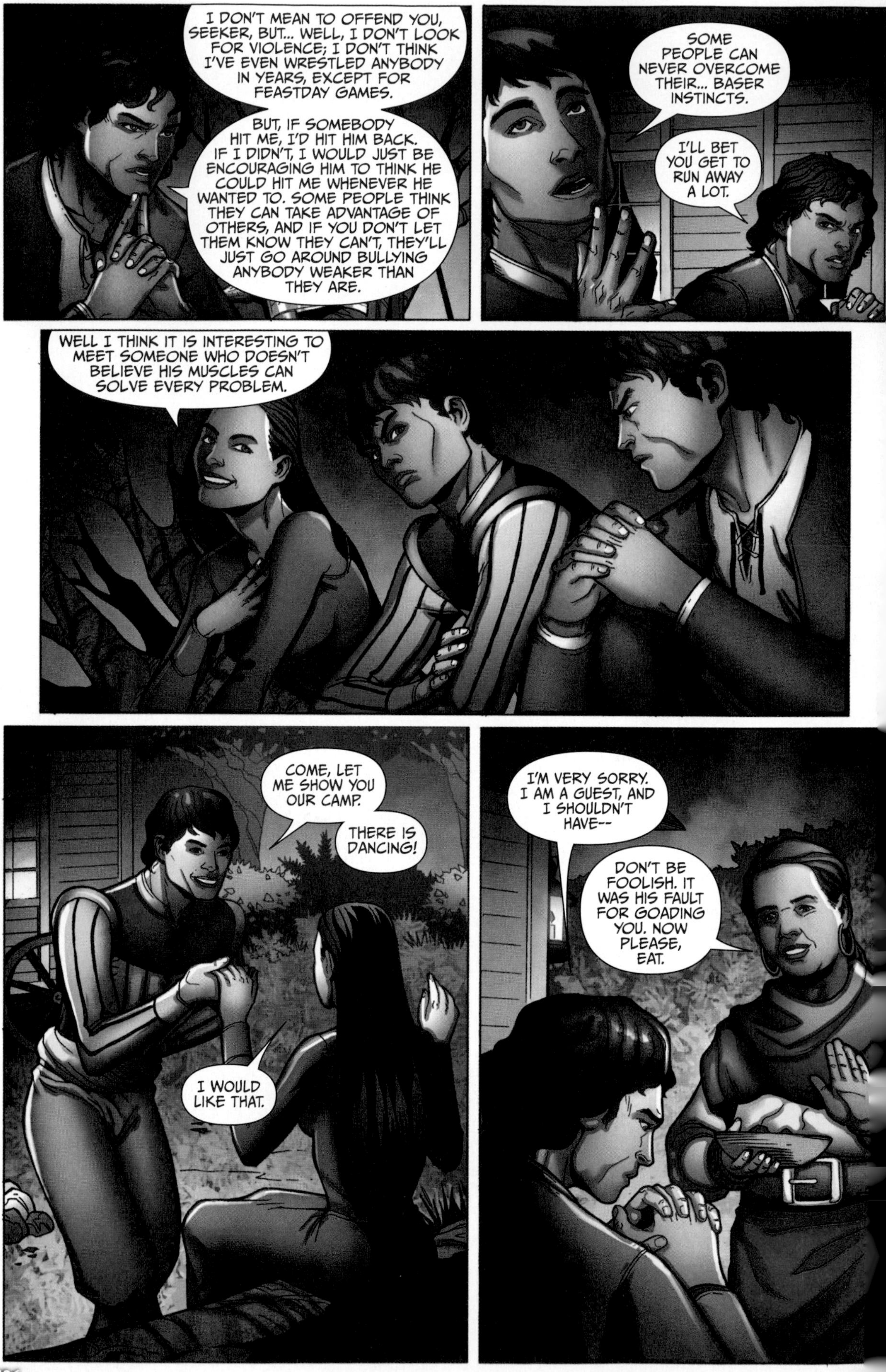
I DON'T MEAN TO OFFEND YOU, SEEKER, BUT... WELL, I DON'T LOOK FOR VIOLENCE; I DON'T THINK I'VE EVEN WRESTLED ANYBODY IN YEARS, EXCEPT FOR FEASTDAY GAMES.
BUT, IF SOMEBODY HIT ME, I'D HIT HIM BACK. IF I DIDN'T, I WOULD JUST BE ENCOURAGING HIM TO THINK HE COULD HIT ME WHENEVER HE WANTED TO. SOME PEOPLE THINK THEY CAN TAKE ADVANTAGE OF OTHERS, AND IF YOU DON'T LET THEM KNOW THEY CAN'T, THEY'LL JUST GO AROUND BULLYING ANYBODY WEAKER THAN THEY ARE.
SOME PEOPLE CAN NEVER OVERCOME THEIR... BASER INSTINCTS.
I'LL BET YOU GET TO RUN AWAY A LOT.
WELL I THINK IT IS INTERESTING TO MEET SOMEONE WHO DOESN'T BELIEVE HIS MUSCLES CAN SOLVE EVERY PROBLEM.
COME, LET ME SHOW YOU OUR CAMP.
THERE IS DANCING!
I WOULD LIKE THAT.
I'M VERY SORRY. I AM A GUEST, AND I SHOULDN'T HAVE--
DON'T BE FOOLISH. IT WAS HIS FAULT FOR GOADING YOU. NOW PLEASE, EAT.

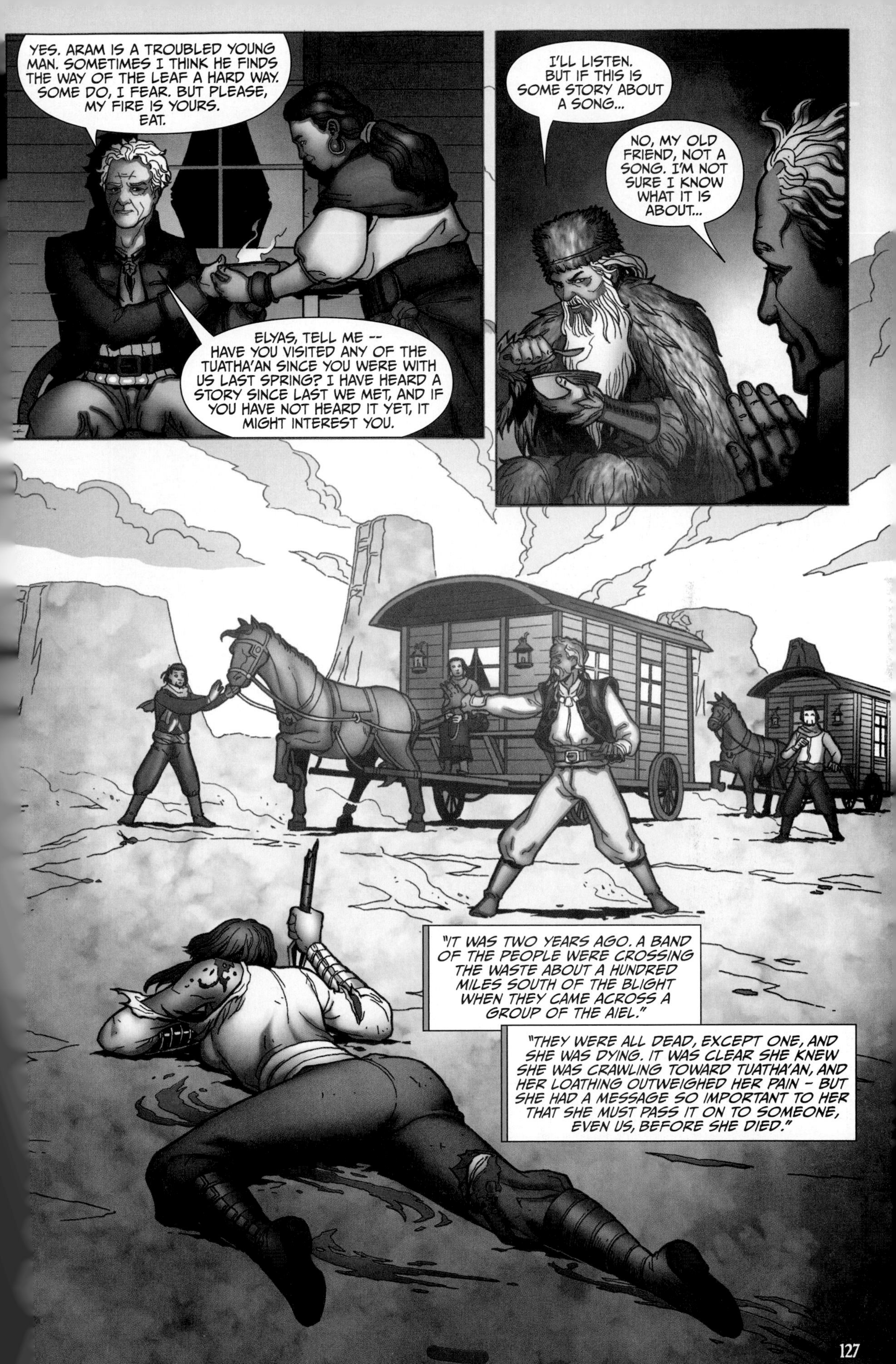
YES. ARAM IS A TROUBLED YOUNG MAN. SOMETIMES I THINK HE FINDS THE WAY OF THE LEAF A HARD WAY. SOME DO, I FEAR. BUT PLEASE, MY FIRE IS YOURS. EAT.
ELYAS, TELL ME -- HAVE YOU VISITED ANY OF THE TUATHA'AN SINCE YOU WERE WITH US LAST SPRING? I HAVE HEARD A STORY SINCE LAST WE MET, AND IF YOU HAVE NOT HEARD IT YET, IT MIGHT INTEREST YOU.
I'LL LISTEN. BUT IF THIS IS SOME STORY ABOUT A SONG...
NO, MY OLD FRIEND, NOT A SONG. I'M NOT SURE I KNOW WHAT IT IS ABOUT...
"IT WAS TWO YEARS AGO. A BAND OF THE PEOPLE WERE CROSSING THE WASTE ABOUT A HUNDRED MILES SOUTH OF THE BLIGHT WHEN THEY CAME ACROSS A GROUP OF THE AIEL."
"THEY WERE ALL DEAD, EXCEPT ONE, AND SHE WAS DYING. IT WAS CLEAR SHE KNEW SHE WAS CRAWLING TOWARD TUATHA'AN, AND HER LOATHING OUTWEIGHED HER PAIN – BUT SHE HAD A MESSAGE SO IMPORTANT TO HER THAT SHE MUST PASS IT ON TO SOMEONE, EVEN US, BEFORE SHE DIED."

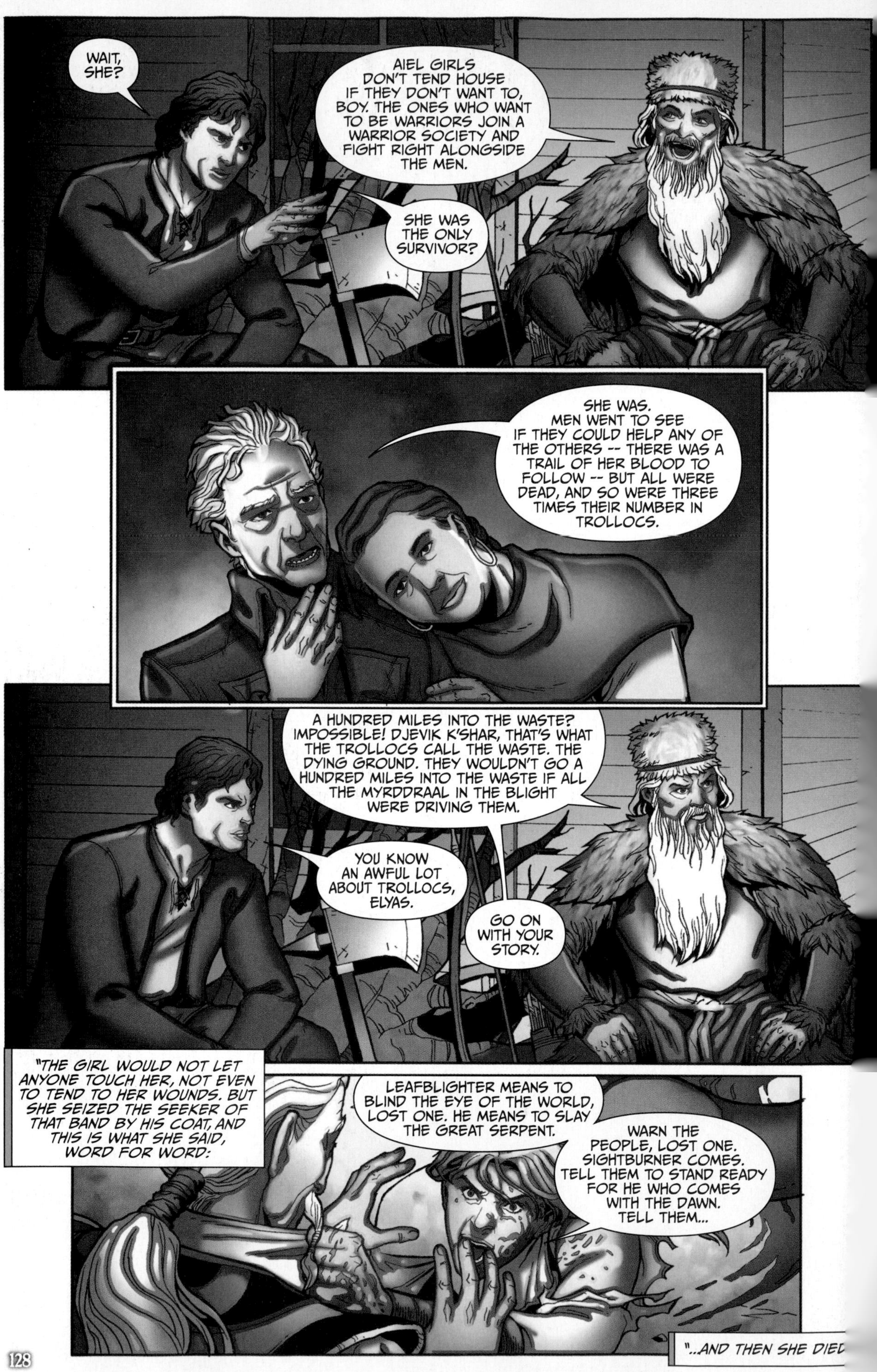
WAIT, SHE?
AIEL GIRLS DON'T TEND HOUSE IF THEY DON'T WANT TO, BOY. THE ONES WHO WANT TO BE WARRIORS JOIN A WARRIOR SOCIETY AND FIGHT RIGHT ALONGSIDE THE MEN.
SHE WAS THE ONLY SURVIVOR?
SHE WAS. MEN WENT TO SEE IF THEY COULD HELP ANY OF THE OTHERS -- THERE WAS A TRAIL OF HER BLOOD TO FOLLOW -- BUT ALL WERE DEAD, AND SO WERE THREE TIMES THEIR NUMBER IN TROLLOCS.
A HUNDRED MILES INTO THE WASTE? IMPOSSIBLE! DJEVIK K'SHAR, THAT'S WHAT THE TROLLOCS CALL THE WASTE. THE DYING GROUND. THEY WOULDN'T GO A HUNDRED MILES INTO THE WASTE IF ALL THE MYRDDRAAL IN THE BLIGHT WERE DRIVING THEM.
YOU KNOW AN AWFUL LOT ABOUT TROLLOCS, ELYAS.
GO ON WITH YOUR STORY.
"THE GIRL WOULD NOT LET ANYONE TOUCH HER, NOT EVEN TO TEND TO HER WOUNDS. BUT SHE SEIZED THE SEEKER OF THAT BAND BY HIS COAT, AND THIS IS WHAT SHE SAID, WORD FOR WORD:
LEAFBLIGHTER MEANS TO BLIND THE EYE OF THE WORLD, LOST ONE. HE MEANS TO SLAY THE GREAT SERPENT.
WARN THE PEOPLE, LOST ONE. SIGHTBURNER COMES. TELL THEM TO STAND READY FOR HE WHO COMES WITH THE DAWN. TELL THEM...
"...AND THEN SHE DIED

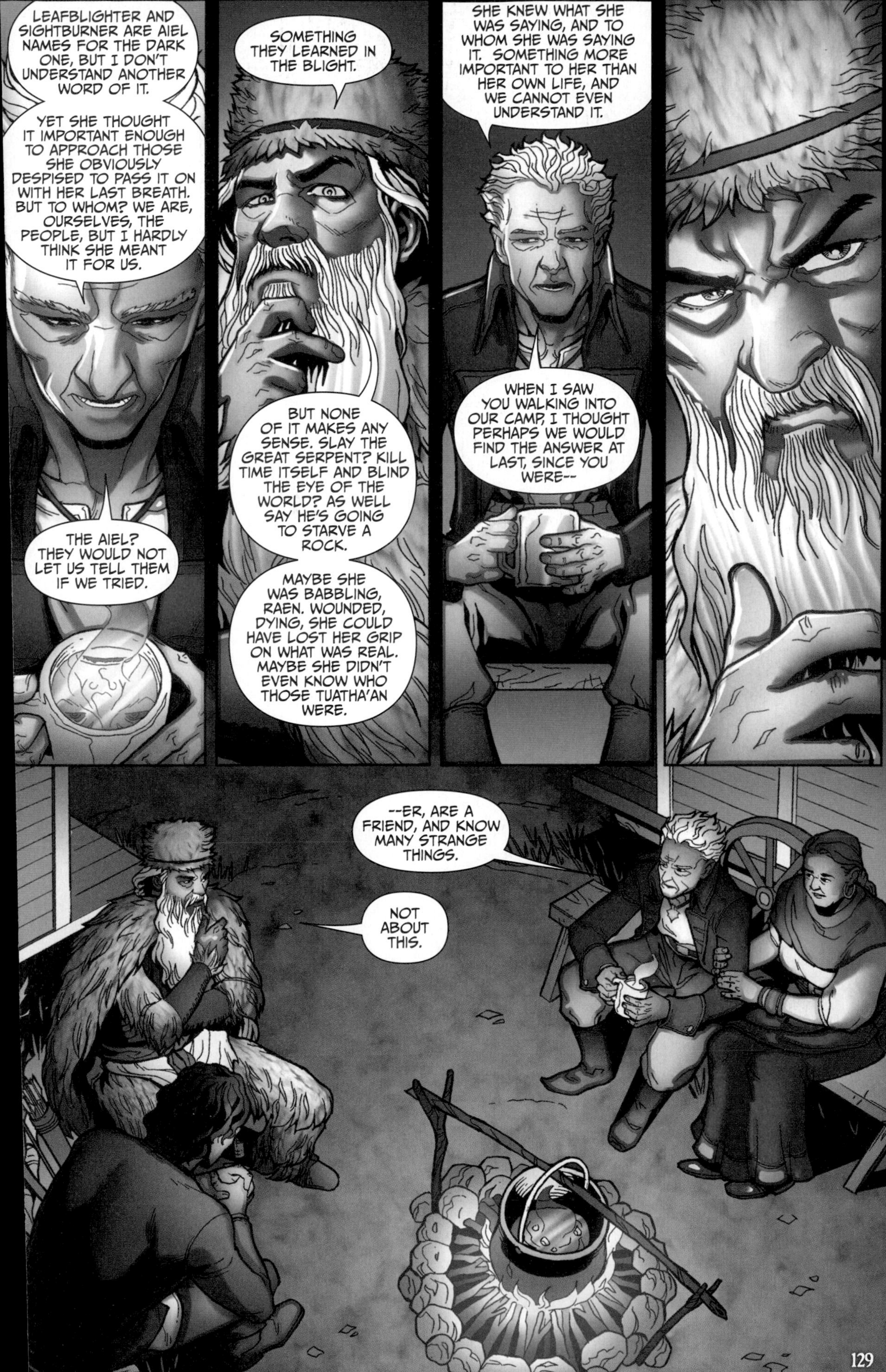
LEAFBLIGHTER AND SIGHTBURNER ARE AIEL NAMES FOR THE DARK ONE, BUT I DON'T UNDERSTAND ANOTHER WORD OF IT.
YET SHE THOUGHT IT IMPORTANT ENOUGH TO APPROACH THOSE SHE OBVIOUSLY DESPISED TO PASS IT ON WITH HER LAST BREATH. BUT TO WHOM? WE ARE, OURSELVES, THE PEOPLE, BUT I HARDLY THINK SHE MEANT IT FOR US.
THE AIEL? THEY WOULD NOT LET US TELL THEM IF WE TRIED.
SOMETHING THEY LEARNED IN THE BLIGHT.
BUT NONE OF IT MAKES ANY SENSE. SLAY THE GREAT SERPENT? KILL TIME ITSELF AND BLIND THE EYE OF THE WORLD? AS WELL SAY HE'S GOING TO STARVE A ROCK.
MAYBE SHE WAS BABBLING, RAEN. WOUNDED, DYING, SHE COULD HAVE LOST HER GRIP ON WHAT WAS REAL. MAYBE SHE DIDN'T EVEN KNOW WHO THOSE TUATHA'AN WERE.
SHE KNEW WHAT SHE WAS SAYING, AND TO WHOM SHE WAS SAYING IT. SOMETHING MORE IMPORTANT TO HER THAN HER OWN LIFE, AND WE CANNOT EVEN UNDERSTAND IT.
WHEN I SAW YOU WALKING INTO OUR CAMP, I THOUGHT PERHAPS WE WOULD FIND THE ANSWER AT LAST, SINCE YOU WERE--
--ER, ARE A FRIEND, AND KNOW MANY STRANGE THINGS.
NOT ABOUT THIS.

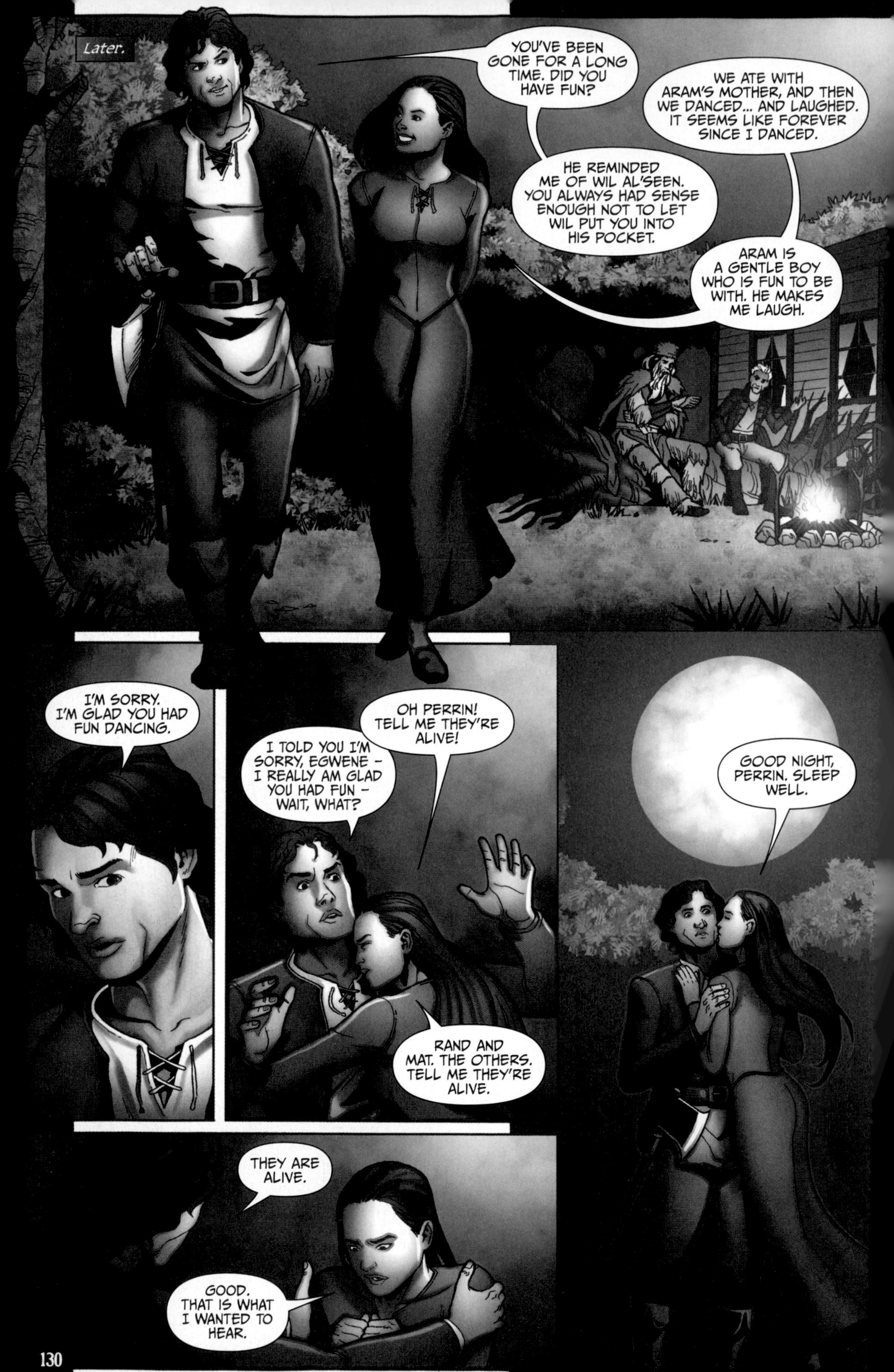
Later.
YOU'VE BEEN GONE FOR A LONG TIME. DID YOU HAVE FUN?
WE ATE WITH ARAM'S MOTHER, AND THEN WE DANCED... AND LAUGHED. IT SEEMS LIKE FOREVER SINCE I DANCED.
HE REMINDED ME OF WIL AL'SEEN. YOU ALWAYS HAD SENSE ENOUGH NOT TO LET WIL PUT YOU INTO HIS POCKET.
ARAM IS A GENTLE BOY WHO IS FUN TO BE WITH. HE MAKES ME LAUGH.
I'M SORRY. I'M GLAD YOU HAD FUN DANCING.
OH PERRIN! TELL ME THEY'RE ALIVE!
I TOLD YOU I'M SORRY, EGWENE - I REALLY AM GLAD YOU HAD FUN - WAIT, WHAT?
RAND AND MAT. THE OTHERS. TELL ME THEY'RE ALIVE.
GOOD NIGHT, PERRIN. SLEEP WELL.
THEY ARE ALIVE.
GOOD. THAT IS WHAT I WANTED TO HEAR.

chapter six

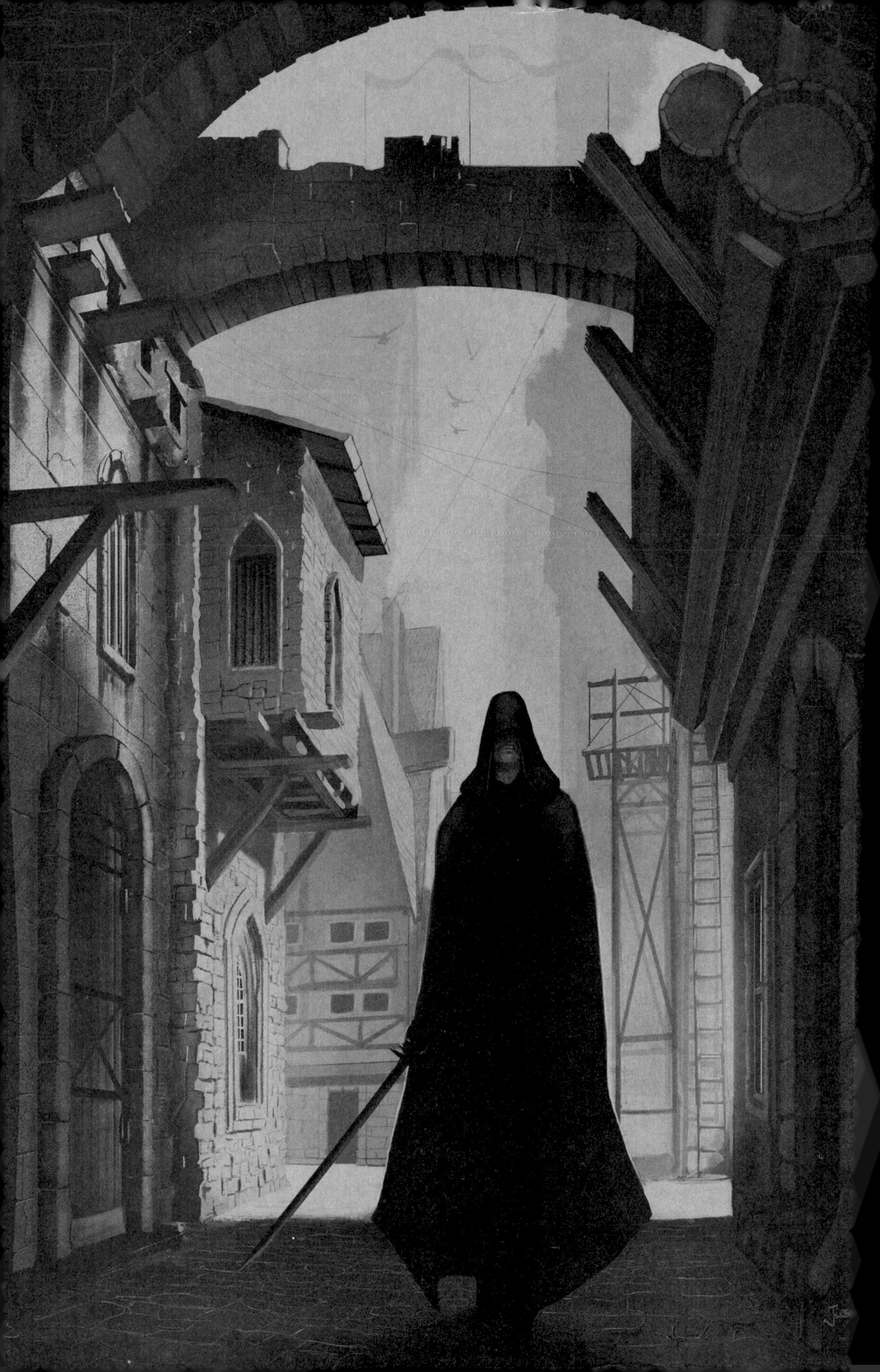

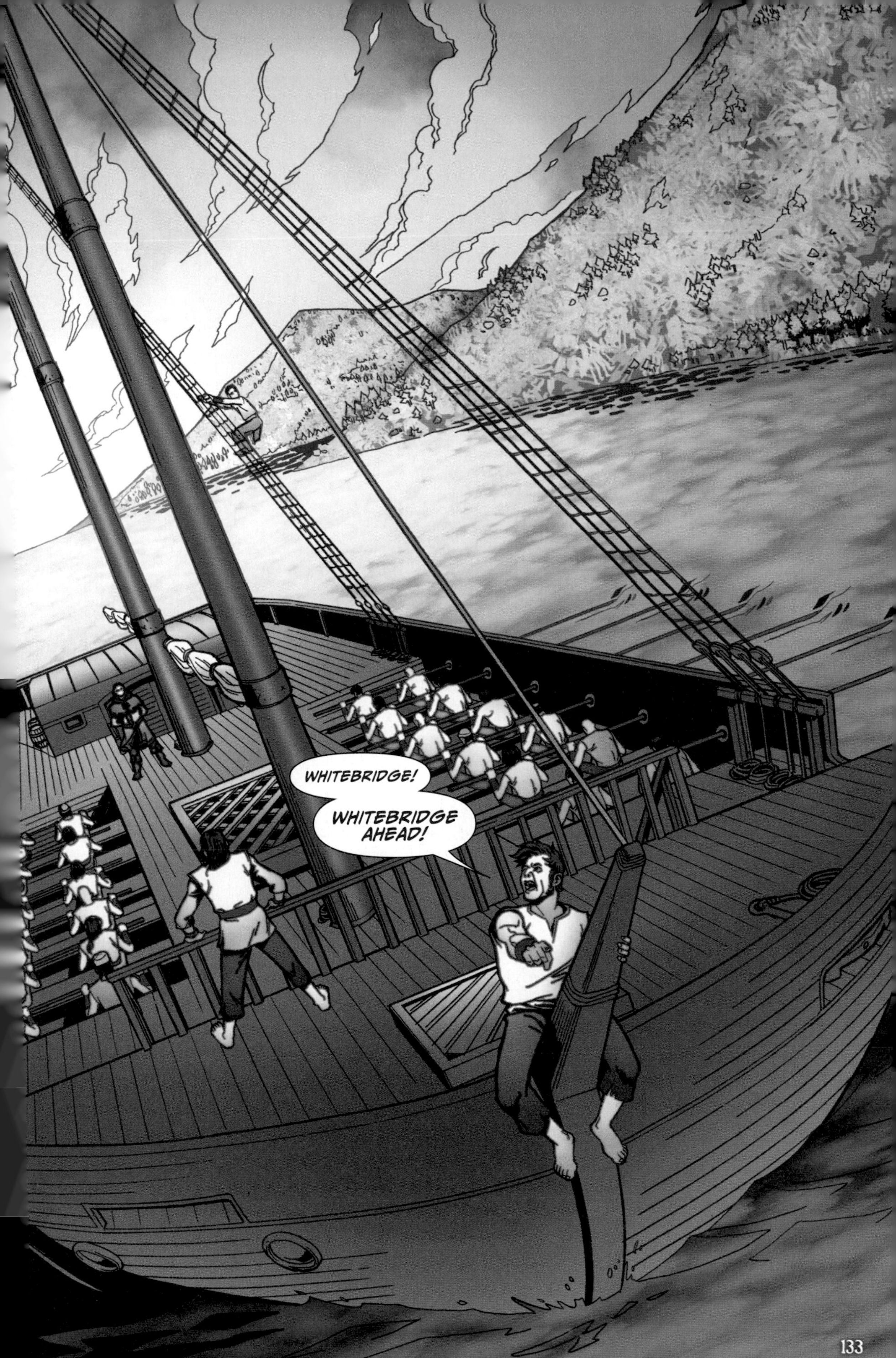
WHITEBRIDGE!
WHITEBRIDGE AHEAD!

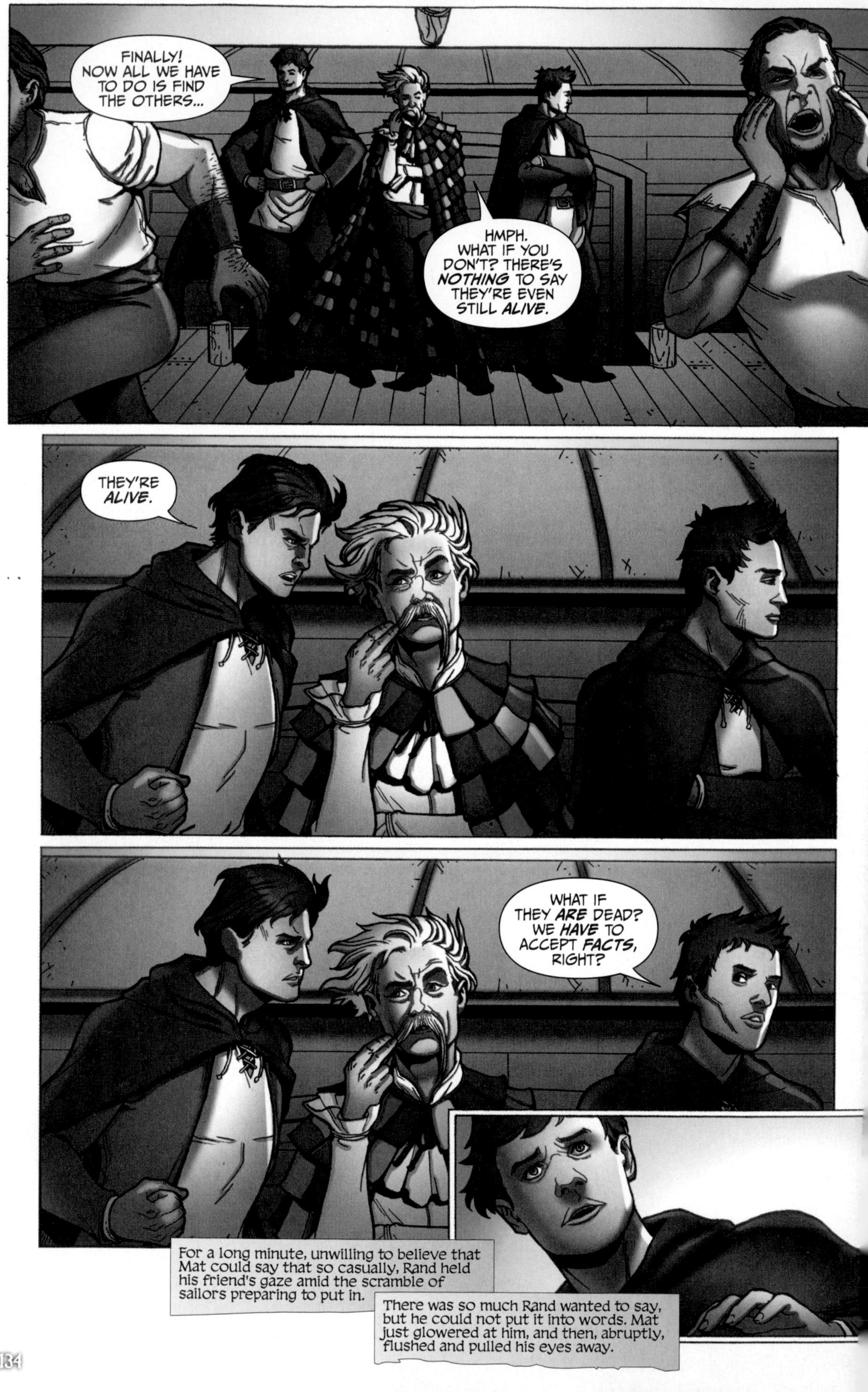
FINALLY! NOW ALL WE HAVE TO DO IS FIND THE OTHERS...
HMPH. WHAT IF YOU DON'T? THERE'S NOTHING TO SAY THEY'RE EVEN STILL ALIVE.
THEY'RE ALIVE.
WHAT IF THEY ARE DEAD? WE HAVE TO ACCEPT FACTS, RIGHT?
For a long minute, unwilling to believe that Mat could say that so casually, Rand held his friend's gaze amid the scramble of sailors preparing to put in.
There was so much Rand wanted to say, but he could not put it into words. Mat just glowered at him, and then, abruptly, flushed and pulled his eyes away.

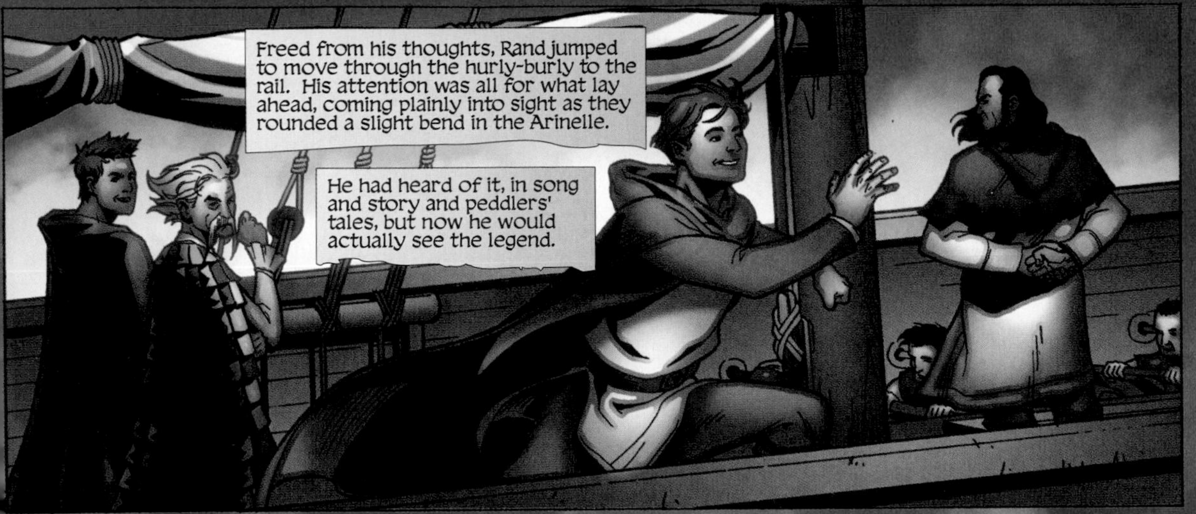
Freed from his thoughts, Rand jumped to move through the hurly-burly to the rail. His attention was all for what lay ahead, coming plainly into sight as they rounded a slight bend in the Arinelle.
He had heard of it, in song and story and peddlers' tales, but now he would actually see the legend.

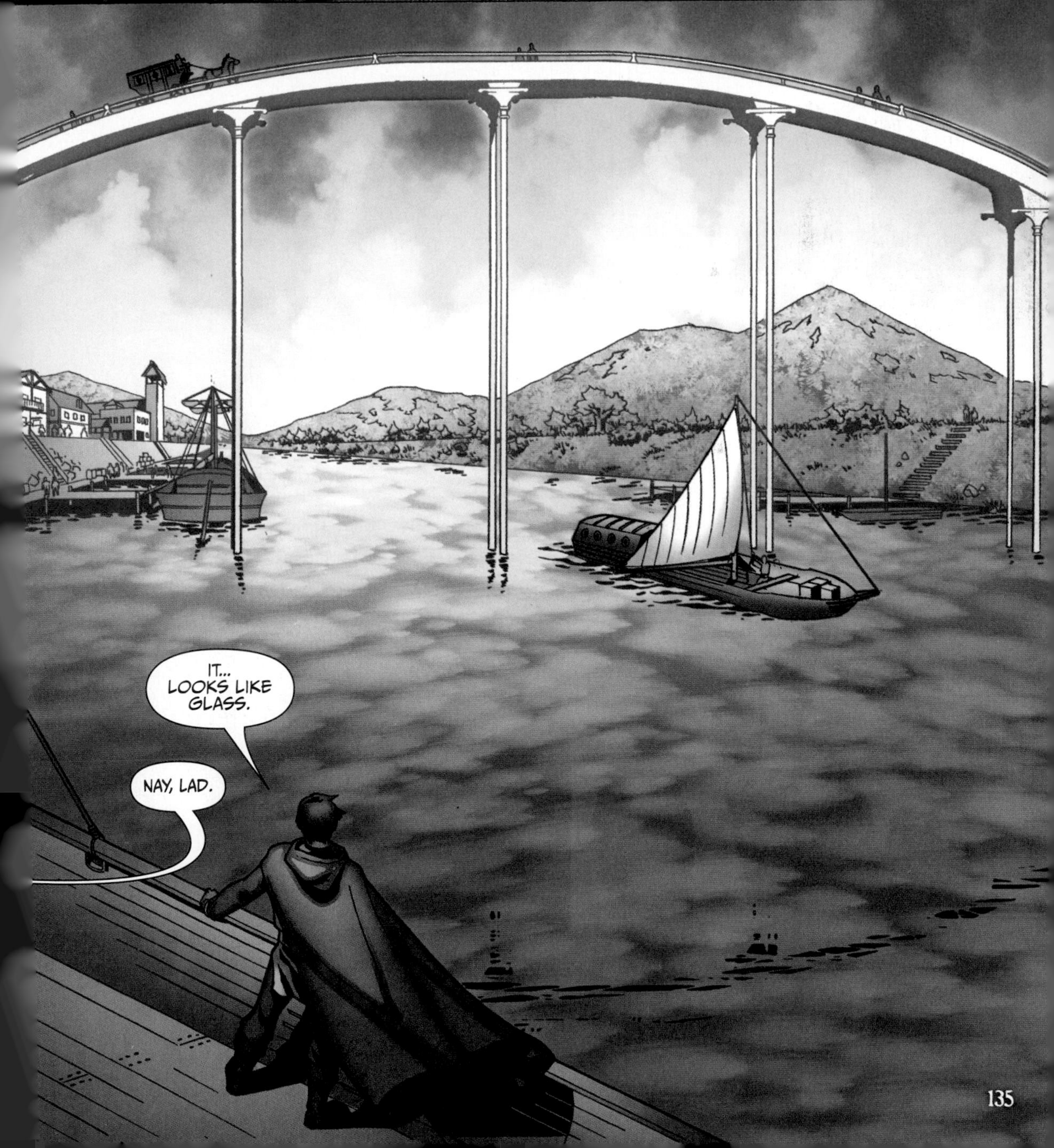
IT... LOOKS LIKE GLASS.
NAY, LAD.

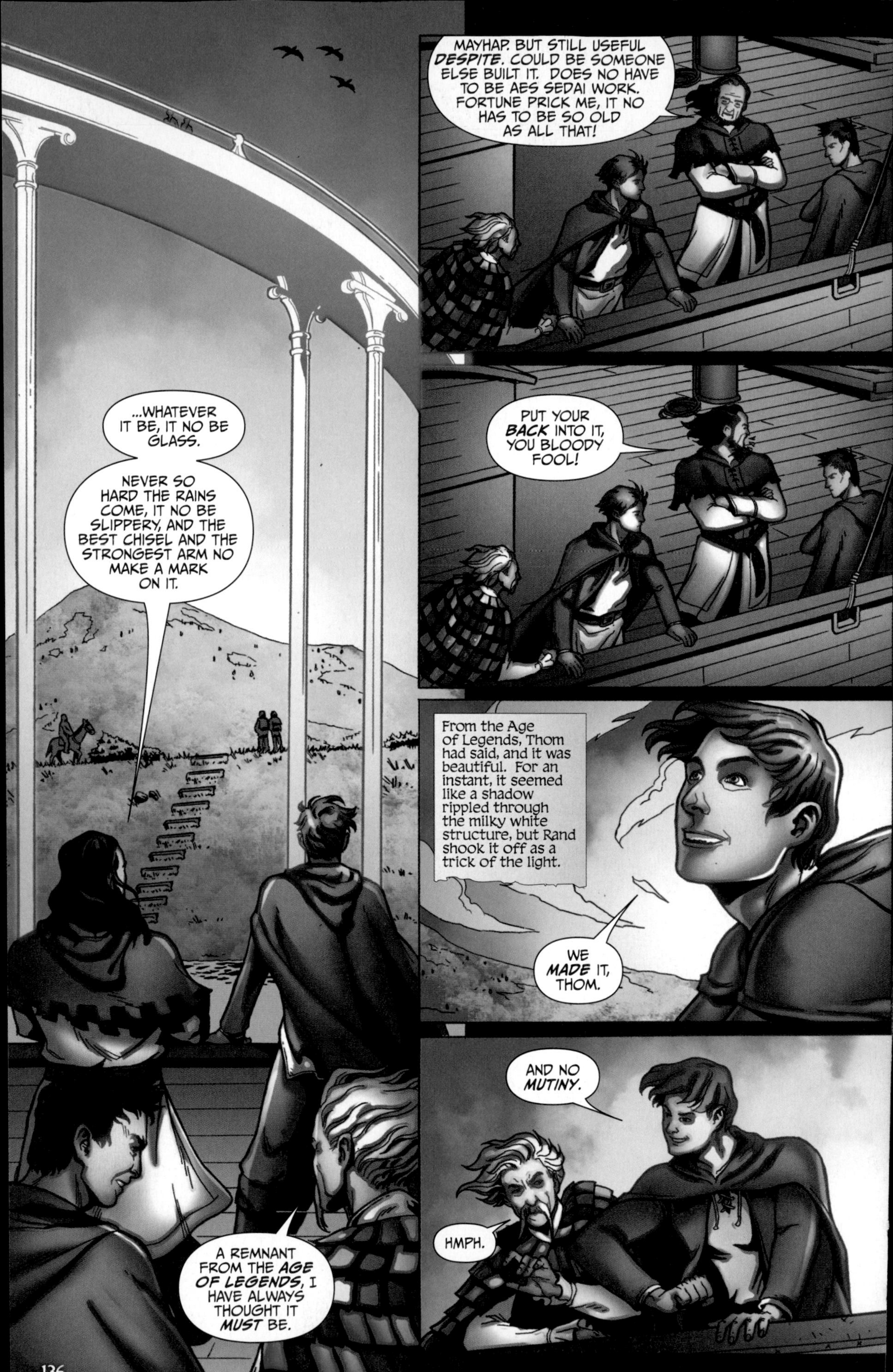

...WHATEVER IT BE, IT NO BE GLASS.
NEVER SO HARD THE RAINS COME, IT NO BE SLIPPERY, AND THE BEST CHISEL AND THE STRONGEST ARM NO MAKE A MARK ON IT.
A REMNANT FROM THE AGE OF LEGENDS, I HAVE ALWAYS THOUGHT IT MUST BE.
MAYHAP. BUT STILL USEFUL DESPITE. COULD BE SOMEONE ELSE BUILT IT. DOES NO HAVE TO BE AES SEDAI WORK. FORTUNE PRICK ME, IT NO HAS TO BE SO OLD AS ALL THAT!
PUT YOUR BACK INTO IT, YOU BLOODY FOOL!
From the Age of Legends, Thom had said, and it was beautiful. For an instant, it seemed like a shadow rippled through the milky white structure, but Rand shook it off as a trick of the light.
WE MADE IT, THOM.
AND NO MUTINY.
HMPH.

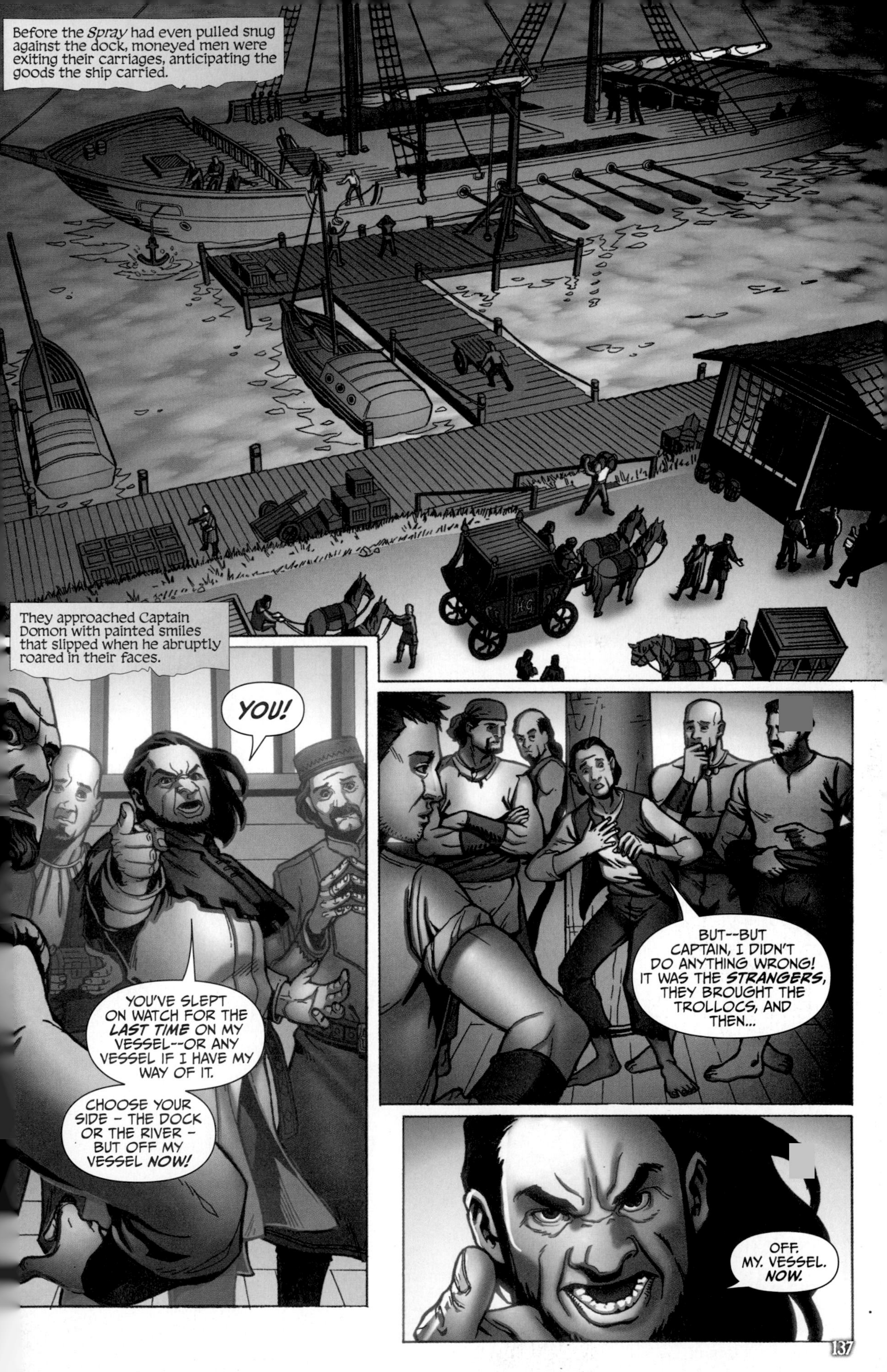

Before the *Spray* had even pulled snug against the dock, moneyed men were exiting their carriages, anticipating the goods the ship carried.
They approached Captain Domon with painted smiles that slipped when he abruptly roared in their faces.
YOU!
YOU'VE SLEPT ON WATCH FOR THE *LAST TIME* ON MY VESSEL--OR ANY VESSEL IF I HAVE MY WAY OF IT.
CHOOSE YOUR SIDE – THE DOCK OR THE RIVER – BUT OFF MY VESSEL *NOW!*
BUT--BUT CAPTAIN, I DIDN'T DO ANYTHING WRONG! IT WAS THE *STRANGERS*, THEY BROUGHT THE TROLLOCS, AND THEN...
OFF. MY. VESSEL. *NOW.*

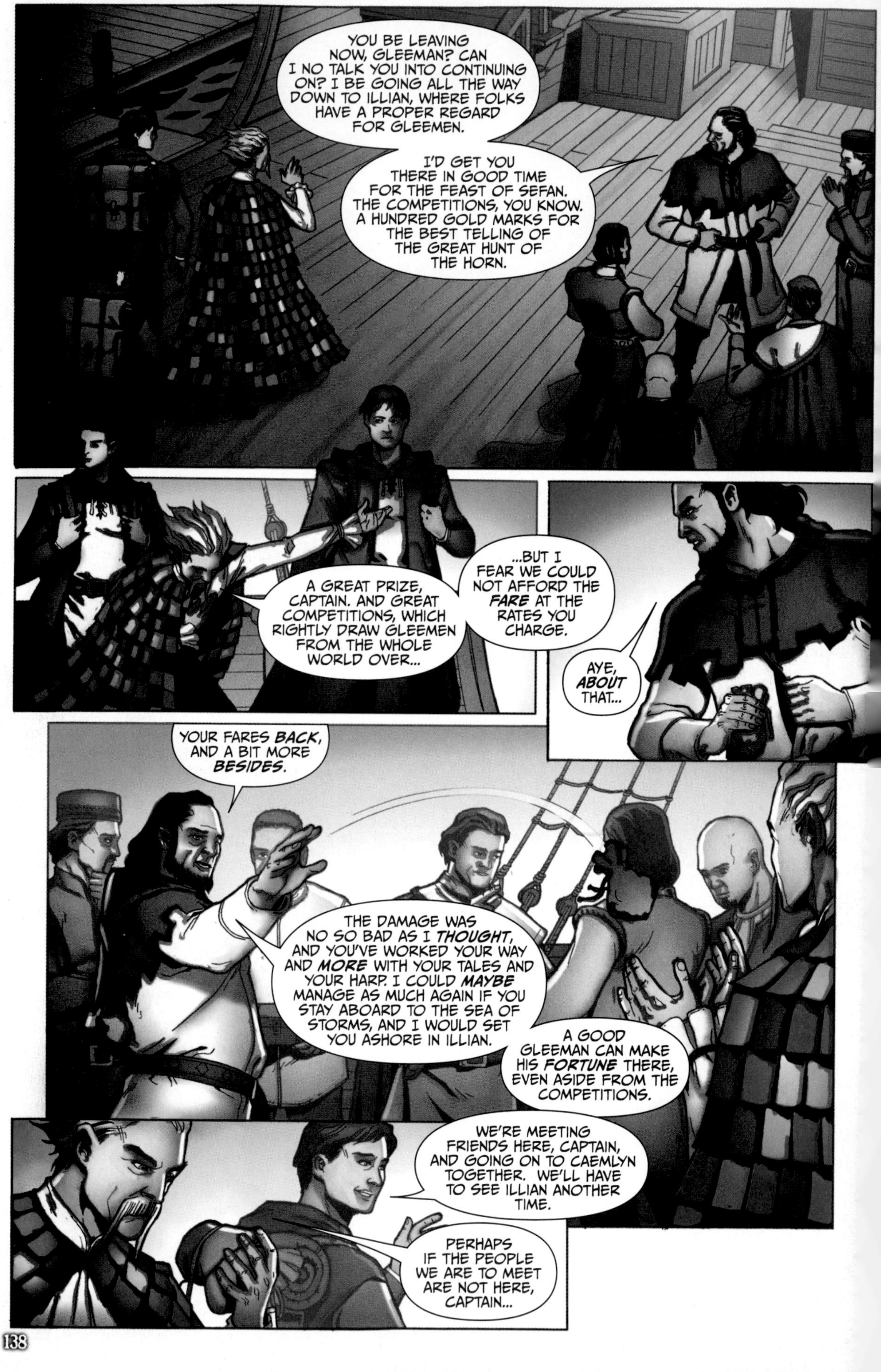
YOU BE LEAVING NOW, GLEEMAN? CAN I NO TALK YOU INTO CONTINUING ON? I BE GOING ALL THE WAY DOWN TO ILLIAN, WHERE FOLKS HAVE A PROPER REGARD FOR GLEEMEN.
I'D GET YOU THERE IN GOOD TIME FOR THE FEAST OF SEFAN. THE COMPETITIONS, YOU KNOW. A HUNDRED GOLD MARKS FOR THE BEST TELLING OF THE GREAT HUNT OF THE HORN.
A GREAT PRIZE, CAPTAIN. AND GREAT COMPETITIONS, WHICH RIGHTLY DRAW GLEEMEN FROM THE WHOLE WORLD OVER...
...BUT I FEAR WE COULD NOT AFFORD THE *FARE* AT THE RATES YOU CHARGE.
AYE, *ABOUT* THAT...
YOUR FARES *BACK*, AND A BIT MORE *BESIDES*.
THE DAMAGE WAS NO SO BAD AS I *THOUGHT*, AND YOU'VE WORKED YOUR WAY AND *MORE* WITH YOUR TALES AND YOUR HARP. I COULD *MAYBE* MANAGE AS MUCH AGAIN IF YOU STAY ABOARD TO THE SEA OF STORMS, AND I WOULD SET YOU ASHORE IN ILLIAN.
A GOOD GLEEMAN CAN MAKE HIS *FORTUNE* THERE, EVEN ASIDE FROM THE COMPETITIONS.
WE'RE MEETING FRIENDS HERE, CAPTAIN, AND GOING ON TO CAEMLYN TOGETHER. WE'LL HAVE TO SEE ILLIAN ANOTHER TIME.
PERHAPS IF THE PEOPLE WE ARE TO MEET ARE NOT HERE, CAPTAIN...

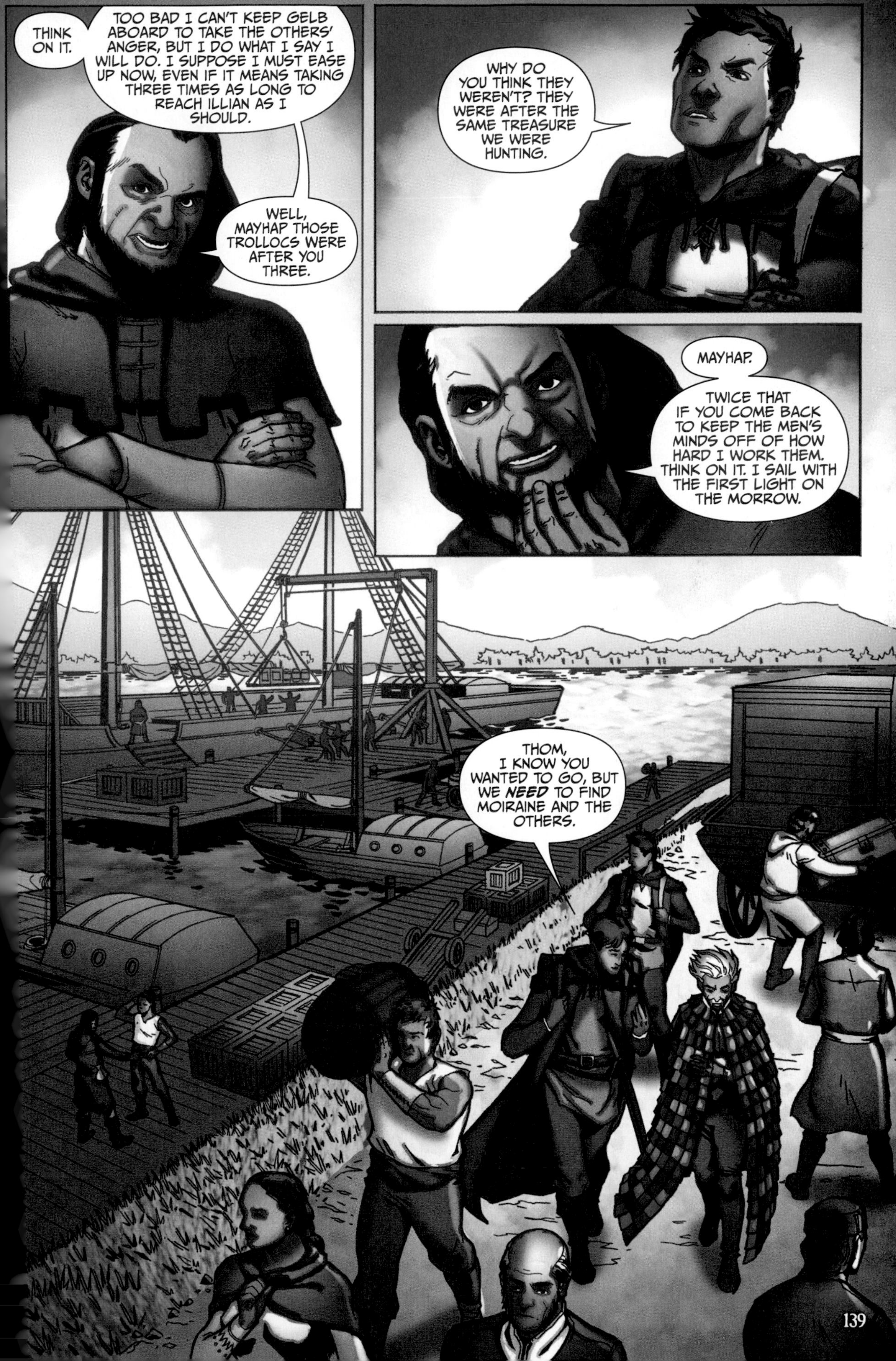
THINK ON IT.
TOO BAD I CAN'T KEEP GELB ABOARD TO TAKE THE OTHERS' ANGER, BUT I DO WHAT I SAY I WILL DO. I SUPPOSE I MUST EASE UP NOW, EVEN IF IT MEANS TAKING THREE TIMES AS LONG TO REACH ILLIAN AS I SHOULD.
WELL, MAYHAP THOSE TROLLOCS WERE AFTER YOU THREE.
WHY DO YOU THINK THEY WEREN'T? THEY WERE AFTER THE SAME TREASURE WE WERE HUNTING.
MAYHAP.
TWICE THAT IF YOU COME BACK TO KEEP THE MEN'S MINDS OFF OF HOW HARD I WORK THEM. THINK ON IT. I SAIL WITH THE FIRST LIGHT ON THE MORROW.
THOM, I KNOW YOU WANTED TO GO, BUT WE ***NEED*** TO FIND MOIRAINE AND THE OTHERS.

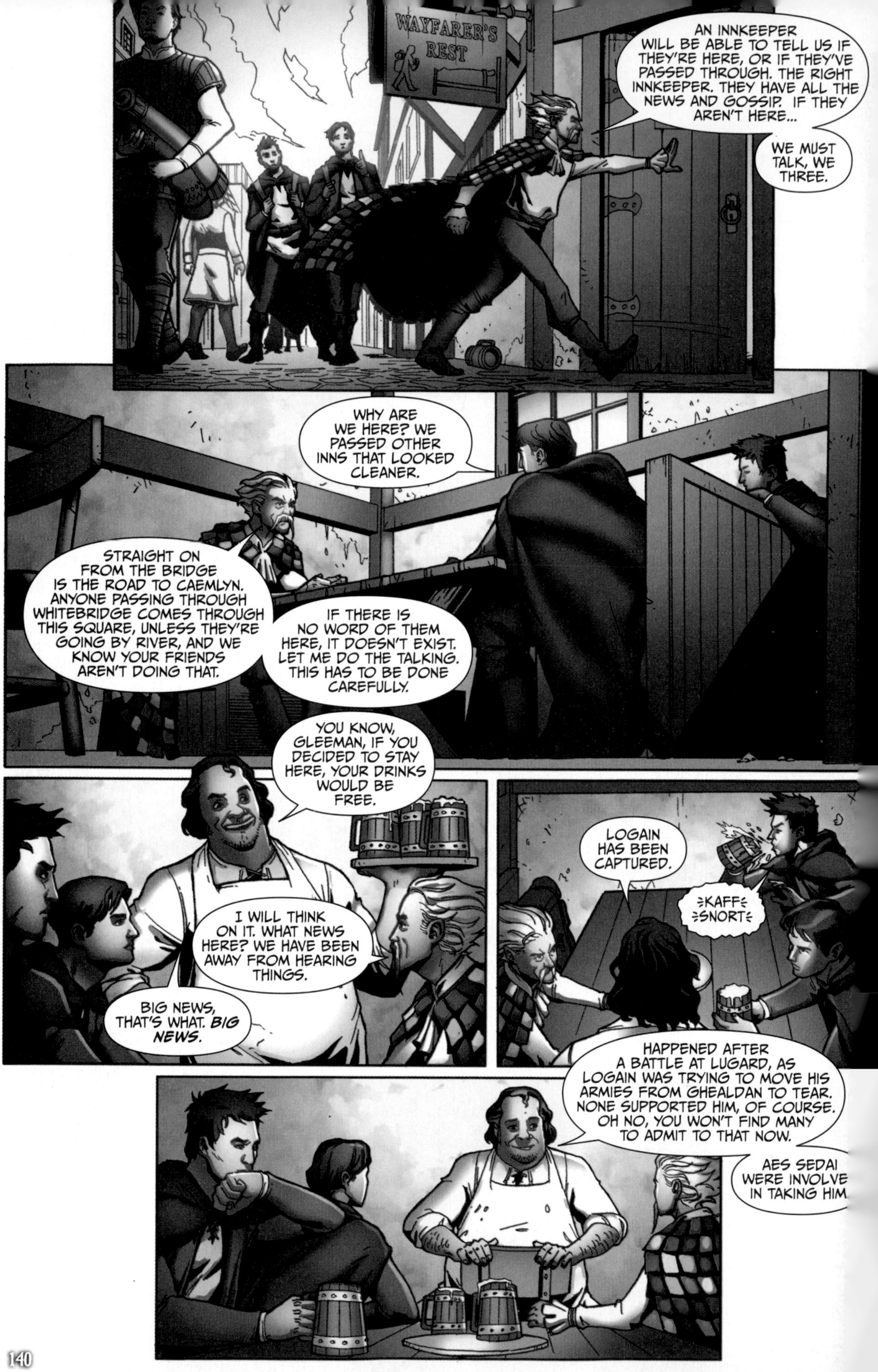
WAYFARER'S REST
AN INNKEEPER WILL BE ABLE TO TELL US IF THEY'RE HERE, OR IF THEY'VE PASSED THROUGH. THE RIGHT INNKEEPER. THEY HAVE ALL THE NEWS AND GOSSIP. IF THEY AREN'T HERE...
WE MUST TALK, WE THREE.
WHY ARE WE HERE? WE PASSED OTHER INNS THAT LOOKED CLEANER.
STRAIGHT ON FROM THE BRIDGE IS THE ROAD TO CAEMLYN. ANYONE PASSING THROUGH WHITEBRIDGE COMES THROUGH THIS SQUARE, UNLESS THEY'RE GOING BY RIVER, AND WE KNOW YOUR FRIENDS AREN'T DOING THAT.
IF THERE IS NO WORD OF THEM HERE, IT DOESN'T EXIST. LET ME DO THE TALKING. THIS HAS TO BE DONE CAREFULLY.
YOU KNOW, GLEEMAN, IF YOU DECIDED TO STAY HERE, YOUR DRINKS WOULD BE FREE.
I WILL THINK ON IT. WHAT NEWS HERE? WE HAVE BEEN AWAY FROM HEARING THINGS.
BIG NEWS, THAT'S WHAT. *BIG NEWS.*
LOGAIN HAS BEEN CAPTURED.
KAFF SNORT
HAPPENED AFTER A BATTLE AT LUGARD, AS LOGAIN WAS TRYING TO MOVE HIS ARMIES FROM GHEALDAN TO TEAR. NONE SUPPORTED HIM, OF COURSE. OH NO, YOU WON'T FIND MANY TO ADMIT TO THAT NOW.
AES SEDAI WERE INVOLVE IN TAKING HIM

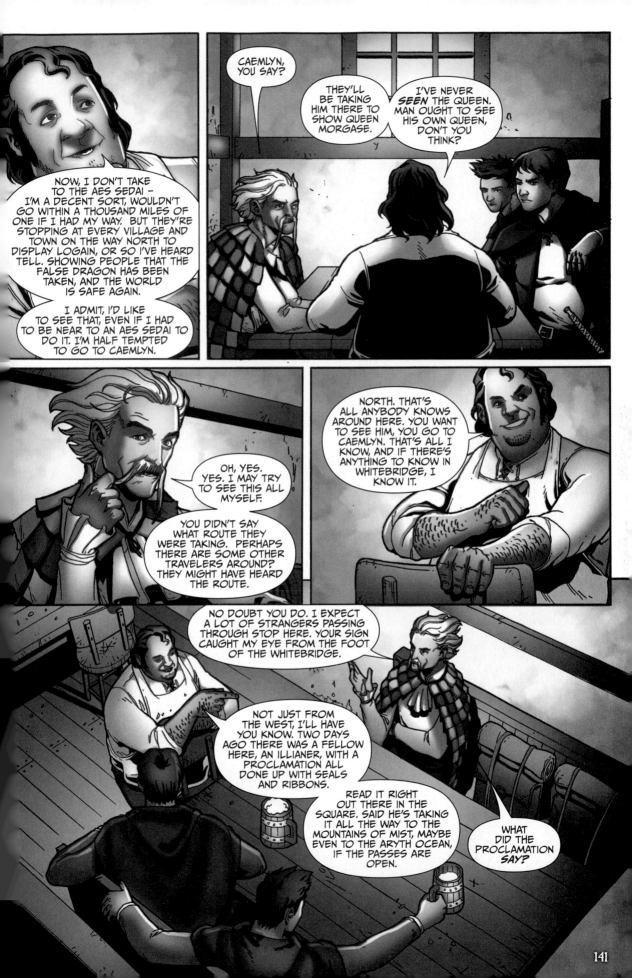

CAEMLYN, YOU SAY?

THEY'LL BE TAKING HIM THERE TO SHOW QUEEN MORGASE.

I'VE NEVER *SEEN* THE QUEEN. MAN OUGHT TO SEE HIS OWN QUEEN, DON'T YOU THINK?

NOW, I DON'T TAKE TO THE AES SEDAI – I'M A DECENT SORT, WOULDN'T GO WITHIN A THOUSAND MILES OF ONE IF I HAD MY WAY. BUT THEY'RE STOPPING AT EVERY VILLAGE AND TOWN ON THE WAY NORTH TO DISPLAY LOGAIN, OR SO I'VE HEARD TELL. SHOWING PEOPLE THAT THE FALSE DRAGON HAS BEEN TAKEN, AND THE WORLD IS SAFE AGAIN.

I ADMIT, I'D LIKE TO SEE THAT, EVEN IF I HAD TO BE NEAR TO AN AES SEDAI TO DO IT. I'M HALF TEMPTED TO GO TO CAEMLYN.

NORTH. THAT'S ALL ANYBODY KNOWS AROUND HERE. YOU WANT TO SEE HIM, YOU GO TO CAEMLYN. THAT'S ALL I KNOW, AND IF THERE'S ANYTHING TO KNOW IN WHITEBRIDGE, I KNOW IT.

OH, YES. YES. I MAY TRY TO SEE THIS ALL MYSELF.

YOU DIDN'T SAY WHAT ROUTE THEY WERE TAKING. PERHAPS THERE ARE SOME OTHER TRAVELERS AROUND? THEY MIGHT HAVE HEARD THE ROUTE.

NO DOUBT YOU DO. I EXPECT A LOT OF STRANGERS PASSING THROUGH STOP HERE. YOUR SIGN CAUGHT MY EYE FROM THE FOOT OF THE WHITEBRIDGE.

NOT JUST FROM THE WEST, I'LL HAVE YOU KNOW. TWO DAYS AGO THERE WAS A FELLOW HERE, AN ILLIANER, WITH A PROCLAMATION ALL DONE UP WITH SEALS AND RIBBONS.

READ IT RIGHT OUT THERE IN THE SQUARE. SAID HE'S TAKING IT ALL THE WAY TO THE MOUNTAINS OF MIST, MAYBE EVEN TO THE ARYTH OCEAN, IF THE PASSES ARE OPEN.

WHAT DID THE PROCLAMATION *SAY?*

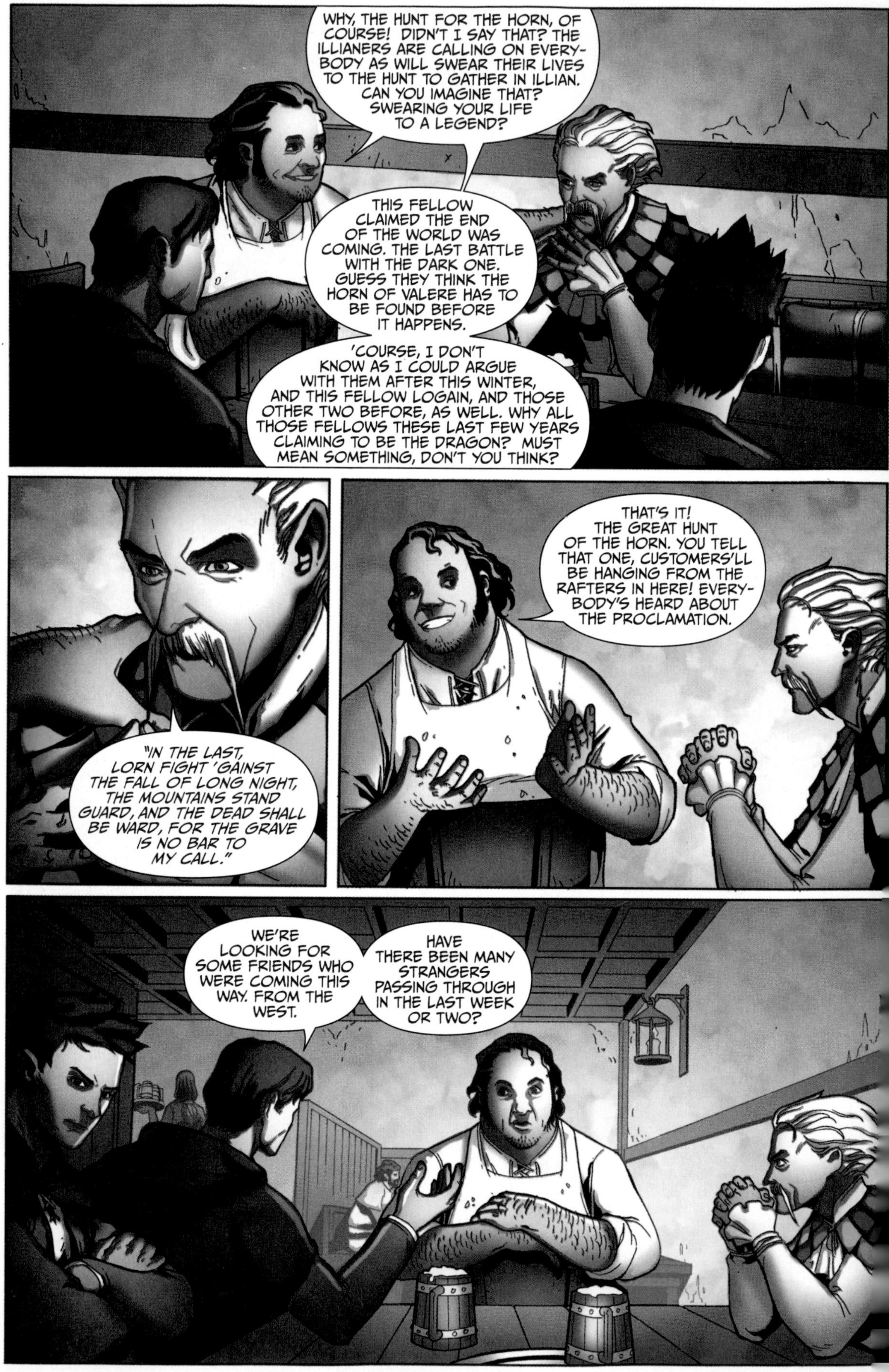
WHY, THE HUNT FOR THE HORN, OF COURSE! DIDN'T I SAY THAT? THE ILLIANERS ARE CALLING ON EVERY-BODY AS WILL SWEAR THEIR LIVES TO THE HUNT TO GATHER IN ILLIAN. CAN YOU IMAGINE THAT? SWEARING YOUR LIFE TO A LEGEND?
THIS FELLOW CLAIMED THE END OF THE WORLD WAS COMING. THE LAST BATTLE WITH THE DARK ONE. GUESS THEY THINK THE HORN OF VALERE HAS TO BE FOUND BEFORE IT HAPPENS.
'COURSE, I DON'T KNOW AS I COULD ARGUE WITH THEM AFTER THIS WINTER, AND THIS FELLOW LOGAIN, AND THOSE OTHER TWO BEFORE, AS WELL. WHY ALL THOSE FELLOWS THESE LAST FEW YEARS CLAIMING TO BE THE DRAGON? MUST MEAN SOMETHING, DON'T YOU THINK?
"IN THE LAST, LORN FIGHT 'GAINST THE FALL OF LONG NIGHT, THE MOUNTAINS STAND GUARD, AND THE DEAD SHALL BE WARD, FOR THE GRAVE IS NO BAR TO MY CALL."
THAT'S IT! THE GREAT HUNT OF THE HORN. YOU TELL THAT ONE, CUSTOMERS'LL BE HANGING FROM THE RAFTERS IN HERE! EVERY-BODY'S HEARD ABOUT THE PROCLAMATION.
WE'RE LOOKING FOR SOME FRIENDS WHO WERE COMING THIS WAY. FROM THE WEST.
HAVE THERE BEEN MANY STRANGERS PASSING THROUGH IN THE LAST WEEK OR TWO?

THERE'S ALWAYS *SOME*. FROM EAST AND WEST BOTH.

WHAT DO THEY *LOOK LIKE*, THESE FRIENDS OF YOURS?

THEY--

TWO *MEN*, THREE *WOMEN*. THEY MAY BE *TOGETHER*, OR MAYBE *NOT*.

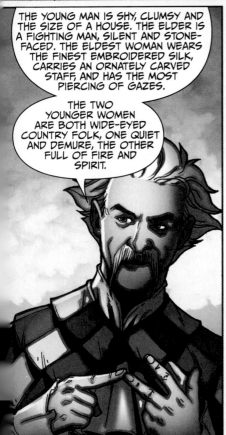

THE YOUNG MAN IS SHY, CLUMSY AND THE SIZE OF A HOUSE. THE ELDER IS A FIGHTING MAN, SILENT AND STONE-FACED. THE ELDEST WOMAN WEARS THE FINEST EMBROIDERED SILK, CARRIES AN ORNATELY CARVED STAFF, AND HAS THE MOST PIERCING OF GAZES.

THE TWO YOUNGER WOMEN ARE BOTH WIDE-EYED COUNTRY FOLK, ONE QUIET AND DEMURE, THE OTHER FULL OF FIRE AND SPIRIT.

I'VE CHANGED MY MIND. FORGET ABOUT PERFORMING HERE. IN FACT, I'D APPRECIATE IT IF YOU DRANK YOUR ALE AND LEFT.

LEAVE *WHITEBRIDGE*, IF YOU'RE SMART.

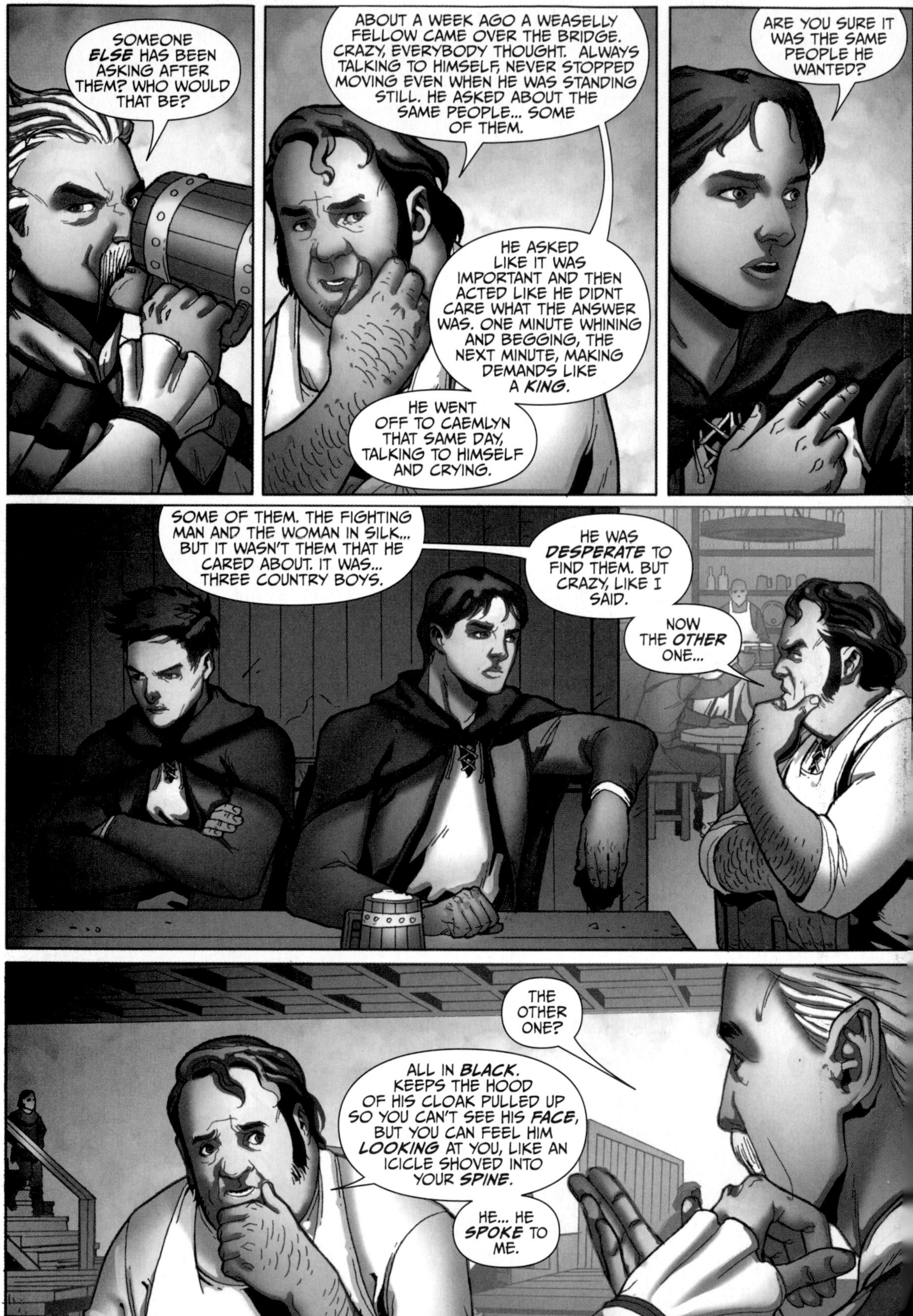
SOMEONE ELSE HAS BEEN ASKING AFTER THEM? WHO WOULD THAT BE?
ABOUT A WEEK AGO A WEASELLY FELLOW CAME OVER THE BRIDGE. CRAZY, EVERYBODY THOUGHT. ALWAYS TALKING TO HIMSELF, NEVER STOPPED MOVING EVEN WHEN HE WAS STANDING STILL. HE ASKED ABOUT THE SAME PEOPLE... SOME OF THEM.
HE ASKED LIKE IT WAS IMPORTANT AND THEN ACTED LIKE HE DIDNT CARE WHAT THE ANSWER WAS. ONE MINUTE WHINING AND BEGGING, THE NEXT MINUTE, MAKING DEMANDS LIKE A KING.
HE WENT OFF TO CAEMLYN THAT SAME DAY, TALKING TO HIMSELF AND CRYING.
ARE YOU SURE IT WAS THE SAME PEOPLE HE WANTED?
SOME OF THEM. THE FIGHTING MAN AND THE WOMAN IN SILK... BUT IT WASN'T THEM THAT HE CARED ABOUT. IT WAS... THREE COUNTRY BOYS.
HE WAS DESPERATE TO FIND THEM. BUT CRAZY, LIKE I SAID.
NOW THE OTHER ONE...
THE OTHER ONE?
ALL IN BLACK. KEEPS THE HOOD OF HIS CLOAK PULLED UP SO YOU CAN'T SEE HIS FACE, BUT YOU CAN FEEL HIM LOOKING AT YOU, LIKE AN ICICLE SHOVED INTO YOUR SPINE.
HE... HE SPOKE TO ME.

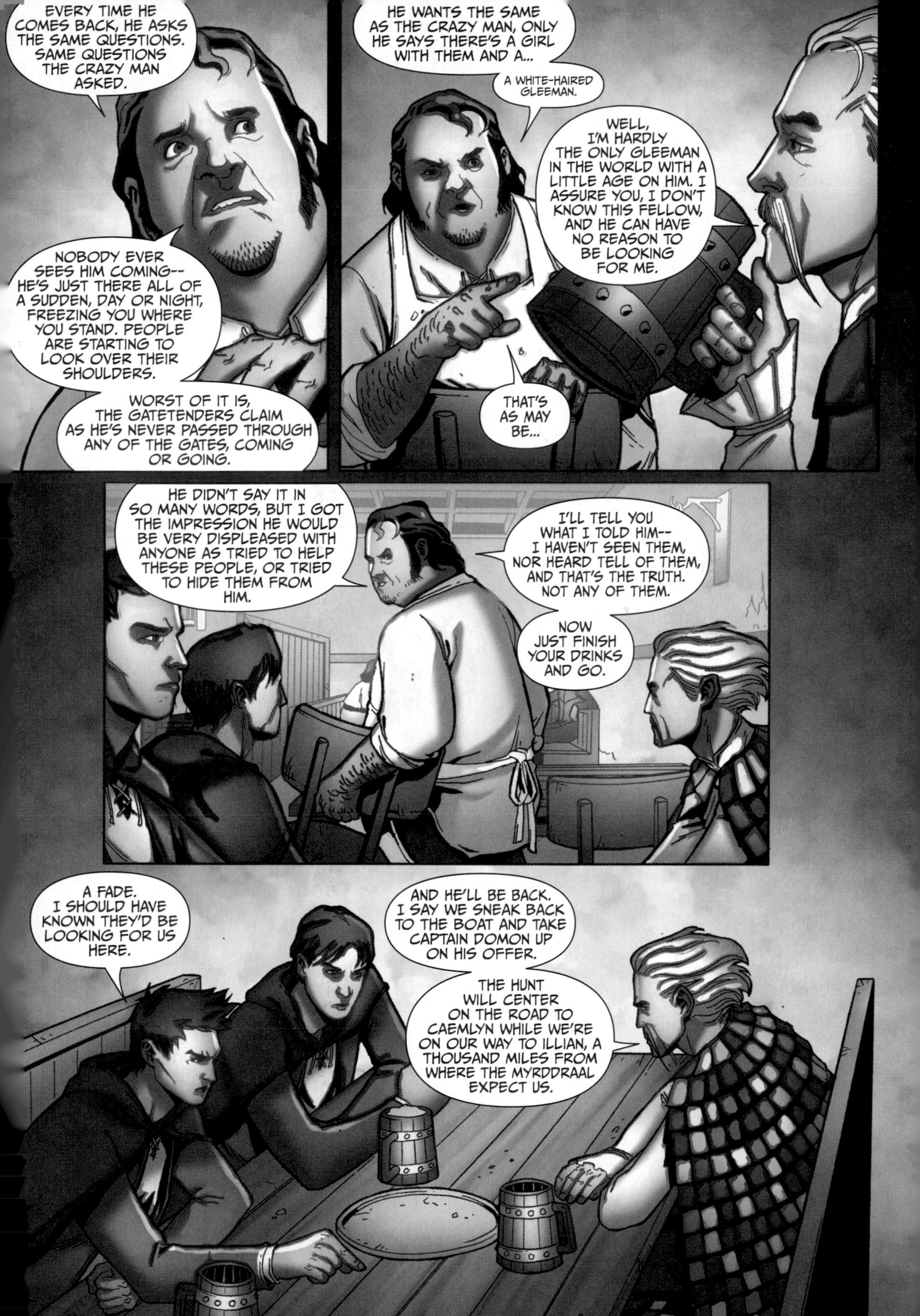
EVERY TIME HE COMES BACK, HE ASKS THE SAME QUESTIONS. SAME QUESTIONS THE CRAZY MAN ASKED.
NOBODY EVER SEES HIM COMING-- HE'S JUST THERE ALL OF A SUDDEN, DAY OR NIGHT, FREEZING YOU WHERE YOU STAND. PEOPLE ARE STARTING TO LOOK OVER THEIR SHOULDERS.
WORST OF IT IS, THE GATETENDERS CLAIM AS HE'S NEVER PASSED THROUGH ANY OF THE GATES, COMING OR GOING.
HE WANTS THE SAME AS THE CRAZY MAN, ONLY HE SAYS THERE'S A GIRL WITH THEM AND A...
A WHITE-HAIRED GLEEMAN.
WELL, I'M HARDLY THE ONLY GLEEMAN IN THE WORLD WITH A LITTLE AGE ON HIM. I ASSURE YOU, I DON'T KNOW THIS FELLOW, AND HE CAN HAVE NO REASON TO BE LOOKING FOR ME.
THAT'S AS MAY BE...
HE DIDN'T SAY IT IN SO MANY WORDS, BUT I GOT THE IMPRESSION HE WOULD BE VERY DISPLEASED WITH ANYONE AS TRIED TO HELP THESE PEOPLE, OR TRIED TO HIDE THEM FROM HIM.
I'LL TELL YOU WHAT I TOLD HIM-- I HAVEN'T SEEN THEM, NOR HEARD TELL OF THEM, AND THAT'S THE TRUTH. NOT ANY OF THEM.
NOW JUST FINISH YOUR DRINKS AND GO.
A FADE. I SHOULD HAVE KNOWN THEY'D BE LOOKING FOR US HERE.
AND HE'LL BE BACK. I SAY WE SNEAK BACK TO THE BOAT AND TAKE CAPTAIN DOMON UP ON HIS OFFER.
THE HUNT WILL CENTER ON THE ROAD TO CAEMLYN WHILE WE'RE ON OUR WAY TO ILLIAN, A THOUSAND MILES FROM WHERE THE MYRDDRAAL EXPECT US.

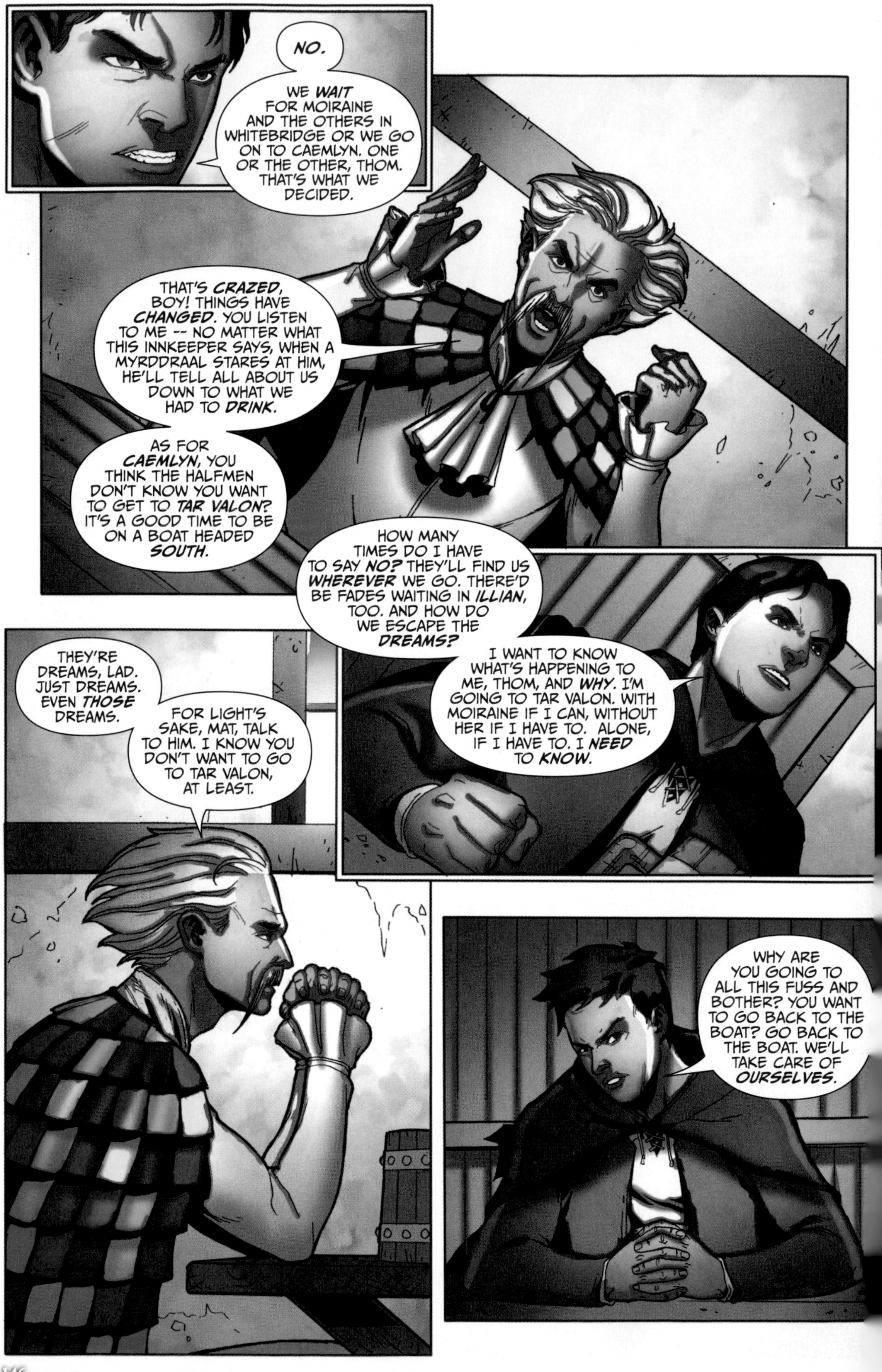
NO.
WE WAIT FOR MOIRAINE AND THE OTHERS IN WHITEBRIDGE OR WE GO ON TO CAEMLYN. ONE OR THE OTHER, THOM. THAT'S WHAT WE DECIDED.
THAT'S CRAZED, BOY! THINGS HAVE CHANGED. YOU LISTEN TO ME -- NO MATTER WHAT THIS INNKEEPER SAYS, WHEN A MYRDDRAAL STARES AT HIM, HE'LL TELL ALL ABOUT US DOWN TO WHAT WE HAD TO DRINK.
AS FOR CAEMLYN, YOU THINK THE HALFMEN DON'T KNOW YOU WANT TO GET TO TAR VALON? IT'S A GOOD TIME TO BE ON A BOAT HEADED SOUTH.
HOW MANY TIMES DO I HAVE TO SAY NO? THEY'LL FIND US WHEREVER WE GO. THERE'D BE FADES WAITING IN ILLIAN, TOO. AND HOW DO WE ESCAPE THE DREAMS?
I WANT TO KNOW WHAT'S HAPPENING TO ME, THOM, AND WHY. I'M GOING TO TAR VALON. WITH MOIRAINE IF I CAN, WITHOUT HER IF I HAVE TO. ALONE, IF I HAVE TO. I NEED TO KNOW.
THEY'RE DREAMS, LAD. JUST DREAMS. EVEN THOSE DREAMS.
FOR LIGHT'S SAKE, MAT, TALK TO HIM. I KNOW YOU DON'T WANT TO GO TO TAR VALON, AT LEAST.
WHY ARE YOU GOING TO ALL THIS FUSS AND BOTHER? YOU WANT TO GO BACK TO THE BOAT? GO BACK TO THE BOAT. WE'LL TAKE CARE OF OURSELVES.

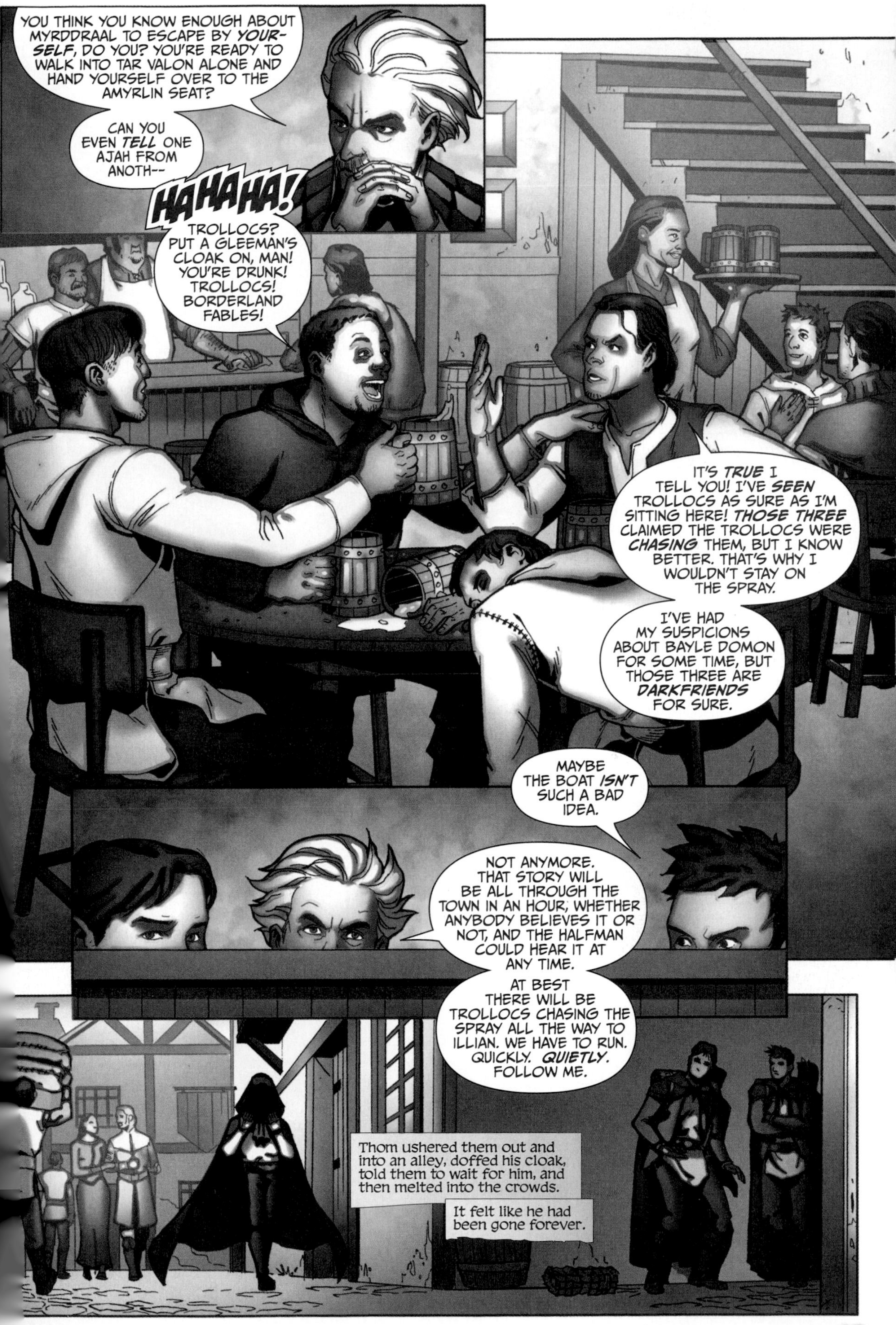
YOU THINK YOU KNOW ENOUGH ABOUT MYRDDRAAL TO ESCAPE BY *YOURSELF*, DO YOU? YOU'RE READY TO WALK INTO TAR VALON ALONE AND HAND YOURSELF OVER TO THE AMYRLIN SEAT?
CAN YOU EVEN *TELL* ONE AJAH FROM ANOTH--
HAHAHA!
TROLLOCS? PUT A GLEEMAN'S CLOAK ON, MAN! YOU'RE DRUNK! TROLLOCS! BORDERLAND FABLES!
IT'S *TRUE* I TELL YOU! I'VE *SEEN* TROLLOCS AS SURE AS I'M SITTING HERE! *THOSE THREE* CLAIMED THE TROLLOCS WERE *CHASING* THEM, BUT I KNOW BETTER. THAT'S WHY I WOULDN'T STAY ON THE SPRAY.
I'VE HAD MY SUSPICIONS ABOUT BAYLE DOMON FOR SOME TIME, BUT THOSE THREE ARE *DARKFRIENDS* FOR SURE.
MAYBE THE BOAT *ISN'T* SUCH A BAD IDEA.
NOT ANYMORE. THAT STORY WILL BE ALL THROUGH THE TOWN IN AN HOUR, WHETHER ANYBODY BELIEVES IT OR NOT, AND THE HALFMAN COULD HEAR IT AT ANY TIME.
AT BEST THERE WILL BE TROLLOCS CHASING THE SPRAY ALL THE WAY TO ILLIAN. WE HAVE TO RUN. QUICKLY. *QUIETLY.* FOLLOW ME.
Thom ushered them out and into an alley, doffed his cloak, told them to wait for him, and then melted into the crowds.
It felt like he had been gone forever.

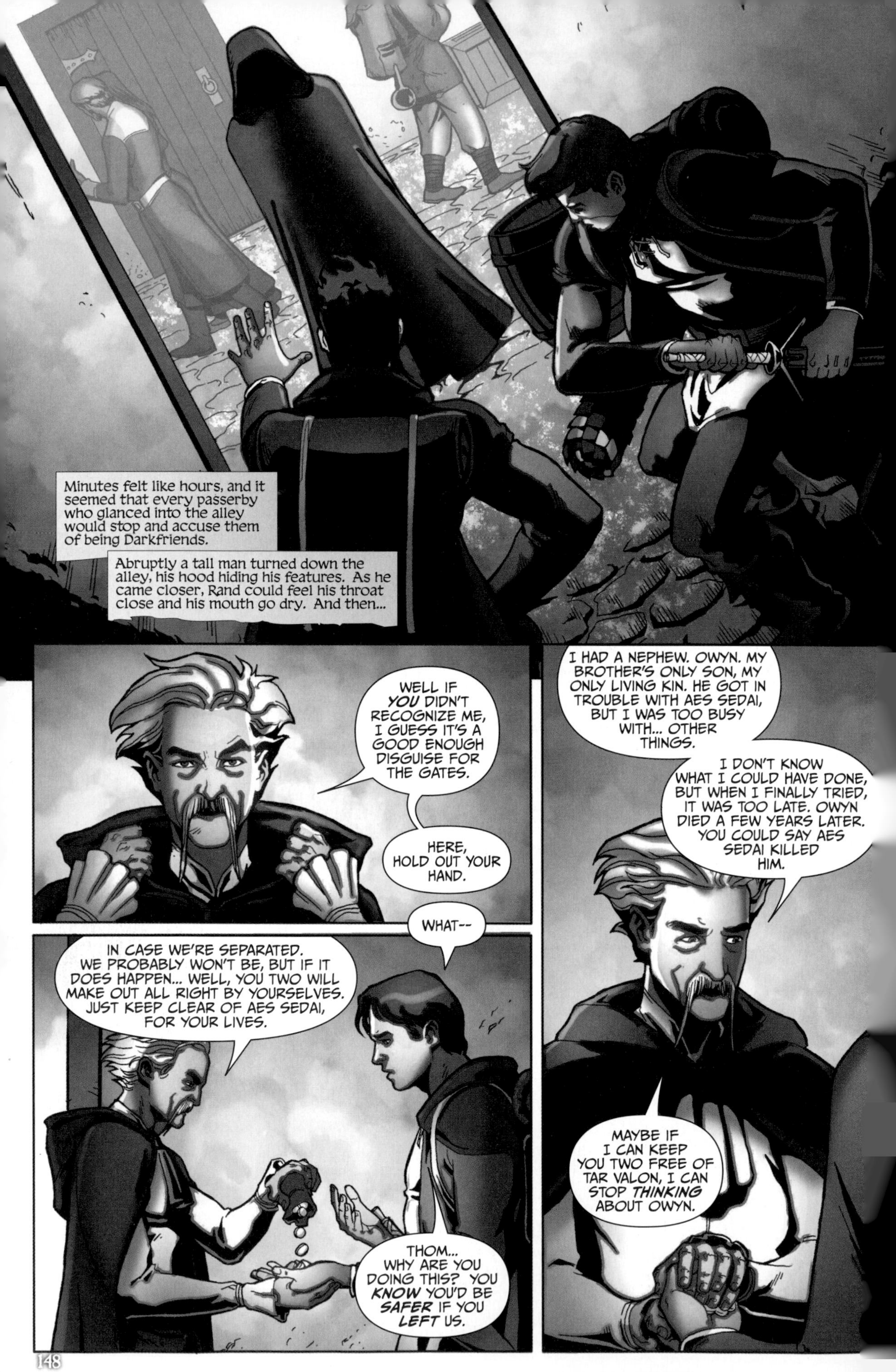

Minutes felt like hours, and it seemed that every passerby who glanced into the alley would stop and accuse them of being Darkfriends.
Abruptly a tall man turned down the alley, his hood hiding his features. As he came closer, Rand could feel his throat close and his mouth go dry. And then...
WELL IF YOU DIDN'T RECOGNIZE ME, I GUESS IT'S A GOOD ENOUGH DISGUISE FOR THE GATES.
HERE, HOLD OUT YOUR HAND.
WHAT--
IN CASE WE'RE SEPARATED. WE PROBABLY WON'T BE, BUT IF IT DOES HAPPEN... WELL, YOU TWO WILL MAKE OUT ALL RIGHT BY YOURSELVES. JUST KEEP CLEAR OF AES SEDAI, FOR YOUR LIVES.
THOM... WHY ARE YOU DOING THIS? YOU KNOW YOU'D BE SAFER IF YOU LEFT US.
I HAD A NEPHEW. OWYN. MY BROTHER'S ONLY SON, MY ONLY LIVING KIN. HE GOT IN TROUBLE WITH AES SEDAI, BUT I WAS TOO BUSY WITH... OTHER THINGS.
I DON'T KNOW WHAT I COULD HAVE DONE, BUT WHEN I FINALLY TRIED, IT WAS TOO LATE. OWYN DIED A FEW YEARS LATER. YOU COULD SAY AES SEDAI KILLED HIM.
MAYBE IF I CAN KEEP YOU TWO FREE OF TAR VALON, I CAN STOP THINKING ABOUT OWYN.

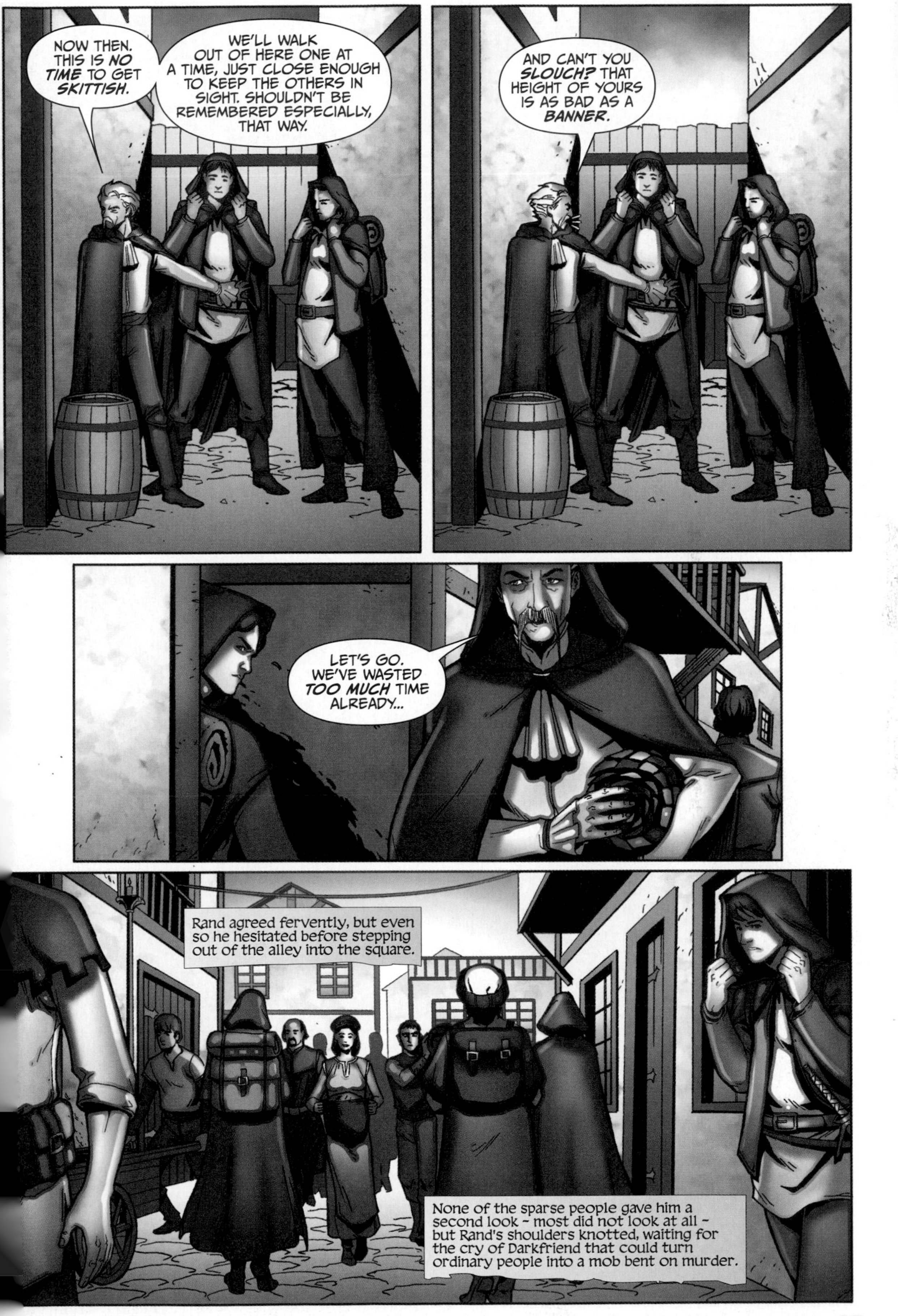
NOW THEN. THIS IS NO TIME TO GET SKITTISH.
WE'LL WALK OUT OF HERE ONE AT A TIME, JUST CLOSE ENOUGH TO KEEP THE OTHERS IN SIGHT. SHOULDN'T BE REMEMBERED ESPECIALLY, THAT WAY.
AND CAN'T YOU SLOUCH? THAT HEIGHT OF YOURS IS AS BAD AS A BANNER.
LET'S GO. WE'VE WASTED TOO MUCH TIME ALREADY...
Rand agreed fervently, but even so he hesitated before stepping out of the alley into the square.
None of the sparse people gave him a second look - most did not look at all - but Rand's shoulders knotted, waiting for the cry of Darkfriend that could turn ordinary people into a mob bent on murder.

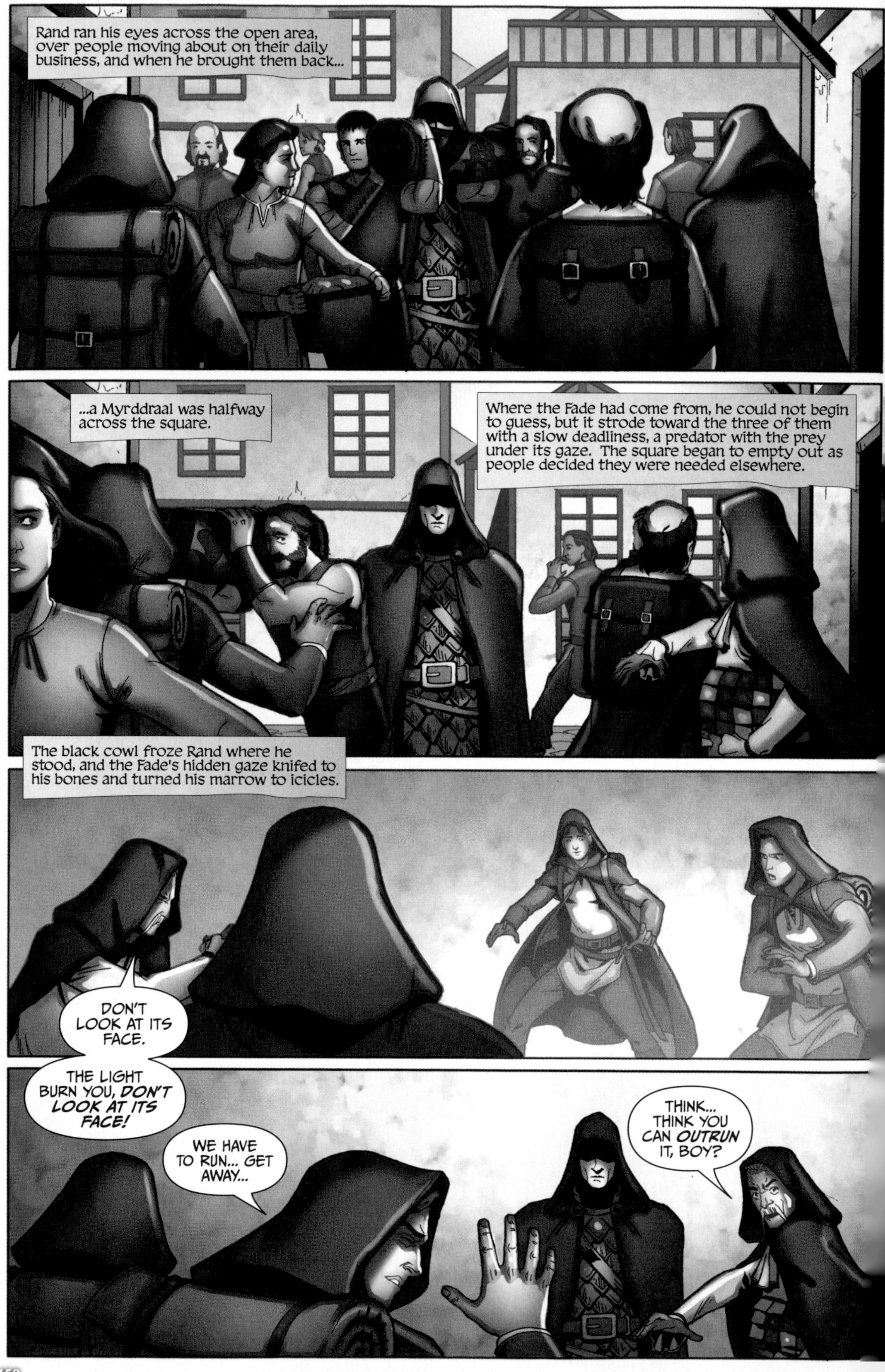

Rand ran his eyes across the open area, over people moving about on their daily business, and when he brought them back...
...a Myrddraal was halfway across the square.
Where the Fade had come from, he could not begin to guess, but it strode toward the three of them with a slow deadliness, a predator with the prey under its gaze. The square began to empty out as people decided they were needed elsewhere.
The black cowl froze Rand where he stood, and the Fade's hidden gaze knifed to his bones and turned his marrow to icicles.
DON'T LOOK AT ITS FACE.
THE LIGHT BURN YOU, *DON'T LOOK AT ITS FACE!*
WE HAVE TO RUN... GET AWAY...
THINK... THINK YOU CAN *OUTRUN* IT, BOY?

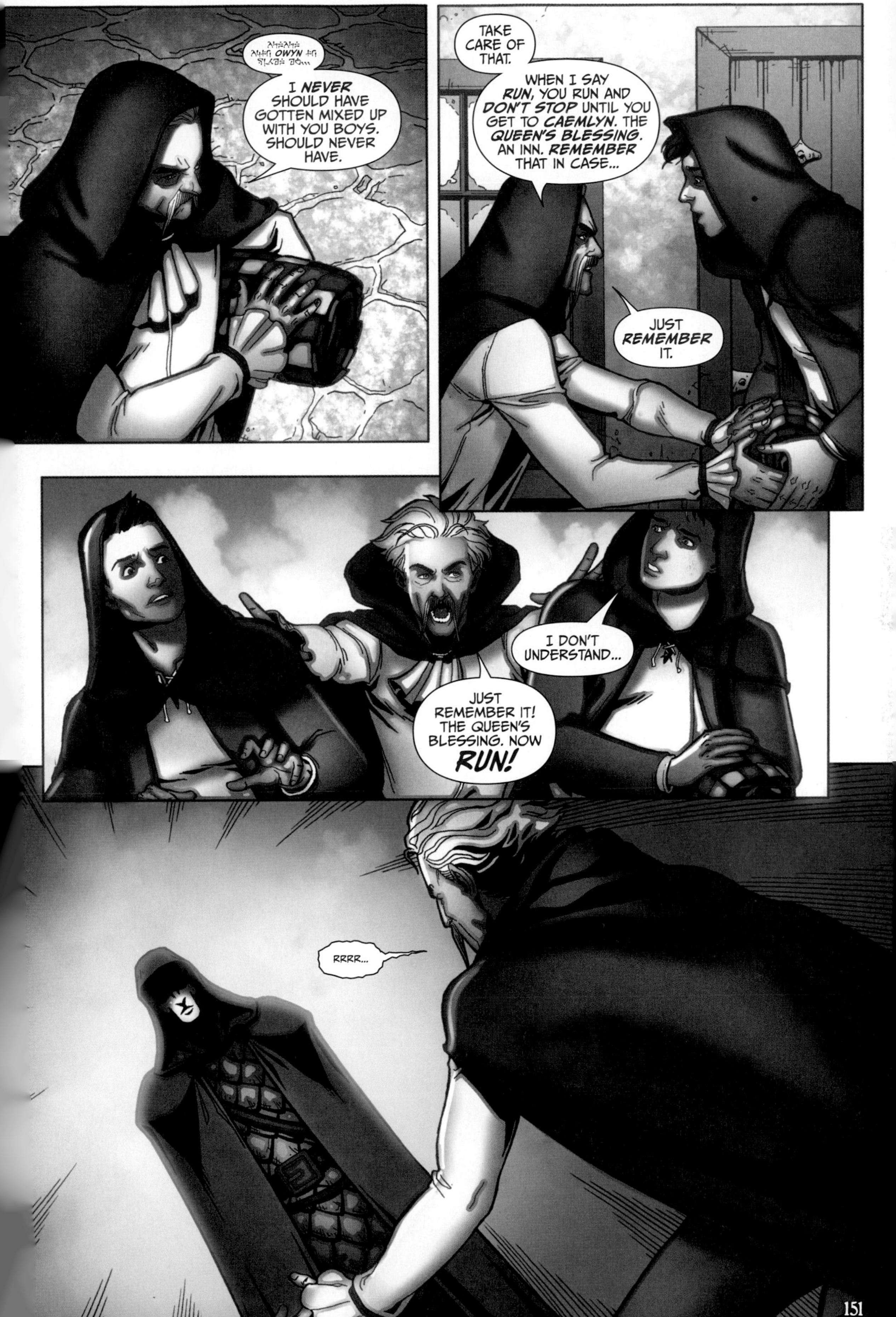
I NEVER SHOULD HAVE GOTTEN MIXED UP WITH YOU BOYS. SHOULD NEVER HAVE.
TAKE CARE OF THAT.
WHEN I SAY RUN, YOU RUN AND DON'T STOP UNTIL YOU GET TO CAEMLYN. THE QUEEN'S BLESSING. AN INN. REMEMBER THAT IN CASE...
JUST REMEMBER IT.
I DON'T UNDERSTAND...
JUST REMEMBER IT! THE QUEEN'S BLESSING. NOW RUN!
RRRR...

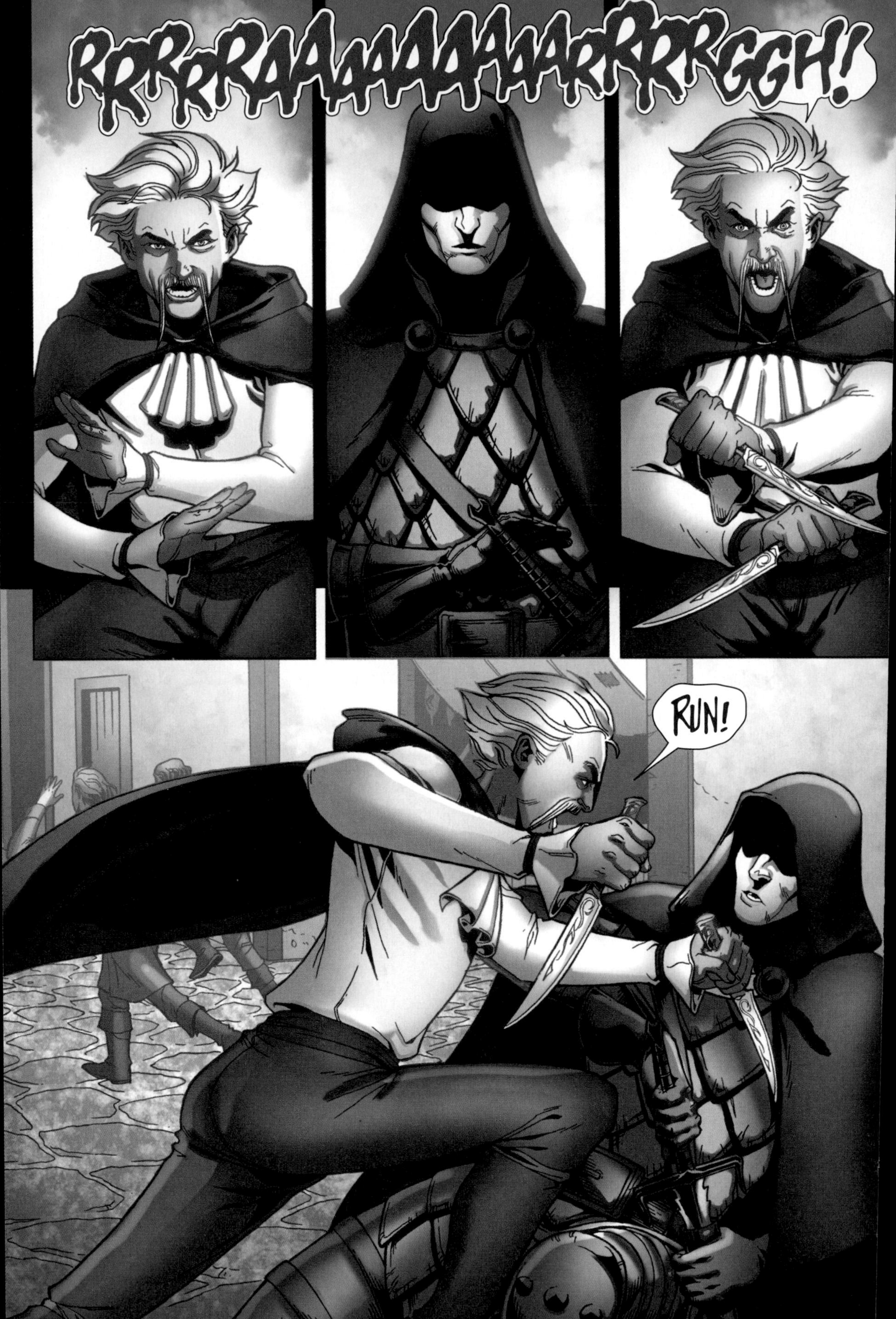
RRRRRAAAAAAAAARRRRRGGH!
RUN!

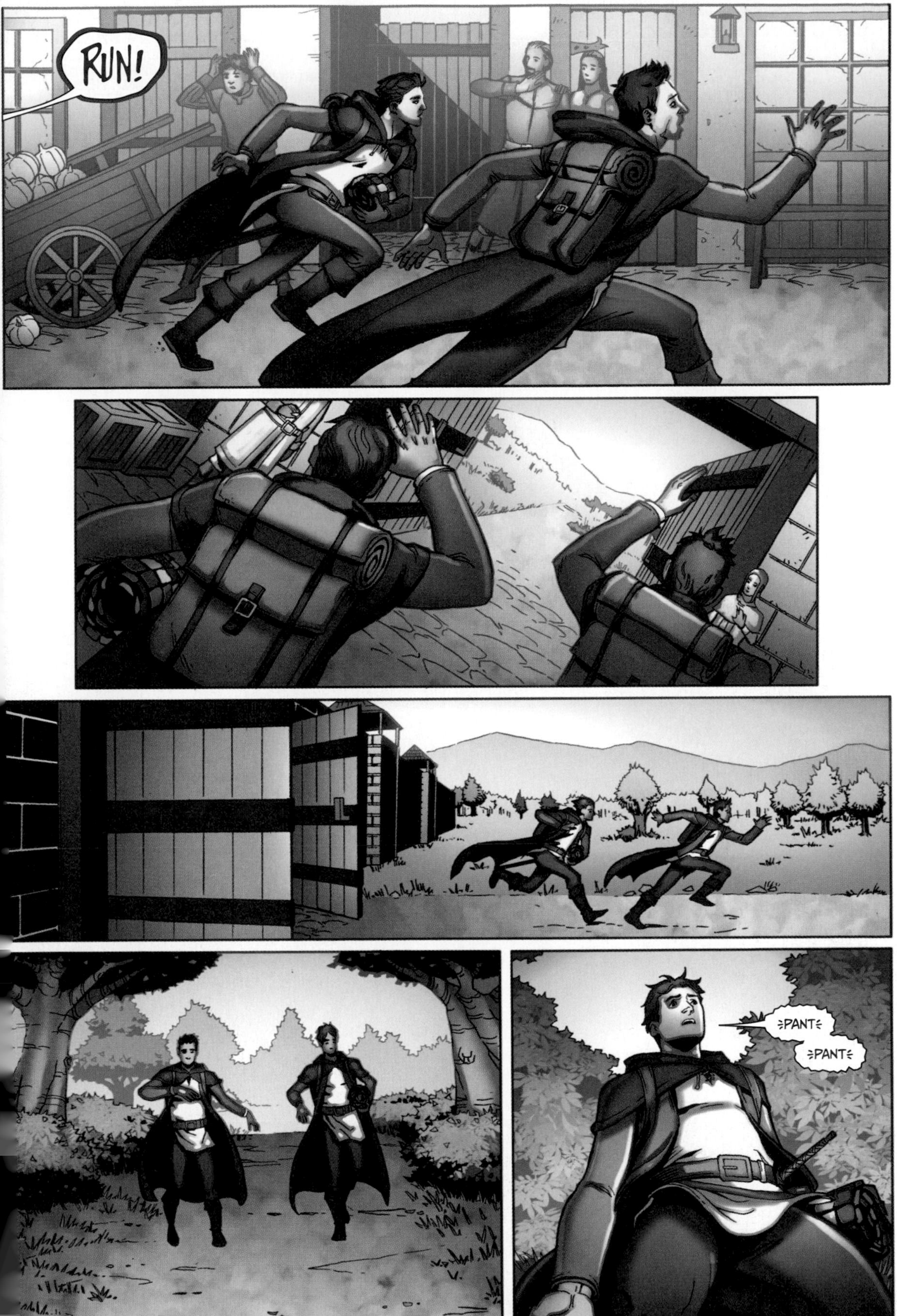
RUN!
PANT
PANT

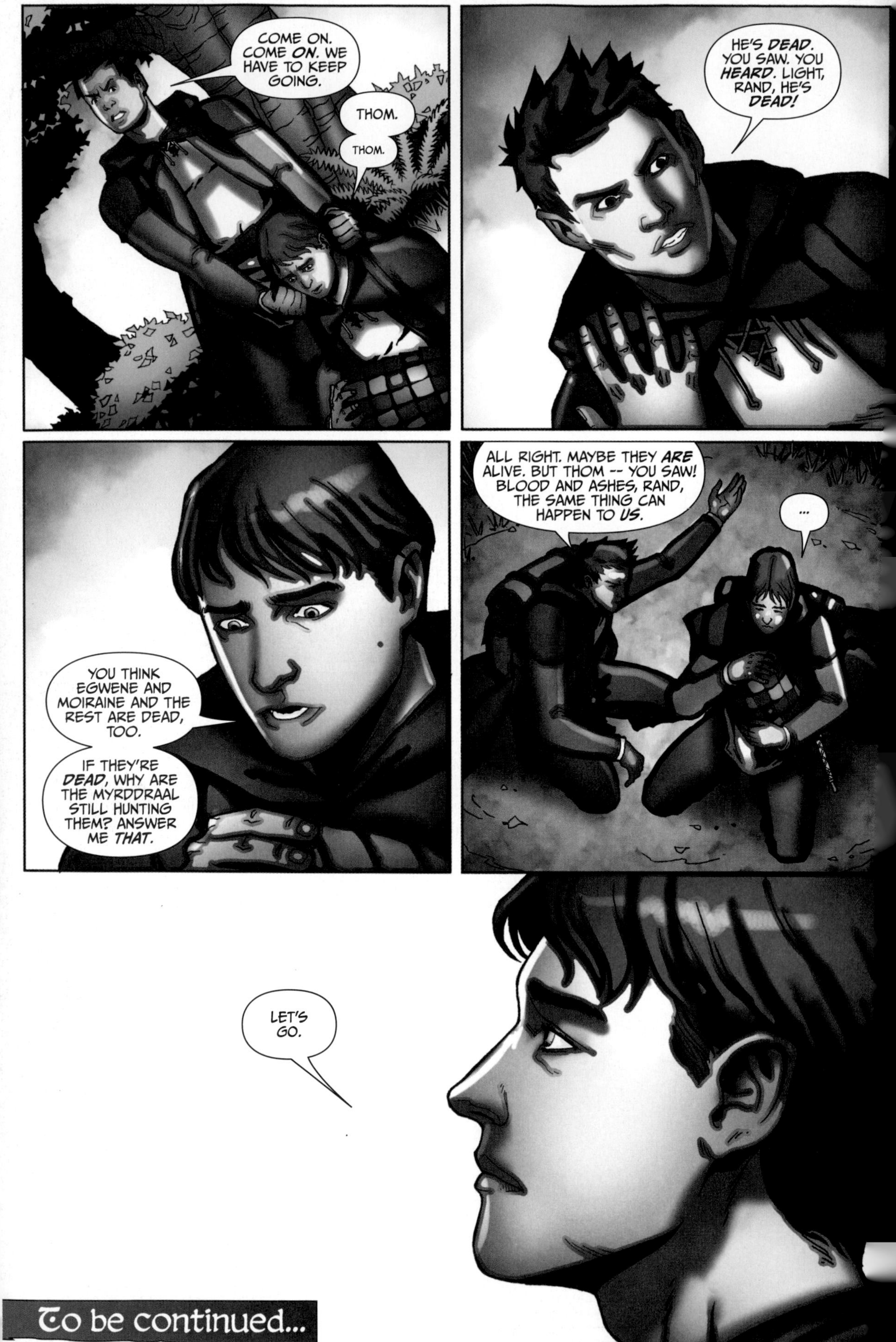
COME ON. COME *ON*. WE HAVE TO KEEP GOING.
THOM.
THOM.
HE'S *DEAD*. YOU SAW. YOU *HEARD*. LIGHT, RAND, HE'S *DEAD!*
YOU THINK EGWENE AND MOIRAINE AND THE REST ARE DEAD, TOO.
IF THEY'RE *DEAD*, WHY ARE THE MYRDDRAAL STILL HUNTING THEM? ANSWER ME *THAT*.
ALL RIGHT. MAYBE THEY *ARE* ALIVE. BUT THOM -- YOU SAW! BLOOD AND ASHES, RAND, THE SAME THING CAN HAPPEN TO *US*.
...
LET'S GO.
To be continued...

cover gallery

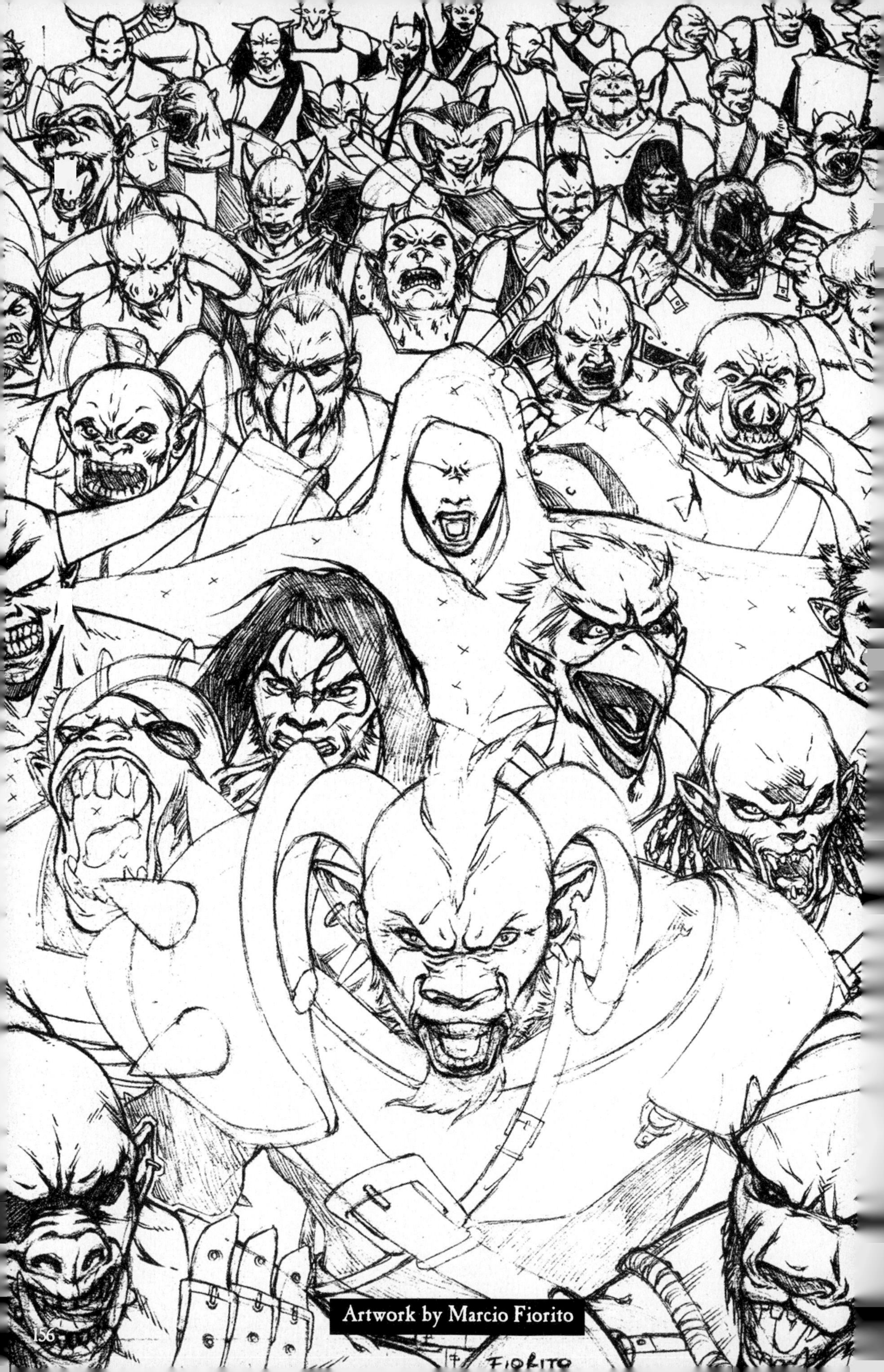
FIORITO

Artwork by Marcio Fiorito

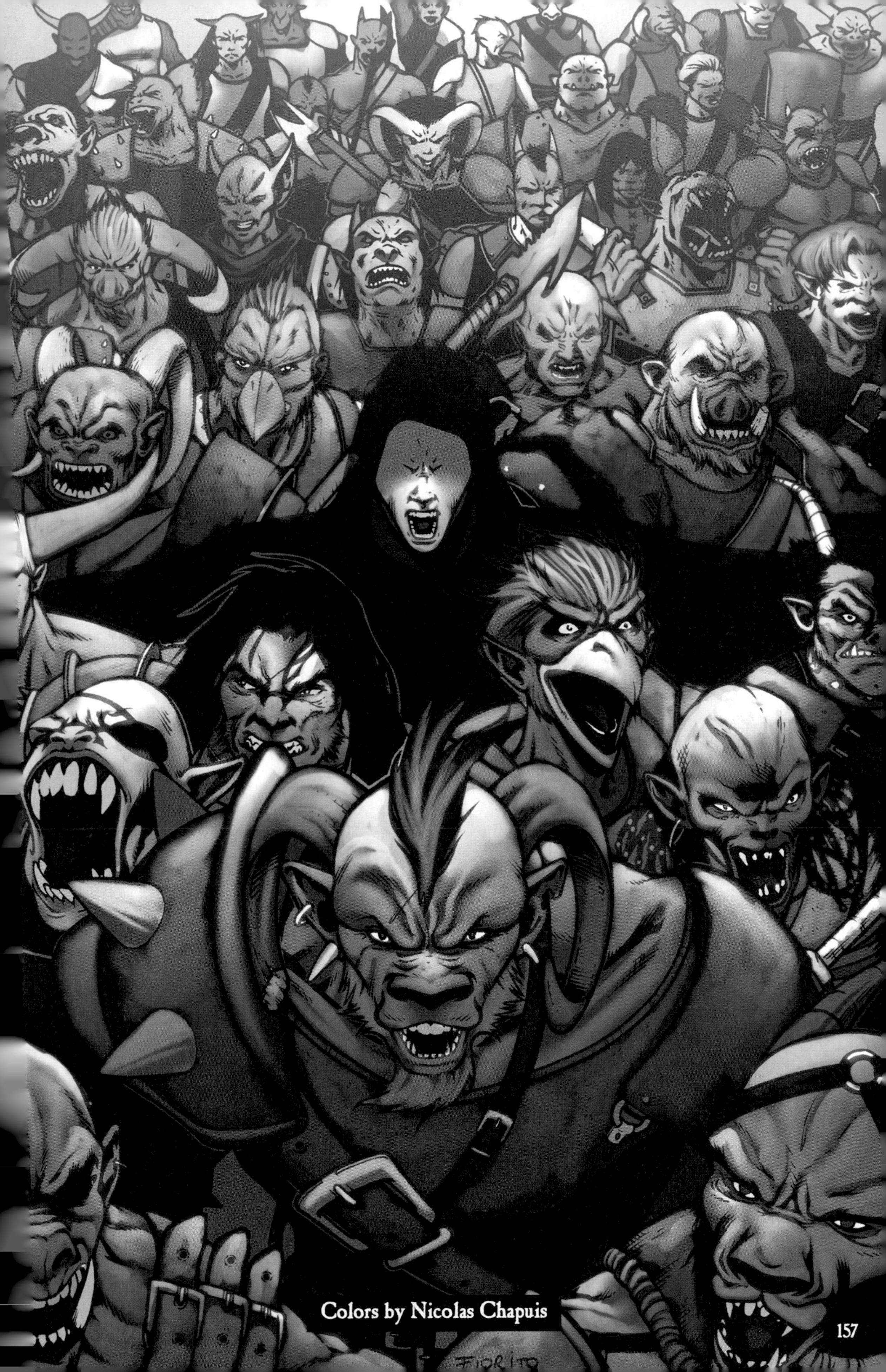
FIORITO

Colors by Nicolas Chapuis

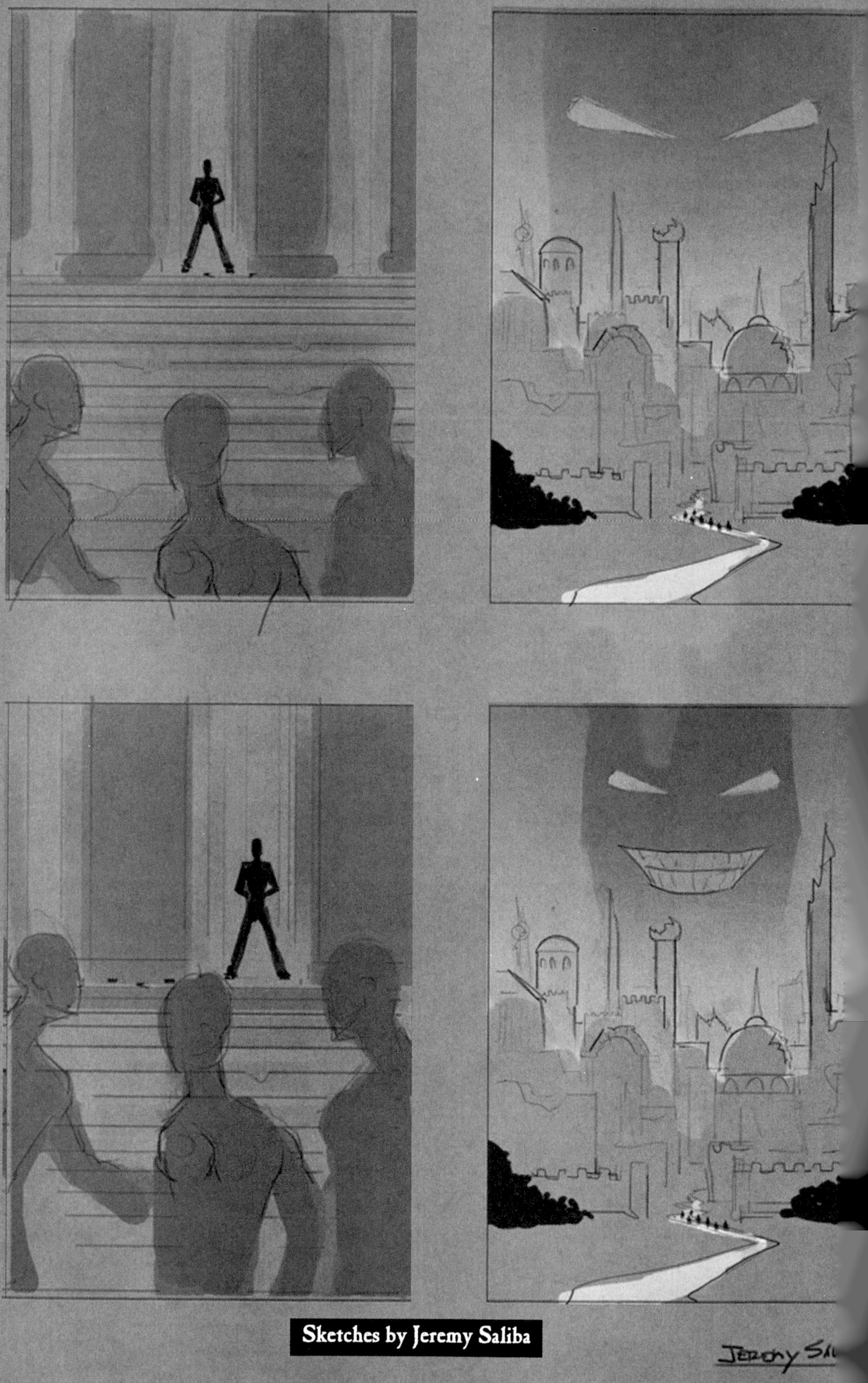
JEREMY SA

Sketches by Jeremy Saliba

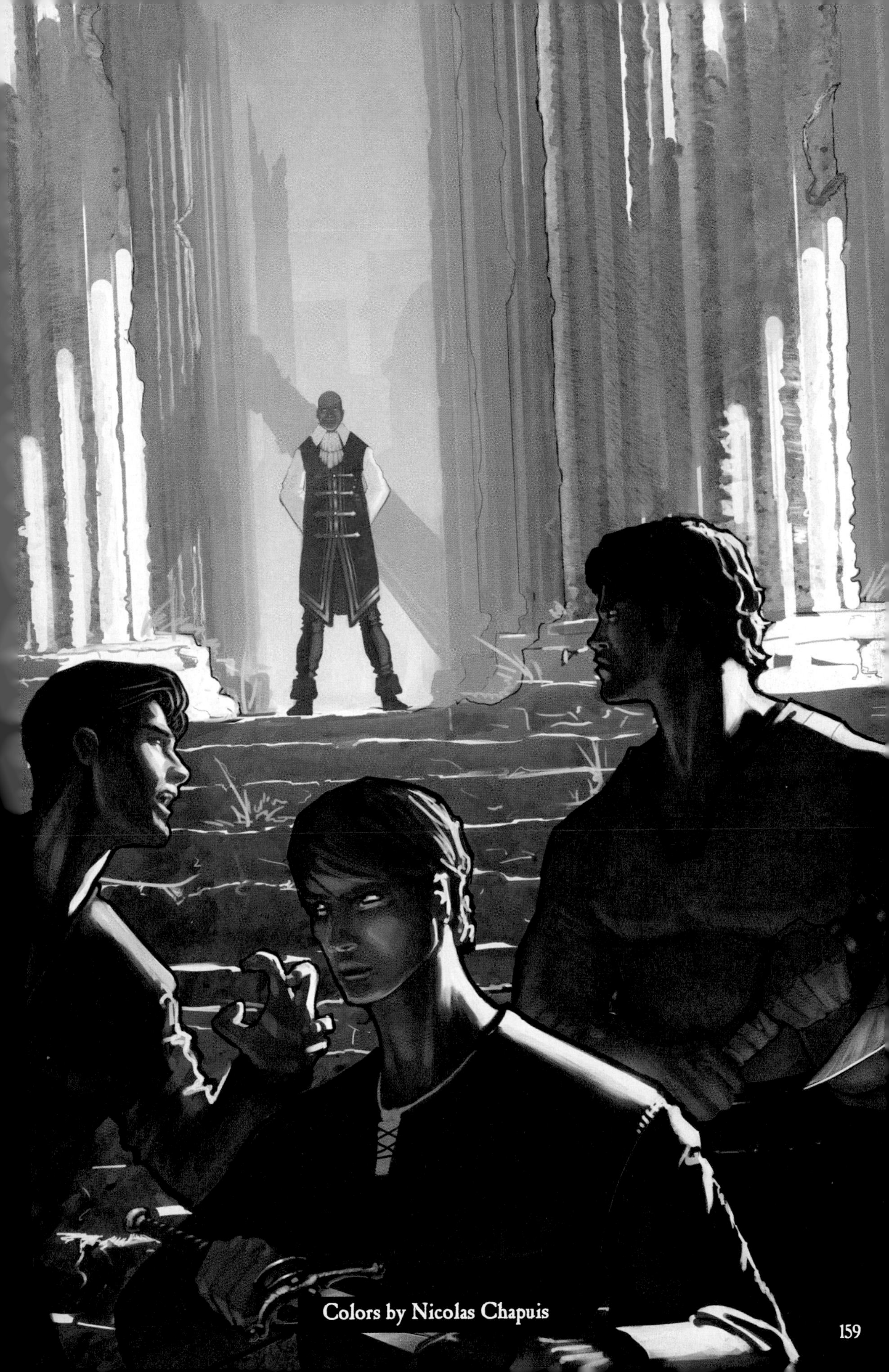

Colors by Nicolas Chapuis

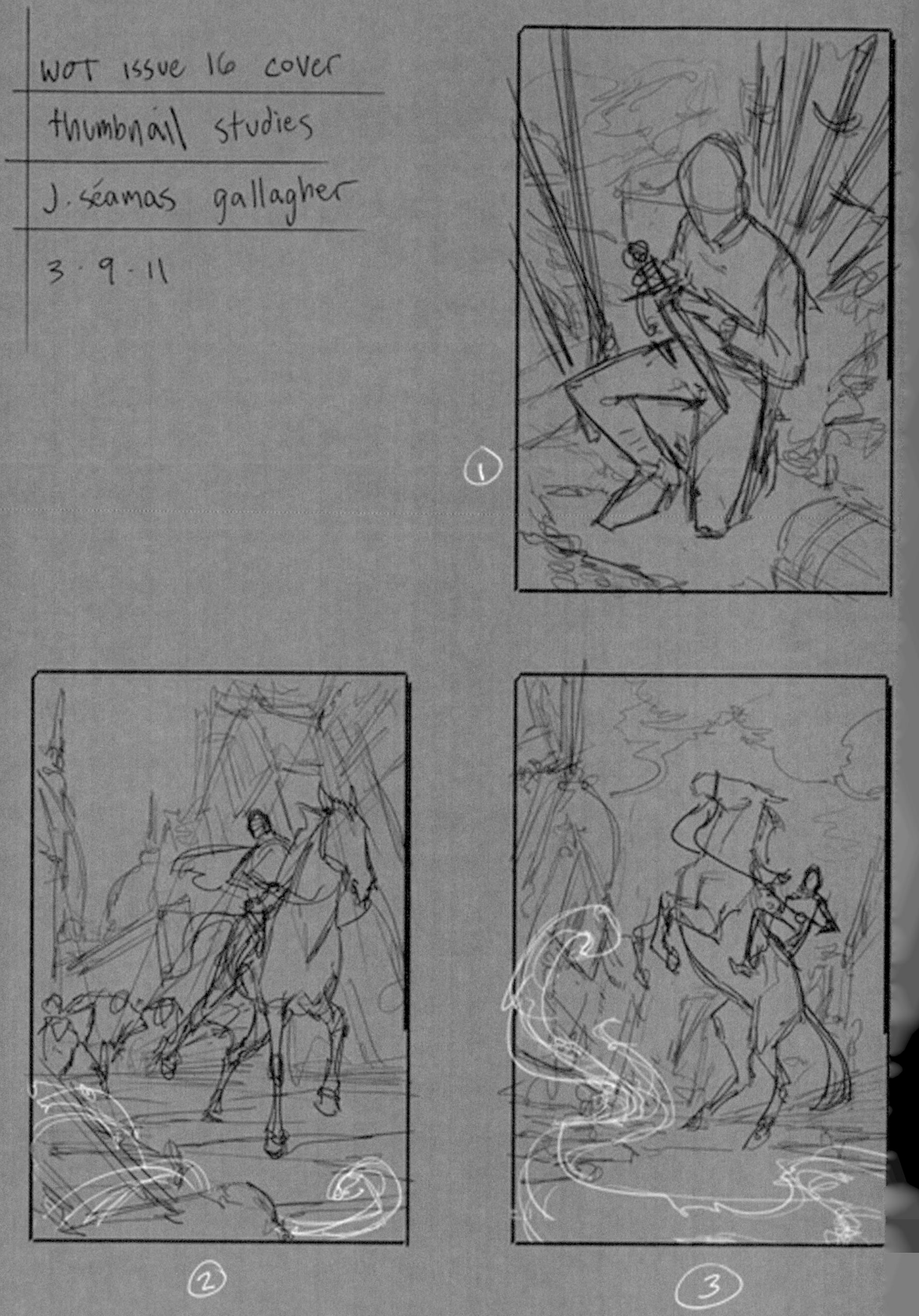
wot issue 16 cover
thumbnail studies
J. séamas gallagher
3 · 9 · 11
1
2
3

Sketches by Seamas Gallagher

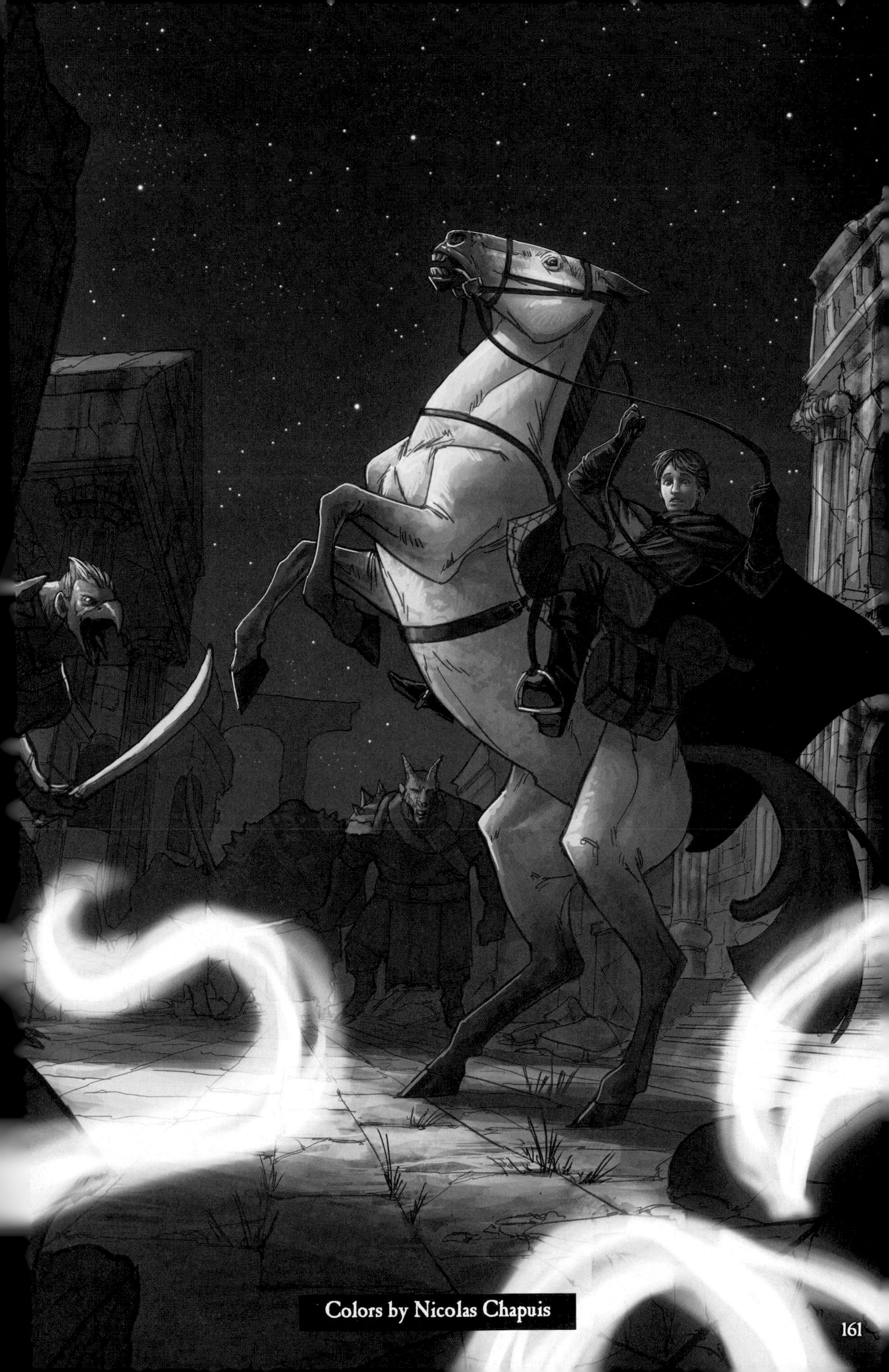
Colors by Nicolas Chapuis

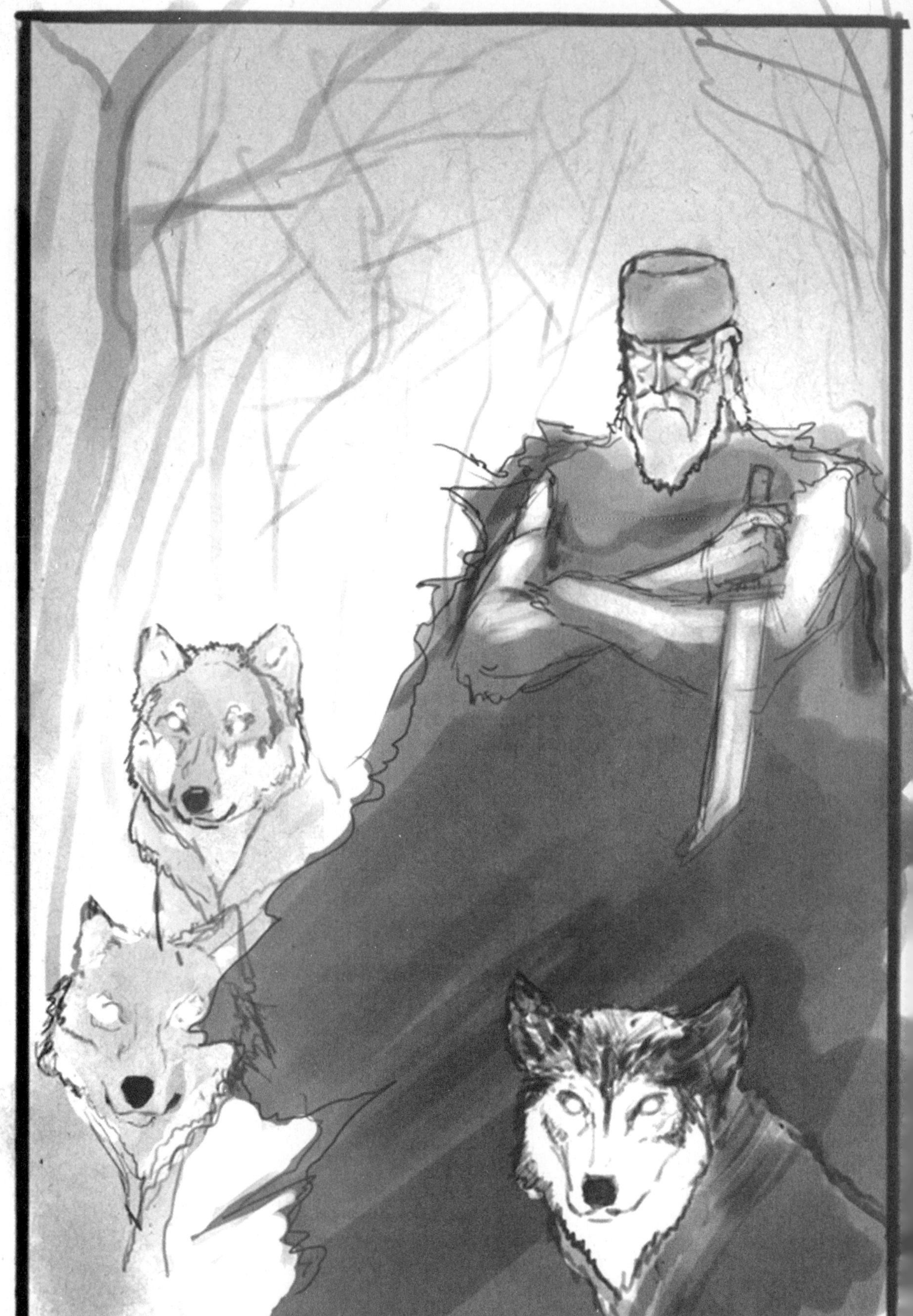

Artwork by Jeremy Saliba

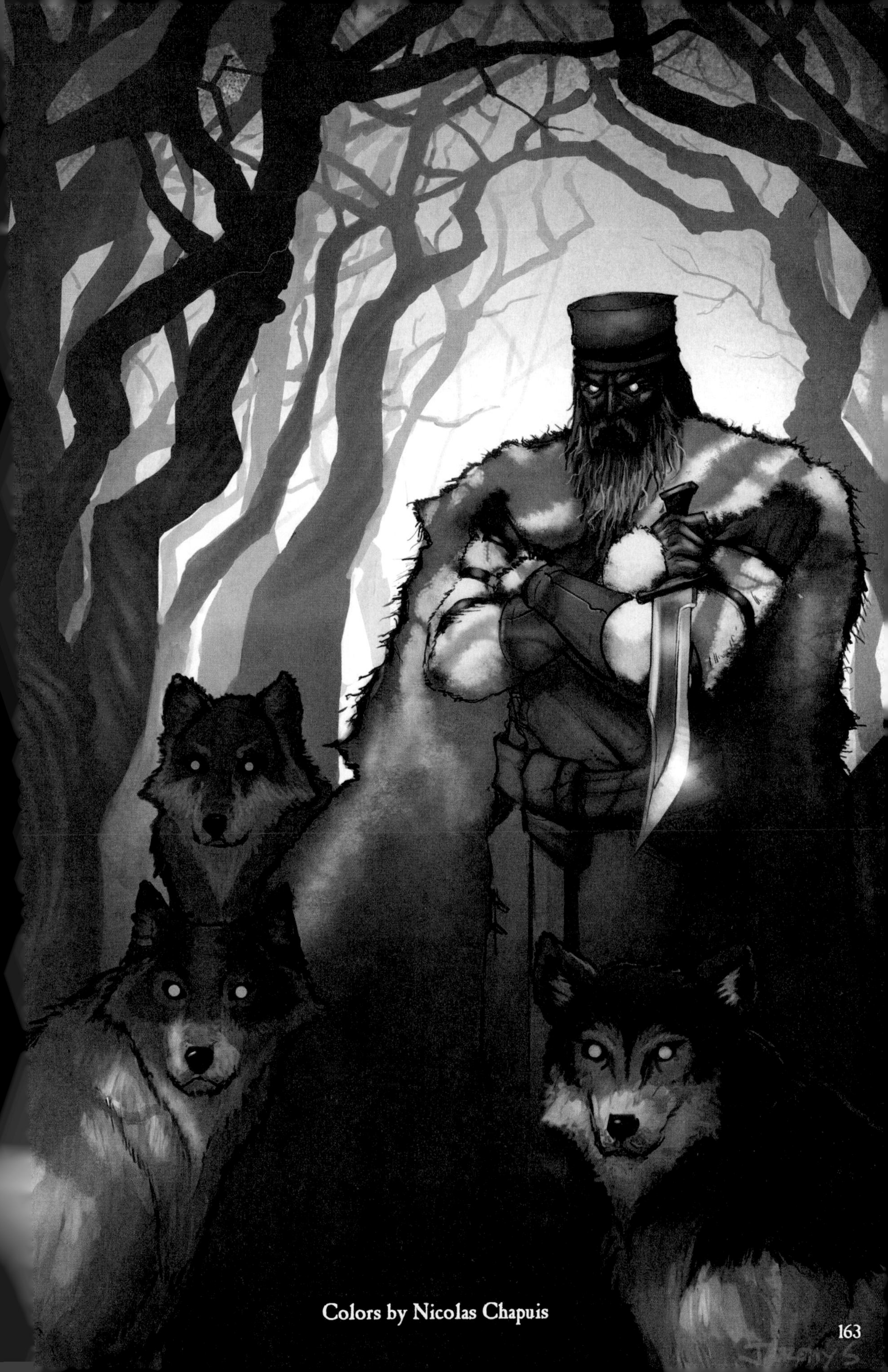

Colors by Nicolas Chapuis

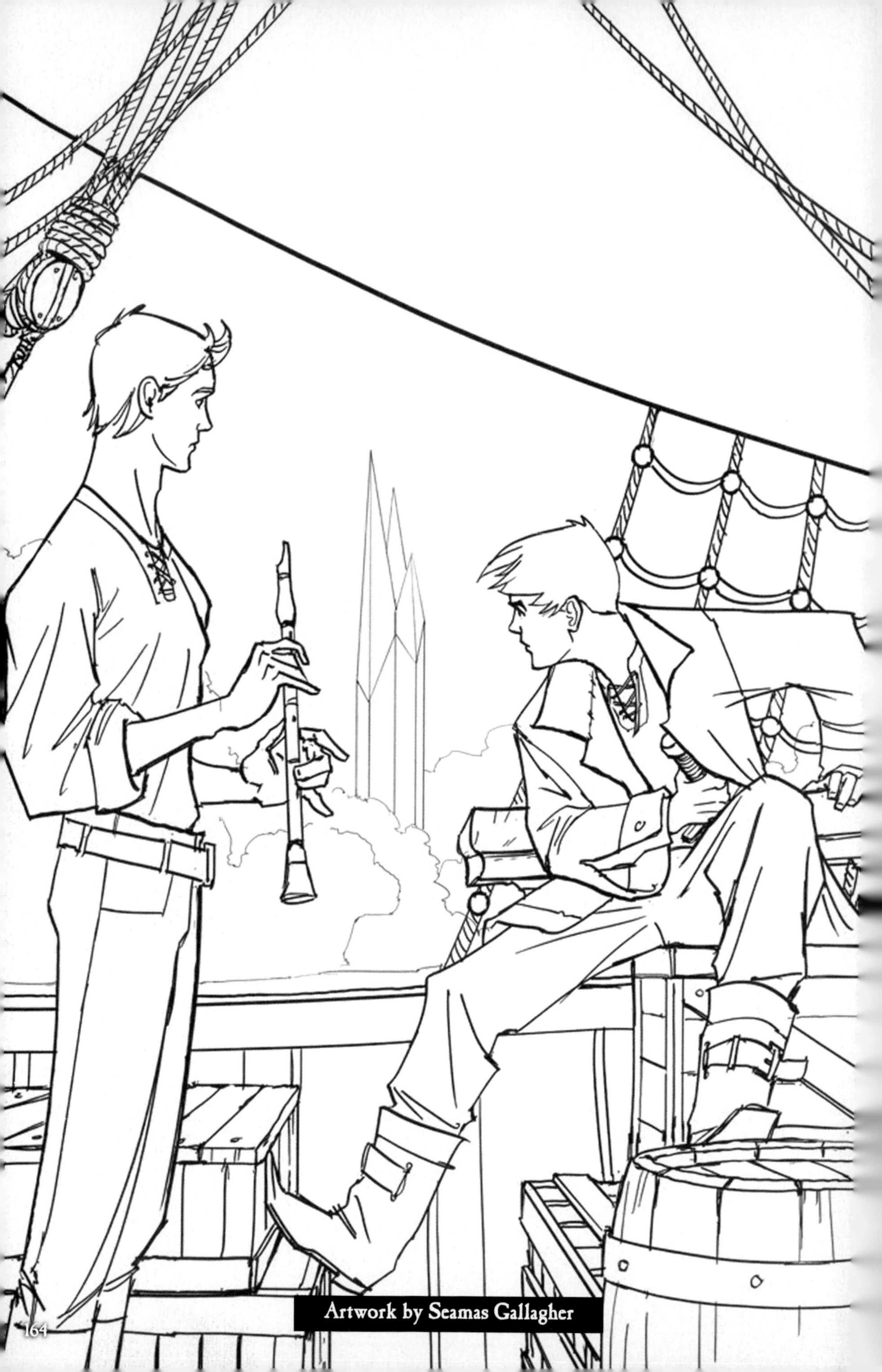

Artwork by Seamas Gallagher

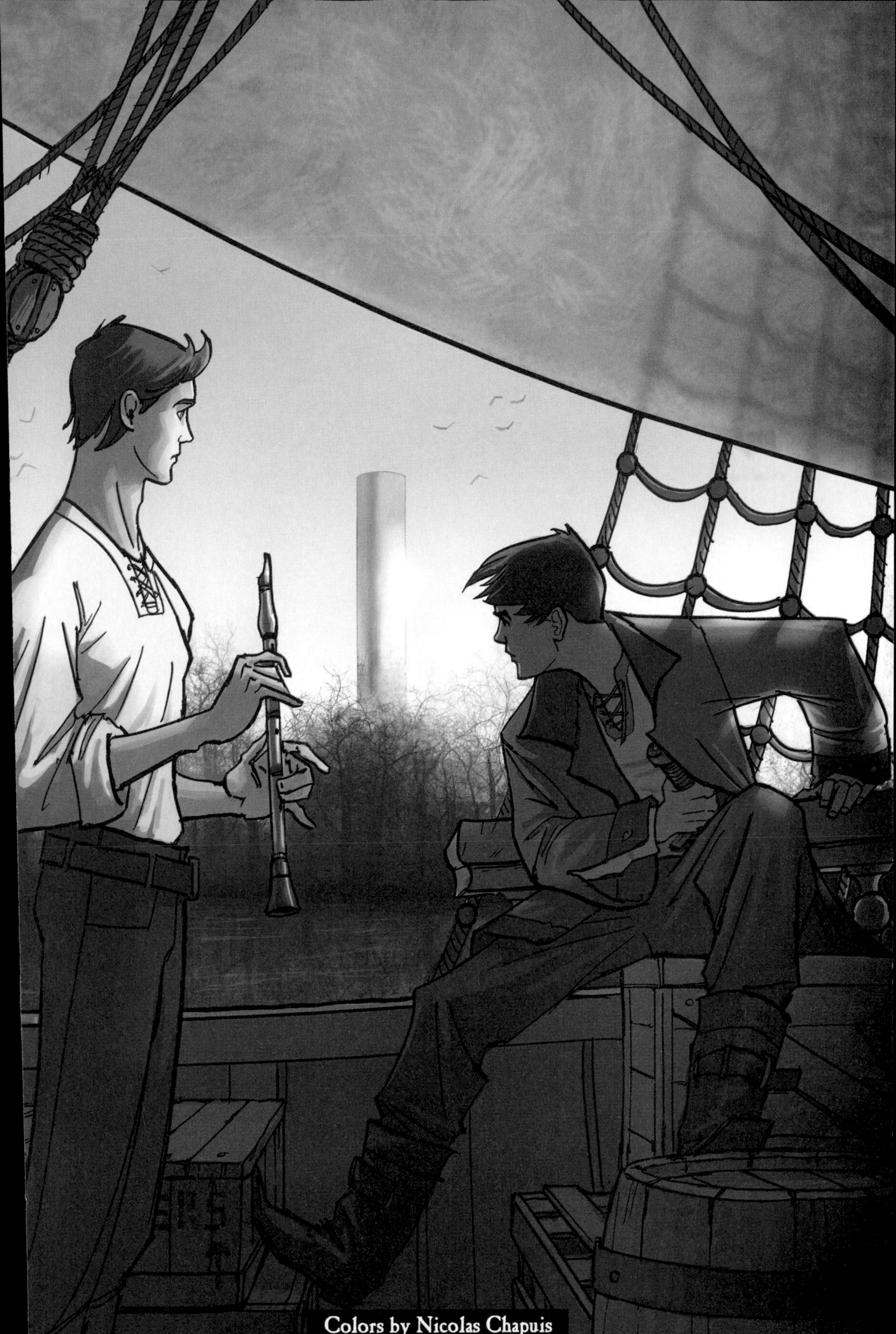

Colors by Nicolas Chapuis

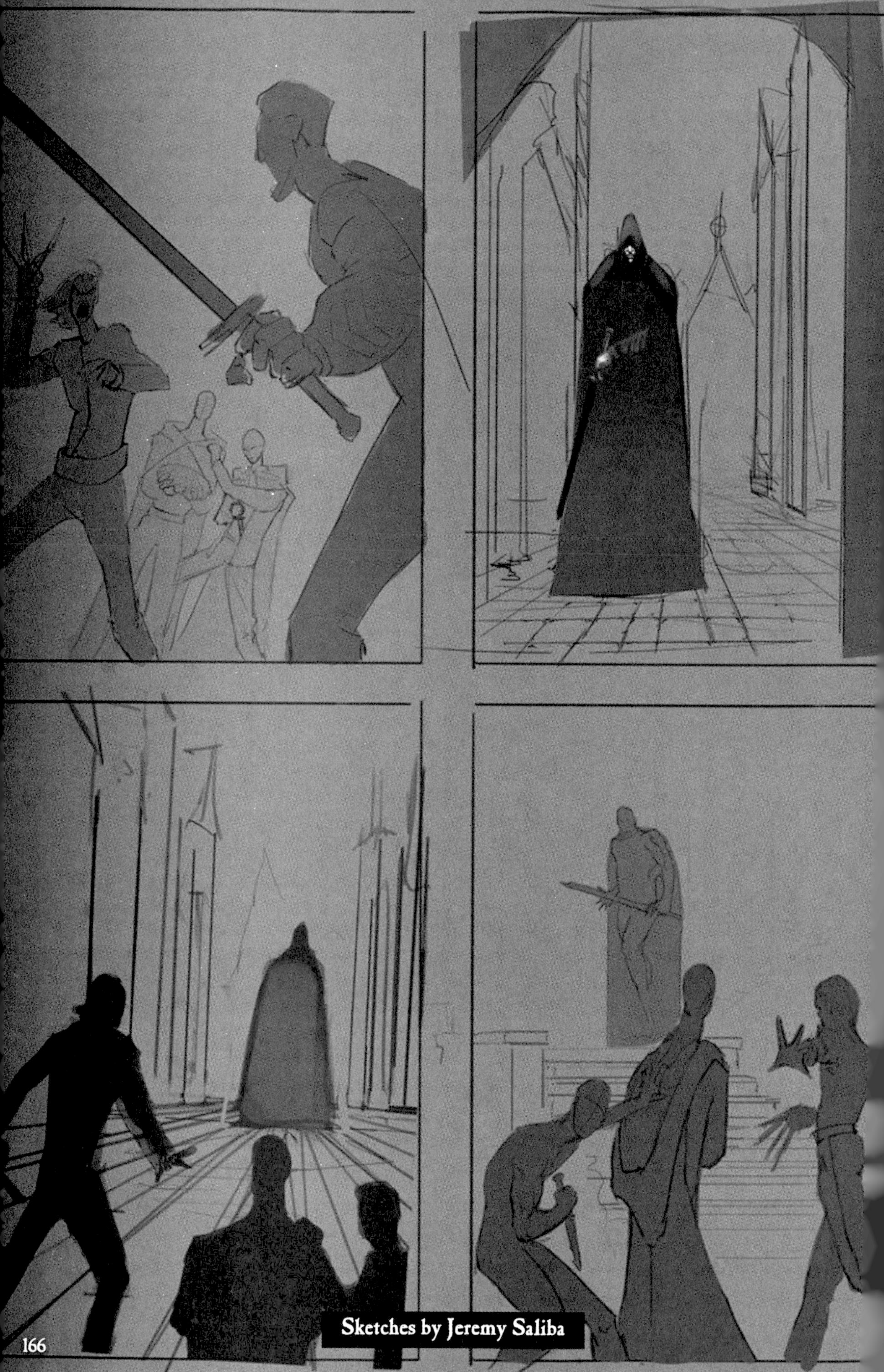

Sketches by Jeremy Saliba

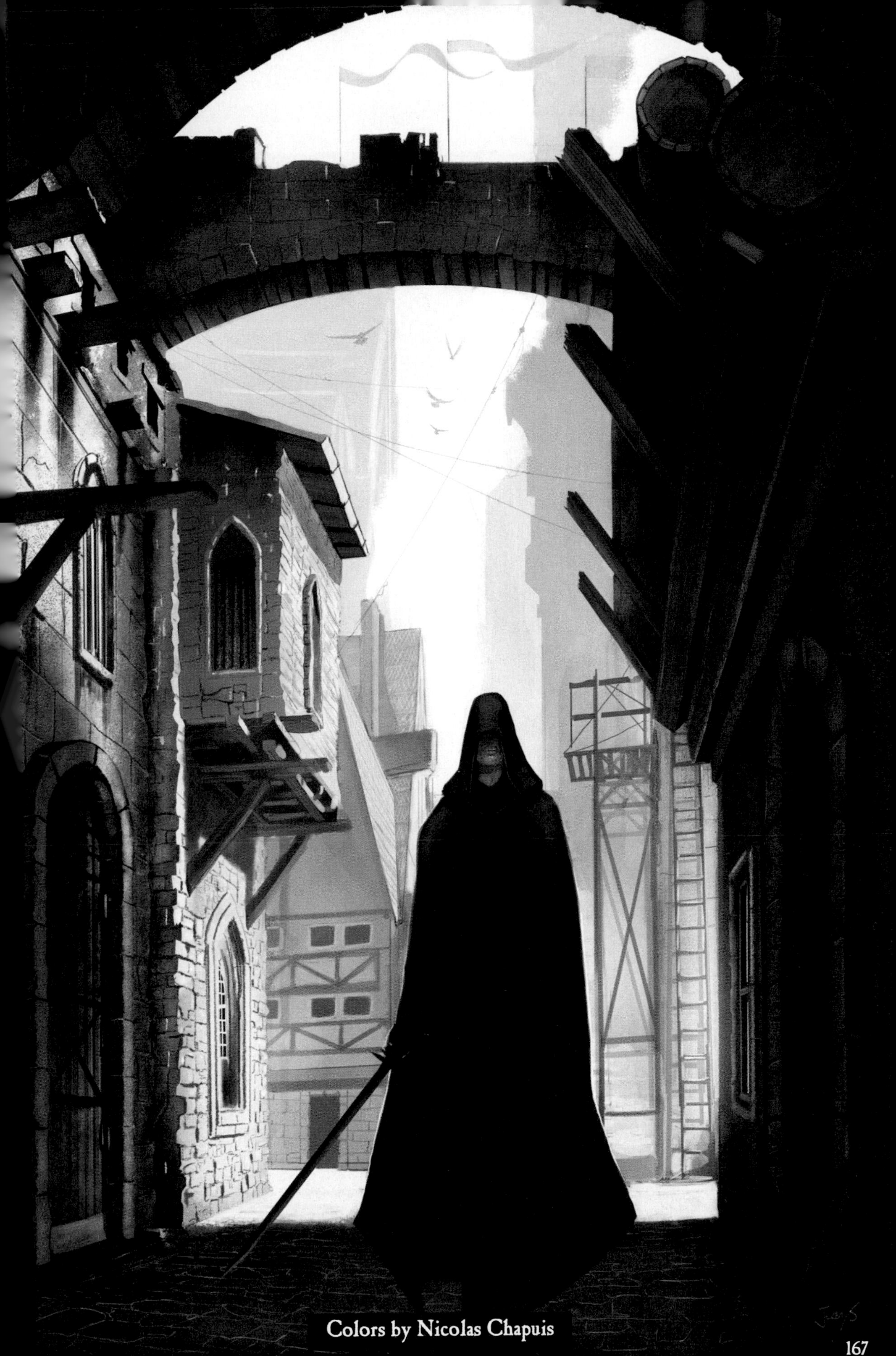

Colors by Nicolas Chapuis

biographies

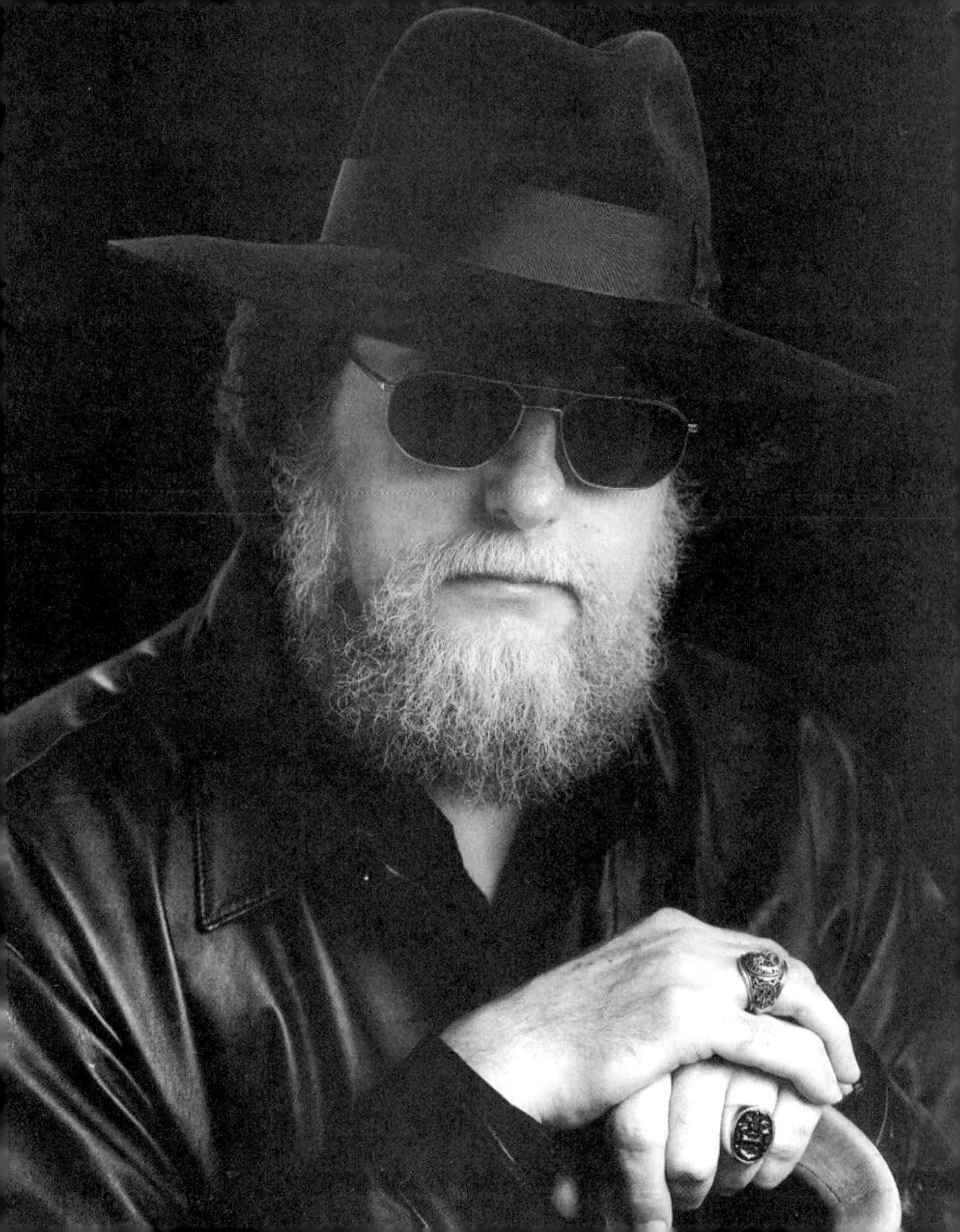

ROBERT JORDAN

Mr. Jordan was born in 1948 in Charleston, South Carolina. He taught himself to read when he was four with the incidental aid of a twelve-years-older brother, and was tackling Mark Twain and Jules Verne by five. He was a graduate of The Citadel, the Military College of South Carolina, with a degree in physics. He served two tours in Vietnam with the U. S. Army; among his decorations are the Distinguished Flying Cross with bronze oak leaf cluster, the Bronze Star with "V" and bronze oak leaf cluster, and two Vietnamese Gallantry Crosses with palm. A history buff, he also wrote dance and theater criticism and enjoyed the outdoor sports of hunting, fishing, and sailing, and the indoor sports of poker, chess, pool, and pipe collecting. He began writing in 1977 and went on to write The Wheel of Time®, one of the most important and bestselling series in the history of fantasy publishing with more than 14 million copies sold in North America, and countless more sold abroad. Robert Jordan died on September 16, 2007, after a courageous battle with the rare blood disease amyloidosis.

CHUCK DIXON

Mr. Dixon has worked for every major comic book publisher as a professional comic book writer. His credits include *The Hobbit* graphic novel, *The Punisher, Birds of Prey, Batman, Catwoman, Green Arrow, Green Lantern, Star Wars, Simpsons* comics, and the comic adaptation of *Dean Koontz's Frankenstein*.

Chuck currently resides in Florida.

FRANCIS NUGUIT

Philippine-based artist Francis R.V. Nuguit, a fine-arts graduate, has worked as a graphic, package, and web designer for several different companies before breaking in as a comic book illustrator. He has worked on a few creator-owned and indie titles such as *Hitless* and *Control Under Fire (Bloodlines)*. He did some character concept art as well, before he started working on the *Wheel of Time: Eye of the World* series.

NICOLAS CHAPUIS

Nicolas Chapuis was born in 1985 and decided to freelance as a comic book colorist after earning a degree in graphic design. His work includes *Robert Jordan's The Wheel of Time, Jonathan Stroud's Bartimaeus: The Amulet of Samarkand*, and *Richard Starking's Elephantmen*.

He resides in Freiburg, Germany.

MARCIO FIORITO

Marcio Fiorito started as a marketing executive for many publishing and telecommunication companies, when he decided to drop everything to fulfill his lifelong dream of becoming an artist. He began doing commercial and book illustrations for several gaming companies such as White Wolf Publishing, Steve Jackson Games, Green Ronin Publishing, Alderac Entertainment, Mongoose Publishing, and many more. Moving on to the comic book industry, Marcio got his breakthrough at Dynamite Entertainment, working on *Anne Elizabeth's Pulse of Power* and quickly moving on to *Robert Jordan's Wheel of Time* series. He is a fantasy and comic book enthusiast, and currently lives with his wife and beautiful daughter in Minas Gerais, Brazil.

BILL TORTOLINI

Already an accomplished art director and graphic designer, Bill began lettering comics more than a decade ago and has worked with many of the comic book industry's top creators and publishers.

Current and past projects include: *Stephen King's Talisman, Anita Blake: Vampire Hunter, Army of Darkness, Random Acts of Violence, Wolverine, Back to Brooklyn, The Hedge Knight, Archie Comics, Riftwar, Battlestar Galactica, The Warriors, The Wheel of Time, The Dresden Files, Transformers, Star Trek: The Next Generation, G.I. Joe, The Last Resort,* and many others.

Bill resides in Billerica, Massachusetts, with his wife and three children.

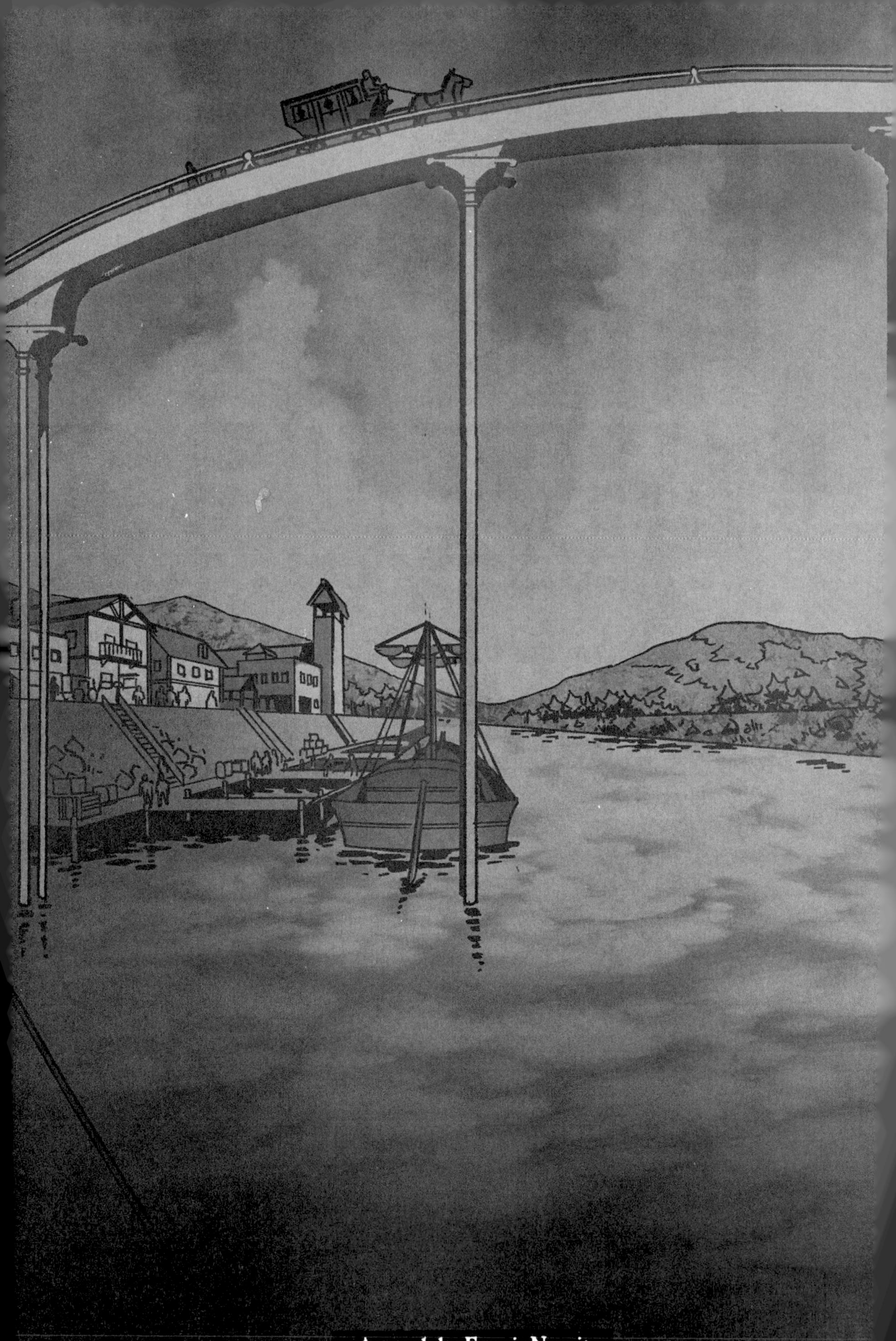

Artwork by Francis Nuguit